Captain Durant's Countess

Books by Maggie Robinson

Captain Durant's Countess

MAGGIE ROBINSON

KENSINGTON
Kensington Publishing Corp.
www.kensingtonbooks.com

KENSINGTON BOOKS are published by

Kensington Publishing Corp.
119 West 40th Street
New York, NY 10018

All Kensington titles, imprints, and distributed lines are available at special quantity discounts for bulk purchases for sales promotions, premiums, fund-raising, educational, or institutional use.

Special book excerpts or customized printings can also be created to fit specific needs. For details, write or phone the office of the Kensington special sales manager: Kensington Publishing Corp., 119 West 40th Street, New York, NY 10018, attn: Special Sales Department; phone: 1-800-221-2647.

KENSINGTON and the k logo are Reg. U.S. Pat. & TM Off.

First Electronic Edition: February 2013

ISBN-13: 978-1-60183-041-8
ISBN-10: 1-60183-041-6

ISBN-13: 978-1-60183-175-0
ISBN-10: 1-60183-175-7

Printed in the United States of America

Chapter 1

London, December 1820

"You cannot go up there, madam!" The butler, whose cauliflower nose made him look like he had once fought—and lost regularly—for a living, tried to block the stairs.

He didn't want to grant her admittance to the house, and Maris really didn't want to enter. What she had to do there was beyond scandalous, and she'd spent her whole life—well, practically her whole life—avoiding scandal like the plague. Never taking a false step or breaking a rule or speaking up for herself.

Except once, and how she regretted *that*.

Would she regret today? She was trying to convince a strange man to come home with her and—and—she stopped herself from thinking any further.

Maris dodged by the butler and stood at the bottom of a vast marble staircase. One good push from above and one could very easily fall, with no hope of recovery. Marble was hard. As hard as her heart needed to be at present.

"I can and I will. You will not hit a lady, I am sure." The Countess of Kelby pinned back her veil and smiled. The effort was nearly painful as her cheek muscles were unused to the exercise. Maris had spent the last ten years caring for her elderly husband Henry and slaving over his ancient texts, and there had been little occasion to turn up her lips to strangers. But now the earl needed something else done, and the recalcitrant man he had chosen to do it was somewhere upstairs in a den of utter iniquity.

She *must* speak with him. It was a matter of life and death—*his* death if he wouldn't cooperate, she was that angry. Let him tumble down the stairs and break his neck. Henry had counted on him. Placed his trust in him. She had been writing to the man for weeks with no response. It was past time he do his duty, go to Kelby Hall, and begin the job for which he'd been hired.

And paid.

Maris stood in the foyer of the most infamous address in London—the Reining Monarchs Society. Even buried in the country, she had heard of the place and the men—and, unbelievably, women—who belonged to the secret club.

Not so secret, after all. It had been a matter of a few shillings and another one of her rare smiles to induce Reynold Durant's valet to reveal where his employer was spending his misbegotten afternoon.

Interesting, since two months ago, Reynold Durant couldn't have afforded a valet or membership in such a place.

The butler crossed his muscled arms before him. "He's not to be disturbed, madam. I'll lose my position."

Maris attempted the smile again. "Then I'll wait. Right here at the bottom of the stairs. Captain Durant is bound to come down sometime."

The man's dismay was comical. "You can't do that! You're a . . . you're a lady! It's not proper having someone like you here at all."

"It's not proper having *anyone* here. You must be desperate to work in such an environment."

The butler's bloodshot blue eyes dropped to the carpet. "It ain't so bad. You get used to it."

Maris could not imagine a more unlikely thing. To *get used to* unending carnal depravity would simply not be possible. She'd rather jump from the Tower of London than bare her breasts like that brazen woman she'd glimpsed through the open parlor doors. Before she'd blinked away, Maris could have sworn there were *jewels* on the woman's nipples—rubies, or at the very least, garnets.

She opened her reticule and fished out some bribe money. She'd have to walk back to her hotel if she had to dole out any more, but it wasn't far. The Reining Monarchs Society was located right in the heart of Mayfair, conveniently close to the best houses. Captain

Durant's bachelor lodgings were only around the corner. One had to conserve one's energy when one was sinning at such a spectacular rate.

Henry had given up his house in town years ago. Maris had not been to London very often since her unsuccessful Season. It had overwhelmed her then, but she didn't have time to be frightened now. It was she who planned to do the frightening.

She passed the butler the coins. "I promise I'll not bother anyone. I'll just sit in silence in that chair over by the wall. Could you describe Captain Durant so I'll recognize him when he comes down?"

Maris's money disappeared with breathtaking speed. "You don't know him?"

"Not at all." And she wished they didn't have to become acquainted. A man who restrained and whipped his women was no one she wanted to meet over the breakfast table at Kelby Hall. Or maybe *he* was the one being bound and beaten? She shuddered at the image.

"He's a tall one, he is. Dark hair and eyes. Has a saber scar on his cheek, but other than that, I s'pose you'd call him handsome. He was wearing a yellow waistcoat, although I don't guess he's got it on now."

She tripped over the rug at that news and arranged herself on the chair. "Thank you. See? I'm sitting." Maris folded her gloved hands in her lap. "I don't imagine there's any reading material I might peruse while I wait?"

"Nothing the likes of you would enjoy, my lady. There's a large library here, but the books are what you might call naughty. More pictures than words, if you take my meaning."

In general, Maris was in favor of expanding her education, but perhaps not in this case. "I take your meaning very well. You've been very helpful, Mr.—?"

"Mick Fisher, at your service. Don't make me sorry I let you wait, now."

Maris crossed her fingers in the folds of her skirt. "I shall be the soul of discretion. Do carry on."

She counted to one hundred after Mr. Fisher shuffled his bulk down the hallway, taking in her surroundings. The club's furnishings were in the first stare of fashion. The carpet was thick and Turkish, the chair comfortably padded, the gilt-framed paintings lurid yet lushly executed. The house was remarkably still for a haven of vice. Maris had lived in the country too long to think that sexual congress, whether committed by humans or animals, was ever quiet.

But it was only two o'clock in the afternoon. Perhaps the society became noisier at night.

Maris had never been touched by her husband unless it was fully dark outside . . . and inside, too. Henry was as anxious as she to blow out the candles to prevent them both from seeing what was going on.

Or not going on.

Their marital bed had held little joy for him, but it was all so many empty years ago. She'd come to terms with her situation and was not going to let herself dwell on it. Maris was a woman of action now, and the stairs beckoned. Time was of the essence, in so many ways. Who knew when Mr. Fisher might be back to check up on her, or a footman would cross through the hall? Or, God forbid, that scandalously naked woman decided to parade along the Turkey carpet, her nipples sparkling?

Or how long her beloved Henry would live.

Maris practically ran up the steps to the next floor, minding the slippery marble. In her experience, when one wished evil on another, evil frequently had other ideas. She did not intend to fall when the object of her quest was so close.

Judging from the open doors she peeked into, she had found the bedrooms, and odd bedrooms they were. Yes, there were beds—rather giant ones that could hold the average family—but the rooms were fitted with equipment that would be more at home in a stable than a family home. The selection of crops and a variety of roping neatly tacked to the flocked walls was astonishing. Where the walls were not wallpapered, they were mirrored, and Maris moved swiftly so she would not glimpse her plain gray walking dress and pale-as-milk skin reflected on them. It had been much more important to focus on her brains than her nonexistent beauty since she'd attained her womanhood, and she generally gave mirrors a wide berth. It was enough she was clean and respectable.

Though respectability would not serve her well there.

When she came to a shut door, she paused. Did she dare knock, or just open it? She heard muffled noises behind the thick painted wood. A steady swish of something, and low groans a second after. Disgusting. Whoever was in there deserved to be interrupted.

Maris turned the doorknob. Unlocked. She pushed the door open a fraction.

The first thing she saw was a man's waistcoat draped over the back of a chair. Yellow, with what appeared to be giant orange chrysanthemums embroidered on the silk fabric. A vulgar waistcoat, entirely unsuitable for a decorated war hero, which she knew Reynold Durant was, for all his lack of duty to his new responsibility. He'd recently sold out and was rutting through London, all on her husband's coin.

Another inch of open door showed a standing glass mirror angled toward the bed and the broad back and taut buttocks of a rather spectacular specimen of manhood captured in its surface. The double image of reality and reflection made Maris swallow and stumble backward. Perhaps this was not such a good idea after all.

"Care to join us?" the specimen drawled, sending shivers right down her spine. He must have eyes in the back of his head, for he didn't turn, just continued stroking the woman stretched upon the bed with a black velvet crop. His voice sounded as if it would taste like warm dark honey blended with the best French brandy. One raspy word from him and a woman would never leave, trapped in its liquid amber depths.

"Captain Durant?" Maris managed to squeak.

"Who's asking?" He turned, fully available for view.

All of him.

His skin was burnished, his root swollen and pointing heavenward.

Maris closed her eyes briefly. Apart from statuary and drawings in antique manuscripts, she had never seen an entirely unclothed male, but this male seemed to be inescapably branded on the inside of her eyelids after only a few seconds. She opened her eyes and assumed a neutral expression. It wouldn't do to have him think she was truly interested in him.

"I am Lady Kelby. You may recall receiving at least two dozen letters from me." She struggled for haughtiness, but was afraid she'd revealed the truth. To her ears, she sounded like the desperate fool she was.

"One almost every day for the past month." Durant tossed his crop to the floor, where it rolled beneath the tester bed. "Patsy, love, you may want to cover up in front of Lady Kelby. It seems I have finally been run to ground."

Maris watched in disapproving silence as he strolled to the bedside table. He opened a drawer and pulled out a knife. Good Lord, he wasn't going to attack her, was he? She had nothing to defend herself with except her hatpin. Mr. Fisher probably would be in no hurry to come to her rescue if she was to scream, but she opened her mouth anyway to do just that.

To her relief, Durant didn't notice her panic as he sliced through the cords that bound his paramour. The woman's bottom was raspberry-pink, the rest of her plump and snow-white. He tugged the sheet up over her, but it was he who needed covering. Surely he didn't expect to converse with Maris in his current state?

He was naked.

And as shameless as she had feared.

"Will she take long, or shall I go, Reyn?" the woman asked.

Durant sighed. "Perhaps we can finish this tomorrow, my dear. But if you are in great need, I think I saw Blivens in the dining room."

Patsy pouted. "But he's not *you,* Reyn."

"Any port in the storm, love. I may not have served in the navy, but that much I'm sure of."

All cats are gray in the dark, Maris thought. But judging from Patsy's expression, she might have said it aloud.

"Very well," Patsy huffed. "I'll hold you to tomorrow, though. Same time, same room. I'll arrange it with Fisher." Still wrapped in the sheet, the woman climbed down from the bed and gathered up her clothes.

"Excellent." Durant kissed Patsy's exposed shoulder and patted her rump. Maris felt a twinge of irritation at his affectionate dismissal.

"Now then," he said after Patsy had flounced out and slammed the door behind her. "Let's get this over with. What do you want?"

"You know perfectly well what I want! I've written to you enough times!"

The man—the still naked man—shrugged. "But I didn't read them all. Refresh my memory."

"You need to come to Kelby Hall . . . as you originally agreed. My husband is not at all well." This was not exactly the diatribe she'd practiced delivering, and it didn't begin to cover all the details that rattled around in her head.

He shook his head and sat down on the bed. Could he not put something over his penis? There were at least half a dozen pillows scattered all over the counterpane.

"But I don't want to leave town right now, or any time soon. I've seen enough of the countryside. Since I was sixteen, I've traipsed all over Europe and the Americas. A dozen years of getting shot at and sleeping in ditches and mud and starving myself to serve the king. I find life in London to be very amusing."

Maris saw how amused he still was. His rampant cock had not wilted one whit as she'd stood there haranguing him. But then, he was still so very young, six years younger than she was if she did her sums correctly.

"You must come! It is your duty!"

"Don't talk to me of duty, madam. I've done my share and have the scars to prove it." Maris's gaze couldn't help but follow his large brown hand, where it rubbed against a muscled thigh slashed with a long red line.

He noticed. "Bayonet wound. There's still a ball in my shoulder, too. Hurts like the devil when the weather is damp, which is pretty much every day in England. Look your fill—I've nicks and knots everywhere. Even my pretty face didn't escape the French. Some ladies like it, though." He grinned rakishly, the saber scar doubling his dimple.

Maris could see where some ladies would.

He was not yet thirty, but there was a worn look about him that went beyond whatever injuries he'd sustained. Dissipation, she thought, but something else as well. She watched as his fingers drummed against his thigh, and quickly realized where her eyes were straying.

A few minutes in this horrible house and she was good as corrupted. But that was necessary, wasn't it, if she were to go through with Henry's plan?

"You *must* come to Kelby Hall, if only for a little while. I'm sure it won't . . . take very long." She felt the color creep into her cheeks.

"I told your husband I had changed my mind. Now I am sure of it."

Damn the man and his implied insult. She knew she was plain and old, but not completely repulsive. "You took his money."

"And I wrote to say I'd pay it all back." Durant rose, went to the chair where his clothes were piled, and reached into a pocket. "Here. I've had some recent luck at the tables. I was mistaken to agree when Mr. Ramsey presented this . . . uh . . . *unique* opportunity to me. He can be quite convincing, you know. Passionate. I've never met a man quite like him, and that's the truth. Odd sort of fellow. Have you met him?"

Maris shook her head in answer. Henry had come up with his cork-brained idea all on his own and had made all the arrangements. She waved away the offered payment.

"Something is not quite right about him. I don't think he is at all what he pretends to be. But when I met him, I thought to—well, never mind. My need for the *position* you hired me for is no longer valid."

His emphasis on the word *position* brought another blush to Maris's cheeks. She could feel the heat sweep clear down to the collar of her high-necked gown. She tugged the fabric up another inch.

The man had the effrontery to catch her at it and smile. It was dazzling, like the rest of him. "Needless to say, I'm sorry I ever replied to the advertisement in *The London List* last fall and put you both to all the trouble. It was a mistake. After I met with your husband, I had a crisis of conscience and realized his scheme wouldn't suit."

Maris had not been present for the job interview. Henry had insisted on handling the meeting himself, and she had relented, hoping to delay her mortification. She had not even permitted herself a peek at Captain Durant as he rode up Kelby Hall's crushed stone drive.

"My husband is dying," she said bluntly. *Thank heavens Cap-*

tain Durant is stepping into his fawnskin trousers. He doesn't seem to wear smalls, though.

"I am very sorry to hear that, Lady Kelby. But it doesn't change my mind. I assure you I will repay every penny now that my luck is turning."

"We don't want the money! We want . . . you." It was far too late to go through the process all over again. It had taken Mr. Ramsey over a year to get even this far. Vaguely worded advertisements. Vaguely worded interviews with the handful of candidates so desperate they had not been bothered by the vagueness.

Henry had been extremely particular. While all cats might be gray in the dark, Lord Kelby did have a care for his wife and the succession. Evidently the two other men Mr. Ramsey had sent him had not compared at all favorably with Captain Durant, for Henry was insistent that no one else would do.

Though Henry might not be so impressed if he knew where Maris had found him. Henry's London doctor would have to be consulted if Reynold Durant decided to go through with this insanity. She was not going to sacrifice herself to the pox.

"I'm not for sale after all."

"Everyone has their price, Captain Durant." She knew she did, and it had been shockingly low. For a roof over her head when her father died and the chance to continue to work on the Kelby Collection, Maris had married a man who was old enough to be her grandfather.

And impotent.

But she had always loved him, ever since she was a little girl. Henry had been kind, caring for her in all the ways he was capable, and they had been happy . . . until two years ago when he became so agitated and determined to cut his wretched nephew out of the earldom. His idea on how to do it had seemed the purest folly. Well, *im*purest. Henry had been impossible to sway, and Maris had never been the sort of woman who could wield her negligible feminine wiles to change a man's mind.

Like right at the moment, for example. Durant seemed obdurate.

"I-I am begging you, Captain Durant. You know of our difficulties. I understand Henry confided in you completely, so he must have trusted you. I confess I don't see why," Maris said, unable to forgive the man his casual effrontery. "My husband's nephew is the worst sort of villain. He's sworn to destroy the scholarly work of my husband's lifetime. All the books in the library—he'll damage every one. Crumple every paper. And . . . and he's a libertine. He'll turn Kelby Hall into a . . . a place just as vile as this one."

Durant raised a thick black brow as he buttoned a cufflink. Maris was delighted to see that he continued to dress as she stared over his head at a painting that featured several bodies writhing in presumed ecstasy. Or indigestion. It was impossible to tell which from their facial expressions.

"Is this supposed to persuade me? I have no time for reading, Lady Kelby. It doesn't matter to me what becomes of Kelby Hall's library."

Maris wanted to scream, but losing her temper wouldn't help. "It matters to my husband. By the terms of the entail, every single thing housed at Kelby Hall must remain on the property to be passed on to the next earl, but it doesn't specify the condition." The Kelby earls had been an eccentric lot. And hoarders, too. It was dangerous to navigate the attics for the jumbled collection of boxed antiquities amassed by generations of globe-trotting aristocrats. Henry's dream was to turn part of the house into a museum, with Maris as its curator. His work would be its centerpiece, but many other centuries' detritus would be on view as well.

"So smuggle out some papers."

"It's not just papers. There are priceless artifacts. By law, Henry's nephew can't sell them, but he's threatened to simply drop them into the lake. They'd still be on the property, wouldn't they?" she asked bitterly. "David knows just how to hurt Henry. My husband spent years in Tuscany at excavation sites. He is the foremost expert on Etruscan civilization in England."

"A worthy endeavor, I'm sure, Lady Kelby. But the Etruscans, like the Romans and the Greeks, are dead, thank the gods. As a schoolboy, I always found classical studies to be quite gruesome. Rape and swans and swallowing one's wife. Daughters bursting out of one's head. Rubbish, really. Why should I—or anyone else living—care?"

The Kelby Collection had been of paramount importance Maris's whole life. Her father had been the earl's secretary and general factotum. She'd accompanied the two men on their digs as soon as she was old enough to be useful, and was an expert on Etruria. Since her husband's eyesight was failing, it was she who did the translating, she who prepared the papers for his lectures and publications.

What she'd been unable to do was provide him with a son.

It was probably too late anyway. She was thirty-four, and had pulled out a wiry white hair from her dull brown curls just that morning.

"Look, it seems to me you can box up whatever's so valuable and hide it somewhere. How's this nephew to know? He's no expert, is he?"

"David knows everything. And it's more than what I've just said." Maris hadn't planned on revealing the worst of it . . . and she wouldn't. Even Henry did not know what she had done five years ago. She had been a fool for all her pride and intelligence, and paid with her guilt every single day when she looked into her husband's proud wrinkled face.

But she could see she wasn't firing up Durant intellectually. He'd even bragged that he was virtually illiterate.

Why was Henry so set on Durant? Henry was a brilliant man, if a bit single-minded. He'd be risking turning Kelby Hall over to a son of this ignorant rakehell.

Though any child conceived might not even be a son. Henry's longed-for heir with his first wife had been a daughter. Poor Jane. Poor *dead* Jane.

"My husband believes his nephew David was responsible for the death of his daughter."

Ah, that stopped the man from thrusting an arm into the ghastly waistcoat. "Why hasn't he told the authorities?"

"It's complicated." The truth was that Jane took her own life, but David might as well have stitched the stones into her hem. Jane had been his victim as much as Maris, but at least she still lived.

"You begin to interest me, Lady Kelby. So what you are saying is this mad scheme is really a noble cause. I'm meant to prevent a murderer from inheriting."

"Exactly."

"Why don't you just hire someone to murder the murderer? Not me, mind you. I'm done with killing for a living. Hire a proper as-

sassin. Surely there's some other male Kelby waiting to be un-
earthed somewhere like one of those Etruscan artifacts you're so
keen on."

"My husband's family seemed to collect things rather than children. There is no one but David. The title and estate would revert
to the Crown."

"Would that be so awful? Surely some provision has been made
for you."

"I'm not worried about myself." *Oh, untrue.*

David was ever edging into the perimeter of her life. Maris was
not entirely certain she could protect herself from him should anything happen to Henry. She wouldn't be safe in the dower house
alone, that was for sure. She'd not been safe from his attentions at
Kelby Hall five years ago. She had lived in the enormous Elizabethan house since she was a little girl. She would miss it, but she
would have to go someplace farther away when David was earl.

Unless she had a baby to care for. But what if she and the child
still were not safe?

"You look pale, Lady Kelby. Why don't you sit down?"

She could hardly sit on the bed after what had just transpired on
it, and his jacket and neckcloth were still folded on the only chair
in the room. She lifted her chin in false bravado. "I am perfectly
well, Captain Durant."

"You don't look it." He swept his clothes to the floor and pushed
the chair at her. "Here. Sit."

"I am not one of your recruits to be ordered about." Nevertheless, she sank gratefully into the chair. The day was proving to be
too much.

Or not enough.

"No, you are as haughty as a queen. I reckon you'd be the one
giving the orders. 'Explore the New World, Walter. Write me a
play, Will. Kill my heir.' That would be Mary, Queen of Scots, not
David."

"I am not Elizabeth, sir," Maris said, irritated and somewhat surprised by his knowledge.

"The Virgin Queen," Durant mused. "You have a virginal look
about you still, Lady Kelby. Lord Kelby was an ancient old bird
even when you married, was he not?"

Maris's spine turned rigid. She was, unfortunately, no virgin.

"You overstep yourself, Captain Durant. I can see it was pointless to waste my precious time and money to find you. A man like you has no sense of honor or accountability. I cannot even believe I am conversing with you in your current state. You are . . . you are . . . words simply fail."

Durant's lips quirked, unruffled by her insults. "Why talk when there are so many other things we might do?"

He was teasing her, but she was horrified nonetheless. "Here? Are you mad? Dream on, you degenerate! If you were the very last man in the kingdom, I would not permit you to put a hand on me in this revolting room!"

"And yet I somehow want to. In fact, I cannot think of anything that would please me more. Please us both." He stalked across the carpet like some kind of feral cat.

Maris scrambled up from her chair and backed into the wall, an instrument of torture prodding her in the back. She stuck a hand behind her, her gloves slipping on the smooth leather whip. She could not get purchase to grab it from its hook and hammer it down on Durant's dark head in time before she felt his warm breath on her cheek.

"Just one little taste, I think. To see what I'll be missing," he murmured, before his lips came down on hers.

Chapter 2

R eyn Durant was a dog. A right bastard, even if his rackety parents had been married. His behavior thus far had been outrageous. He knew it, but how was he supposed to have recognized the very proper Countess of Kelby? She was the last person in the world he expected to see at the Reining Monarchs Society.

It was not uncommon for an interested party to wander into a discipline session, and the unpredictability of the place had amused him for a time. However, once she'd identified herself, he should have insisted she leave immediately, then crawled into the bed to shock her further if she wouldn't. Or draped himself in a fringed curtain. At the very least, hollered for Fisher.

He'd done none of those things. He'd flaunted himself like an actor on a stage in his vain attempt to drive her away. And instead of firmly refusing her offer and leading her to the door, he was pressed against her, the quivers of indignation unbelievably tempting.

Damn it, the woman needed kissing in the worst way. Reyn had been in enough scrapes with uncertain outcomes to have learned to always seize the moment, so he touched her lips intending to teach her a lesson and scare her away for her own good.

And was rewarded for his trouble by a sharp knee to his groin.

Fortunately his reflexes were excellent and he avoided the worst of it. The least of it was still painful. He took a deep breath and steadied himself against the wall.

He was an idiot. He should be putting yards between himself and Lady Kelby, but her struggle against him only intensified his desire to master her.

He wasn't sure why. Despite her finding him in such a compromising position, he did not naturally need to subdue a woman. The Reining Monarchs Society was simply one of those ports in a storm for him, an amusement, nothing more. He had no intention of going through with the unamusing proposition and attempt to impregnate a woman who obviously held him in contempt. A plain, shriveled-up bluestocking to boot.

No, that was wrong. Perhaps she wasn't so plain now that her color was high and her brown eyes sparked in anger. Up close, he saw her eyelashes were long and batting like butterflies trapped against glass. Beneath her ugly gray dress she was lushly curved, and if she hadn't partially unmanned him, he might have appreciated her figure more.

She was handsome enough, but totally unsuited for what her husband had in mind. If she couldn't bear his kiss, how could she endure the rest?

Reyn had been damn near his wit's end when he responded to the oddly-worded advertisement in *The London List*. The owner of the newspaper, Mr. Ramsey, had been evasive, but had vetted him thoroughly, asking him so many questions Reyn felt like he was sitting for all those exams he'd so spectacularly failed at school. That strange fellow Ramsey knew more about him than his own mother had. Whatever Reyn had said had pleased him, and the newspaperman had arranged for him to meet with the old earl two months ago. Reyn couldn't believe his luck at the money that was dangled before him just to go to Kelby Hall.

The travel expenses—and what was promised if he had a satisfactory interview—were much too generous. Reyn had known from the first that something was off, but his sister Virginia needed his help, and he needed money to help her. His efforts had come late, but at least her days were being spent in what little comfort he could provide. He'd hired a nurse and leased a cottage with clean air outside Richmond. He'd given her a dog, because Ginny had always wanted one from the time he could remember. Their parents had never set down roots anywhere long enough to acquire one. An animal was an expense, something Anthony and Corinne Durant could ill afford after their excesses at the tables.

Reyn was really no different. He'd lived everywhere and nowhere, deserting his responsibilities to his sister as he marched through Europe and Canada. But he still had *some* scruples. He'd never, ever been serious about following through with the Earl of Kelby once he learned what the old man wanted. The worst that could be said about him was that he'd borrowed money under false pretenses. So what if he'd reneged. The earl could never prosecute him for its return. The scandal would kill the old fellow outright and turn society against his shivering countess.

Reyn would pay the earl back somehow. He'd had a run of good luck in the hells lately as if he was being rewarded for his bad behavior. His parents would have been envious if they still lived.

Something had happened to him since he'd sold out, something he didn't care to examine too closely in the light of day. Whatever it was—boredom? despair?—had made him reckless. He'd always been a restless soul, unable to stick to anything but soldiering for very long. But the war was over, had been for ages. The dull routine of peace had brought him no comfort. In fact, it had driven him slightly mad. All he'd done the past year since he'd been posted to London was parade in uniform like a wind-up doll for the king's pleasure. The army was no place for him, anymore.

Civilian life had not been much better. He'd even bought a quarter-year subscription to the Reining Monarchs Society to see what all the fuss was about. But he still didn't know. When granted absolute power over another human being, he still felt powerless. He told himself that denying the earl's dying request was actually a good thing. He was not the wastrel decent people thought he was. He'd once had character. Perhaps he'd regain it again.

"Get off me!"

Lady Kelby didn't shout. No one would come to her aid, anyway. Shouting was de rigueur at the Reining Monarchs. That was part of the fun.

"I am not precisely *on* you, Lady Kelby. You'd know it if I was, and I wager you'd not object. Isn't that why you are here?"

She was tall for a woman, but somehow ducked under the arm that pinned her to the wall. Her hat was tipped at a crazed angle which made her look much less starchy, but no less angry. Damn but he wished he had succeeded in kissing her. There didn't seem to be much hope of that now.

"You are d-disgusting! I cannot for the life of me imagine why my husband thought you might be s-satisfactory."

Reyn wasn't quite sure either. He was nobody in particular, not titled, not educated, not accomplished. His father had been a cousin to a bankrupt marquess, and his mother was the youngest daughter of a disgraced viscountess who'd run off with her dresser. It was amazing to think his old granny had been a follower of Sappho, but he remembered her and her companion Grace as being very kind the few times he'd met them.

Scandal and sloth had been bred into Reyn from the earliest age, and he'd been thrown out of more schools than he could count. Both his parents had been good-looking, and he had no complaints when he caught his reflection in the mirror. Perhaps the earl had chosen him as he might choose a thoroughbred to cover a mare. Reyn was showy and spirited, and came from good bloodlines even if no one had won prize money in a race lately.

He picked up his neckcloth from the carpet and began to strangle himself with it. "I have no idea, Lady Kelby. Did you not discuss this whole affair with him?"

"I told you he hasn't been well," she snapped. "He's so worried I cannot believe he is clear-headed, else he never would have selected you."

"Consider me deselected. I shall return the advance at the earliest opportunity."

"Why did you take the money if you did not plan to honor your word? Do you find me so unattractive?"

Reyn felt a stab of annoyance. He was not going to do the pretty when the woman had kneed him in the groin. "Don't fish for compliments, Lady Kelby. You can hardly expect me to tell you I desire you when it's clear you loathe me. I had need of the money. Still do. My sister is—well, she's dying, just like your husband is—only she doesn't live inside a thousand acre park with a thousand servants to tend her and a devoted spouse who will do anything, no matter how repulsive, to make her happy. You must love your husband very much to come here to find me."

Lady Kelby flushed. "I-I do. He . . . he's a wonderful man. Henry is very dear to me."

"I'm sorry for you then. My sister is dear to me also, and I neglected her for years. I was quite desperate when I met with Mr. Ramsey. I really would have done most any job he offered to make my sister's last months easier. But not this one."

"N-no. I am sorry for you, too."

Reyn smiled. "We're quite a pair, aren't we? I'm a thief, and you were ready to let me steal your virtue if there's any left to steal."

Oh, he'd gone too far with that. The lovely blush that had stained her cheeks retreated. He expected her to curse him, to strike him, or flounce out of the room in high dudgeon like Patsy did.

Instead, Maris's lips trembled and her large brown eyes filled with tears. "How dare you," she whispered. "You cannot know the agony—" Her sob choked her words away.

Tears were usual at the Reining Monarchs Society as well as shouts, but Reyn had never been able to harden his heart against them. He walked over to Maris, intending to hand her his handkerchief and straighten her hat, but somehow put his arms around her and got a nose full of gray organdy ribbon. His cravat would have to be retied, for Lady Kelby clung to it as if it were a lifeline.

"There now. I'm sorry," he said, patting the buttons on the back of what surely was the most unbecoming dress he'd ever seen on a peeress before. Did not her husband still have his eyesight? Perhaps he didn't, although the man had stared quite sharply at him the day they met.

Henry Kelby's eyes were black as a crow's, much like Reyn's own. Reyn had seen a portrait in the library of the earl in elaborate court dress from the last century, his hair covered by a wig. Maybe when the Earl of Kelby looked at him, he saw a resemblance to his younger self. It was impossible to know.

"Please don't cry."

Lady Kelby gave a great shuddering hiccup and continued to dampen Reyn's shirtfront. The woman had been pushed to the edge over the impossible situation.

Durant was ashamed he'd made it worse. "I didn't mean it, Lady Kelby. I always say the first foolish thing that pops into my head. I need a keeper, I do. Or a muzzle."

All his life, he had spoken too soon, acted too soon. The latter had been useful in battle, but it wasn't always welcome in civilian life. Sometimes he felt his skin itch from the inside out. Heard bees in his head. Couldn't sit still. Couldn't read a book without falling asleep or flinging it against a wall.

He also couldn't walk away from a dare or a challenge. If he had a brain in his head, he'd set the woman aside and stride out the door. Find Patsy and fuck her if Blivens wasn't already at the task.

Reyn didn't have a brain. Not a useful one, anyway. He held Lady Kelby until she stilled in his arms, then lifted her chin. Her dark eyelashes were wet and spiky, but the little lakes that had pooled in each brown eye had dried. She stared at him so hard he thought he might forget what he wanted to do.

"Forgive me," he said, and kissed her.

There was no kick, no struggle. Her lips opened in surprise and he swept in. She tasted of tears and tea. And innocence. She was inexpert at kissing him back, and that only made him more regretful that he'd started the whole thing.

What on earth was wrong with him? Lady Kelby was not his type, pale and gray and brown as she was.

She was married and loved her elderly husband. Reyn didn't dally with married women unless they were free of such nonsense. Patsy and the others looked for him to replace the boredom of their arranged marriages with a bit of wicked spice. He'd been happy to oblige, even if he'd had to use a cane or a crop or wield his cock as a welcome weapon. He didn't seduce innocents.

Lady Kelby's reluctant tongue touched his, sending an electric jolt to his groin.

He frowned. He didn't even know her first name. But there were so many things he didn't know, and he'd managed to get along in life perfectly well. Well enough, anyway.

His mind might be a perfect blank at the moment, but his body was fully engaged with the woman in his arms, whose kidskingloved hands trembled against his throat. In fact, every bit of her shook as if she were immersed in a Canadian snowbank, which set off an avalanche of response within him. Her mouth was soft and yielding, allowing his very thorough exploration.

Reyn held her closer, his fingers busy with the line of fabric-covered buttons at her back, her bountiful soft breasts snug against his shirt. He brushed up past boned linen to the scoop of warm skin above her chemise, hoping the lush kiss might distract her into wantonness.

The touch of his fingers to her flesh alerted her to his intention, causing her tongue to stop mid-tangle. Reyn opened his eyes to see hers, dark as coffee. They blinked, and he felt her pull away.

He was still mostly a gentleman, so he released her, stepping back and banging his bad knee against the chair.

"W-what are you doing, Captain Durant?" She wiped the wet from her swollen lips.

He shrugged. "I'm sorry for that, too, if you didn't like it."

She said nothing.

He was not so full of himself to believe his kisses could leave someone speechless, but it had been a damned good kiss once the woman relaxed into it. He wondered if she still kissed her husband . . . or anyone else. Somehow he doubted it.

"Did it . . . does it mean you've changed your mind about coming to Kelby Hall?"

He should tell her no. What kind of man would he be to father a child and then walk away? The whole idea was insupportable. Reyn had no particular yearning for marriage and fatherhood, but that didn't mean he was completely without honor, no matter what Lady Kelby said. What was the lesser of two evils—taking unearned money or abandoning a child? He opened his mouth and then shut it.

Lady Kelby stood proud, her chin raised despite the wobble of her bonnet. She would lose it soon, and good riddance. But her eyes betrayed her. They were damp again with desperation. Whether she was desperate for him to say yes or no, he wasn't quite sure.

Reyn was certain she had not been in favor of her husband's scheme, no matter how devilish David Kelby was. Saving books and silly statues was not enough for her to commit adultery with a complete stranger. Lady Kelby did not seem to be the sort to break *any* of the commandments.

"Let me do up your buttons."

"You have not answered me." She turned her back in acquiescence.

"I haven't." Reyn was never much of a thinker, but he felt obligated to make some sense of his scattered thoughts. He concentrated on each gray button, covering up inches of snow-white skin and linen. Would he want to release her from the confines of an equally ugly dress in the future? He just didn't know. He placed his hands on her shoulders and turned her gently.

"Give me a day to think this over again. Where are you staying?"

"Mivart's Hotel on Brook Street."

"I assume your husband is not with you."

She shook her head and the hideous hat collapsed to her shoulder. "He does not know I'm here."

"Here in London? Or *here?*"

Lady Kelby struggled to untie the double knot on her gray organdy ribbon. Her hands still shook, and Reyn felt it necessary to assist her. He was good with his hands, liked to keep them busy, even if it meant he played lady's maid.

She stood solemnly still as he made quick work of the difficulty and drew the hat away. "He knows I am in London. I told him I had some shopping to do."

Good. She needed new clothes. Lady Kelby looked like she was in mourning already.

"So he doesn't know you came to find me?"

"He did not send me. I'm not sure he would approve."

"I should say not. It's very shocking that you are here," Reyn replied. "Have you a chaperone lurking somewhere downstairs?"

"I sent my maid back to the hotel once I found out where you were. Bad enough one of us had to enter this place," Maris said tartly, taking back her hat from him and pinning it back on with a wickedly sharp hatpin.

Reyn picked up his yellow silk waistcoat. He was in need of a shopping trip himself. Now that he was no longer constrained by a uniform, his taste in civilian clothing had yet to be discovered. He feared the waistcoat was undoubtedly a mistake. "You were foolish to come, and I don't believe you are usually a foolish woman."

"I wrote," she reminded him. "That seemed to do no good."

He was not about to explain the trouble he had reading her handwriting. It was probably perfectly formed, but it had given him a headache. He had enough difficulty with a printed page without trying to decipher Lady Kelby's pretty loops and curlicues.

He *could* read. Barely, and certainly not for pleasure. The number of books in the Earl of Kelby's library had failed to impress him.

"Let me escort you back to Mivart's."

"Won't Patsy miss you?"

Surely Lady Kelby was not jealous. "I'm sure she's found an adequate substitute," he said, squeezing himself into his coat. He saw her hesitate, then drop her veil.

"All right. The quicker I can get out of here, the better."

He offered an arm and they left the room. "How is it you got past Mick Fisher?"

"I lied, sir. Just as you have."

"Ouch. I don't suppose you even need a knife to cut your dinner when your sharp tongue will do. I also take it lying does not come naturally to you?"

In the long hallway, she took a misstep, causing them to careen toward a marble-top table.

"Easy, Lady Kelby. One foot in front of the other. Don't worry if anyone sees us. The Monarchs are a discreet bunch, believe it or not."

"D-do you require all those peculiar implements on the wall to . . ." Her words faded.

Reyn wished he could see her face clearly. She must think the absolute worst of him. He laughed. "To perform? You need have no fear, Lady Kelby. I bought a subscription to the club as a lark. A dare." He had beyond bored, and it had seemed a good idea at the time. He was as normal as the next man, more or less, with some significant exceptions.

"Shouldn't the money you spent have gone to your sister?"

Yes, he should have settled the extra sum on Ginny, but she had been safely set up in the country before he won his little windfall. Lord Kelby's gold had seen to that. Reyn was spared from answering by the sight of a contrite Mick Fisher at the bottom of the stairs.

The butler began his effusive apologies from the hallway below as Reyn steered Lady Kelby down the marble steps. "Beggin' your pardon, Captain. I told the mort not to go up to bother you. She promised me she'd stay put." Fisher gave Maris a pugnacious glare.

"No bother at all, Mick. Really, it was quite delightful to have her join me."

Lady Kelby stiffened under his hand, but did not contradict him.

"Mrs. Rumford weren't none too pleased to be interrupted, Captain, I can tell you that. You'll have some fences to mend there. Lady Kelby, I believe Mrs. R. said her name is?"

Damn the man, and damn Patsy. The countess's reputation would suffer if it was discovered she'd been entertained at the Reining Monarchs Society even for so short a time as a brief conversation.

And especially after that kiss.

"I think you misheard, Mick." Reyn stuck his hand in his pocket and brought out the coins Lady Kelby had refused, dropping them into the butler's open palm and praying he kept quiet. The man must be getting quite rich working there, and it was easier than getting pummeled nightly in a boxing ring. "Is Mrs. Rumford still about?"

"Went home, she did. Called a hack for her myself. If I was you, I'd go visit her with a peace offering right quick."

"Thank you, Mick. I shall do that immediately. Lady *Trilby*, shall we leave?"

In what passed for a sprint in so large a man, Mick made it to the front door before they did and held it open. "Good afternoon, Captain Durant. Good afternoon, Lady *Trilby*."

Reyn took a left turn at the sidewalk.

"Mivart's is in the other direction," Lady Kelby objected.

"I know that. We're giving Mick some misdirection. He may seem as if he's been hit in the head too many times, but he's very shrewd. Did he see your face?"

"Oh. Oh dear."

"I take it that's a yes. We'll just have to hope my little bribe was sufficient. Patsy will be more difficult to silence, but leave her to me." Reyn patted Maris's arm confidently, hoping his words were true.

"Do you have a paddle in your pocket to persuade her?"

"Lady Kelby, you have a very prurient mind. I trust my natural charms are sufficient to assuage Mrs. Rumford."

Maris sniffed as they passed gated front gardens with pruned boxwood and urns of hardy pansies. The neighborhood was lovely, if one liked bland and orderly—with the exception of the Reining Monarchs in its midst, of course.

Reyn looked around. "Is it not a lovely day?"

"I am not going to waste my time discussing the weather with you, Captain Durant."

Ha. That was his usual reaction to such talk, was it not? Conversations about the weather put him to sleep, unless he was on patrol in Halifax, where it paid to wear some extra layers and complain accordingly. "How are we to get to know each other better, Lady Kelby?"

"I don't *wish* to know you."

Her kiss told him otherwise. "If I agree to your husband's plan—

and that's a big, Mt. Olympus–sized if—it will be easier if we are friends."

"Friends!" Maris stopped dead on the street and dropped his arm. The tiny flowers stitched across the lace covering her face made it difficult to see her expression, but Reyn could well imagine it. "If you *do* change your mind, I would expect nothing but an efficient effort on your part. No friendship would be necessary."

"You have the oddest idea of coupling, Lady Kelby. I'm not a dancing bear to be brought into the circus ring to perform and then put back in its cage."

"No one called you any sort of animal! You will be well compensated. You already have been, may I remind you. You'll have food and lodging and anything you like, within reason. But not my friendship."

She was not making the venture any more enticing. Reyn would not have minded a little flattery or flirting, two things which Lady Kelby seemed incapable of.

"How do you expect to explain my presence at Kelby Hall?"

Maris resumed walking, her stride nearly as long as his. She was not some mincing debutante.

He pictured her racing down the long, straight avenue that led to Kelby Hall, wavy brown hair flying behind her. She probably always kept it pinned back, though. Everything about her was pinned, tight, buttoned.

He could change that.

If she let him.

"My husband will say you are a fellow antiquities enthusiast, come to help me catalogue what's stored in crates in the attics. His father and grandfather—in fact, all the Earls of Kelby—were avid collectors, although not the scholar Henry is. If it wasn't Etruscan, Henry had no interest in it. But now he's curious. He would like to know exactly what's up there before he dies. All you need do is be found with some notebooks and a pair of spectacles and dust in your hair and people will presume you're an expert."

It was Reyn's turn to stop walking. "You're joking. You expect me to *catalogue* that junk?" He could hardly think of anything more horrifying, unless he was asked to unwrap a mummy. There might even be one in some box stored in the attic.

"I shall be doing the actual cataloguing. I would never expect a man such as yourself to appreciate ancient history and civilizations. But it will give us an excuse to be together. No one will bother us while we're working."

"Why, Lady Kelby. Are you proposing to compromise me in broad daylight?"

"My eyes will be closed, Captain Durant. I expect you to close yours, too."

Chapter 3

R eyn had a difficult evening. Patsy Rumford had not been
fobbed off with a few cuddles and kisses, and he was ever so
glad to see her husband return early from his club before being
forced to go further. She may have been wanton at the society, but
she was a dutiful wife at home. How she explained his visit to her
husband he had no idea, but likely she would find her movements
restricted in the future.

It would be something else she'd resent him for. Reyn was not
convinced she'd keep her mouth shut about Lady Kelby, even if
he'd promised her unlimited punishment and pleasure at a later
date.

Worse, Lady Kelby had tattled on him. He'd come home to a
tersely worded note from Mr. Ramsey on *London List* stationery,
who urged him to keep his commitment to the Kelbys. It did not
take a genius to read between the neatly printed lines. He had
threatened to reveal Reyn's recent coronation as a Monarch in one
of his wretched gossip columns—not that anyone but his sister
Ginny would care.

Reyn was already sorry he'd joined the society, for it had done
nothing but make him feel a bit ridiculous, whacking at women—
and some men—like a mad villain from one of the demented gothic
Courtesan Court novels Ginny liked to read. If he hadn't been at
such loose ends . . . but there was a solution to all that. He could go
to Kelby Hall and impersonate a bloody classics professor.

The Kelbys were collectively insane. While they may both be
experts in Etruscan civilization, they knew nothing about Reynold
Durant in the nineteenth century. He would never be able to pull off
such a deception. Apart from his youth, there was his ignorance to

deal with and his inability to examine anything for any length of time before he lost interest. The idea of being trapped in an attic with the Countess of Kelby and remnants of ancient dead people's things collected by somewhat more recently dead people held absolutely no allure.

She had told him he was not really expected to do any scholarly work, so there must be a couch or an old feather mattress she planned on using for sexual activity, however. Reyn wondered how many times a day she would expect him to service her. It gave him something to contemplate as he drifted off to sleep.

He woke up the next morning—not that he'd slept very long or very well—almost convinced to do as hired, or at least go to Kelby Hall for a day or two and see where that led him, though he was a little annoyed with Ramsey. He didn't like thinking of him and Lady Kelby conspiring against him like two strict schoolteachers with a naughty boy in their charge. He wasn't even all that naughty, when one examined all the facts.

Blast. That was what came of trying to adjust to civilian life without adequate income or occupation. Throw poor Ginny into the mix and he had been between a rock and a very hard place.

He had plenty of time to ride out Richmond to see his sister before he made his final decision. Ginny wouldn't judge him, not that he'd tell her what he'd been up to lately. She still thought of him as a hero, and he didn't want to disabuse her of that preposterous notion, particularly on the front page of *The London List*. What he'd done on the Belgian battlefield five years ago was steeped so deep in the mists of time he could barely remember it. He may have won his captaincy as a result, but his career had been distinctly downhill from there.

He'd managed to hang on to his old charger Phantom through thick and thin, and Reyn walked to the stables where the horse was housed. After a few words with the groom, he found his horse waiting, long nose poked over the stall. The gelding seemed pleased to see him, whickering and tossing his coarse gray mane in greeting. Reyn pulled an apple from his coat pocket and watched while Phantom enthusiastically chomped down on it. The horse didn't have a care in the world. He was warm and fed and dry, no longer evading bullets or sabers.

Not faced with a moral dilemma, either.

Reyn dealt with the tack himself and wended through London's morning traffic. The December day was bright and clear, with just enough nip in the air to make the ride to Richmond pleasurable. It was not long before he came to Ginny's cottage. A few very late roses climbed bravely up the lattice by the door. The house was altogether charming, much nicer than anywhere Ginny had lived in a long time. Their parents' financial circumstances meant that year by year their accommodations were reduced in size and restricted by neighborhood.

When Reyn had come back to London from Canada, he'd found his little sister pale and coughing her head off, living above a butcher shop belonging to their old cook's brother. He'd done what he could, moving her to better lodgings along with Mrs. Clark the cook. Thanks to the Earl of Kelby, the cottage and the extra servants were a vast improvement.

After tying Phantom to a bare sapling in front of the house, he strode down the path and knocked on the door. Ginny wasn't expecting him, as he usually visited on Sundays. Most of the time she was too ill to attend church services, but the earnest young vicar stopped by Sunday afternoons and she seemed to take comfort from his visits.

Reyn had endured the homilies and platitudes over tea for his sister's sake, but was not convinced God was watching out for any of them. If anything, the Old Boy must have lost patience with him years ago, when he could not sit still in church to save his life. His mother had swatted him after he looked up at the ceiling one Sunday and said during a lull, "That's enough, God. I want to go home." Some in the congregation had tittered; most had not. But it was not long afterward that his parents were evicted from the manor house they leased and had moved to yet another parish where Reyn endeavored to say nothing but "Amen."

Molly, the maid of all work he'd hired, opened the door and blinked in surprise. "Good morning, Captain. It's not Sunday."

Reyn doffed his hat. "I trust you'll let me in anyhow, Molly. Is Mrs. Beecham about?"

"She's upstairs with Miss Virginia. They neither of them passed a peaceful night, I'm afraid."

"How bad was it?" Reyn asked, afraid to hear the answer.

"Mrs. B. worried she'd cough up blood this time, but she didn't, praise God. Cook's gone out to get a beefsteak to build up Miss Virginia's strength."

Beefsteak probably would not help, but Reyn was grateful to his family's longtime loyal cook and the other two women who attended his sister. He'd been lucky to get them through Mr. Ramsey's *London List.* When he'd explained to the newspaperman why he was applying for the Kelby job, the man had worked a miracle, finding the cottage *and* the nurse and maid. Ramsey had taken pity on him then, but was not so happy with him now.

Reyn followed Molly up the narrow stairs, ducking his head. The cottage was sturdy, though built a century ago when people must have been considerably shorter—or knocked unconscious regularly by the low beams. Reyn heard his sister gasp for breath, then the comforting murmur of Mrs. Beecham before he entered the little bedroom.

Ginny was propped up against half-a-dozen pillows, her face gray, her dark curls damp beneath a lace cap. To his mind, she was much too young to wear a spinster's cap, but she might never live long enough to be anyone's bride.

Poor Ginny. She was just twenty-two, and had spent half her life in poverty and illness. He'd escaped when he was barely more than a boy, but he should have given her a thought before he ran off to enlist.

"Reynold!" Her face lit at the sight of him, but then the coughing spasms began. Her little terrier Rufus thumped his tail, but remained in Ginny's lap.

"Captain Durant, this is a surprise. But a welcome one." Mrs. Beecham patted Ginny's face with a dry cloth. Despite the open window and the breeze wafting through it, beads of sweat shimmered on his sister's forehead and throat. "Do you want me to leave the two of you alone?"

"If you don't mind. I promise I won't tire her too much." Reyn pulled a chair up closer to the narrow bed and rubbed the dog's ears. "Good morning, sweetheart. Don't try to talk. Promise?"

Ginny bit a lip and nodded. Her eyes were fever-bright beneath dark brows as formidable as Reyn's. She resembled him greatly, from the curl and color of her hair to her long, straight nose to the dimple in her cheek. Where he was handsome, she was handsomer still, or would have been if her pallor did not betray her. But she'd never had a season to show off her dark good looks, never danced, never flirted.

And never would. Reyn restrained himself from punching one of her pillows. It was so unfair. She'd done nothing to deserve her fate. Their parents had died in a house fire two years ago while he was still in Nova Scotia. Ginny had not succumbed, but her lungs had been so damaged the doctors who treated her were not optimistic she would ever fully recover.

It was really a miracle she was still here. She had never been strong, even before the accident, catching cold with every shift of the weather, struggling to breathe in London's wet yellow fog. He'd been foolish to think the recent move to Richmond might make a difference.

But it had only been two months. He had money for better doctors now, better food, better care. Their old cook Mrs. Clark had done the best she could with limited resources until he'd come back a year ago. The woman was a saint, a better mother to Ginny than Corinne Durant had ever been.

"I may have to go away on business for a little while, Gin. Not far, though, just outside Guildford. If you need me, I can be back here in a trice."

"Business?" she whispered. "What sort of business?"

"I told you not to speak."

She grinned up at him. "I never follow orders."

Nay, she hadn't. Reyn had had a willing accomplice in his younger sister as they made mischief for their parents. She'd been a lively little girl before he'd gone away. Before her asthma became so troublesome. The damage to her lungs made those earlier breathing difficulties seem like child's play.

"Have you a promise of a real job?" Ginny had not been happy to learn that Reyn was earning his living by gambling as their parents had. In her eyes, Reyn should have been doing something respectable—clerking for some great man or seeking a position as a steward. The fact that he had trouble tallying up numbers larger than the ones to count the points in his hand was unknown to her. He was good with figures in his head; it was just the sitting down to tote them into neat columns that defeated him. The damned numbers would not stay where he put them no matter how careful he was.

He managed his money well enough now that he had some, except for the purchase of that unfortunate waistcoat. He'd have to make it last and hope for more luck, as any avenue of gentlemanly employment seemed blocked for him by his vexing stupidity.

No. He was not stupid. Just . . . different.

"Yes. A *real* job. I'm to help an old earl clean out his attics."

She pinched his coat sleeve. "Don't bam me, Reyn."

"It's the honest truth. The man wants an accounting of the treasures he has up there before he sticks his spoon in the wall."

"That sounds exciting! I wonder what you'll find."

"Loads of dust and probably dead mice, love. Over the centuries, I gather his ancestors brought back everything that wasn't nailed down from three continents. Perhaps I'll discover the Holy Grail."

"I wish I could help. I'd love to see such things." She gave him a wistful look, then turned her attention to Rufus, who snorted happily on the counterpane as she scratched his belly.

"Perhaps I'll sneak something out for your inspection."

"Don't tease. You wouldn't want to lose this position, Reyn. Perhaps the earl will keep you on permanently."

Reyn couldn't imagine such a thing, but he nodded and joined her in indulging Rufus. He had wondered at first if the dog might upset her breathing, but the comfort the little animal provided seemed worth the risk.

"Rufus hasn't had a proper run since you were here Sunday."

Reyn took the hint and scooped the dog up. "It will do us both good to get some fresh air, then," he said, kissing his sister's damp forehead. Some days she was well enough to leave her bed and take the animal out herself, but today was not one of them.

Once outside in the walled back garden, he plopped Rufus on the grass to do his business and picked up a handful of acorns, rolling them around in his palm. The oak in the center of the lawn was stripped, brown leaves curling on the ground.

Reyn had not been impressed with the recent English autumn. He missed the breathtaking fall foliage of Nova Scotia. After Waterloo, he'd spent almost four years with what was left of his regiment in Canada. He'd not much cared for the ocean crossing, but once he was there the blunt natural beauty of the place had awed him. The primeval forests, rough Atlantic coastline, and abundant wildlife—even the winter hardships—had touched something within him. Canada had nothing like the manicured countryside of Kelby Hall. That civilized place had made him feel like a savage. Everything about the estate was managed, from the formal gardens to the geometrically clipped yew hedges to the uniformity of the pea stones on the drive. The long façade of the house itself, with its glowing honey-colored stone and scores of windows, was designed to intimidate. Rumor had it that one of the Kelby earls rebuilt the original dwelling to please Queen Elizabeth, who had been a frequent guest.

Reyn had seen nothing but the enormous entry hall and the library on his visit. He'd felt dwarfed by the high coffered ceilings and long windows. Somehow the rugged cliffs and roar of the ocean on Cape Breton did not frighten him quite the way silent, elegant Kelby Hall did.

Reyn turned to his sister's snug cottage and tossed an acorn up to her bedroom window as he'd done from the time they were children. In the old days it was the signal for her to slip out of bed and join him on an adventure. Now it just garnered him a puzzled look from Rufus.

"I know, boy. You want me to throw something for you." Reyn cast around for a proper stick to throw and found one amidst the fallen leaves. He spent the next ten minutes running the dog from one end of the garden to the other until his arm ached. When he looked up, Ginny was standing at the window, her thin white hands pressed against the glass. He gave her a jaunty wave, as though the sight of her wasn't a bit spectral.

"All right, Rufus. Fun's over for us, I think. Time to return to town and face the Gorgon." Not that Lady Kelby was Gorgonish at all. From what he'd seen when her hat fell off, her hair was not snakelike but molasses-brown. She was not exactly beautiful, but no single feature was objectionable. She was tall and well formed, her face a near-perfect oval with dark eyes and a wide mouth. He'd not seen her smile yet, but wanted to.

What in hell was the matter with him?

Oh, what wasn't? He was beyond bored. Still. And in desperate need of an adventure. He must be desperate indeed, if he thought mounting grim Lady Kelby would be any sort of adventure. Where was Napoleon when one needed him?

Nothing might come from his trip in the country, and that suited him perfectly. It was rather repugnant to think of himself as that dancing circus bear. He might get some country air and shooting in though, if an antiquities expert was allowed to hold a modern gun.

Reyn rubbed his shoulder, wishing he could pluck out the ball inside. It was so inconveniently lodged that the army sawbones had been reluctant to go digging any further for it. After six years, it was a part of him, tangled in muscle and blood.

Everyone carried some sort of secret inside, didn't they? Reyn wondered what Lady Kelby's was. He supposed he'd soon find out.

Chapter 4

Maris sat on the divan in the hotel room, giving thought to the night before. Captain Durant had come to Mivart's in person to tell her he had changed his mind. Again. And she'd had an additional request. It had been a tricky thing getting him to cooperate, and a horribly awkward conversation, but she had been adamant, insisting he see Henry's London physician before he left the city.

She could see that Durant had been torn between humiliation and apoplexy. The muscle in his scarred cheek had jumped a mile. To his credit, the man did not lose his temper, although his black brows struggled to remain level. They really were quite terrifying things, like glossy, overfed caterpillars.

She'd been impressed with the control he'd exhibited, but then, he'd been a soldier. Soldiers were supposed to be stoic at orders they doubted, were they not? He'd opened his mouth and quickly shut it, nodded and held his hand out for the address she'd written on a piece of hotel stationery.

To her relief, he had said nothing about her meeting Mr. Ramsey, either. Perhaps it had been a bit underhanded of her to have enlisted the newspaper editor's help, but Henry had depended upon the man's discretion. Maris had asked him to continue to look for a suitable candidate, just in case, God forbid, Captain Durant didn't come up to scratch after Ramsey's little threat. Perhaps another gentleman could be found to perform in his place.

But that had not been necessary. Reynold Durant would join them within a few days if he were not afflicted with some gentleman's gruesome complaint. The captain had been punctiliously correct at their meeting in her hotel suite last night, with nary a sign that he wanted to steal kisses or pursue "friendship" with her. Maris took that as a good sign. What was between them was no more than a business transaction—unusual business, to be sure—but there was nothing of a personal nature between them, nor could there ever be.

Maris stood. With the prospect of an heir for Kelby Hall looking somewhat brighter, she had delayed her own departure for home. Henry thought she was in town to do some shopping, so shopping she would go. There was no time to stand about in one's underthings to get pinned and poked, but if she could find some ready-made garments, why not? She had not ordered new dresses in years.

It had not mattered what she wore lately—she was bound to drop ink on her skirts or trail a sleeve through fixative. She'd become adept piecing fragments of linen and stone together, her hands steady. Maris was proud of her hands. They were strong and her one true beauty, with long, slender fingers and smooth white skin. She kept them covered with white cotton gloves when she worked with her artifacts, and kid and silk when she did not. Maris decided she'd buy new gloves to go with her new dresses, too.

She called to her maid Betsy and they set out for Madame Millet's, only to find the shop taken over by a wine merchant. *It truly has been a long time,* Maris thought ruefully. She was about to give up and go back to the hotel when she felt a tap on her shoulder. She turned at the audacity, but her sharp retort died upon her lips.

"Good afternoon, Lady Kelby. It's a lovely day for shopping, is it not?" Captain Durant held up several parcels tied with string. Maris could only hope one of them contained a suitable waistcoat.

She was not prepared to see him again quite so soon. He was bare-headed, his black hair gleaming like a crow's wing in the bright December sunshine. Soberly dressed, apart from the lack of a hat, he looked reasonably respectable, nothing like the wicked crop-wielding man she had first seen the day before yesterday.

"I-I w-wouldn't know." Damn, the man always made her stutter. It was a good thing they would have to do very little talking to each other. If she could insist he keep his eyes closed when they fornicated, she would ask him to do the same with his mouth. She didn't need to hear flattering falsehoods from him.

Or be kissed. Really, there was no need for kissing at all.

"The d-dress shop I hoped to patronize seems to have

d-disappeared," she continued, feeling flustered. "And g-good afternoon, sir." She sounded like her poor stepdaughter Jane, who
had been unable to string a sentence together without tripping over
her tongue. A vow of silence in Captain Durant's presence was definitely in order.

"Madame Millet's? She moved to a larger establishment about
six months ago. But you don't want to go *there*."

"I don't?"

"You don't. She dresses nothing but dowds and is quite *de trop*
amongst those in the know."

"If she's so awful, why did she have to expand the size of her
shop?" Maris asked, swallowing the insult. Madame Millet had
made the perfectly serviceable dress and matching spencer she was
wearing. Six years ago, but still. The stitching had held fast and the
trimmings looked fresh enough to her eyes.

"There are ever so many more dowds in England than there
should be, I suppose. But you don't have to be one of them, Lady
Kelby. Allow me to escort you to a much better dressmaker. It's not
far."

How on earth would he know? Patsy and the other women he'd
dealt with at the Reining Monarch Society were not wearing any
clothes at all as far as Maris could see.

"Do you consider yourself an expert on ladies' attire as well as
antiquities, Captain Durant?" It was best to convince Betsy that
Durant was who they would say he was.

"Not especially. You know my first love is all that old historical
rubbish, as some might say," the captain replied, taking the hint. "But
I had a few things made up for my sister from Madame Bernard.
She was very sympathetic and not too expensive. Although I don't
suppose cost matters much to the Countess of Kelby. You seem
willing to pay top dollar for what you want."

"Not in front of my maid," Maris murmured, taking the captain's
proffered arm and putting some distance between them and Betsy.
"You cannot say such vulgar things when you come to Kelby Hall.
You'll arouse suspicion."

"Well, I presume you'll tell people you hired me to muck out
your attics. No man works for free."

"You know nothing of those who are obsessed with history.

Some would pay *us* to get a chance to go through the Kelby Collection." Henry had been turning away supplicants for years.

"You're right. I know nothing. That might be a bit of a drawback."

"I can give you some books. You can read up a little, drop a phrase or two, and the staff should be satisfied." Maris was quite pleased that she had managed the conversation without stumbling over her words. She was always safe talking about the Kelby Collection.

Captain Durant said nothing for over half a block, but then rounded the corner and paused at a shop window. A collection of small silver objects glittered in an amazing display of craftsmanship. Even Maris, who, unlike generations of true-blood Kelbys, had no appreciable trace of magpie within her, was impressed. He pointed to a velvet-lined tray. "You should buy some hatpins here. I hear they come in handy to repel unwelcome advances from bad men. Speaking of which, what about the villain David? How am I to convince him of my scholarship?"

Maris wished she'd had a dozen hatpins to repel David Kelby five years ago. But they wouldn't have been enough. The truth was, she hadn't wanted to repel him, idiot that she was. "He does not live at Kelby Hall. But he does visit when he wants something, which is much too often. You'll have to be on guard against him." She turned away from a lacework butterfly with reluctance.

"Did he serve?"

"What? Oh, you mean in the army? Oh, heavens no. He's much too in love with himself to get in harm's way." Maris tried to imagine David killing anyone with a weapon other than his vicious tongue and came up short. Henry believed his nephew was the cause of Jane's death, but David would never bestir himself to actually put his hands around someone's throat. He would somehow convince his enemies to strangle themselves.

Well, that wouldn't work, would it? Once one was deprived of oxygen to the brain, one's hands would drop and—

Oh, good grief. Where was her mind taking her? Captain Reynold Durant unsettled her even as he continued to steer her down the fashionable side street.

"Here we are. I told you it wasn't far." He opened the door, and a delicate bell above tinkled. The shop was empty, thank goodness, because the vexing man was still at her side. No gentleman accompanied a lady to a dress shop unless he was her protector or her husband. Surely he was aware of that.

"Thank you, Captain. You may leave us now." Maris hoped the chill in her voice was clear enough.

"What, and deprive myself of all the fun? Come in, come in—what is your maid's name, Lady Kelby?"

Maris was too shocked to speak.

"Betsy, sir," her maid supplied unhelpfully. If she was worth a fraction of what Henry paid her, she'd push Captain Durant out the door to protect her mistress. But alas, Betsy had a moonstruck expression on her face as she took in the blackguard's impressive physique and dashing smile.

"Don't worry about indiscretion, ladies. Madame Bernard has a back room for her best patrons, which you are about to be. I'll just tuck myself in a corner and offer some advice. Ah, Fleur, *ma cher!* Here you are. See whom I've brought. The Countess of Kelby who is in desperate—one might even say dire—need of you."

The bell had summoned a large, forbidding Frenchwoman who looked like no one's *"cher,"* or much of a flower, for that matter. Her hair and eyes were iron-gray and the rest of her resembled a battleship ready to launch a hundred deadly cannon balls. She glanced at Maris with disapproval.

"Pah. I do not believe this drab could be the Countess of Kelby. I do not dress your loose women on credit, Reyn, so turn about and try to charm another hapless *modiste.*"

"On my honor, Fleur. You must apologize at once."

Maris started at Captain Durant's blistering tone. He had been the epitome of lazy, careless charm since she bumped into him on the street, but he was suddenly rather frightening. Those black eyebrows!

Oh, what if her baby inherited those eyebrows? She'd have to get a special brush.

Fleur Bernard dropped to so deep a curtsey Maris worried if the older woman could rise up again. "Pardon, your ladyship. This coxcomb is ever one for playing tricks upon me. He and his army friends—well, I shall spare you the tales. You are a most respectable woman, yes? I am covered in shame. Please forgive me."

Not having been born to the peerage, Maris had always felt uncomfortable when a fuss was made over her rank. She thought of herself as her husband's secretary first and his countess much further down the list. "It's . . . it's all right. Please do get up."

Reyn extended a hand and helped return Madame Bernard to her not inconsiderable height. She was exquisitely dressed. Her dress was black, but there was nothing funereal about it, trimmed as it was with thick lapis and silver braiding which shimmered in the shop lights. If Madame's own clothes reflected what she could do for her customers, Maris was ready to forget her earlier rudeness and submit to her intense gray stare.

"Come into my private parlor, my lady. Yvonne! Some tea and biscuits for our special customers," she called to her assistant.

Damn. That was another witness to her folly. But soon people at Kelby Hall would see her with Captain Durant. Maris would pray that if he was successful, her servants, and more important, David, couldn't count.

"That's not necessary, Madame Bernard. I'm not at all hungry."

"*C'est rien.* Choosing clothes is hard work, Lady Kelby. One must be fortified. Captain Durant, will tea be sufficient, or shall I have Yvonne fetch some brandy?" The dressmaker pronounced his name in the French manner. Maris imagined from his dark coloring he had Norman or Celtic blood. Henry had both. Was that why Durant had been chosen? Or had none of the men Henry interviewed been desperate enough to undertake this particular mission?

No, that wasn't right. Henry had not explained the nature of his need to the other two. He told her he'd been taken with Captain Reynold Durant from the instant he spied him riding up the drive.

"You do think ill of me to offer me brandy at this hour, Madame. It's not yet dusk. In fact the sun is shining."

"It is dusk somewhere, Captain, and you are not known to follow the conventions."

Captain Durant gave a husky laugh, which to Maris's ears seemed quite wicked. "No, I am not. But I'm giving up my ramshackle ways. The countess's husband has consented to employ me for a few months, and I'm on my best behavior."

"If that is the case," Madame Bernard said archly, "then I invite you to leave my shop at once. Thank you for bringing her to me, but you will not wish to compromise the lady's reputation and anger her husband. You might lose this desirable position."

Maris suppressed her grin at Captain Durant's obvious dismay. He had been most effectively routed. He was not her lover—yet—and had no right to sit and watch her shimmy into dresses.

"But of course. What was I thinking? Ah! I never think things through, Madame. Lady Kelby, forgive me for being so presumptuous. Betsy, I commend the countess's care into your capable hands. Oh! And just one more thing. You will be pleased to know, Lady Kelby, that the appointment you arranged for me was a smashing success. I visited with the gentleman just this morning. There will be no impediments whatsoever to my performing successfully in my new occupation. I am clean as a whistle. What can that mean, anyway? One would think whistles would be most unhygienic. All that spittle. *A bientot.*" He tipped an imaginary hat and left.

Some of the air in the room went with him. Maris put a gloved hand on a display case to steady herself. The captain's casual confession that he was not syphilitic was welcome, of course, but to announce it in such a way was preposterous.

He was so very improper. Impulsive. Indiscreet. Maris had never met anyone like him.

"Good riddance, *oui*? Right this way, my lady. The captain, he is full of so boyish charm. *Très charmant.* One could forgive a woman for losing her virtue to him. You must forgive me for coming to an entirely incorrect conclusion earlier. I should have recognized at once that you are not his type at all."

The pendulum had swung in an equally insulting direction. First, Madame Bernard had thought her a lightskirt; now she was too unattractive to capture the captain's attention as his lover.

Maris regretted she had ever sought to improve her wardrobe. She was tempted to leave in a justifiable huff, but somehow was swept into the private room and seated in a plush velvet chair.

"Now tell me what you have in mind, my lady."

"I don't really have time for all this," Maris said, waving her arm at the squares of fabric and pattern books that were artfully stacked on a large drum table. "I was hoping to find something ready-made. My husband is expecting me home tomorrow. And I don't like to . . . to fuss over my clothing. I like simple things."

"Ah. I see you are a practical woman, but you do have a lovely figure." Madame Bernard stepped back in contemplation, a finger on her chin. "I may have one or two dresses in the back that might suit you. But you would be much happier—and more *à la mode*—if I took some measurements and made a new wardrobe just for you."

"Oh, no. That won't be necessary." Maris didn't need an entire new wardrobe, just a few things so she wouldn't be such a *dowd.* Not that she cared one jot what Captain Durant thought of her. He would soon be taking those dresses off her, anyhow.

There was a knock on the door, and Yvonne entered with refreshments.

"Very well. But humor me, my lady. Allow me to send you one special dress. You will trust me to select the fabric and the color, yes? Think of it as a sample of what I can do to show you to advantage. When you come back to London and have the time, we can sit down with fashion plates. It will take Yvonne no time at all to get her tape. She is very efficient. Please make yourself comfortable. I shall return with the dresses I have on hand, and Yvonne can measure you after you try them on."

"I . . . all right." Maris felt beautifully bullied into agreement. Madame Bernard was skilled beyond her artistry with silk and scissors. "I shall pay you for the sample dress, of course."

Madame Bernard smiled. *"Naturellement."* She followed Yvonne out of the room, chattering in rapid French which exceeded Maris's schoolgirl understanding.

Maris poured the fragrant tea into two cups and passed one to Betsy. The young maid helped herself to an iced cake, but Maris was much too nervous to eat. She always felt awkward at the dressmaker's. If she had any skill with a needle and thread she would have preferred to sew her own clothes, but she was hopeless.

"This is a fancy place," Betsy whispered. "Imagine that captain knowing about it."

"Captain Durant is a most unusual gentleman. Lord Kelby is anxious that he get started on the inventory as soon as possible. He might be staying with us for a month or so."

"Ooh. He's very handsome, isn't he?"

Maris shrugged. "I suppose. But he's being hired for his historical expertise, not his pretty face."

"And it *is* pretty. He's ever so much nicer than my John." Betsy bit into her cake, cheerfully deriding the footman she was carrying on with. Maris should have no knowledge of Betsy's love life, but her maid couldn't seem to keep her indiscretions to herself. Sometimes Maris felt like the girl's mother. She *was* old enough.

Drat. The female servants would probably be swooning every time Captain Durant strutted through the hallways. But by and large, they were grateful to be working in an earl's household, knew their place, and would keep to it. Henry was a generous employer, as long as someone didn't meddle with his library.

The household ran like clockwork under the supervision of Amesbury, the butler, and Mrs. O'Neill, the housekeeper. Maris barely had to lift a finger, which was a good thing. Although she'd been raised at Kelby Hall, the intricacies of being a proper countess sometimes eluded her. She was certain a proper countess would not don breeches and dig through hillsides, sweating under the hot Tuscan sun .

Or solicit sexual favors from a complete stranger to perpetrate a fraud.

No, he wasn't a *complete* stranger. She was beginning to know the captain a little, even if he flummoxed her.

Maris drank her tea and did not have too long to wait before the women returned, each carrying three gowns.

Maris objected immediately to the rainbow of colors. "I usually wear gray or brown, Madame Bernard."

"As if I could keep my clientele with such dismal stuff," the dressmaker said dismissively. "You are still young, if not in the first blush of youth. Thank heavens, for white would wash you out."

Maris agreed. Her come-out dresses had made her look like a sickly ghost. The earl had financed her debut, cajoling his now-deceased maiden sister to sponsor her and Jane. At twenty, Maris had already been on the shelf and mortally shy in society. Seventeen-year-old Jane had not taken either. Despite being the daughter of a wealthy earl, she was even more reticent than Maris, crippled with a stutter that made the simplest conversation impossible.

Tails tucked between their legs, the girls had returned to Kelby Hall, swearing never to leave its confines again. Within four years, Maris was unexpectedly its chatelaine. Her friend Jane remained a confirmed spinster until David Kelby seduced and abandoned her.

"We shall try the wine silk first, I think," Madame Bernard said, scattering Maris's unhappy memories. "Your skin is fashionably pale, so you need no powder. But some rouge and lip salve would not go amiss. Yvonne, show Lady Kelby's maid our pots and brushes. Between the two of you, you should find the perfect colors."

Betsy rose, brushing cake crumbs from her black skirts. She wouldn't know one pot of paint from the other. Maris didn't require much from her but to do up her hard-to-reach buttons and brush her mud-brown hair free of tangles. Not a proper countess, she did not have a proper lady's maid. Betsy had helped Monsieur Richard in the kitchen until she'd dropped one too many platters, and Maris had taken pity on the girl, spiriting her upstairs.

"I've told you I like simple things," Maris said.

"Simple is one thing—ugly is quite another. There is no reason for a lady with your standing in society to appear so plain. You are *la comtesse*. This dress? Bah! It is not fit even for your little mouse of a maid. Take off that dreadful hat."

For an instant, Maris wished for Captain Durant's presence. Surely he would not let Madame Bernard hector her so? But she had no champion, not even her "little mouse of a maid." Maris pulled the pin from her hair and placed the hat on top of the tower on the drum table.

"Ah. Just as I thought. You are a brunette, Lady Kelby, and fortunate that you can wear bold colors without them overpowering you. The woman should wear the clothes, not the other way around. Garnet, emerald, bronze—these will suit you. No pastels. No blue, although perhaps a deep navy." Madame Bernard made quick work of Maris's buttons and Maris found herself in her plain linen underthings, earning a disapproving cluck from the dressmaker.

"Even if no one sees what is underneath, it improves a woman's confidence to know good quality is next to her skin. I shall get Yvonne to pack up some pretty chemises for you. And a proper corset. This one will not do."

Any response Maris could have made was blocked by a wash of dark ruby silk over her head. When her face emerged, her arms were being thrust into long tight sleeves. When she was hooked into the dress, most of her bosom was exposed by the low square neckline. The design was simplicity itself—as she had requested—but surely she would not be expected to show so much flesh?

"I see from your expression you are not happy. But does your husband not wish to admire his wife?" asked Madame Bernard.

"He . . . I . . . we lead a very quiet life. He is a scholar, madam, and we do very little socializing. He has not been well." Henry would not be smitten with this gown or any other.

"Poor soul. All the more reason to cheer him up, *n'est pas*? Your breasts, they are *formidable,* even in this sad corset. But if you wish, we might add a little ruffle on the bodice. I have some scraps of the fabric still and it would be a matter of minutes to have Yvonne run something up for your modesty. You will remain in town until tomorrow?"

"I plan to leave early in the morning."

"*Bien.* We shall manage. Now the green next, I think."

Maris endured Madame fitting her into three more dresses. She had to admit she looked uncommonly well in all of them, or would when minor adjustments were made. Betsy returned with Yvonne and watched with concentration while the junior dressmaker applied a subtle hint of color to Maris's lips and cheeks. Something was done to her hair as well, which made Maris almost reluctant to put her hat back on.

As it happened, she was not given that choice. Once she was measured, Madame decided the violet walking dress and matching coat needed no alteration and Maris would be wearing them out of the shop. A tiny pouf of matching velvet and feathers was found in the back room and affixed to her head. Maris could only blink at her reflection. She had never been so stylish.

Or so very purple.

"*Et voila!* Now you are fit to take the town by storm. I shall send everything round this evening to your hotel. Your own things as well, although I do hope you will not ever wear them again."

Somehow Maris agreed to gloves and stockings and a host of other fripperies in addition to the four new dresses. The afternoon would prove costly, and it was utter nonsense to try to make lamb out of mutton. She was four-and-thirty, well past her prime, and no one cared how she dressed.

"Oh, Lady Kelby," Betsy gushed. "You do look a treat!"

"Handsome is as handsome does," Maris grumbled. Feeling ridiculous, she swept out of the shop with Betsy at her heels. At least her half boots were still her own and comfortable. She hadn't gone but half a block when she heard a shrill whistle behind her.

"It's that captain, my lady!"

Whistling at me on the street? "Keep walking, Betsy, and don't look back."

"But he's running down the street after us!"

Damn. Even worse. Whistling *and* running. What was the matter with the man? They would attract attention. No one knew her in London, and that was the way she wished to keep it.

Captain Durant was at her elbow in seconds. "I almost didn't recognize you, Lady Kelby," he said, smoothly taking her arm and matching her stride. "If it wasn't for little Betsy here, you might have escaped my notice altogether."

"Why are you still here?" Maris hissed.

"It takes more than one fussy Frenchwoman to get rid of me. I say, Madame Bernard has outdone herself. You look absolutely *magnifique.*"

"Oh, do shut up." Maris could feel a natural blush augmenting the rouge.

"It's only right that I escort you back to Mivart's now that I took you out of your way."

"I can find my own way back, I do assure you." She found it impossible to disentangle her arm from his.

"I also wanted the opportunity to give you this." He thrust a small box into her hand.

"What is it? You should not be giving me gifts, you know. It isn't right."

"Be forewarned. Anyone can tell you I never do the right thing."

That was certainly true so far. The captain stopped walking, and Maris stumbled.

Betsy barely avoided careening into them, looking far too interested in the box once she righted herself.

"Betsy, I believe I left my handkerchief in Mrs. Bernard's shop. Could you fetch it for me, please?"

The maid's disappointment was obvious, but she left them alone.

"Open it."

"On the street? You're mad."

"Indubitably. I'm here with you, am I not? Here, I'll do it if you won't." He quickly opened the box. The butterfly hatpin twinkled on a bed of midnight blue velvet.

"How did you . . ."

He couldn't have known it had caught her eye unless he was a mind reader. And if he *was* a mind reader, she devoutly hoped he couldn't untangle her jumbled thoughts.

She was unused to getting gifts of any kind. Henry gave her unlimited pin money, but had never had a sentimental inclination in his life. Birthdays and Christmases had passed unacknowledged.

Maris closed the box. "You shouldn't have. I cannot accept this."

He smiled at her, unperturbed. "Yes, you can. Consider it an apology. We met under rather indelicate circumstances. I was, to put it bluntly, a cad. One small gift cannot even begin to express my shame."

Maris stared at him. Hard. There was a definite spark of mischief in his eyes. "You are no more ashamed than I am Queen Elizabeth."

Reynold Durant's smile broadened. "I see I cannot put anything over on you, Lady Kelby. But it's a pretty little thing, and it suits you. Here, let me." He took the package from her hand and pulled the pin from its velvet. Before she knew it, he was sliding the butterfly into the purple cap on her head.

Right on the street. Where anyone might see them. The act was so intimate, Maris lost her power of speech, which seemed to be a recurring condition in the captain's presence. Betsy had been goggling at them, but her eyes would be rolling straight out of her head to the pavement below if she was there.

Durant stepped back. "There. Now you are truly à la mode." He tucked the box into a pocket and placed her leaden arm into the crook of his elbow. "I shall make arrangements to join you at Kelby Hall by the beginning of next week."

It was Thursday. Maris would spend all the next day traveling. Thank heavens the captain would not be shut up in the Kelby coach with her. She would need a day or two simply to recover from the day's attentions.

How on earth would this all work? She needed to talk to Henry. But what could she say that wouldn't worry him? He was so desperate to deny David his birthright. Damn primogeniture and entail. It was not as if men were any wiser than women in estate management. Maris left the running of the house itself to her capable staff, but had long helped Henry and Mr. Woodley with estate matters. Henry was a generous landlord and employer, but more out of indifference than anything else. He assumed money would smooth the way so he wouldn't have to be bothered with petty domestic details.

Well, this one domestic detail he'd have to discuss. Captain Reynold Durant's improper deportment was a complication they couldn't afford to ignore.

Chapter 5

When the crested coach rolled up the long copper beech avenue, it was close to midnight. Maris had finally fallen asleep some miles back, but was gently shaken awake by Betsy.

"We're home, my lady."

Flambeaux were lit, and footmen scurried out into the dark, joining the outriders in divesting the carriage of its occupants and baggage. The December night air was chilly, and Maris wrapped the fur carriage robe closer before she abandoned it altogether. She must look a fright. She'd discarded her hat hours ago, and her gray traveling costume was wrinkled. Her new clothes were safely packed in the trunk in the boot, but she picked up the book she'd purchased for Henry. He would be up despite the hour. It seemed he slept less and less lately, but did not lose a fraction of his keen intelligence despite his fatigue.

Maris knew where to find him, but wasn't sure she'd find the words to tell him what she had done. She waved away Betsy's offer to freshen up and headed straight for the library. The room was bright as daylight with candelabra on all flat surfaces. Her husband's face lit with a smile as she approached, and he pushed himself up from his chair.

Where he had once been tall—as tall as Captain Durant—he now stooped a bit. His black hair had turned silver before Maris married him, but he was still a handsome man. When she was a child, he'd treated her like an extra daughter, but she had worshipped him, making her own father a little jealous.

Apart from their difficulties in the bedroom, the marriage had been everything Maris had ever hoped for. They shared common interests, and he was the only man who did not make her nervous. The seventh earl of Kelby respected her mind and treated her as an equal. Henry knew her better than she knew herself, as he proved immediately.

"Maris, my dear, what have you been up to? You look guilty as sin. And don't try to fob me off with a book, even if it's one I've been longing to get my hands on."

Maris put the book on the desk and sidled around it, enfolding herself in Henry's open arms. She was safe there, had always been. She cupped his thin cheek and kissed it. While he had been unable to perform in the strictest sense, their marriage bed had not always been cold. Much to her embarrassment, Henry had tended to her in the earliest stages of the marriage, and she knew what it felt like to flame under a man's touch.

David Kelby had ruined that comfort for her.

She searched Henry's face, pleased to see his dark eyes bright and unclouded. "How are you feeling? Have you been eating?"

"Mrs. O'Neill has been even more terrifying than you are. I've behaved just as I should in your absence. I missed you."

"And I you."

He raised a white brow. "But?"

"Oh, Henry. I may have done a foolish thing."

"Sit down, my love, and tell me all about it. Shall I ring for tea?"

She shook her head and left the warmth of his embrace with reluctance. Her gloved fingers picked nervously at her gray skirts. She couldn't sit down and face Henry's sympathetic gaze, didn't deserve his affection. She'd betrayed him once to her regret, and was about to do so again. This time, at his bidding.

Maris was heartsick, but knew how much a child would mean to Henry to carry on Kelby Hall's mission. David was no fit steward for the treasures within.

But would Captain Reynold Durant's son have appreciation for its history?

"I-I went to London, as you know," she began, once her husband was seated back in his chair.

He pushed aside the papers he'd been working on and folded his hands in expectation. "Yes. I hope you didn't spare any expense on your purchases. You've worked too hard lately."

Maris was certain Madame Bernard's bill would be astronomical. "I did buy a few things. But that was not the true purpose of the visit." She took a breath. "I found Captain Durant."

The only sound in the room was the quiet rumble of the fire. The room was overwarm, but Henry said his old bones craved the heat of the Tuscan sun. He was staring at the leather blotter with particular intensity.

Maris stole a glance at him. "Aren't you going to say anything?"

He raised his black eyes to hers. "I asked you to leave it to me, Maris. This business is not fit for a lady. Perhaps there's still time to find someone else."

"Henry! You are forgetting I'm smack in the middle of 'this business.' " She would leave aside his claim of sufficient time. Mr. Ramsey had not been especially encouraging about procuring another gentleman for this deviant purpose. "C-Captain Durant has agreed to come to Kelby Hall within a few days."

"How did you ever persuade him? His last letter was most definitive. He did not want the job after all."

"I didn't seduce him, if that's what you are implying," Maris said, stung.

Henry chuckled. "Nay, you haven't an ounce of seduction in you, my love. You're a good girl, more's the pity. If we had met when I was a young man, things would have been different. You've always been an apt pupil." He sighed and picked up his spectacles. "So Durant changed his mind. He doesn't want more money, does he?"

"I don't believe so."

"He said something about a sick sister."

"Yes, so he told me. His concern for her is in his favor, I suppose." It went some way to explain why he had ever agreed to this scandalous scheme to begin with.

"What did you think of him, Maris?"

She felt like she was treading into quicksand. She loved Henry, but there was no denying Captain Durant was an attractive man. Henry would know at once if she was lying. His illness and age had not robbed him of any of his acuity. She ceased her pacing and dropped into a chair. "He's very handsome."

"That should make it a little easier to bear, then. The intimacy," Henry clarified, as if she needed explanation. "I fully appreciate the sacrifice you'll be making for me, Maris. This goes well beyond humoring an old man. You've been a good wife to me, a great help-meet. Some might say you've thrown your youth away on me, missed opportunities. Captain Durant will go a little ways to making it up to you."

"I don't need any making up! You've been everything that is kind and good. Even when you are consumed with your studies, I've been consumed right along with you!"

"My little bluestocking," Henry chuckled. "There is more to life than books and bits of shattered pottery. Even *I* know that." He placed the spectacles on his nose and shuffled the papers he'd been reading back into order. "You must be exhausted. Go on to bed. We'll talk about this more in the morning."

"W-Won't you come to bed with me?" They no longer shared a room, but if this fiction of creating a child together was to be preserved, they needed to appear close again.

"I suppose you are right. It is very late, isn't it? But you know how restless I am, Maris. You won't get a wink of sleep."

"I don't care about sleep. I just want you to hold me, Henry. Like you used to."

"It would be my privilege," he said softly. "Go on upstairs. I'll join you shortly."

But when Maris woke at dawn, she was alone.

It took Reyn two days' travel to join the Kelbys. As usual, he visited his sister on Sunday, but stayed the night to break up the journey and give old Phantom a rest. He'd purchased two sober, scholarly-looking waistcoats, and a pair of clear glass spectacles that, in his own eyes, did nothing to make him appear any smarter. But if they helped trick the servants at Kelby Hall—and the villain David—they were a small price to pay out of his ill-gotten gains.

It was still afternoon when he rode down the beech avenue, the golden façade of Kelby Hall glowing in the sunlight. Despite his disinclination, he'd read up a bit on the house in one of those "great families of Britain" books. The old earl's ancestors had stolen the honey-colored stone from a nearby monastery. The building had an ecclesiastical look about it still, with winged stone angels over the carved oak front door and long gothic windows on the ground floor. What Reyn was about to do beneath its gabled roofs flew in the face of most of the Commandments.

The massive front door was opened by several footmen in silver and green livery well before he was anywhere near it. A groom appeared instantly to lead Phantom away, and Reyn was ushered into the vast paneled entry hall by the butler Amesbury, who was almost as old and starchy as the earl.

At one time, the room would have welcomed travelers with banquets and minstrels, but it was empty save for some massive paintings, tatty tapestries, and a couple uncomfortable-looking chairs before a sputtering fire at the far end. A waste, that. Who would sit there waiting for someone to knock on the door? Not that one would even need to knock. The staff at Kelby Hall seemed frighteningly on top of things.

That might prove to be a problem. Reyn took the spectacles out of his pocket and slid them onto his nose, hoping the length of it would keep them up. Durants tended to have long noses, giving them a Continental look. While in the army, he'd been teased for resembling the enemy. The back of his ears itched already from the metal stems.

Amesbury bent slightly at the waist. "We were expecting you, Captain. If you follow me, I'll show you to your room. I trust you will find everything to your liking."

Reyn followed Amesbury up a wide oak staircase, sure he'd be satisfied with the accommodations. He could tell the butler a thing or two about sleeping on the ground, and being glad of it—glad to be alive.

Reyn's new London lodging was pleasant enough, but nothing compared to the elegant suite of rooms he was led to, once they'd climbed another set of stairs and walked to the end of an endless hallway. Old Amesbury was a bit breathless, but pointed out the desk in a corner of the sitting room, fully equipped for a man of letters with pens, pots of ink, a stack of foolscap, and clean ledgers. An open door led to a light-filled bedroom, which overlooked the tree-lined avenue. Through yet another door was a dressing room with its own copper tub and cedar wardrobe. A brace of maids entered with towels and jugs of water for the washstand, and a footman delivered Reyn's well-stuffed saddlebag.

"I trust your trunks will be arriving shortly?" Amesbury asked.

Reyn had packed his most essential needs within the confines of the worn leather bag. He supposed it all looked inadequate for a month's stay, but he wasn't sure yet he'd be staying a month. If he did, he'd get a Christmas in the country out of it.

"My valet has it all in hand." Reyn shrugged. Likely Gratton was drinking himself silly at that very moment in relief over not getting sacked. It had been a near thing once Reyn found out the man had directed Lady Kelby to the Reining Monarchs Society. If Reyn needed anything else for this "visit," he could send word. The valet's wages and his rent were paid up through the end of the year.

By January, Reyn might have a better idea how to spend his time as a civilian. Inventorying might prove interesting, if one didn't want to read legible penmanship.

"Lord Kelby will see you in the library once you've refreshed yourself. Dinner will be brought to your rooms at eight o'clock, if that suits you."

So, he wasn't to dine with the family. Just as well. Reyn was not there as an honored guest, and he certainly did not have evening clothes with him. He was an employee, nothing more.

Not the sole hope of Clan Kelby.

"That suits me perfectly, Amesbury. I think I can remember where the library is."

"Should you need assistance, sir, just ring. The staff is at your disposal. When it comes time for you to begin your duties, a set of stairs to the attics is convenient just through the door opposite your suite. You need not trouble yourself navigating all through the house."

Clever of Lord Kelby to keep him confined to one end of the house like a mad uncle. But there must be other ways to gain entry to the attics, or Lady Kelby was going to attract unwanted attention coming too near his bedroom.

His meager belongings were swiftly unpacked and stowed, his face and hands cleaned of their road dirt, and his coat brushed, leaving no excuse not to locate the library. The architecture of the house was straightforward. Kelby Hall was one long rectangle of yellow stone divided by a center hall and numerous stairways. Everything eventually led back to the entrance hall in the middle of the house.

Reyn traversed it for the second time, noting its relative emptiness. All of the other ground floor rooms he passed had been overly furnished. It was as if Kelby Hall deliberately went out of its way not to make a grand impression, except for the sheer size of the room and its large fireplace. He could fit nearly all his friends—and there were a great many, for he was a good-natured fellow—in its interior, and they wouldn't even have to duck. At one time, entire animals must have been roasted within, but the room now held an unwelcome chill.

He passed numerous footmen, standing tall along the corridors as any of his regiment on parade. How incredibly tedious. He would go mad rigged out in stiff livery, standing around waiting to be summoned.

The hurry up and wait of army life had been bad enough. Reyn was never so happy as when he was in the midst of battle or exploring a forest expecting the natives to jump out from behind the trees. Everything came into focus for him then. His objectives were clear—to save his scalp and preserve what was left of his skin, and keep his men safe. Such activity was not precisely restful, he realized. Ordinary people would find his delight in fright incomprehensible.

He wasn't frightened as he tapped on the library door, but there was an unexpected constriction to his throat. He half expected one of the footmen to jump forward and open the door, but he managed to pull the knob all on his own.

The Earl of Kelby was hunched over a massive desk, strewn with papers from one corner to the other. He held a magnifying glass in his hand as well as wore half-moon spectacles. Presumably his weren't for show. Reyn's fingers went automatically to his own glasses and took them off. The earl followed suit and rose unsteadily from his chair.

"Camouflage, Captain Durant? I suppose Maris suggested them."

Maris. Up till that moment, Reyn had not known her name. It suited her somehow, a firm name, but soft upon the tongue. Unusual, just like its owner.

"Yes, my lord, she did. But it will take more than clear glass to make a scholar out of me."

"We're not interested in your bookishness, as you know. It will be enough to *appear* as if you are working for me. Sit down, my boy, sit down." The earl slid back into his leather seat.

"I'm not sure I've really changed my mind about this whole

thing," Reyn blurted. He remained standing, wondering if in fact he should bolt out the door and run by the army of footmen.

Kelby gave him a lopsided smile. "Crisis of conscience? That's what your letter called it."

Reyn had labored over that letter with painstaking care so as not to show his true ignorance. It had taken him hours to write it. "You must admit your offer was most singular."

"It was. It is. I understand Maris has explained the situation more fully than I did at your interview." The earl frowned at Reyn. "Captain, you're going to give me a crick in my neck if you don't settle yourself on that chair behind you."

"I'm sorry, sir. My lord," Reyn amended. He was not much used to conversing with such exalted personages. He collapsed into the chair and tried to look composed, but there was no disguising the whole situation made him nervous. Absently, his hand rubbed against the long scar on his thigh.

"Maris will be joining us shortly. I want to alleviate any awkwardness there might be. We're all adults, are we not? With a common goal. I understand why this position may be somewhat distasteful to you, and I'm prepared to offer you an additional stipend, beyond what we discussed earlier, if you are successful. You have a sick sister, I know, and no means of support except for your gambling."

Reyn swallowed hard. It was bribery, and the earl was good at it.

"Our original agreement was sufficient to my needs."

"One can never have too much money, Captain. Don't deny yourself and your sister out of pride."

Reyn could see it was pointless to argue with the old man. "Very well. But I may not be successful."

"I pray that you are. My nephew David killed my daughter, or as good as. She drowned herself in the lake because of him." The earl's hands shook as he spoke. "That is, of course, confidential. One more secret we have armed you with to destroy us."

"I would not do such a thing!" Reyn was tempted to get up and leave, ride all the way back to London.

"No, I don't believe you would. In fact, I am sure of it. I have every confidence in you." The earl gave him a ghostly smile. "We put it about that it was an accident. To have David step into my shoes"—Kelby shook his head—"no, I cannot let that happen. The thought of it comes close to killing me right now where I sit. Even if Maris is blessed with a daughter from your union, at least she'll have someone to comfort her when I'm gone."

"She could marry again." Reyn wished he could bite off his impulsive tongue.

The earl nodded. "So she could. She's young enough, and her widow's portion will be a lure to every fortune hunter in England. But my Maris is shy."

Reyn harkened back to the avenging angel who ferreted him out at the Reining Monarchs Society. Shy was not quite the word he would have used to describe her, so he said nothing.

"You will have to be careful with her," the earl continued.

Reyn could feel his ears going hot. He had never in his life had such a strange conversation. The earl was amazingly sanguine about giving instructions to another man as to how to bed his wife. It was clear from his tone and the careful words he used that he had great affection for Maris.

Reyn stood up abruptly. "How can you sit there and give me such advice?"

"What would you have me do, Captain? I'm dying. I don't have time to pussyfoot around. I need an heir, but I'm not heartless. Maris is a special woman. I'd like her to have some enjoyment over this thing I've asked her to do for me. She's . . . inexperienced. My fault entirely. Consenting to this goes against every rule she's ever followed, and believe me, she's a rule follower. Has been since she was a little girl, except when she's donned breeches to help me in my excavating." The earl smiled at the memory, and Reyn instantly pictured the tall Lady Kelby's long legs encased in tight gentlemen's trousers.

"But I know she loves me, or thinks she does," Kelby continued. "She's been loyal. Faithful. I won't have her mistreated."

"I would never—" Reyn stopped himself. A week ago he'd wielded a whip on Patsy Rumford's white behind and thought nothing of it except that it was a bit boring. "I will treat your wife with all due respect and consideration."

"Good. Then we understand each other. Let's hope your seed takes and we can be quit of each other soon. I imagine you'd like nothing better. Sit back down, Captain, and try to relax."

As if he could. "Why did you pick me? Did you think I was the sort of man who would do anything—even this—for money?"

"I had you investigated, Captain Durant. Beyond Mr. Ramsey's recommendation. You are remarkably honest, even to your own detriment. Honorable. You were brave in service, if a bit foolhardy. Restless. Ready for action. I want any child of mine to be curious about the world, not just sit around waiting for things to happen. I haven't always been buried behind a stack of books in this library, you know. As a young man, I was active. Spent a great deal of time on the Continent. In Italy, specifically."

The earl placed a pale broad hand on an ornate stone box anchoring a sheaf of papers. "The Etruscan civilization is my specialty. I dug this *cista* up myself when I was about your age. Just look at the details! It was my first major find, but not my last. I plan to give a lecture series on all my discoveries next spring at Oxford, if I'm still alive. Publish a book for posterity. Maris has been invaluable helping me get my notes in order and doing some illustrations."

"Your experiences on the Continent were far different than mine," Reyn reminded him. "I joined the army when I was sixteen. But it was not a Grand Tour by any means."

Kelby chuckled. "I dare say not. But you learned a thing or two, did you not?"

"Nothing I could write a book about." *Nothing anyone could read, at any rate.*

But if the earl had looked into Reyn's background, surely he must have discovered his difficulties in school.

"This restlessness of mine you seem to favor—I must tell you, it does not spring from intellectual precocity. Studies bored me stiff. I was the despair of a half dozen headmasters."

"Perhaps you had not yet found your niche. Some people bloom late."

"I'm afraid my garden's overgrown with weeds at this point."

The earl waggled his fingers. "Nonsense. Learning is a lifelong endeavor. I'm almost in my eighth decade on this earth, and every day brings new information."

Reyn shrugged and changed the subject. "This inventory you wish me to begin—won't the work take Lady Kelby away from your own efforts?"

"I'm nearly done with the last chapter. She'll have plenty of time to get it all shipshape for me. And apropos of new information, I'd really like to know what's upstairs in all those crates before I shuffle off this mortal coil. You'll be killing two birds with one stone for me." The earl chuckled. "I'm afraid my father and grandfather—and nearly every other Kelby earl collected more than they ever could display in the house properly. I understand the housemaids complain about dusting all the *objets d'art* as it is. That's why it's critical we add a gallery wing to Kelby Hall and curate the truly valuable pieces. Another project for the spring, God willing."

"You would turn the house into a museum?" Reyn asked doubtfully. He couldn't imagine strangers wandering down the long corridors, rooms roped off and defended by the footmen.

"Not all of it, of course, but some of the greatest houses in the land are open to the public. There are too many treasures here to hoard in dusty attics and packing crates."

"Why not simply donate them?"

"I thought my wife had explained the unusual stipulations of the entail to you."

Had she? Reyn had been too busy trying to shock the stuffing out of Lady Kelby to remember everything she'd said.

He did remember the kiss, though, and the way she'd felt in his arms. The softness of her lips. The scent of soap and rosewater. The silk of her exposed skin. The way her body shuddered against his, ever so briefly.

"I'll try to pay closer attention to Lady Kelby in the future, my lord. I swear to you if I do this thing, you will have no cause for worry. I shall treat her with consummate care."

The earl raised a feathery white eyebrow. "If?"

"I will try, Lord Kelby. That's all I can promise. Your wife might not be agreeable in the end."

Maris Kelby had made it plain from the first moment she'd tracked him down that she wished to keep Reyn at a considerable distance.

The earl nodded and pointed to a bellpull not far from where they sat. "Would you ring for Lady Kelby? She is awaiting our summons. We shall all take tea together. I reckon you are tired from your journey and could use some refreshment before dinner."

"I'd rather have a brandy, and that's the truth," Reyn said, rising.

"Dutch courage? My reports did not reveal you to be a habitual drinker, Captain."

It should bother him more that Kelby had picked apart his life, but Reyn supposed it was understandable. *Blood will out.* "I am not. I've always preferred to have my wits about me." *Scattered as they sometimes are.*

The occasion was so damned uncomfortable, Reyn welcomed a little blurring of his senses. He imagined Maris Kelby might like to take the edge off her fear as well.

She didn't wish to get to know him any better or become his friend. He could understand that, but he was damned if she thought they could simply fit together like stiff wooden puzzle pieces. He had to woo her in a way that wouldn't alarm her, and woo himself, too, since she was far from the kind of woman he was used to taking sport with, lately.

"Help yourself to the drinks table then." Cut-glass decanters on a low sideboard twinkled in the sunlight.

Reyn rose, wishing he wouldn't have to sit down again and make idle conversation with the Kelbys. How long could tea last? And when would they expect him to begin this infernal job? It was all so very wrong.

He poured amber liquid into a glass, not bothering to read the silver tag on the bottle. It didn't matter what kind of liquor it was. It would never be enough.

Chapter 6

Maris smoothed the wine-colored ruffles on the bodice of her new dress, took a deep breath, and followed the servants with the tea cart into her husband's library. Both men stood at her entrance, Henry rising much more slowly than Captain Durant. She kept her eyes on the earl's face so Durant was just a dark smudge on the periphery of her vision.

The earl smiled. "Ah! Good afternoon, my dear. Would you do us the honor of pouring our tea? Or would you like another whiskey, Captain Durant?"

"No thank you, my lord. Good afternoon, Lady Kelby."

The captain seemed subdued, which was a good thing. Kelby Hall could have an intimidating effect on the most well-connected visitor, and by Captain Durant's own account, he was a nobody. Maris sat on the tufted leather sofa in the center of the room and waited for the maid and footman to arrange the tea table in front of it. Once they left, the men crossed the room, Henry leaning heavily on his stick as he made his way to her. Maris wondered where his bath chair was. He had been using it more and more of late, complaining that every time he took a step he could hear his knees and ankles crack like rifle fire. No doubt he didn't want to appear at a disadvantage before Captain Durant. Henry had once been a vigorous man, and it was difficult for him to accept his limitations. When she had been a little girl, he'd been very dashing.

She prepared Henry's cup as Captain Durant took the seat to her right. That might have been rude to her guest, but it was her foolish way of letting him know that her husband would always come first, no matter what lay ahead between them. "How do you take your tea, Captain?" she asked, once she had given Henry a plate of small sandwiches and biscuits.

"Just a bit of sugar, my lady."

Maris's hand shook only a little as she dropped a lump into the captain's cup. She'd skip the sugar in her own. The tongs felt clumsy between her fingers today.

Durant helped himself to a piece of fruitcake as she sat back and swallowed a mouthful of strong India tea. Henry had already relegated his untouched plate to the table next to him. She would not nag at him, but hoped he would do justice to their dinner later on.

"Your trip to Surrey was uneventful, Captain?" she asked politely.

"Quite. I stopped to see my sister yesterday and stayed the night."

"And she is improving?"

"That is my fondest wish, though it's too soon to tell. I found her in good spirits, at any rate, entertaining the vicar. I begin to think the man does not simply visit each Sunday out of concern for her immortal soul."

Maris smiled a little at the captain's grimace. "You suspect a romance then?"

"I do after yesterday. Perhaps I was just too blind to see it before." Durant did not look especially pleased at the prospect of having a man of the cloth as a brother-in-law. Little wonder, after his most recent activities and what he was about to embark upon.

"I wish your sister every happiness. I'm sure she deserves it." Maris examined the bottom of her cup, wishing she could interpret the dregs as some gypsies did. What did her future hold, and how quickly could she get through this awkward present?

Well, there was always the weather, the last refuge of conversational inanity. "Today was ideal for traveling on horseback. December travel can be so chancy." Maris wished Henry would say something, anything.

His black gaze flicked over his tea cup from her to the captain, but he was maddeningly quiet.

"It was very pleasant. The countryside hereabouts is delightful." Durant turned to Kelby. "Do you ride, my lord?"

Henry set his cup down. "On occasion. Not enough to suit me, but my wife worries. I admit my stamina is not what it once was.

Maris is quite a good horsewoman. I taught her myself when she was just a little bit of a thing. Taught her and Jane, though Maris took to the saddle far better than my daughter. Perhaps you both should spend some time together exploring the area before the snow flies."

By God, Henry is playing matchmaker. Maris couldn't bear it. "We won't have time for that, Henry. What about the *inventory?*" She charged the word with the meaning they had agreed upon, but Henry deliberately ignored it.

"I've waited a lifetime to see what's up there. A few hours in Captain Durant's company in the fresh air won't hurt you, my dear. Winter will come, and then you'll be shut up indoors. You permit yourself so few amusements."

"I am perfectly amused by helping you, Henry."

"And what sort of life is that for a young woman, holed up within these four walls, day in, day out?"

"I'm hardly a young woman anymore," Maris muttered.

"You're not yet in your dotage. And a very handsome woman, don't you think, Captain Durant?"

"Henry!" His name came out as a wild plea. For something. A stop to the discussion, for sure. Maris's cheeks were so hot they matched her dress. It was a mistake to wear it. To show off. Everything was a horrible, horrible mistake.

"You are a fortunate man, Lord Kelby," Durant said, not falling into Henry's trap. No matter what he said, he couldn't win that disastrous game.

"Maris, why don't you show the captain the attics after tea? You may as well get started today while there is still light."

"T-today?" Maris had not expected to begin *today.* Tomorrow perhaps. Or next week.

Or never.

"Just show the captain around a little. You need do no more than that today, Maris," Henry said, his tone gentle.

"I . . . I . . . Oh blast it, Henry! This is . . . this is all so *awful!*"

Henry's dark eyes held steady and clear. "I know, love. But it's the only way. We agreed."

Indeed, she had, desperate to ease his agitation over David. But now that she was minutes away from being shoved at Captain Durant, she found she could not screw up her courage. Her heart was inextricably bound to her husband, whom she'd loved ever since she was a little girl.

She didn't want flattery and flummery. She'd had that from David in the short weeks she'd lost her head and embarked on the affair with him. How could she ever manage to become intimate with this stranger, no matter how charming and handsome he was?

"I hear some ladies are instructed to think of England," Captain Durant said in a quiet voice. "In your case, think of the Kelby Collection. Kelby Hall. Generations of mad old earls—present company excepted, of course—bringing home the loot for future generations to marvel over. Let's go up and see what's in those boxes, Lady Kelby. You may be pleasantly surprised." He fished a handkerchief out of his pocket. "Don't cry, please. I cannot guard myself against a woman's tears."

Maris sniffed and wiped her cheeks. "I-I'm sorry I'm such a coward," she said to her husband. To them both, really.

"Nonsense, my dear. You are the bravest woman and best wife in England. I quite like the captain's advice. We will not speak of this arrangement any further. I'm satisfied I picked the right man for the job, Maris, and you needn't tell me the details of what transpires between you. In fact, I forbid you to. I find I'm much more possessive than I expected to be, ridiculous as that may be when I'm the architect of this plan. I do wish to be informed, however, if you come across some artifact you think might be important."

"O-of course." As if she could ever *tell* Henry . . .

"I will see you at dinner, Maris. Captain, I've instructed the staff to take your meals to your suite. I hope you're not offended, but things are bound to become only more peculiar the longer you stay here. I thought for all our sakes we would keep unnecessary fraternization to a minimum."

"I understand, my lord. I'm only an employee, after all." There was no trace of emotion in Durant's voice, but Maris thought he struggled to keep his expressive face neutral.

"Good man." Henry pushed himself up from his chair. "I'm back to work. I suggest you both do the same." And just like that, he hobbled to his desk and Maris and the captain were dismissed.

Maris returned her cup and saucer to the tea cart. "Shall we begin, Captain?"

"I'm ready when you are."

Maris was *not* ready. Might never be ready. But she picked up her wine-colored skirts and moved swiftly down the central corridor running the length of Kelby Hall, taking the narrow staircase at the end that led to Captain Durant's rooms. The captain followed at a respectful distance.

She wondered what he was thinking? What would he do when they climbed that final set of stairs?

She had ordered the whole of the attics swept and all the windows washed when she'd come back from London. In one of the chambers near the entry, cast-off furniture had been arranged into an office area, a long table serving as a makeshift desk with two sturdy chairs brought up from below. There were inkpots and reams of paper. A row of well-thumbed history books. Sets of tools and rags and cleaning solvents. A spirit stove for making tea. The chaise behind a torn screen would be a logical place to lie down when one's head was swimming with measurement figures and descriptions.

It was a proper workspace for the highly improper business they were about to conduct. Anyone inspecting the room would be convinced it was Captain Durant's new office, but Maris had instructed the servants that they did not want to be disturbed. The sooner they finished the inventory, the sooner the earl could be satisfied as to what the entire Kelby Collection contained. The staff knew of Henry's frail health, and if knowledge of what all the boxes held could add to his life, they were all for it.

A bit breathless, Maris climbed the last stair and opened the heavy door. A rush of cold air greeted them.

"I was half asleep in school, but I could swear the masters told us hot air rises," the captain quipped behind her.

"There is a working fireplace in the room . . . the room you will use," Maris replied. "You should be quite comfortable."

"It's not me I'm worried about."

"It is not *I*."

"What?"

"The verb *to be*—think of it as an equal sign. The subject and the pronoun must agree."

"Ah. You've fobbed me off as an historian. I cannot be responsible for grammar and mathematics as well."

So, he was not entirely stupid, and had a bit of wit as well. But she refused to smile back at him. "Do you want to tour the attics first, or . . . or . . ."

"I am not going to leap upon you, Lady Kelby. Not today. Perhaps not even tomorrow. When were your last courses?"

Maris stopped in her tracks. "I beg your pardon?"

"Your menses. I believe that's a correct term. There's been a debate over the centuries when a woman's optimal time to conceive is. Augustine of Hippo even waded into it. St. Augustine, you know. I'm afraid my schoolmates and I ignored his philosophy, but were very interested in his views on conception. We all wanted to have carnal relations, but none of us wanted to be fathers, as you might expect. We were children ourselves. I believe the prevailing theory is that a woman is the most fertile directly after her courses have ceased for the month, but one cannot be sure of anything when it comes to the mysteries of women."

Maris pulled a face. "Well, it's pointless then. It's been well over a week. I can*not* believe we are discussing such a subject. It's . . . unseemly."

"I'm afraid we're apt to get *unseemlier* as the days go by. Do you suppose that's a word? If it isn't, it should be."

"Stop making jokes, Captain! This is serious business."

"Aye, it is—which is why jokes are so necessary. You are thinking far too hard, Lady Kelby. You shouldn't be afraid. Coitus is ridiculous in itself. 'To shoot betwixt wind and water,' 'to dance the goat's jig, ' 'to take a turn in Cupid's alley' are all euphemisms for what is sweaty and messy and necessary for the continuation of the human race. But not dignified. It's never dignified. You can forget all those paintings of angels and amorous couples in their flowered bowers. Cupid is having a chuckle at all our expense, stripping us naked with all our warts and bumps and lumps on display."

If that was Durant's attempt at getting her to relax, he was failing badly.

"You forget I've seen you naked already," Maris pointed out.

"And did you like what you saw?"

Odious man. "I am sure you are adequate for the occasion."

The captain rumbled in laughter. "I see you will be a difficult mountain to climb, Lady Kelby. You are obdurate—granite itself—

with lots of icy patches to keep me unbalanced. I believe it will be a worthwhile trip to your summit, though. I've been entrusted with your safekeeping . . . and your pleasure."

"M-my pleasure!" Maris did not intend to derive one moment's pleasure out of the next few weeks. "Do you think likening me to rock will smooth your path?"

"I'm just being honest. I think we owe that to each other."

"We owe each other nothing." *Except the extra money he will get once this was all done.* Maris didn't approve of Henry's generous impulse to sweeten the already sugary deal, but one couldn't argue with Henry and win very often.

"Suppose we stop disagreeing. Why don't you conduct me through all this? Are the boxes we are to open all in the same place?"

Maris shook her head. "Not really, but they're all clearly marked. Most of the storage rooms contain the usual sort of thing—old toys, ball gowns, and bad pictures. The other end of the attics are the servants' quarters."

"They won't be taking turns with their ears pressed against a wall?"

Maris flushed. "We shall have complete privacy. You know how long Kelby Hall is. There's plenty of space between the inhabited portion of the attic and the workroom. It's just through that doorway."

The captain let out a low whistle when he saw the arrangements she'd made. "Very nice. You've thought of everything."

Rectangles of bright sunlight slanted through the room's newly scrubbed west-facing windows. "I tried. I will be doing all the real work up here, after all." She thought of the pillows and blankets stacked neatly on the chaise behind the screen, praying he wouldn't go looking into that corner quite yet.

"Oh, I don't know. I'm sure my brawn will be good for hauling crates and jimmying them open. I'll leave writing down all the historical details to you. I wouldn't know a Roman frieze from a Greek one. Shall I start a fire?"

There was a plain brick fireplace along the south wall. One of the servants had already laid it. A basket of wood, as well as several hods of coal were nearby.

"I haven't a tinder box with me."

"I do. In my room. Make yourself comfortable while I go get it."
Maris shivered despite standing in a patch of sunlight by the
window. She felt she'd never be warm again.

Perhaps she wouldn't have to disrobe entirely, just hike up her
skirt as she had with David. Their few encounters had been hurried
and somewhat brutal. The whole thing had been sordid, which only
seemed to make him enjoy it more. She had been scared to death of
discovery and had never achieved with him what Henry had been
able to do with his hand in the early years of their marriage.

She and Jane had been used for David's own sense of consequence. He had toyed with them—the sheltered wife and daughter
of the man who held so tight to his purse strings. Henry was not as
generous with David as he was with his tenants and servants, and
rightfully so. David had run through his own inheritance in the
blink of an eye.

While he could be charm itself, Maris had come to know his
ruthlessness. But Jane's suicide seemed to have sobered him a little, and he'd ceased bedeviling Maris with constant threats to reveal their affair. Over the years, she had given him most of her pin
money for his silence. Unlike David, she had more than she could
spend.

Were men born evil or did they learn it? Could one do evil and
still be good? Maris felt the beginning of a headache but turned
from the window at Captain Durant's footfall. She watched as he
shucked his jacket and knelt before the hearth, rearranging the carefully laid fire.

So, he liked to put his mark on things. Most men did. It was why
Henry could collect artifacts thousands of years after their makers
were long in their graves.

The captain poked and prodded until a merry little flame sprang
to life. "There. That should take the chill off once it gets going." He
bounced back up and rolled up his sleeves. "Let's get at some of
these boxes. Lay on, Macduff." He grabbed the crowbar from the
table.

"Most people say 'lead on,' " Maris said with surprise. "It's one
of the most misquoted phrases from Shakespeare."

"Good to know something sank in after all the canings."

Maris knew corporal punishment was common. "I take it you
didn't like school much."

"School didn't like me either. I was thrown out six times, if I can count correctly."

"You were expelled from your school *six* times?" That must be some sort of record. Maris pictured Captain Durant as a mischievous boy, not all that different from the present.

"Only once at each institution, but there were six of them. The army kept me, however."

Goodness. He must have been a handful. "I see. I don't think we need open anything up today, so you can leave the crowbar. I'll just point out the boxes. As I said, they're labeled, but you may want to add some sort of notation of your own." She handed him a stick of charcoal from a box on the table.

"Hold still." He pulled a handkerchief from his waistcoat pocket and Maris gaped as he wiped the black dust from her fingers . . . taking a little longer than was absolutely necessary.

It was just her hand that he touched, nothing more. His own hands were steady. Callused. He had fine dark hair along his knuckles and forearm, so different from her pale body with its golden fuzz. His nails were clean and standing so close, she could smell whiskey and leather and the special soap she had milled for Kelby Hall.

"Good as new." He didn't drop her hand, but held it between his own, rubbing his thumb idly over her palm.

"Generally, they're ink-stained. But th-thank you." Maris made no effort to step back and disengage. Their arrangement was beginning, and there really was no point in fighting it. She was curious where he would take his perceived duty to bring her pleasure. Surely Henry had not told him to provide it, had he? The thought of them discussing her like that was very vexing.

"I understand you are a great help to your husband. He told me about how you are assisting him with his book. That's a bit unusual for a countess."

She met his eyes, trying not to show her nervousness. They were very nearly black, much like Henry's. In an odd way, that was comforting. "I wasn't bred to be a countess. My father was Henry's secretary, and I 'helped' them as soon as I could read. Both of them indulged me, and when I was old enough, took me on their digs. It was an unusual upbringing."

Durant bent down and whispered, "I understand they let you wear breeches. I'd like to see that sometime."

"I've given them up."

"That's a great pity."

"What does it matter what I wear? You're here for one thing, and one thing only," she said, spoiling his flirtation.

"Am I? Then let's get to work." He drew her hand to his lips and kissed a fingertip. His mouth was warm, almost hot.

He had kissed her before. She remembered that kiss. It had practically crippled her until she came to her senses when she realized he was trying to disrobe her. His hand had slid under her chemise, gently stroking her as if she were a pet. Who knew the skin on one's upper back could flare up in desire? One's back could not be a source of pleasure, could it? She was familiar enough with the usual locations, although she'd not tried to bring herself to climax for five years.

Guilt. She was full of it and about to overspill. She had betrayed her husband, who'd been nothing but kind to her all her life, who had raised her with the same care he showed his daughter Jane. And who had saved her from a penurious spinsterhood by marrying her and making her a full partner in his academic endeavors.

Maris owed him everything. If that included a liaison with Captain Durant, she'd better get used to it.

The boxes could wait a few minutes more. Maris raised her face. "K-kiss me."

Chapter 7

If the Countess of Kelby had asked him to conjugate Latin verbs, he could not have been more surprised. Reyn felt as if he was being tested, and he'd never done well when he had to think about something very long. If she'd just kept quiet, he would have kissed her anyway. It was where the delicate dance had been going.

But she stood stiffly with her big brown eyes closed and her lips pursed like she was some kind of fish.

He cleared his throat. "Where?"

Her eyes snapped open. "I beg your pardon?"

"Where would you like me to kiss you, Countess? On your hand? On your lips, or perhaps somewhere more intimate?"

"What do you mean? Just the usual kind of kiss, Captain. Nothing f-fancy."

"But we've agreed you're unusual. And when we're alone together, I think you should call me Reyn."

"I don't think that's a good idea."

"There's no one to hear you. Say it. It's just one syllable."

The Countess of Kelby looked like she wanted to turn tail and flee the cozy workroom. But she took a deep breath. "Reyn."

"Thank you. May I be permitted to call you Maris when we're up here?"

She flushed, but nodded.

He'd never seen a grown woman color up so often. The earl was right. His wife really *was* shy. "Even your name is unusual."

"My father was nearly as Etruscan-mad as Henry. That's how he came to be hired. My parents married late, and there wasn't hope of a boy, so they named me Maris, the Etruscan version of Mars."

"You don't seem at all warlike." Except when she was storming the Reining Monarchs Society. He felt he should explain in more detail about all that at some point, but not right now.

"Mars was also the god of agriculture. In Etruria, that meant fertility as well. Ironic, is it not?"

He touched her cheek with the barest of pressure from his thumb. "Maybe not."

"We had better hope I'm fertile so this dreadful business can come to a conclusion."

"Dreadful business? And yet just moments ago you asked—no, *told*—me to kiss you."

"That was a mistake. It won't happen again."

He could feel her withdrawing into herself. What had she been like as a young woman, before she married a man older than her father? The earl said she'd been a rule follower. A good girl. There didn't seem to be an ounce of frivolity or wickedness in her. She was so damned serious about doing her *duty*.

"What do you do for fun, Maris, when you're not up here being long-suffering?"

"For fun?" She pronounced the word as if it was foreign. "And I am not being long-suffering. You must admit we are in an impossible situation."

"Nothing is impossible. Your husband said you ride. What makes you laugh?"

She stared at him, her brown irises edged with blue-gray, and lit with gold around the pupils. If there was a child, he or she would likely have dark eyes.

"You know. *Laughing*. Ha-ha."

"Things have not been funny around here for some time, Captain. My stepdaughter—my best friend—died, and my husband's health was seriously affected. We've been busy trying to bring his life's work to print. I haven't had time or inclination for *fun*."

"That's a pity. I'll have to see what I can do about that."

"You don't have to do anything! My life is perfectly fine the way it is."

"If you say so." The moment for kissing was lost, and it was all his fault. "Let's see about these crates, eh?"

The attic had been divided into chambers, one leading to another. Some of the rooms had fireplaces, but most had been boarded up. The wooden floors were crammed with trunks, old furniture, and boxes. As she made her way through the slender path winding through them, Lady Kelby's red dress caught on corner of a wash stand and she tugged it free.

"As I explained, the Kelby earls are expected to keep every blessed thing they've ever acquired, even if it needs mending," Maris said, pointing to a broken chair. "But what we're looking for—or to be more accurate, what *I'm* looking for—are the boxes with white ribbons on them. Those were shipped home from all over Europe and Asia over the last couple centuries. Henry's father got as far as tying the ribbons on them before he passed. The Kelbys had very eclectic taste as you can tell from the furnishings throughout the house. Henry is convinced there are still hidden treasures to be found."

"I don't think the true treasure up here is in the boxes." Lord, that seemed lame even to his ears. Maris Kelby was not the sort of woman whose head could be turned by a few honeyed words.

To prove it, she snorted at his attempt at flattery, shoved an ancient rocking horse out of the way and kept picking through the path, until she reached the last storage space. "We can take boxes into the workroom with a wheeled cart. Some of them are too heavy, even for you. I shan't expect you to do much besides move things around."

"Good." Reyn gripped the charcoal stick, wondering what she had intended him to do with it. He'd seen enough white ribbons. He estimated there were at least sixty boxes of various sizes to go through.

That was it. He'd number them and open them in order. That would be one way to make sense of the project. He began by writing a big black 1 on a box.

"Oh! That's a good idea. But when we begin uncrating things, let's start with the room closest to your office. We'll be warmer."

"Whatever you say." Even if it was long sleeved, she must be freezing in that flimsy silk dress, although it looked lovely on her. "Is that one of your new frocks from Madame Bernard?"

"Yes."

"It suits you. The color is very nice."

Her face and lips were absent the rouge she'd worn the last time he'd seen her, but she didn't need the artificial enhancement. Her lips were rose-pink, and she'd blushed all afternoon.

"Thank you."

There, they both got through his mild compliment.

"But perhaps not suitable for working up here. You must be cold. I won't keep you anymore this afternoon. I'll just continue to mark the boxes and we can get started in the morning."

He expected her to flee, but she stood uncertainly, steepling her long fingers in front of her. "You *do* understand how difficult this is for me, don't you?" she asked quietly.

"I think I do. The whole situation is nothing I'm accustomed to either. I expect we'll find our way. I promise I will do nothing that you do not wish." He reached his left hand out. "I'll take that kiss now, if you still want to give it. To seal the deal."

She hesitated, then placed her right hand in his. Took a step forward. Lifted her face. She did not close her eyes or look anything like a fish. Damn, but there were tears again, threatening to spill down her cheeks.

"No tears. I forbid them."

"I-I can't help it."

Reyn felt a compulsion to touch his tongue to her skin, to taste the salt and sadness. She was a woman who had almost everything—a stunning stately home, occupation, a husband who loved her. But Reyn might be able to give her the one thing she didn't have, and the burden upon him to do it with care was nearly overwhelming. He felt he owed her something, and wasn't even sure why.

He didn't think it was just the money the earl had already given him, or the comfort it had provided for his sister Ginny. Maris Kelby had pulled him into her orbit even while she tried to repel him.

She wasn't any kind of siren. Reyn wasn't swept away by her appearance, although she was attractive in her own quiet way, especially now that she was dressed properly. He'd like to remove that dress, loosen her hair from its prison of hairpins, but all that would come in time. It was much too soon, but it *was* time to kiss her. He dropped the charcoal from his right hand where it splintered on the floor, then wiped his hand on his breeches. He would try not to touch her with it, though he wasn't sure that was possible.

Angling his mouth over hers, he gave the hand he still held a reassuring squeeze.

She squeezed back.

The kiss was velvet and lush moisture. Her tongue turned from tentative to determined, as though she was deconstructing the art of his kiss and making it her own. Gone was the uncertainty and the shyness and, he hoped, the tears. One couldn't cry when one experienced a surge of lust so powerful it nearly rocked one off one's feet, could one?

But perhaps he was alone in that surge, although he didn't think so. Her breasts brushed against his chest as he brought her closer, and he could swear he felt her nipples harden against him. He could find out for sure, but he didn't want to frighten her off, not when she was so languid in his arms, touching the back of his neck with those long white fingers. Reyn felt a shiver down his spine that had nothing to do with the chill of the room.

There were servants on the other side of the wall. But it wasn't likely they were lounging about in their rooms in the afternoon. There was plenty of work to be done in a house that size . . . from before dawn to well after nightfall. And he could spend all that time in the coming days with Maris Kelby at the other end of the attic. Alone, undisturbed. Tangled before the fire, her ivory skin sheened in sunlight and dew.

Hang the boxes and the ledgers and the pens. The only things Reyn wanted to discover and catalogue were the secrets of Maris's body.

She made a slight noise—a satisfied sound so quiet he could barely hear it, but he felt it *inside* him. She was unraveling and quite frankly, Reyn had very little to do with it. He felt so witless he had forgotten to use his tried-and-true seduction methods and his kiss was just as eager and unpracticed as a schoolboy's. She tasted so damn good and felt even better, her height perfect for his, touching him in all the right places. He fisted his charcoal-stained hand on the small of her back and held her close, mentally stripping them both so they were skin to skin . . . in his mind, at least. Her nipples would be brown against her creamy skin, the color of cocoa. Small? Large? He didn't care. Reyn just wanted to suckle, but that would mean leaving her lips, which would be a travesty. His cock nestled against her lower belly, and he swore she thrust the littlest bit at him. The friction was exquisite yet maddening. There were too many layers of fabric between them.

But he would stick to kissing just a "usual kiss—nothing fancy." Odd that such a simple embrace was nearly flattening him on his arse. Lady Kelby's innocent enjoyment was a heady thing, and Reyn savored each nip and nibble. It gave him hope that they would be able to manage with some degree of compatibility.

He had never and could never take a woman against her will, but for Reyn, that had never been a problem. Females had been throwing themselves at him since he was fourteen, and he had grinned and caught every one. It had boosted his confidence that while he might have been a disaster in the schoolroom, he knew his way around the bedroom very, very well.

So well, in fact, that he had gotten a bit bored. Hence the Reining Monarchs. To his chagrin, he discovered he did not have the necessary sin inside him to "rein" for very long. When he returned to London, he wouldn't renew his membership.

London was far-off, and thoughts of being with anyone other than Maris held no allure at the moment. He opened his eyes a sliver and saw that a brown curl had escaped and fluttered against her cheek. He brushed it back with his thumb, marveling at its softness, then closed his eyes again and let the kiss take him on its course. He didn't know where it might lead, only knew that it was not his to command.

Not the countess's either. She seemed as bewitched as he was. Reyn released his fragile control and held her tighter. There was not a space of air between their bodies, and his was alight with sensation, his cock marble-hard. He didn't want to alarm her, but he wanted *more*.

More for her.

His own pleasure could wait.

Reluctantly he broke the kiss, but not the embrace. "I want us to go to the workroom, Maris," he whispered into her ear.

She showed her alarm immediately and pulled away. "But you said—"

"I will not bed you, not yet. I will only when you are ready. But I wish to continue to kiss you. Where it's warm and we can be private." He hoped he'd make her scream and didn't want to take the chance that some housemaid was right next door laid up with a toothache.

She frowned. "I really should go."

"Give me five more minutes. Ten at the most."

"That's a very long time to kiss, Captain."

"Reyn," he reminded her. "And if I take too long and you become disinterested, I shall stop immediately."

"Y-you kiss very well. That is unlikely to happen."

"Maris, you won't believe me, but I feel as though I've never kissed a woman before today. You kiss very well, too."

She gave him a skeptical look, then navigated the crooked path through the attics.

As he followed her, he gave thought that Maris Kelby had probably never been kissed by any man save for the earl. That they had great affection for each other was obvious. But physical passion was not apparent. *God. Had her marriage ever been consummated?* The earl must have been well into his sixties when they married. Reyn knew that people aged differently. He sure as hell hoped when he was an older man he'd still be able to perform. But from what little Kelby had implied, relations were impossible between them now.

Reyn was definitely not prepared to take a thirty-four-year-old virgin to bed. Or any virgin, for that matter. He was sure he'd never fucked an entirely inexperienced woman in his life. If Maris Kelby *was* still untouched, it explained her shyness, and made the next ten minutes absolutely critical.

He couldn't ask her. He didn't know her well enough. And if he didn't know her well enough to ask that question, he certainly did not know her well enough to kiss her where he planned to in the next few minutes. The absurdity of the situation almost brought him to laughter.

Chapter 8

Maris could feel the captain's dark eyes boring into her back. *Reyn.* It had taken her years to remember to call her husband by his Christian name instead of Lord Kelby. She wasn't sure she could use Captain Durant's first name. It wasn't proper.

Oh, good grief. She was a first-rate idiot. Why was she bothering to think of propriety? They were both well past that. She was about to commit a sin so great it would bar her from Heaven, if there was such a place. Even if she was doing this to please Henry to secure the earldom, God would punish her.

But she'd been raised on many gods and goddesses. The Etruscans had a list as long as her arm, and believed that they directed all activity on earth. Perhaps she was meant to be having carnal relations with Captain Durant. Perhaps it was not even her choice or Henry's, but some long-forgotten deity's.

Maris put a hand to her lips, which still buzzed with stimulation. Something had turned hot and liquid inside her. Of course, Durant was a practiced rake who must know how to do all sorts of horrible things to a woman. He had restrained Patsy Rumford, although the woman didn't seem to mind. Tied her and *whipped* her. How could anyone find that pleasurable? Maris wished with all her heart she could forget that first encounter with the man who was to be her loveless lover.

He was so *big.* He was not fleshy, but well-formed, his arms corded with muscle, his scarred body brown and defined. When she was in those arms and against that body, he made her feel slight. Delicate.

And his manhood—well, that was not slight or delicate.

Maris wished she could throw a switch and shut off her brain for the next few weeks. Be more like the captain, who didn't seem to give anything a deep amount of thought. Six schools!

She was being unfair. Durant was no scholar—*bragged* about that—but he did seem to have some native intelligence and wit. He'd kept himself alive in an army career that had spanned more than a decade, so that meant something. He was kind to his sister and when he wasn't tying up women and beating them, he could be quite charming.

She should have mentioned the Reining Monarchs Society to Henry, but her courage had failed her. Henry had not asked where she had found the captain, and she had not volunteered the truth. He would have been furious—worse, disappointed in her—for lowering herself to enter such an establishment.

They entered the warm workroom. Maris stood before the fire and rubbed her frozen fingers, wondering if she should have moved the chaise in front of it. But they could kiss standing up again. They were old hands at that already.

Reynold Durant stood behind her. She could feel his breath on her neck, and goose bumps washed over her. It seemed to be colder in the attics than it was outside, which made no sense at all.

Nothing made sense.

She turned slowly to face him. "What are you waiting for?"

He caught her off guard as he placed his hands on her shoulders, his thumbs grazing her exposed collarbone. Durant said nothing, just pressed her as if he wanted her to sit down on the floor. At the same moment, his lips touched her forehead. "Lie down before the fire with me, Maris."

She should mention the chaise and its pillows and blankets, but the very fact of it revealed that she had capitulated days ago. The gentle pressure of his large hands and the brush of his lips over her right eyelid caused her to sway, and he pushed her straight down to the moth-eaten hearth rug. They were both on their knees, nose to nose. His expression was unreadable.

"You promised—"

"Hush. I keep my promises." He tipped her backward, spreading the silk of her skirts under her to keep her hair from touching the rug. The front of her dress rode up as well, and Maris tried to cover herself.

He pulled her hand away. "No. Let me see. Let me taste."

What on earth was he talking about? They had a bit of a tussle as he slipped his hand under her dress and tried to part her legs.

"No! Not like this! We're on the floor, for heaven's sake!"

"I suppose I could have you sit on the worktable. You might be more comfortable. This rug's none too clean. Yes, you're a genius, Lady Kelby."

"And you! You are a—"

"I am a man who is about to make you very happy." He pulled her to her feet, swept her up, and deposited her on the edge of the makeshift desk.

"You are insane! You said you were going to kiss me, not toss me about like a ragdoll!"

"And so I am. Hold still, please. I swear I won't hurt you." He dragged over a chair and sat down in front of her.

His mouth was nowhere near convenient for kissing, and it was turned up in a sly smirk. Odious, *odious* man.

If she didn't know better she'd think he was going to kiss her . . . *Sweet heaven.*

He bunched her dress and petticoats up in a fist and petted her nether curls with his free hand. "Scoot toward me just a little bit."

"W-what?"

He reached around her bottom and gave her a push. Maris gripped the edge of the table before she fell off.

"Beautiful. Roses and your own musk. You smell good enough to eat, Maris." Then his face disappeared and all she could see was his glossy black hair at the juncture of her thighs.

And all she could feel . . . she yelped at the first swipe of his hot wet tongue along her seam. *Sweetest* heaven. What was he *doing*? He'd dropped her dress to one side and both his hands held her folds open for his silent, serious assault on her wits. She could do nothing but meet his thrusts with feeble spasms of her own. Her legs fell apart—exactly like a ragdoll's—and she allowed herself to focus on his fingers and remarkable tongue.

Never in her thirty-four years had she ever imagined anything like this. The salacious act that Reynold Durant was performing on her should fill her with disgust. Him, too. Yet his long nose was buried in her curls and his tongue was curling up inside her, and his hands—oh, his hands were doing things that drove her wild.

Once upon a time, Henry had stroked her like this, though never with such diligence or precision. But he had never kissed her as Reynold Durant was doing, never took the morsel of flesh that was the key to her undoing gently between his teeth, then sucked *hard* as his fingers slid into her. Maris rocketed up from the table and gasped, holding the edge of the table so she wouldn't fly right off. She bucked helplessly as each wave washed over her. She was finished, done for. Surely he knew that. But he kept kissing her center as though he found her to be delicious. Delectable. Showed her no mercy. She climaxed again and again, begging him in a ragged whisper to stop.

But is that what she really asked of him? She was incoherent at the moment. Unreliable. Perhaps she told him to continue. Whatever he heard, he simply did as he pleased, which seemed to involve giving her more pleasure than she had ever deserved.

She was hot and wet and in a sort of heaven that she doubted a Judeo-Christian god would approve. "You must stop," she hissed. She couldn't remain upright or relatively quiet one minute longer.

In an instant his tongue disappeared between his lips and his hands rested damply on her knees. Reynold Durant—Reyn—looked up at her, his black eyes gleaming. "Must I? Very well. Did you like it?" His lips were rough. Red. Beads of perspiration etched his forehead and his black hair was tousled. He looked as if he'd run a mile.

She had no words to answer him. Not a one.

"I see you're speechless. It was a success, then." He grinned, looking like a very naughty boy.

Maris nodded, almost against her will. She was every bit as depraved as Patsy Rumford, only she didn't need him to tether her to the table to gain his mastery over her.

"Has no one ever done this for you before?"

"No."

"Ah. Well, I'm honored to be the first."

She felt a finger trace a pattern on her right thigh. She'd noticed the few times they'd met his hands were often busy. She'd thought it a nervous trait, but found his circular touch pleasant. She tried to still her breathing to the light downward curve as his fingertip swirled.

Seconds ago that fingertip and two more had been snug inside her, working her into a near-frenzy. Now Reyn was spelling something with her own moisture on her skin in a language she'd never learned.

But what they had done would not get her with child, so it was all a waste of time, wasn't it?

Even if she'd never felt so exhilarated, she was falling into herself, her back muscles tightening in tension, her bare arse chafing against the rough wood of the old table. Her crumpled new dress would require ironing, her mind retrieving from wherever Reynold Durant had sent it. Maris had sworn to herself she would take no joy in their arrangement, and she'd broken that vow already, on his very first afternoon at Kelby Hall. She was *worse* than Patsy Rumford.

She pushed his hands from her body and smoothed her skirts over her stockinged legs. "It's late." The room was no longer bathed in bright sunlight, and shadows deepened in the corners.

"Don't go yet." He wasn't satisfied.

Did he want her to return the favor? She knew that women could kiss men down there, even if she'd never suspected the tables could be turned. David had tried to make her do it, and a ghastly business it had been.

"I-I really must. I have a thousand things to do before I have to dress for dinner." She couldn't remember a single one.

His hand slipped into her disordered hair and pulled out a loose hairpin. "I feel guilty, Maris. I tricked you. You were expecting an altogether different kind of kiss, weren't you? Something 'usual.' Although I don't think anything between us will ever be *usual*."

"There is no 'us,' Captain Durant." She meant to sound superior, but her words rang hollow.

"Oh, there's going to be an 'us,' if only for a few minutes every day. Maybe several times a day to make sure we've given this mission all our efforts. I'm willing to make the sacrifice."

He was teasing her! Did the damn man not know his place?

And it wasn't between her legs in whatever form he happened to choose.

"I need to go," she said firmly.

"A good-bye kiss then. For luck." He waggled a black eyebrow at her. It needed some smoothing down after his recent activity.

"I am only going downstairs to my rooms, Captain, not off to war."

"Luck always comes in handy. We will need as much of it as possible in the weeks ahead. Come, Maris, just a quick kiss and then you can scamper off while I go back to numbering boxes."

She slid off the work table, surprised her legs were strong enough to support her. Before she could refuse his offer she was in his arms again, tasting herself on his lips. She was shocked—and something more.

The kiss was not long in length, but not short on sensation, either. Reyn was very gentle, teasing her again, but not with words. A butterfly kiss, that's what it was called. She'd read about it somewhere, but had not understood.

Now she did.

And knew she was in trouble.

Chapter 9

Reyn's chair before the fire was comfortable, his dinner delicious, the accompanying wine truly spectacular. A man like the Earl of Kelby must have a cellar anyone might envy and a kitchen staff imported from damned France. Reyn was no connoisseur of the finer things in life, but they were all around him and inside him, digesting happily. Even a heathen like he could appreciate his new position.

Especially since it involved seducing the countess.

Maris.

The afternoon had been promising. He'd been valiant in his effort to make her come, and come she had. Repeatedly. Her taste still resonated through the vintage port he held in his hand. Reyn had always enjoyed giving women their pleasure. He'd never been a selfish lover. In his experience, the more one gave, the more one got back.

He had been willing to try anything—hence the Reining Monarchs—to feel sated. Find peace. There had to be some fun in life beyond bayonets and tradesmen's bills. He was good at three things—cards, making men laugh, and making women breathless. Resentful as he might be over the earl's investigation, Reyn's reputation as a lover must have been discovered and found acceptable.

Maris Kelby was not quite the buttoned-up biddy she'd first appeared. For one thing, now that she was not dressed in drab grays and browns, she was more than passably handsome. With her wavy hair loosened, her cheeks flushed, and her lips swollen, she could rouse any man's desire. Reyn had been in such agony when she'd left him that afternoon, he'd sat back down on the chair and jacked off, imagining those swollen lips around his cock.

However, teaching her to do that was not part of the plan. They were not having an ordinary affair, after all. He was there for one reason and one reason only. His own pleasure was incidental, but he wanted Maris Kelby to find hers . . . to help ease her regret about their liaison and find it less sordid.

A little less cold.

She was a virtuous woman. Virtuous women were hard to come by nowadays. From what he could gather, she had been raised in this house with the earl acting as a second father to her. How she wound up marrying him was an oddity he couldn't fathom. What young woman would throw her youth away on an impotent old man? Reyn supposed he was being silly. Lots of girls married for money and position. Those things didn't seem to matter to her, though. Perhaps it was access to the Kelby Collection that made her subjugate herself to Henry Kelby. Maybe she had preferred scholarship to sexual satisfaction. If so, he pitied her.

He put the port back on the tray unfinished. Well, what was he going to do with the rest of his evening? It was hours yet before his usual bedtime, but there were no army friends to carouse with, just a shelf full of oxblood leather-covered classics he hadn't bothered to read when he should have a dozen years ago. No point to picking one up tonight, although it might put him to sleep. He *should* be tired. He'd ridden half the day and pushed boxes around and twitched under the earl's sharp-eyed scrutiny.

It was a relief he'd be excused from further contact with the man, though that might seem strange to the servants when Reyn had been hired to assist him. Poor Maris was to be their go-between, reporting on whatever rubbish they found in the sixty-seven boxes upstairs. It was too cold and dark to go up to the attics and get started, but he had managed to carry some of the smaller boxes into the workroom for inspection tomorrow.

He wouldn't know how to begin, anyway. There must be some sort of method one used when describing artifacts. Did one pull out a tape measure and count the inches? Write down colors and country of origin? He knew his numbers and red from green at least. Advantage Reyn.

He rang for someone to take away the remains of his dinner. He felt a little like a princess walled up in a castle tower since he didn't have free rein to wander about the house looking for amusement. Maris was not apt to come to him to begin their other project, either. He'd already stroked himself to blessed oblivion earlier, so even self-abuse seemed a bit redundant. What the devil was he going to do with himself for the next few hours?

A fresh-faced young footman came to reclaim the dinner tray. Reyn was almost bored enough to engage the boy in conversation, but that would have been considered odd. Everyone had their place at Kelby Hall. Reyn might not be good enough to eat with the earl and countess, but he was much too grand to gossip with a footman. So there he sat. He poked at the fire and rubbed some dust off the side of his boot onto the patterned carpet. His hands itched for a deck of cards, if even to play solitaire. Getting up, he rummaged through the drawers and was rewarded by emptiness, not even an overlooked ball of fluff.

Probably nothing was overlooked at Kelby Hall. The place was run with an efficiency any army officer would long for in his own troops. The old butler Amesbury was even frostier than the earl. Between the two of them, they must scare the wits out of everyone within a ten-mile radius.

Maybe Reyn needed to get out of their range. It was a fine, crisp night with a three-quarter moon. There was no reason he couldn't take a walk and enjoy some fresh air. Take a turn in the garden he'd seen from the windows of the library.

His old army cloak hung in the dressing room, gloves and scarf stuffed in the pockets. He wouldn't ask for a lantern. His night vision had always been good—useful in his previous line of work. He dressed and took "his" staircase down several flights to the ground floor. The earl's library was at the other end of the house, and Reyn wondered if the old man was in there fiddling with his papers, or if he was still dining with the countess. The house was quiet, but sconces were lit all along the corridor and a few footmen were visible at their positions farther down the hallway.

One of them raised a hand to Reyn and hurried down the oriental runner that seemed to go on for miles. "May I help you, sir?"

"Where's the nearest door to the garden?" Reyn felt he should know this already. Good reconnaissance had always been a habit.

"You want to go *outside,* sir?" The footman sounded as if it was a rather outrageous plan.

True, it was chilly, but Reyn had toughened up in Canada. "I do."

"Do you wish for a guide and a torch, sir?"

"To walk in the garden? Don't be silly. I'm not exploring the pyramids. Just show me a door and make sure no one locks it so I can get back inside in an hour or two."

"Are you sure, sir? I could bring a brandy up to your rooms."

"I've had enough to drink." Reyn never overindulged. He found he preferred being clear-headed, especially since the world was such a confusing place. "But you might fetch me a cheroot. I'm afraid I forgot mine upstairs."

"Certainly, sir. Wait right here, sir."

Reyn leaned up against a wall and stared at a hideous painting of an unfamiliar allegory. All this sir-ing was stirring up nostalgia for his army service. Maybe he shouldn't have sold out, but asked for a transfer. He might be playing *vingt-et-un* with a bejeweled maharaja right this very minute. But then where would poor Ginny be? *No, I've done the right thing,* he decided.

The footman returned less than two minutes later. "If you'll just follow me, sir, there are French doors from the music room to the garden and we shall get you settled."

The music room was dark, but moonlight spilled in through a wall of windows. The footman opened a glass door, handed Reyn his cigar, and lit it for him.

"Thank you. What is your name?"

"John, sir. All the footmen at Kelby Hall are called John."

"Are they indeed? What does your mother think about that, John?"

"She's dead, sir. But I'm sure she wouldn't mind."

What rot. What sort of people were the Kelbys to rob their servants of their own names for convenience? He forgot his earlier vow not to try to fraternize with the servants. "You feel fortunate to be employed here then?"

"Oh, aye, sir." John continued to hold the door, but Reyn resisted stepping over the threshold onto the stone terrace.

"An easy job, is it?"

"Oh, no, sir! There's plenty to do, and long hours. But I don't mind. The master's a very fair man."

"And Lady Kelby?"

"She . . . she's lovely, she is."

She was indeed.

"Thank you, John, for your assistance." Reyn dug into his pocket for a coin, which disappeared with alacrity. "Tell me, what's your real name?"

"Aloysius, sir. Mr. Amesbury says it's a burden, but I do feel sorry for the Williams and Roberts who work here. Nothing wrong with *those* names."

"Nothing wrong with yours either. Good evening to you, Aloysius."

"And to you, sir."

Reyn stepped out into the night. The moon hung low and stars sprinkled the sky. After getting his bearings, he could see the gleaming crushed stone path that led from the patio to a corner of the formal garden. That way wasn't much of a challenge. He'd seen squares and rectangles, all tidy and tamed and pruned back for the spring. He could march around their borders as if he were on parade, but that wouldn't do much for the inexplicable yearning he felt. He rested his hand on the balustrade and took a puff of his very fine cigar.

People who claimed the country was quiet had never listened. Reyn heard a fluttering above—probably a bat—and the distant hoot of an owl. Bushes rustled in the light wind.

He heard the lap of water in the lake on the property, the place where the earl's poor daughter had ended her life. He'd seen it in an illustration in the guidebook he'd bought to learn more about Kelby Hall. Always be prepared, that was his motto, but the place itself had exceeded all his preparation. It was a very, very grand house. Reyn supposed these sorts of places owned the men who lived in them, not the other way around. The lords were temporary caretakers for future generations of temporary caretakers. Ridiculous when you thought about it.

And a son of his might be one of them.

He stepped off the terrace onto thick, springy grass. For a mad moment, Reyn wanted to remove his boots and sink his toes into its cushion, but the bite of night air drove that thought from his mind. He headed in the direction of the moving water with only the light of the moon and glow of his cigar's end to lead him.

To have one's child die must be an insurmountable grief. Maris had said her husband had changed, and it explained some of the urgency of the task before him. Not that Lady Jane Kelby could have inherited Kelby Hall, but at least the earl would have left something behind for posterity besides the book he was writing. A flesh and blood legacy. Reyn had never thought that far ahead as to what mark any future descendants of his would leave upon the world. When one's life was regularly in danger, one didn't have time to think beyond the present.

He was thinking too much. He was deliberately—with the earl's full approval—going to try to feather the Kelby nest with a Durant cuckoo. His own long nose—hell, his bushy eyebrows—might be passed down through the ages.

And he wouldn't be around to see it. There was something terribly wrong about it all.

He clamped the cigar between his teeth and batted a bush out of his way. It had been a while since he'd been on a night patrol, and his instincts had gone soft. But it was peacetime, and he wasn't about to be attacked on the manicured grounds of Kelby Hall.

He passed by all the regimented clipped hedges and came to a vast expanse of empty lawn. The ground beneath his feet sloped gradually down to the lake, which was lit with a shimmering stripe of moonlight. A folly with vine-covered columns rose like a stone ghost on a tiny island in the middle of the black lake. A rowboat was tied to a matching stone pillar at the water's edge. At one time people had rowed out to the folly on a sunny summer day and picnicked, but that seemed pointless to him. A man-made lake, a man-made ruin, all very picturesque and all very false.

Even if Reyn had not known of the tragedy that had occurred there, an aura of sadness pervaded the place. Weeping willow trees shivered all around him, anticipating the winter to come. Did the lake freeze up? He wondered if the countess skated, her long legs gliding from shore to shore. Probably not. As she kept saying, she had no time for recreation, and it would not be fun visiting the place where her friend died.

Judging from the condition of the little boat, it had been ages since someone had gone out in it. Leaves floated on water that covered its bottom from the last rainfall. Rowing might be good for his bad arm. Despite the pain of it, Reyn didn't want to lose what mobility he had left. Exercise was important.

Bedsport could be very athletic, but Reyn anticipated he and the countess would be restrained, as proper as one could be under the circumstances. Even with the privacy of the workroom, they could be discovered and then the entire plan would fall to pieces. He bent and booted the cigar stub into the ground. Tomorrow would arrive soon enough to test his amorous abilities. He'd made enough headway today—at least Maris Kelby had been satisfied. Even her slender white thighs had been flushed, as lovely as her cheeks had been.

Reyn turned to walk back toward the house and stopped when he saw movement between a gap in the hedges that surrounded the formal garden. Someone else was enjoying the country air and moonlight. He could make out enough to know that his fellow nature lover was a woman.

A tall woman with darkish hair and fair skin that fairly glowed under the moonbeams.

He didn't want to alarm her, so made plenty of noise as he walked up the lawn, whistling off-key and crunching his boots down hard on the fallen leaves and twigs that had scattered on the lawn. He heard her own feet on the crushed stone path. She was trying to make a rapid retreat.

Should he let her go? It might be less embarrassing all the way around. What did they have to say to each other, after all?

Reyn found himself loping up the lawn and through a break in the bushes. "Lady Kelby!"

Maris Kelby stopped at once and turned, nervously fingering the knot in the pale fringed shawl that had first attracted his attention. She wasn't wearing gloves, and her hands were white as the tall obelisk not two feet away from her. She must be freezing.

"Good evening, Captain. I didn't expect to find anyone out of doors at this hour."

The implication was that he was trespassing on her privacy, which he was, but Reyn didn't care. "It's a beautiful night, don't you agree? I stepped outside to enjoy one of your husband's cigars."

"Smoking is a filthy habit."

Reyn ran a tongue over his teeth. Tobacco, like leather, whiskey, and horse, was a perfectly acceptable male odor. But he could give up smoking if it bothered the countess. There would be enough vice for him without it.

"Most everyone enjoys a pipe now and then. It's a huge cash crop all over the Americas. It's even grown in Canada now. Tobacco financed the American Revolution, you know."

"All the more reason to avoid it. We want no more wars."

"Amen to that," Reyn said, although his heart wasn't quite in it. War had been the making of him. "You are much too young to remember King George's War."

"My husband is a historian, Captain."

Reyn was not used to discussing history and revolutions with lovely women in the dark. The night was designed for better things. "Come sit with me for a few moments, Lady Kelby."

A silence hung between them before she said, "I should get back."

"Are you in the habit of walking in the garden at night?"

Lady Kelby—Maris—sighed. "If I tell you I am, will you seek me out and rob me of my peace?"

"I don't want to do anything to upset you further," Reyn said quietly.

"I am upset! I've never been in such a state! I can't think. I can't eat. I can't rest."

Her words were as quiet as his, but he heard the tremor in her voice. Reyn placed a gentle hand on her shoulder. "You should talk to your husband. He cares for you. If this is all too much for you, I'm sure he'd understand. I know I do."

"I must do it," Maris whispered. "I promised him. I owe him everything, you know."

"You don't owe him—or anyone—your soul, Maris. Walk away from it. Walk away from me."

She took a ragged breath. "I-I cannot."

"Well, then. Think of all this as bad medicine you must swallow to be well again."

She shook his hand away and leaned against the marble obelisk. "How can you j-joke?"

"It's what I do, I'm afraid. It's meant to boost your morale. Is it working?"

There was no hint of a smile on her moonlit face, but at least she wasn't in tears again. "No, not really."

"I'll do better tomorrow. I'll leave you to your second thoughts. Good night, Lady Kelby."

"Wait! Don't go."

Reyn paused. He really ought to go to the earl straightaway and tell him he was leaving in the morning. The man was still up. The lights from the library windows cast pale rectangles on the grass beyond the garden hedges. Reyn was beginning to feel like a fish that was reeled in, only to discover the line had gone slack.

"I think you were right."

He quirked an eyebrow, a dependably devilish expression, which was wasted in the dark. "About what?"

"We . . . we *should* be friends. It will make it easier."

"All right." He held his hand out. "Let's shake on it."

Her hand was ice cold. Reyn brought it to his lips and blew a warm breath across her knuckles. She trembled and took a step forward.

Another kiss was a much nicer way to cement their new friendship. He covered her lips and eased into a tender tangle. No wildness, no wanton pressure, just a soft brush of skin and tongue which brought its own innocent pleasure. He could get used to kissing Maris Kelby. She'd improved by miles since their first encounter at the Reining Monarchs Society a few short days ago. Who knew how expert she'd be once they were done with each other?

The obelisk in the center of the hedges shielded them from prying eyes, so he was in no rush to end their friendly kiss. Neither, it seemed, was Maris. She had not pulled away from his embrace in with any sort of revulsion. If anything, he thought she was remarkably relaxed, her fingertips delicate upon on his jaw, her breathing just shy of steady. Reyn's groin tightened in response to the very unexpected turn of events.

And then he felt a little push. With the greatest reluctance, he withdrew from the kiss and stared down into her pale face.

Her eyes were huge and fathoms dark, her lips still parted. She licked them, causing Reyn to clamp his own mouth shut.

Her words were even more unexpected than her kiss. "I can't wait until tomorrow. I'll never sleep anyway, worrying over it. Will it be all right if I come to you tonight?"

Reyn loosened his tongue from its knot. "Is that wise, Lady Kelby?"

"None of this is wise. I want to get it over with. The beginning of it, at least. Once I know what to expect, I'll be more—" She shook her head. "I don't know what I'll feel. I hope to be less afraid, I suppose."

"You have nothing to fear. I promise." Reyn hoped he was telling the truth.

Chapter 10

Take my medicine. Get on with it. Get it over with.

The more time she had to think about it, the more agonized she was. Yes, it was much better to go to the captain's rooms tonight and do what they were supposed to do.

Maris was sure Reynold Durant would be a better lover than David. Durant's kisses had been masterful. No wonder woman waited to be whipped by him. Maris would almost consider the crop herself.

Good Lord. What was happening to her mind? Since London, she'd been unable to be of any use to Henry. Her agitation grew daily, her concentration shot to pieces. It was a good thing her husband was in the final stages of compiling his book, for she had been no help at all since she returned from town with her silly dresses.

She would wear none of them tonight. Maris had dismissed Betsy once the girl had brushed through her knotted wavy hair and braided it. She had sponged herself clean with a second bath and scented her body with rosewater. Dressed in a sensible white lawn nightgown, she covered it with a dark blue brocade robe. Madame Bernard had said navy could suit her, did she not? Maris had chosen it not for the color, but to traverse the dark hallways without attracting notice.

Captain Durant was on the floor above her, just a few steps up the narrow staircase at the end of the house. She had left the countess's suite at the opposite end of the corridor five years ago, when the fiction was that Henry's nocturnal restlessness made it impossible for her to sleep next door.

To some degree, it had been true. Henry wandered back and

forth from his library to his bedroom all night long, and being a man, was never quiet about it. His old valet Chambers had left Henry's service because of it. The man had been so bleary-eyed he was walking into walls toward the end. Now Henry made do with a young ex-soldier who was grateful to have a job. Sullivan claimed he took naps when the earl was busy at his desk for hours. Clever lad to make the best of Henry's erratic schedule.

Maris wouldn't take a candle; she knew every nook and cranny of Kelby Hall. It was only a few doors down to the stairwell, only a few steps up to the deserted wing where she had placed Captain Durant. But she wouldn't make a habit of the nighttime excursion. Her luck would only hold so far. The house was crawling with servants, though most of them should be asleep at that hour.

In the garden, her idea had seemed a good one, but as she hurried up the stairs, she wondered what Reynold Durant *really* thought. Of course he had not refused her, just cupped her cheek and stared into her face until she felt he could see every thought in her head. He nodded once, then absurdly kissed her forehead as if she were a child.

As Henry used to do. But the captain's kiss did not bring her the same comfort.

Maris hesitated a moment at the door, but before she had a chance to knock he opened it and pulled her into his well-lit sitting room. She'd been hoping for dark. Pitch-black, actually.

Durant locked the door behind her. He was still dressed, the fire going strong. He'd procured a bottle of wine, which sat next to one stemmed glass on a piecrust table.

"I didn't dare ask for another glass. We'll have to share," he said, smiling.

"I don't need any wine, thank you." Her throat was so dry her words came out as a croak.

"You're nervous. I confess I am too, a little."

"You? I don't believe it." She'd seen what he looked like naked and randy . . . and what he was capable of.

But perhaps she didn't appeal to him.

He walked to the table and filled the wineglass almost to the brim, then took the first sip. "Believe it, Lady Kelby. See? I even have trouble calling you by your Christian name. You quite awe me."

Maris took the glass from him, but set it back down. "Don't be ridiculous."

"You're a countess. I'm no one in particular."

"My father was the earl's secretary. My mother was a vicar's daughter. I'm no one in particular either." She took a deep breath. "I did not come here to discuss genealogy, Captain Durant. I didn't come here to *discuss* anything."

He took another swallow of wine. "Shall we take a vow of silence then?"

"I think that's an excellent idea." It would be far less embarrassing than making idle conversation through this thing.

"Very well. But you will tell me if you do not like something, won't you? Don't just lie there and endure."

Maris shrugged. That was precisely her plan.

She followed him across the carpet to his bedroom door. The fire was roaring in there as well, the bedcovers turned down, though just a single candle burned. Maris blew it out without thinking. She much preferred the gray gloom of this room to the sitting room, though she was not anxious to unbelt her robe yet.

Reynold Durant did that for her. He slid the garment from her shoulders, his thumbs stroking her arms before he tossed it on a chair.

"Get into bed, my dear. I'll get ready in the dressing room."

Maris told herself she was not disappointed that he would not strip before her. It was too dark to see clearly anyhow, and that was the point, wasn't it? The dark was welcome.

Necessary.

She climbed into the captain's bed. A waft of bluing and lavender rose up, as it would from all the sheets at Kelby Hall. She pulled the coverlet up to her chin and willed herself to stop shaking. A warming pan had recently been run over the mattress. The captain's doing? She knew he was trying to make her feel comfortable, hopeless a cause as that was.

Maris shut her eyes and began to count, not out of impatience, but as something to do to divert her overactive mind. The brass clock over the mantle struck one, causing her to jump a foot. She started over, reaching two hundred thirty-six before she heard the click of the latch on the dressing room door.

The mattress was not as firm as it could be, sagging at the captain's weight. As a good hostess, she should have tested the bed out herself. She'd never envisioned lying in it, just on the tufted chaise in the attic. But here she was.

Captain Durant was here too, and he was naked. No dressing gown for him. His hair was a bit rumpled and he smelled of tooth powder and sandalwood. Had she brushed her own teeth? She couldn't remember. He lifted the blanket from her, tugging a bit before she released her grip on it.

"Maris."

She couldn't think of a thing to say. Then she remembered she wasn't going to say anything.

His kiss made speech a moot point. Again, he was gentle. Tender. His moves were not abrupt or startling. He touched her with the barest contact and kept his body away from hers.

He was close enough to touch, though she wouldn't. Maris felt the heat of him, was aware of every lazy lick of his fingers and tongue. He seemed to be spelling something on her lawn-covered shoulder, but she couldn't make out the letters. She concentrated on the faint whorls as if they were a sort of code.

She expected the stroking and kissing to stop soon enough. The captain was in no apparent hurry for the main event, however. *The inventory.* The reckoning of her body. She hoped he permitted her to keep her night rail on. She was not ready to be inspected, dim firelight or not.

The kissing really was very nice. Nearly relaxing. Maris tried to give in to it, to accept its claim on her, but she was thinking too hard to do so.

What was *he* thinking about? Could a man rise to any occasion?

Maris had been taught their appetites were insatiable. Duchess or dairy maid, it made no difference. Their male equipment knew no impediment, no class distinction. *All cats were gray in the dark.* She had discovered Captain Durant in the midst of perversion in a heightened state of excitement. Would this gray darkness be enough to rouse him?

Good heavens. Why was she worrying about him? He was being well compensated for the night and all the other days that would follow.

His fingers stopped their spiraling. Belatedly, Maris realized his mouth was still on hers, but his tongue had stopped dancing as well.

He drew back. "I can practically hear the gears grinding in your head. This won't work if you cannot accept it. Focus on just the physical. The pleasure. *Stop thinking.*"

"I cannot stop thinking, Captain." She sounded querulous even to herself.

"Reyn."

"Whatever."

"Remember, this was *your* idea. I was willing to wait for tomorrow."

He's right, damn him. Maris was not giving her best effort. She had no best effort, no real experience of how it was meant to be between a man and a woman. While Henry had given her a measure of satisfaction, she'd been hopeless at doing the same for him.

And David didn't bear thinking about.

"I'm sorry, Captain. Reyn. I don't know what to do."

He squeezed her shoulder. "You don't have to *know.* You only have to *do.*"

"I'm sorry if I cannot distinguish the two."

"Am I not sweeping you off your feet just a little?"

Maris realized she still had her worn needlepoint slippers on. "Obviously, I'm off my feet."

"And in my bed, yes. Some progress has been made, I grant you. But you're coiled tight as a clockwork spring. You are not kissing me back."

"I certainly was!" What had her tongue been doing then if not touching his? Tasting wine and tooth powder and his Durant-ness? Kissing was an intimacy she'd had very little practice with. It almost seemed more important than the other thing they would do once he stopped arguing with her.

"I know when you really kiss me, when you lose yourself. When you toss all those rules you've lived by away and when you let that beautiful body of yours have its way for once."

Pretty words. He couldn't mean them.

Maris sat up. "Perhaps you're right about the wine. Go fetch some. Please," she added. She had sounded exactly like a Countess of Kelby ordering a minion about. Maris didn't do that, and no one in their right mind would think Reynold Durant was suited to be a minion, even if he was in her husband's employ.

Deep down she knew the wine wouldn't help, but it would get rid of him for a few seconds. His insistent nearness confounded her. He wanted something she couldn't give.

He padded across the room and opened the door to the sitting room. When he returned with the glass of wine—no bottle, wasn't he optimistic?—his rangy body was limned with light, his erection unmistakable. The captain pushed the door closed with his bare arse and the bedroom returned to dusk.

"Here you are." Maris took the goblet from him, her hands brushing his. "Th-thank you." She took a tentative sip. It was very good, but then everything at Kelby Hall was of the finest quality.

Even Captain Durant.

He cleared his throat. "Perhaps after you drink some, you should go."

"Do you want me to?"

"No, Maris, I don't," he said with impatience. "But I will not force myself on you. You seem too preoccupied to enjoy yourself."

"I'm just unaccustomed to—" She couldn't finish the sentence. What words could she find to describe what was—and wasn't— between them?

"I know. Believe me, I know. It's nearly as awkward for me, Maris. I've never rented myself out before." He sounded bitter, not at all like the teasing rake he'd been.

"I think we are both overthinking. You accused me, but you are just as bad as I." She passed him the glass.

"It won't work. There's not enough wine left for both of us."

"Then bring in the bottle. We can . . . talk for a while." There went her vow of silence.

He put the glass of wine on the bedside table and walked over to the fire, rubbing his shoulder. He truly was a beautiful man despite the scars on his skin, and seemed amazingly at ease in his natural state. She envied him.

"Maris, I've had a long day. I'm tired. You forget I rode for hours to get here. Maybe I should go back to London tomorrow."

"No!" She surprised herself with the vehemence. She didn't want him to go.

She didn't know *what* she wanted, but knew she could not endure this all over again with another strange man. She was being unfair to him. She couldn't seem to help it. It was she who had been forward in the garden, she who had invited herself up to his room. She who had kissed him back, no matter what he thought. Maris did not mean to trifle with him. She knew she was not the only one perplexed by their situation.

If she could give herself to that rotter David, surely she could engage with Reynold Durant. He was superior in every way.

And he had made her feel things she'd never felt before.

That was part of the problem. Maris felt her loyalty—her old life—slipping away after less than a day. She was on an unfamiliar plane. One false step and she might plummet into the unknown and never be able to return.

Reyn was right. She had to stop thinking. It did her no good. True, she was facing a moral dilemma, but her vacillation was doing nothing but confusing him. He probably thought she was one of those ninnies one found in romance books, a woman who thought the villain was the hero and the hero the villain.

She'd always been a straightforward sort of woman. Straitlaced too, but it was time to cut all the laces. She fumbled with the hem of her night rail, then drew it over her head. "I'm ready. If you'll have me."

Chapter 11

Reyn steadied himself on the chimneypiece. However he'd expected the evening to go, this wasn't it. His throat dried. Maris Kelby sat up in his bed, a long loose braid covering her left breast. And what a breast it would be if it matched the right. Her clothes and his previous explorations had only hinted at what lay beneath. She was made lushly, slender yet sturdy, her shoulders broad. He could see her scrabbling up Italian mountainsides and digging, smiling under the scorching sun with each new discovery.

She was a goddess, or as close to one as pictured in all those rubbishy mythology books. A bit stern, just as she should be. Unyielding. Her innate confidence had been restored in the firelight. She wasn't tripping over her words at this invitation—it was if she finally knew her own worth.

Reyn didn't ask her if she was sure again, and he certainly didn't want to ask her to leave. He couldn't send her packing after she'd revealed herself to him in all her exquisite vulnerability.

It was pointless to be overly polite. Solicitous. All he wanted to do was pounce on her soft white body. To inhale the heady fragrance of roses and her sex. Sheath himself where he was meant to be.

For the time being. It wouldn't do to get too attached to the Countess of Kelby. She was not for him, yet tonight she was his.

She looked at him with her wide brown eyes, *really* looked at him. Even in the dim light, she must see he was hard as the marble he leaned on.

It was better not to speak, to simply act, and it would not be difficult to demonstrate desire.

He was across the room in seconds. She shivered as he drew her underneath the blankets, warming her with his rough hands. The urge to touch her everywhere he could reach was strong. He lifted a breast to his mouth, savoring the sweetly ruffled nipple against his tongue. She gasped and dug her nails into his bad shoulder. It didn't matter.

Reyn felt *he* was making the valuable discovery, uncovering Maris Kelby's sensuality one nibble at a time. Her breast was heavy in his hand, smooth and soft as a pillow. He could lay his head upon it and contemplate the mysteries of life if he could bear to stop kissing her, which he couldn't. She tasted of rose petals, not that he'd ever eaten one. He knew some flowers were edible— candied violets. Nasturtiums. Why was he thinking of eating flowers when he had this lovely woman to devour?

He could lick her secret hollow again and taste her honey. Would do so, but not when his cock ruled supreme. As he suckled, his hand snaked down her belly. Her breath hitched and she parted her thighs without his request. His fingers slid between her folds.

She wasn't quite ready, despite her reassuring responsiveness. His thumb sought the little bud beneath her silky nether hair. Reyn wished she'd touch him as he touched her, but her hands gripped his shoulders as if she was afraid he'd get up and go away. No chance of that. He took a deep tug on her nipple as he circled pink flesh into her pubic bone, causing her to cry out in the quietest way.

His forefinger slipped into her tight channel and she clenched around it. By all that was holy, she would squeeze the life out of him and he'd die a happy man. He stroked until she writhed and twisted, heedless of her dignity.

Good. She wasn't a countess now, just a woman. He gave one last pull to her breast, then nipped his way up her throat to her parted lips. Reyn was desperate to get inside her, but he wanted to be kissing her when he took the plunge, united from top to toe. For their first time, he wanted nothing fancy, as Maris would say, just the elemental. The simple. The beautifully basic.

She seemed to agree as she bucked up to him, her hands scrabbling on his back. His finger was coated with her slick wetness, so he added a second to ready her, all the while swirling her stiff swollen button. He knew to the second when she came apart for him, and he took advantage by replacing his fingers with his cock.

To his shame, he used no finesse, just seated himself in one brutish thrust. He paused, waiting for her objection. Instead, he felt her heels dig into the small of his back and press him closer. She wasn't quiet, moaning into his mouth as he deepened his kiss, deepened their connection. Slow. Steady. Gliding in and out as though the morning would never come.

Until she begged, although not with any words, They still had not spoken one. She begged with her body. Those wretched fingernails of hers scored his back, but he'd bear her marks as another badge of battle. He'd won her, for now.

They climbed and crested together until Reyn couldn't hold back another minute. He didn't need to. She'd had her pleasure— still thrummed with it—and wanted his seed. It was blissful freedom to empty himself into her, to lose their delicate rhythm in his all-encompassing fierceness. He swallowed his victory and muffled her cries in their kiss, driving home.

Marking *her*.

She was his. At this moment. In this bed.

And it might not be enough.

Maris would *not* cry. She had got what she wanted. More, really, than she bargained for.

Much more.

Her skin was on fire, her heat beat wildly. Reynold Durant lay on top of her, his long nose buried between her throat and shoulder. She had no desire to throw him off despite the musky perspiration that clung to their bodies. His manhood was growing regrettably soft inside her, but she did not want him to move an inch.

So *this* was what all the fuss was about.

Maris was well-read, even if she'd lacked proper experience. She had never expected to find any satisfaction in this arrangement despite what the captain had promised.

She had been wrong.

Somehow her wanton response made the whole thing more difficult. How could she face Henry tomorrow—today—over the breakfast table? He would know what she'd done.

And how much she'd loved it. Every sticky, messy minute.

Maris had felt like she was flying, truly unfettered, for the first time in her life. The sensation was still not quite over. Her inner walls drummed a tattoo that echoed inside her whole body.

She had sought this before with David. She'd been nearing thirty and feeling a bit sorry for herself. Empty. Unwomanly. He had picked up on all her cues, even though she hadn't meant to send them. He'd flattered, cajoled, teased. The affair had lasted only a few guilt-inducing weeks before Maris realized she was making the biggest possible mistake. She'd been so lucky that she'd not been caught like poor Jane.

Pregnant. Abandoned. David had refused to marry his cousin, not that Henry would have welcomed the connection.

David had never made her feel like this. In less than twenty-four hours, Reynold Durant had stepped into her orderly world and set it on end. The afternoon had been a revelation. The night was indescribable.

Maris wanted to begin the procedure all over again, and they'd not exchanged an intelligible word between them.

She waited to feel the guilt wash over her. It didn't. How could she regret something that had made her feel so very wonderful? Alive?

She was wicked. And didn't really mind.

She didn't want to hurt Henry, though. He'd picked well for her. Too well. Reynold Durant was an amazing lover. Maris was sure that even if she didn't have much to judge him against, he would top anyone's list. No wonder Patsy Rumford had been so petulant.

With a final kiss on her collarbone, he raised his head. "May I speak now?"

"I wish you wouldn't." His careless words might bring her down to earth and ruin everything.

He nodded, unsmiling, and inched away, retrieving the counterpane from the floor. They had been very energetic and the bed was disarranged accordingly. Maris was not cold, but lay motionless while he tucked the covers around her, though she was well past modesty. He flipped to his back and stared at the shadowy ceiling, still naked. His member had shrunk in its nest of ebony hair, although shrunk was a relative term. Maris believed him to be very well endowed even in repose. The fire lit the broad planes of his chest and the bronze of his skin. She remembered he had a ball in his shoulder, and was ashamed she had squeezed it so hard that she could see the half-moons her fingernails had left.

Maris turned her head away at his beauty. She'd have other

chances to see him in daylight, to examine the silver and angry red scars that quilted his body. To think she had once hoped to keep her eyes closed. To pretend it wasn't happening.

She was beset with an unfamiliar languor. It wouldn't do to fall asleep. She should get up and dress. Go back to her empty bed. But when she tried to sit up, Reyn's arm shot out to stop her.

"Don't go yet."

She shook him away and climbed out of the bed. To her horror, his fluid gushed down her thigh. Did he notice? Would it matter? Maybe she should have lain in place, waiting for a miracle to occur.

"I-I must. Thank you, Cap—Reyn."

He shut his eyes. "Think nothing of it."

Most unlikely. What they had done was all she could think about.

In a few hours, they might do it again.

Maris buttoned up her nightgown and put on her robe. At some point, she'd kicked off her slippers and had trouble finding them on the dark rug. The Countess of Kelby couldn't wander about Kelby Hall barefoot, but she was too proud to disturb Reyn and ask him to help her find them. He looked peaceful, his lashes black crescents against his cheekbones. He couldn't have fallen asleep yet, could he?

It was tempting to bend over and kiss him to find out. However, they'd kissed enough for one day, and she really wanted to get back to her rooms, barefoot or not. She slipped out the bedroom door into his sitting room. Before she blew out the blaze of candles still burning, she tidied herself in front of a mirror between the windows. Her lips were stained as if she'd eaten raspberries, and her braid had come unraveled. Anyone seeing her would suspect what she'd been up to.

So she daren't risk being seen. She poked her head out the captain's door like a faithless wife at a naughty house party and listened. The hallway was empty . . . as it should be. No one but Reynold Durant was occupying that wing of the house.

Kelby Hall's nighttime silence was almost a noise of its own, and Maris's rapid heartbeat added to it. She flew down the stairs and breathed a deep sigh of relief when she reached her suite and shut herself in.

Her own sitting room and bedroom beyond were in darkness.

She was meant to seem retired for the evening and had sent Betsy off to bed hours ago. Maris sat in front of her fitful fire and brushed out her hair again, unsnarling the knots Reyn's busy fingers had woven. The other tangles in her life would not be so easily dealt with.

Reynold Durant. Reyn. He wasn't a complicated man, yet he was going to complicate everything.

She couldn't let the flutter he caused inside her consume her. They had other things to do besides fornicate.

What a harsh word. What they had just done did not warrant such biblical opprobrium. While she might have sinned, she'd never felt better in her life.

How absurd. She was thirty-four years old, a very grown woman, allowing a few minutes of physical release to overtake her good sense. Her lack of experience was a true handicap. Perhaps when one was bedded regularly, one got used to feeling such euphoria. It didn't last very long, did it?

She'd tasted a bite of the apple. She wanted more.

She hit herself on her muddled head with the hairbrush. "Enough, Maris," she muttered. "He was right. I think too much."

She would have to set some ground rules while they worked together, for their other project needed attention, too. Was it best to couple quickly at first, then uncrate antiquities, or work and then play? However was she going to concentrate with the captain at her elbow, radiating masculinity and mischief?

She was much too tired to think straight, never mind think too much. The morning ahead would unfold as it was meant to . . . by decree of the pagan gods or Reynold Durant's tantalizing kisses. Maris tossed the hairbrush aside and crawled into her feather bed and prayed for sleep and forgiveness, not necessarily in that order.

Chapter 12

It was Reyn's birthday, not that he celebrated such things anymore. He was nine and twenty on that frosty December day, an age he never thought he'd live to.

He'd already gotten his gift in its early hours. He expected to get at least another one, so he'd taken care shaving and dressing before he made his way upstairs to his new "office." It was just past nine, yet Lady Kelby was not present to order him about. A fire had already been laid and started by unseen hands, taking the chill from the room. Maris had promised they would be undisturbed up there and he hoped Kelby Hall's staff could restrain themselves from seeing to his every need.

He'd never encountered more solicitous servants in his life, from his dismissed volunteer valet—Reyn could dress himself, thank you very much—to the footman and housemaid who'd brought him so enormous a breakfast it took two of them to deliver it.

He would rather have slept longer than deal with people and porridge. He wondered if Maris had been able to fall asleep. He'd lain in bed for hours after she left, replaying their encounter in his mind until he'd been forced to take himself in hand again and spend against the sheets.

The night had gone better than he'd dared to hope. Once Maris had talked herself into the thing, she had been beyond responsive. Beyond compare in Reyn's checkered experience. Yet there had been an innocence, which made Reyn wonder about her history.

At some point she and her husband must have had a real marriage. She had not been a virgin, thank God. Reyn was sure he'd know such a thing. Maris had been tight, but not untried. She'd gloved him with a surprising intensity that almost blew his head off. As a member of the Reining Monarchs, he'd not gone so long without a woman that the usual carnal act should affect him so. But it had.

He shook his head over the neatly sharpened quills lined up on the penholder. If he was not careful, he'd wind up under the spell of a happily married woman, and then where would he be? He was here for a *job*, not to have a case of calf-love for Maris Kelby.

Where on earth was the word *love* coming from, modified by calf or not? They did not really know each other, and he couldn't imagine a woman more ill-suited to him. She was far too proper, too contained, too shy when she wasn't being bossy. Especially when her heels dug into his back to guide him to her will.

Altogether she was formidable. A countess who helped her husband write books had nothing in common with an ex-soldier who couldn't even read them.

He left the worktable and walked to the window. The formal garden was far below, its regimented hedges separating each garden room. Two smocked men were digging up a plant past its prime, which marred the estate's unnatural perfection, their breaths little puffs of white air. Reyn found the obelisk where he'd kissed the countess and realized they'd need to be careful if they were outside in daylight. Any servant quartered in the attics had a perfect view of the garden and the glistening lake beyond. The little rowboat bobbed against the shore as a brisk wind skimmed the surface of the lake. It looked to be a clear day, and he was sorry he would not be going out in it.

He tensed as he heard a squeak on the stairs, and turned toward the doorway. Maris's footsteps were inaudible as she walked through the first attic room and pushed the door open. Her instant blush told him she had not expected to see him there so early.

"Good morning, Lady Kelby." His voice sounded measured, belying the sudden constriction of his throat.

"Good morning, Captain Durant. I didn't think you'd be up here quite yet."

They were back to *Lady Kelby* and *Captain Durant*. Perhaps that was better. They wouldn't slip into intimacy in front of anyone.

"Early bird, worm, and all that. I haven't started on anything. I wasn't sure what you'd want to do first."

From the looks of her, it would be business. She wore a dark brown dress covered over with a pinafore, just the sort of attire one would wear to muck around in dusty attics. Her hair was hidden beneath a plain linen cap. If Reyn didn't know she was a countess, he'd take her for a superior housemaid. She certainly was not a silk-clad seductress come to deliver another birthday present.

"I trust you've had breakfast," she said, moving to the fireplace. Her shadowed brown eyes focused on a space just to the right of his left ear, not the rug at her feet where they'd begun their affair.

So she hadn't slept much either. "Indeed. I couldn't do it justice. I'm used to simpler fare, you know."

"Tell them what you like, and you shall have it. The staff has been instructed to cater to your wishes."

"You're too generous, Lady Kelby."

"You are our guest, Captain."

"I am your *employee.* I don't want to forget my place." *Bought and paid for, fed like a pig destined for slaughter.* A full stomach wouldn't make death any sweeter. No matter how much he was indulged, he'd never be at ease.

Maris twisted her fingers nervously.

Is she recalling where they had been and what they had done just hours ago? Reyn shook his head. *Best to stop thinking of that.* He grabbed a box from a stack and thumped it on the table. "Shall we begin with this? It's number twelve."

"Shouldn't we begin with one?"

"That box was too heavy for me to bring here by myself. It will have to be opened in the room it sits in, or transported on that cart you mentioned. How will we go about this, Lady Kelby?"

She frowned. "I suppose the best way is to unpack each crate, number, and describe the contents, then put everything back except for what might interest Henry."

The whole thing sounded ridiculous to him. If they were only going to put all the things back in their dark little boxes, what really was the point? A generation from now, someone might decide to throw the lot away as a fire hazard, though perhaps their inventory might dissuade them.

Maris moved over to a chair at the long table and handed Reyn a pair of large gardeners' gloves. "Please wear these."

"I'll be fine."

"It's not you I'm worried about. Some of the artifacts might be too delicate to hold up against human touch." She pulled a pair of white cotton gloves from her apron pocket and put them on.

Reyn followed suit, then picked up the crowbar and pried box number twelve open. His first thought was there was indeed a mummy inside, for strips of fraying linen were wrapped around a giant misshapen lump. The box didn't smell as if it contained a desiccated body, however, so he gingerly removed the lump from the box and set it before the countess. "You do the honors."

Her expertise was evident. Each piece of fabric was painstakingly removed with tweezers that also came out of her pocket. He wondered how she opened *her* birthday presents. Was she as careful or did she rip into things with abandon like a greedy child? He'd bet the former.

Reyn was no wiser what the object was once she'd uncovered it. The heap of linen rags on the table looked more valuable. "What the blazes is that?"

"The statue is South American, quite ancient, I wager. I believe it must have been sent here by Henry's brother. His ship escorted the Portuguese Court to Brazil when they fled Napoleon's invasion in 1808."

"David's father?"

Maris nodded. "Yes. He was in the Royal Navy. He died on the return voyage, poor man. He was nothing at all like his son."

"Why isn't David in possession of this clay thing?"

"If it was delivered here, it was intended for Henry. He's interested in comparative civilizations. This is primitive *vis-à-vis* his Etruscan treasures from the same era. I think we'll put it aside, although he must have seen it once." Maris made a bed of cloth and laid the stature on top of it.

In Reyn's opinion it looked like a mud pie any half-wit child could make. He watched as Maris removed her gloves and wrote in one of the blank ledgers. She lined up a ruler next to the thing and squinted, then pulled out a pair of spectacles from the same capacious pocket. Reyn wondered what else could possibly be in there.

With the glasses perched on her nose, the countess resembled a no-nonsense governess, not that he'd had one. He had been sent off to school at an early age once the local curate washed his hands of him. The curate was the first in a long line of scholars who had very clean hands after dealing with young Reynold Durant.

Lady Kelby was spending an inordinate amount of time with the reddish-brown thing. She scratched out its description, then paused to measure and cluck over it some more. What was he supposed to do with himself between "finds?" Reyn dug his hand deeper into box number twelve, but there seemed to be nothing but more fabric wrapping . . . until he touched something hard.

Hold on. Reyn pulled out a polished green stone the size of a robin's egg. Its multiple facets glinted in his palm. "Maris."

"Umm?"

"Look."

Her head was still bent over the ledger. "I need to finish with the relic first. You'll have to learn to be patient. I'm very thorough."

She was that. "I think you'll want to see this."

"Oh, bother. What is it?" She placed the pen in its holder and looked over her lenses. Her brown eyes widened and her mouth dropped open. He could not have asked for a more satisfactory reaction.

"I think it's an emerald," Reyn said with some confidence. He'd rubbed shoulders lately with some bejeweled ladies. Sometimes the jewels were *all* they wore. The Marchioness of Stitham had an emerald set she wore regularly to the Reining Monarchs Society, tiara and all. But none of her stones could compete with the color, cut, and clarity of the huge rock in his hand.

"Good Lord. It's enormous."

Reyn set the stone in front of her. "It was at the bottom of the box."

She picked it up as if it might bite. "I suppose it really belongs to David."

"Why? You said the box was intended for your husband."

"Henry's brother must have hidden it for transport. I'm sure he would have unpacked it himself had he lived."

"You don't believe in finders keepers?"

Her lips turned up in almost a smile. "If I did, the emerald would be yours, wouldn't it?"

"Not at all. I am merely the hired help."

An emerald that size must be worth a fortune. If Reyn had a brain and fewer scruples, he would have pocketed the thing while Maris was scribbling and no one would have been the wiser. Ginny could have lived out her days in luxury and he need not worry about ever finding a proper job.

Maris looked at him as if she could read his thoughts. "Thank you for your honesty."

Reyn shrugged. "I'm an honorable chap. Mostly. What will you do with it?"

Maris's brows knit. "I don't know. I don't think I want to disturb Henry over it just yet. I'm sure he would say it was David's and it would gall him no end to turn over so valuable an object to him."

"I'd like to meet this blighter David."

"No you wouldn't. Although I suppose he's due any day now. He always turns up when you want him least."

"Tell me about him again so I can prepare myself for the eventuality." Reyn sat on the edge of the table watching Maris Kelby's cheeks flush. He didn't think he'd ever get tired of her blushes.

"He's Henry's heir, of course. A few years older than I. He can be very charming," she said with bitterness.

"Were you raised together here?"

"Oh, no. His parents lived in one of the other Kelby properties in Hampshire. Near Portsmouth, convenient to the Admiralty. His father was at sea for much of his growing up. I supposed that's why he doesn't recognize boundaries. His mother spoiled him dreadfully. David thinks he's entitled to do just as he pleases, no matter who it hurts."

"I gather his marriage to Lady Jane would have been unacceptable."

"Cousins do marry. Henry would have swallowed the pill and approved the match. But David refused, even though—" Maris broke off.

"I'm sorry. It's impertinent of me to ask."

"No. You *should* know. It will help you to understand why my husband is so set against David inheriting. You were right. It's not just about the disposition of the Kelby historical artifacts and books, or even that David trifled with Jane's affections." Maris took a breath. "She was pregnant when she took her life. I didn't know how desperate she was, nor did Henry. We blame ourselves for not understanding what she was going through."

Reyn shook his head. Something was off. "It doesn't make sense to me. Surely David would have been guaranteed his position if he'd married the earl's spinster daughter. Why would he refuse?"

"Because he could. I told you, he likes to do as much damage as possible."

"Well, he doesn't deserve this emerald then, does he?" Reyn picked it up and held it to the window. Even to his untrained eye, it was extraordinary.

"No, he doesn't." She held out her hand. "I'll put it under lock and key until we decide what we should do."

Reyn dropped the bauble onto her palm. "We?"

She blushed again. "If it wasn't for you rooting around in the box, I'd never know it was there, would I?" She put the jewel in her apron pocket, picked up the pen again and set back to work.

Most women would have been dazzled by the green stone, placing it like an imaginary ring on their finger, but not Maris Kelby. She returned to her measuring and analyzing, and it was a good ten minutes before she finished with the pre-Columbian lump. Reyn bided his time with a stroll to the window. The gardeners had moved to a different section of plantings and were inserting something into the ground rather than pulling something up.

There was a career for him. Of course he knew nothing about plants whatsoever, but it was good honest labor and out of doors instead of being shut up in grim book-lined rooms. Fresh air. Sunshine. Reyn didn't mind the rain, either. His brawn would come in handy and he knew his way around a shovel, having dug a trench or two in his time. Ginny might think it a comedown for him, but once he explained his difficulties to her—

Damn. He'd never remember all the Latin names of herbs and flowers. Maybe he wouldn't need to. He wasn't too proud. He could be the under gardener.

Reyn realized he didn't hear the pen scratching behind him anymore and turned. Maris Kelby smiled up at him, and he felt his heart turn over just a little.

"You seemed so lost in thought I didn't want to tell you I'm ready for the next box."

"Forgive me for shirking, my lady." He strode across the room and lifted up box number six. If there was a gap between their stations, it would be a yawning cavern if he became an under gardener. At least now he was an ex-military officer, the son of a gentleman.

And he wasn't a thief. He could have pocketed the emerald so easily.

The next two boxes held no more jewels or treasures of any kind. Reyn poked at the fire while Maris catalogued the odd assortment of objects that had caught Kelby eyes over the years. She explained what she was doing, but Reyn could work up no interest over chipped pottery and blackened candlesticks. When she was done and the items rejected, Reyn rewrapped everything but a Chinese plate and put it all back in the boxes. He walked the length of the attic returning the crates to their stack and brought a few more to the workroom.

Maris was tucking an errant brown curl back under her cap and had managed to smudge some ink on her cheek. Her hands and her cotton gloves were no longer white, and her spectacles had migrated to the end of her nose.

Reyn couldn't help himself. He pulled them off, disentangling her cap and hair. "It's time for a break, Lady Kelby."

"We've only gone through three boxes!" Maris objected.

"Yes, and you've filled up half a ledger. You'll get eyestrain. Your fingers must be numb, aye? And I'm bored to death standing around watching you work."

"Well, now that you've observed the procedure, perhaps you could be trusted to work on a box of your own."

Not bloody likely. "I have a better idea. It's time for our other task."

"Right n-now?"

She should not look quite so appealing. Her cap was askew, her face dirty. Reyn had been fighting an erection for half an hour.

Well, that's what he was there for, wasn't it?

He took her grimy fingers in his hand. "Now. The more often we have relations, the better your chances are for conceiving." He hoped he was sounding reasonable, though he felt anything but.

Something was wrong with him . . . beyond the usual. Being shut up with Lady Kelby all morning had made him lose what little concentration he had. He'd have to take up whittling or something while she worked. He was going mad.

"I . . . there is a chaise behind the screen."

He smiled down at her. "I know." He'd noticed it yesterday as he was organizing boxes. He found the embroidered pillowcases a charming touch.

"We're just going to get up and—" Her blush deepened.

"Oh, there will be some preliminaries, never fear. I'm not going to fall on you like some crazed animal." He hoped.

Her hand was still in his and he bent to kiss it. She trembled a little. How gratifying that it was sensitive to his touch. All he had to do was make sure the rest of her was.

Chapter 13

Maris had wanted to remain clothed, but had been overruled. Oddly enough, she was still wearing her garters, stockings, and one shoe. The rest of her clothes—the cap, the pinafore, the sensible brown dress, her petticoat, corset, and chemise—had been removed layer by layer.

Reynold Durant had proved very efficient in her undressing, folding each item with the precision of the best lady's maid, whispering over her skin until she thought she would burst with impatience. Then there had been slow kisses. Everywhere. He had repeated what he'd done on the work table, but she had been sprawled in comfort on the chaise, dazed and drenched as he licked her as if she were the tastiest sweet.

He had capped that delicious assault with a blissful, blunt entry into her body, resulting in a particularly effervescent kick on her part that resulted in the loss of the other shoe. Losing her footwear around the man was becoming a dangerous habit.

Losing her wits, as well. He had made her press her own fingers between them to stroke herself to sharp bliss as he surged inside her.

Maris was still beneath him, heart beating erratically. She could not imagine going back to the table and working. Pretending all was normal. Reynold Durant had ignited something inside her she hadn't known existed.

She'd received some pleasure in the past, and had been curious about receiving more. Hence her miserable affair with David. But she really hadn't had a clue.

She wasn't about to embark on a sonnet, for this wasn't *love*. However, she liked Captain Durant—Reyn, she reminded herself—

very much. He had a sense of humor at work and was unfailingly solicitous of her when he joined with her at play. Maris felt treasured for the first time in her life. Henry had always been indulgent, more like a father than a lover, though she knew he cared for her as much as he was able. David had simply used her for his own amusement—to thumb his nose at his uncle and line his pockets with Maris's pin money.

Perhaps if she gave him the emerald he would leave her alone for good.

"What is it? That was not a sigh of satisfaction. Are you well?" Reyn lifted himself up and stared down at her, and Maris missed his warmth immediately.

The puckered starburst on his shoulder caught her attention and she touched it lightly. "You say this hurts when it rains?"

"And snows. You're changing the subject. What's wrong? I wasn't too rough, was I?"

Maris felt the heat in her cheeks. He had been splendidly rough. And gentle too. "You were perfect. Must I praise your performance like a schoolmistress? You must know you are the schoolmaster here."

Reyn grinned. "It never does a fellow any harm to hear how content he's made his lady."

"I am content. Content as I can be under the circumstances."

"That's all right, then." He rolled to the wall and took Maris with him. She found herself snuggling against him, an entirely unfamiliar, yet cozy, position. It was what most post-coupling couples did, wasn't it? She felt no urgency whatever to jump off the chaise and get dressed and go back to the mountain of boxes. In fact, she didn't believe she could stand up at the moment.

"So what was that somber sigh about?"

"You never give up, do you?"

"Oh, I've given up on any number of things. Just ask the *real* schoolmasters. Solving problems is not my forte. I'll make an exception for you, though." He kissed her nose. How absurd. But it was rather sweet all the same.

"I don't want to spoil what we have between us right now. It doesn't matter."

He pulled her closer. "Now, you've done it. My sister Ginny has a terrier, did I tell you? His name is Rufus. He has a typical terrier's tenacity, but the dog cannot hold a candle to me when it comes to ferreting out secrets."

"Can a dog actually ferret? That doesn't seem right. They are two different species, surely." How silly she was being, but there was something about talking to this man that called for levity.

"Don't confound this conversation with science. I might get bored to death and then you'd have to dispose of my body in one of those trunks."

"I don't think I could manage it. You are far too . . . large."

He gave her a naughty wink. "Said the girl to the soldier. Thank you, madam."

"Oh! I was referring to your height, you wretched man."

He was still large, even in repose. From a purely artistic standpoint, Reynold Durant was exquisitely sculpted.

"So, tell me what is wrong. Perhaps I can help."

"There's nothing wrong. I was just breathing. Did you find my slippers? I could not find them in the dark last night."

"Ah, yes. I should have told you and saved you some worry. I hid them in my saddlebag. None of the servants will be the wiser. I should tell you, I'm not used to such coddling. A veritable parade of footmen and maids came in this morning with breakfast and oceans of hot water and fresh sheets. I'll be spoiled before this is over. Ruined for my humdrum life."

Maris was afraid he was ruining her too. She disentangled herself from his arms and felt her hairpins slip down her back as she sat up. "Bother."

Reyn caught a curl as it tumbled from her brow. "You have lovely hair."

"It's nothing special, just brown."

"It's soft. And smells like roses." He tucked the loose strand of hair behind her ear.

She would have to remember to bring up a brush and comb to the attics so she could make herself presentable after their interludes. Maris supposed some disorder was inevitable moving and unpacking boxes, but she suspected her recent activities would be plain to anyone who had two eyes.

She felt hot.

She felt *happy*.

"You'd better help me dress. It must be time for luncheon." She swung her feet to the chilly floor and reached for her chemise. "You can ring for something to eat from your room. I'll meet you back up here in two hours so we can work a little while longer before we finish for the day. The light won't hold forever." She pulled the chemise over her head and struggled with the buttons.

Reyn noticed, then took over the job. Somehow he got his own large hands to behave over the tiny bits of bone and fabric far better than she. "Will you be joining the earl?"

"Oh, no. He takes a tray in the library so he can write and read and eat. He's very devoted to his work." She had better luck with the strings of her front-lacing corset and the petticoat tapes.

"That must be lonely for you."

"Well, that's one reason I've helped him all these years, otherwise I'd never get to see him," Maris admitted. It had been a grand adventure accompanying him to digs, but organizing and writing about their discoveries was much less stimulating.

"Why can't we follow suit and have some food sent up here?" Reyn asked.

"I've told the servants not to disturb us, and I don't want to take the chance they'll find out what's going on. Look at me!"

"I am. And I quite like what I see."

Maris waved him away. "You needn't stoop to flattery. My hair is a nest."

"Let me fix it for you. Put your dress on and let me get to work as your maid."

She really didn't have much choice. There was no mirror except a shattered one in a fine gilt frame three rooms over. Another thing to tote upstairs with a brush and comb.

Reyn gathered up the fallen pins amongst the pillows and made her sit at the worktable. And then he did an extraordinary thing. He rubbed her head, slipping firm fingers through her loose hair, pressing onto her scalp in hypnotic motion. For a minute Maris wondered if he might make even more of a tangle of her hair, but the head massage was so wonderful she held her tongue. The tension she felt now that she was no longer prone in his arms disappeared and she felt the coiled springs along her spine relax.

He seemed to know it, dropping a light kiss below her left ear. Then he got busy braiding and pinning.

"It is with the greatest reluctance that I'm giving you this abomination," Reyn said, handing her the cap. "Why do women wear such things? You can't imagine men like them. You might as well be wearing a nappy on your head."

Maris shrugged as she tied it under her chin. She wasn't sure why caps were the custom. Perhaps that was something she could research in the future. There were biblical admonitions to cover one's head, and Maris supposed fashion could stem from fear of God as well as anything else.

She wasn't much for fashion, wasn't even wearing one of her new dresses. Maris felt a little silly thinking they had been a necessary purchase to make her more palatable to Captain Durant. He seemed to like her just fine as she was.

Did it matter what he thought of her? He said he wanted to be friends, and they seemed to have reached some sort of understanding. At least enough for him to make his job look close enough to pleasure.

She hadn't closed her eyes, but he had, as she'd asked him to that first day. Reyn had been beautiful as he'd strained over her, each perfect, hard thrust accompanied by a near prayerful expression on his face.

If he'd opened his eyes and looked down, he would have caught her spying.

Those eyes were so dark. Penetrating. Maris was afraid he'd see inside her, know somehow the secrets she kept. She imagined he didn't have to terrier or ferret much. Something about the man made confession almost inevitable.

"You look very respectable, madam." He began to step into his own clothes with a fluid grace Maris would never manage. "Well then, I propose we share a lunch. Not in that gilded barn you call a dining room of course. I expect Kelby Hall has something more modest—a third or fourth best dining room as it were."

Maris imagined sitting opposite him in the cozy paneled room where she usually took her daytime meals, sunlight shafting through the windows. Despite its relative informality, there were always footmen about, waiting to jump at her every word. "I-I don't think that would be wise. We don't want to engender talk amongst the servants."

"Don't you think I can keep my hands to myself? I swear I won't give you one longing look of lust in public. None of this." He made a face at her, which was a close approximation of a sleek, worshipful hound.

She smiled in spite of herself. "Maybe I worry about what *I* might do."

"Nonsense. You'll chew your food and pass the peas and be the perfect countess."

He didn't know her at all. For one thing, she loathed peas. "Oh, Reyn. I've never been a perfect countess. I just don't think Henry would approve of us eating together." She caught the look on his face and hurried on. "I know it seems absurd after what we've just done. What we'll do again. The . . . the intimacy. But he was specific about you dining in your suite."

Reyn looked more annoyed than hurt, but nodded. "All right. I'll meet you back here at two-thirty. I don't need two hours to eat lunch, you know."

"The servants will require the time to prepare and deliver your meal. Cook is very particular."

"Some bread and cheese and a pickle or two are just fine. I've marched on much less." He was dressed, and did not look as rumpled as she felt.

"Ask for anything you want."

"I don't think I can have what I want," Reyn said quietly, and disappeared through the door.

Maris swallowed. *Blast.* He hadn't said the last sentence with any kind of teasing flirtatiousness.

She was not prepared for the man to become serious. Maris was thinking enough for the both of them. Reyn was much easier to deal with when he was playing the boyish ne'er-do-well without a thought in his head.

She reached into her pocket for a handkerchief to blot any trace of his kisses away and came upon the emerald. Hard to believe she could have forgotten about such an amazing find, but she had. Reyn had swept her mind free of everything but the scent of his skin and the sureness of his touch.

What was she to do with the thing? It must be ridiculously valuable. She would put it in her safe before she went down to eat.

Alone.

Chapter 14

Reyn looked at his watch for the fourth time in ten minutes. He'd been at the little table in his sitting room for most of an hour, staring at the empty gold-rimmed dishes. Fancy dinnerware for his requested humble fare, but he wasn't used to a heavy meal in the middle of the day, particularly after such a huge breakfast. At this rate, they'd have to roll him out of Kelby Hall. Poor old Phantom would buck him right off.

He wondered how the horse was faring in the stable block. Probably eating his head off, too. Everything was first-rate at Kelby Hall for humans and animals alike. Perhaps once he and the countess finished the day's work, he'd give himself and his horse some exercise and ride out to explore the Surrey countryside. A few minutes of fucking was not enough to quell the need his body had for release.

Reyn frowned. There had to be a better word for what was happening with Maris Kelby. Something not so crude. It had been anything but.

Would she want him to do it again this afternoon? Truly, he'd have no objection.

He sensed she was unused to such activity. He'd probably made her sore already. She was tall and well made, but there was a delicacy about her which made him feel protective. He wished he could have a frank conversation with her, but didn't want to pry. He'd have to settle for what her body told him.

She came to orgasm easily, a rarity for a woman, as he knew from experience. He'd often had to labor much harder—labor that was entirely pleasant, naturally—to achieve such responsiveness.

Maris Kelby held nothing back when she was in his arms. It was out of them when she armored herself in a protective shell of hesitance and propriety.

That was probably for the best. In a month he would be gone, and she could go on with her privileged life. He pictured her lounging in her boudoir, long fingers busy with needle and thread, making neat stitches on a baby's cap. Did countesses even sew?

She would be a careful mother, of that he was sure. Nothing like his own. Corinne Durant was too busy with cards and cotillions to pay much attention to her two children. When the debts rose and invitations stopped pouring in, his parents had slipped from one strata of society to the next below, until there was very little space between hell and their unpaid-for shoes.

Ah. That reminded him. He went to his dressing room, all traces of his earlier ablutions removed by efficient servants. His saddlebag hung on a hook on the papered wall and he reached inside. He needed to return Maris's embroidered bedroom slippers. They were much more interesting than most of the objects he'd seen that morning, save for the emerald. A little worn, they were exquisitely sewn with tiny forget-me-nots and curly ribbon. Had Maris made them herself?

She had biggish feet—not that he'd ever say so—but he managed to fold the thin-soled slippers into his pocket. He would go upstairs even though it wasn't time yet, for he was desperate for something to occupy him. He could move a few more boxes into the workroom.

There would be more waiting around in the attics, too, as Maris hunched over the table examining all the ugly objets d'art with her spectacles sliding down her nose. Reyn was not much good at waiting but he'd make the effort. For her.

What in hell was happening to him? It really wouldn't be wise to fall in lust with the Countess of Kelby.

Reyn rang for his dishes to be removed. One of the Johns—not Aloysius—appeared almost instantly. Reyn waited until the hallway was empty, then went upstairs. He took off his jacket and cravat and rolled up his sleeves. He had a feeling Maris had not seen too many male forearms. Even the gardeners he'd seen earlier were covered in long-sleeved smocks against the cold. A gentleman did not remove his coat to work in front of a lady. Actually a gentleman did not, as a rule, do manual labor, unless he made an appearance at the haying to impress his tenants. Even Reyn's own father had dirtied his hands on occasion when he had tenants to impress as he won—then lost—one ramshackle country property after the other.

He was thinking nonsense. Of course Maris had seen her husband at work. Presumably the Earl of Kelby had not worn evening clothes as he tramped the Tuscan hillsides with a spade. From what Reyn pieced together, in his prime, the man had been a force to be reckoned with.

Reyn felt a stab of jealousy, not for the man's position and possessions, but for the loyalty of his countess . . . whom he vowed to leave alone this afternoon no matter how much he didn't want to.

He trotted back and forth until he'd brought in almost everything that was light enough for him to handle. At the snail-like pace Maris was going, they would be at it for weeks. He picked up the ledger and marveled at her handwriting. He couldn't read half of it but it was very pretty. She had drawn illustrations of some of the more decorative things in the margins too, and her artistic skill was impressive. The dents on a chalice, the scrollwork on a knife handle—all of it detailed and precise. Exacting. He looked at the tower of boxes and groaned inwardly.

There were perks to the job, however, perks that made up for the tedium. He brightened as he heard Maris's tread on the steps at last. She was late according to his timepiece.

"I've been working like a slave," he began, and then saw her white face. "What is it? Did something happen?" Was the old earl—

"D-David is here."

She was clearly frightened, and he sought to soothe her. "You said he was apt to turn up. I'm surprised your husband allows it."

"Henry doesn't know he's here yet. David knows better than to bother him. He's come to see me. Someone told David you were at Kelby Hall. He must have a spy on the estate in his employ to carry gossip," she said with bitterness.

"Hold on a minute. Is he banned from coming here?" Reyn would take the utmost pleasure in throwing the man out.

Maris shook her head. "He receives a quarterly allowance according to the terms of his father's will. He used to come in person to collect it, and much more often, just to be a nuisance. Since Jane died, he's been too smart to try to see Henry, but he's written to him. The threats . . . " Maris took a gulp of air. "I don't want my husband disturbed by his visit. If he knew David was here, I can't imagine what he'd do."

Reyn supposed it was perfectly possible that in a house this size, one might have a houseguest for months without ever laying eyes on him. Nevertheless, it seemed odd that the earl wasn't informed of his nephew's presence. The old fellow would no doubt instruct a few of the Johns to throw him out on his arse.

"Did he come for his money?"

"I gave it to him last month."

"Well, then. Send him on his way."

"I-I can't. He says he's staying until he's assured you won't make off with any Kelby treasures."

Reyn was dumbfounded. "Me? Run off with such rubbish? I should be offended he thinks I'm so stupid. And I thought he didn't care about the Kelby Collection anyway."

"He doesn't really, but he doesn't know what might be in the attics. No one does. May I remind you, there *was* the emerald."

"Which I hope you are not going to turn over to him. What have you done with it?"

"It's in the strongbox in my bedroom."

"Good. Keep it there. I don't mind meeting with the man, Maris. Let him snoop his fill and then go away."

"You c-can't call me Maris. David is very sharp. If he discovers you are not who you claim to be—" She shivered.

Reyn was across the floor in a second, and Maris was in his arms the next. "I will do nothing to arouse his suspicions. I'll even wear the damned spectacles if you want me to." They were jammed in his pocket just in case.

"Oh, Reyn! I thought we'd have more time to prepare for him. What if he asks you questions?"

"I've only been up here a day, haven't I? It's not like we've had time to find much. And so I'll tell him." He smelled roses and starch as he tucked her into the crook of his arm. "When do you want me to see him?"

"Right now, if you can. He's waiting in my sitting room. David has reserved a bed in Kelby Village for the night, but maybe he'll go away tomorrow if he's satisfied."

It irked Reyn that there was another man in Maris's private space, but at least he'd get to see how she lived. It was unlikely he'd ever receive an invitation to enter her boudoir again.

Reyn dressed in haste, taking care to muss his hair and put the useless spectacles on his face before he followed Maris downstairs. He was going for the distracted scholar look. He'd seen plenty of masters so wrapped up in their studies they sometimes didn't even notice the dark-haired boy in the back of the room sticking his tongue out at them and lobbing spitballs.

His hands were dirty, so he shoved them in his pocket along with Maris's slippers, praying that David Kelby had never heard of Captain Reynold Durant, late of His Majesty's Army. His best bet was to say as little as possible, which would be easy as he had no real knowledge of the junk upstairs.

The door to Maris's suite was open. Her maid Betsy was standing rather nervously at the entrance as though she was preventing their unwanted guest from leaving.

"There you are, my lady. I told Mr. Kelby you'd be right down and there was no need to go upstairs."

David Kelby did not look as if he meant to go anywhere anytime soon. He was sprawled out on a striped pink wing chair and took his own sweet time standing as the countess entered the room. "Aunt Maris, I had begun to despair of ever seeing your fair face again. Whatever took you so long?"

Reyn wished his clear lenses weren't so smudged, though he could see Kelby well enough. The man bore an uncanny resemblance to his uncle, same angular build, dark eyes and hawkish nose. His hair was auburn rather than silver, though his temples were dusted with gray.

It was his voice that set Reyn's teeth on edge. It was deceptively mellow, yet Reyn could hear the barb behind the words. In an instant, the bumbling professor disappeared and he straightened up. "I'm afraid I don't have time to entertain your guests, Lady Kelby. I answer only to Lord Kelby. What do you want to speak to me about?"

Perhaps he'd overdone it. David Kelby's face suffused with color. "Good Lord, Maris. The man is a rude savage. Where did Uncle Henry dig him up?"

"He has impeccable credentials. Captain Durant, may I present my husband's nephew, David Kelby. As my husband's heir, he believes he has a right to stick his nose in where it doesn't belong."

"Come now, Maris. You didn't mind me sticking my . . . nose in before."

Maris stiffened at Reyn's side.

Holy hell. Reyn balled his fists, his mind racing at Kelby's blatant implication. But as ordinary hired help, he was meant not to know anything about Lady Kelby. He'd be a fool to defend her honor.

When she might not have any.

No. Maris Kelby was not a loose woman. Reyn would swear to that on a stack of Bibles he couldn't read.

What had transpired between them? Nothing good, he was sure. A few seconds in Kelby's presence and Reyn yearned to knock the man down. The man was . . . oily, even if he was handsome. Reyn supposed some women might be persuaded by such charm, but he couldn't imagine Maris falling for it.

"I'm very busy, Kelby. While your concern for your uncle is admirable, I assure you I'm not going to make off with the family silver. My interest is purely academic. When the inventory is complete, perhaps the countess will share it with you. If that's all, my lady, I'll go back upstairs while there is still enough light to do my work."

"Not so fast, Durant. Captain, is it? How did you find time to study ancient history while you were in the army?"

"I was not born in boots. I went to school, of course." *Please don't ask me how many.*

"Cambridge or Oxford?"

"Neither." Reyn made it sound like neither institution was worthy of him, not that either place would have enrolled him. "I was privately tutored." His Majesty had provided him with a Grand Tour of some of the best sites in Europe.

"Do you share my uncle's mania for Etruscan artifacts?"

"That is not my area of expertise." *Please don't ask me what is.*

"David," Maris said impatiently, "Captain Durant came highly recommended. Henry is satisfied with his honesty and integrity. His employment is really none of your business."

"My uncle is an old man, Maris. I won't have him taken advantage of. Who knows what the man is really doing up there?"

"You don't give a fig for Henry! If you did, you wouldn't come to Kelby Hall." Maris was about as indignant as she'd been when she'd found Reyn at the Reining Monarchs. Anger suited her, brought color to her cheeks and a flash to her eyes.

"You cannot keep blaming me for Jane. I never made her any promises. Not once."

Reyn felt like he was an unwilling actor in a play. The conversation was far too personal and charged to be overheard by the stranger he was supposed to be. "If that is all, Lady Kelby. You two may discuss your family business in private."

"There is no family business to discuss. I want you to leave now, David. You've seen what you've come to see."

Kelby raked Reyn with a considering stare.

Reyn felt his hair lift on the back of his neck. The man was dangerous, to the countess especially.

"Yes, I believe I have. You've been warned, Durant. Maybe I should volunteer to assist you in your task to speed the process up and protect my interests."

"No!" Maris cried.

"That won't be necessary. The work is tedious, Kelby. I doubt a man like you would enjoy it." Reyn certainly wasn't, except for the time it afforded him with the countess.

"You're probably right. I understand you've already got a willing worker anyway. My aunt is such a ferocious bluestocking, she must be in transports rummaging through the attic alone with you."

Damn. Kelby made it sound like they were doing exactly what they were doing. Reyn pretended not to understand. "Lady Kelby has been an enormous help so far. For a mere woman, she is very knowledgeable." Reyn prayed she wouldn't elbow him in the gut.

"I'll be back soon to check on your progress. Maris, a word."

Reyn was dismissed. What he really wanted to do was drag Maris upstairs to get her out of Kelby's clutches. However, she would have to fight this battle without him if they were to maintain their ruse.

But when she did come upstairs, he wanted a word with her, too.

Chapter 15

"Who is he? I don't like him." David was sprawled in the chair again. His informality was insolent, deliberately so.

Maris would not let him rattle her again. One word could summon a fleet of footmen to remove him from the premises, but first she wanted to know how he came to be there.

"Henry's f-friend in London found him." David didn't have to know about Mr. Ramsey and *The London List*.

"He doesn't look much like a spindly scholar, long nose buried in some book. All those muscles. And he's young, too."

"I haven't noticed his appearance," Maris lied. "We've been much too busy. There's a great deal of lifting involved, you know. Some of the boxes are very heavy."

"Found any treasure yet?"

"Nothing that would interest you. You've made your opinion known about the family's artifacts, haven't you?" She would never give up the emerald to him. Never.

"Don't hold out on me, Maris. As heir, I have a right to know what's going on here."

"A miracle could happen to prevent that," Maris retorted.

A mistake. David's bronze eyebrows lifted. "Are you enceinte, Aunt Maris? It was my understanding that you and Uncle Henry no longer shared a room."

"One doesn't need to share a room for intercourse, as you well know, David. Where are you getting this information anyway? It is incorrect. Your informant is leading you on."

"I don't think so." He smirked. "Here I am in your boudoir. It's as devoid of passion as a nun's cell. Look at you, all dull in that brown sack. No wonder you don't entice my uncle."

Maris reminded herself that David was out to hurt her, to trip her up, to poison her life. How could she once have found him attractive? Oh, physically, he was handsome enough, but his tongue was vicious. When he'd used it spin tales about the ton, she'd found him amusing, shut away at Kelby Hall far from society as she was. Maris was no longer amused.

"And like a nun, I'm on my knees in prayer thanking God you no longer have an interest in me," she said stiffly.

"I didn't say that. I wouldn't mind picking up where we left off, my dear. Before you got that inconvenient conscience. There's a great deal more I could teach you."

"I would rather die than let you touch me again." Maris would never repeat her foolishness with him, especially now that she knew what could be between a man and a woman. She'd jump from the attic window if she had to.

"Brave words, but you'll change your tune if I decide to tell your husband about our little affair."

Once his threat would have struck her with terror. She'd heard it often enough, but today it was robbed of some of its power. "Oh, David. You disappoint me. Again. You are so predictable. How much money do you want this time?"

He smiled with no warmth. "Do you doubt I'd tell Uncle Henry? You shouldn't, you know. I have nothing to lose by doing so, He can't do anything about the entail, and before you start telling me he'll get a baby on you at this late date, spare me. You've been married ten long years, Maris."

Thank God he did not know he'd taken her virginity. That would have been the ultimate mortification for her. There had been no blood, and not even any pain. All her years of riding and climbing up and down the Tolfa Mountains must have taken care of that little detail.

He'd known she was vulnerable, though. An easy mark for his flattery and courtly concern. All false, as it turned out, but Maris had been such a needy, willing victim. Henry had left her home while he attended a symposium at the University of Edinburgh, and she'd been resentful. All her work for him, years and years of it, and she was "a mere woman," as Reyn had said, unwelcome in his scholarly circle. David had pounced, and she'd not jumped away.

Henry had been away for over a month. Within the first week, Maris knew she'd made an unforgivable mistake, but it had taken her another to extricate herself from David Kelby's arms. She'd been damned lucky to escape a pregnancy.

Maris could not imagine a worse fate than to bear David Kelby's child. Jane was proof of that.

"I wouldn't count my chickens, David. Stranger things have happened." She flinched under his black stare.

"You're up to something, aren't you? Perhaps with that Durant fellow? I wager you think you can pass a bastard brat on to my uncle. I'll tell him that, too."

Maris felt her bravado evaporate. He was much too close to the truth, although at least he didn't believe Henry to be complicit in their scheme. "You are ridiculous! I would never break my vows to Henry!"

"You did with me, Maris. Why wouldn't you again?"

"I just wouldn't." Her words sounded empty even to her. "Captain Durant is only an employee. I don't even know him. I'm not likely to invite him to my bed." She tried to laugh and was not especially successful.

"See that you don't. For I'll find out, Maris. I'm paying good money to someone right in the bosom of your household," he said, smug.

"If I find out who—"

"You won't."

Dear God. This is unconscionable. Maris had planned to be careful with Reyn, but now she had even more reason to worry.

If David suspected, what would he do when he *knew*? He thought he could carry tales to Henry. Wouldn't he be surprised to learn her husband was the architect of this plan? But David could cause trouble for the child, whisper his doubts to the ton, and ruin the Kelby name. True, any child born to Maris would be acknowledged as Henry's legal issue. There were plenty of children who were accepted yet did not have an ounce of their "father's" blood. Some escaped society's gossip, but others were under a cloud for life. The ton had a long memory.

"You are desperate. Grasping at straws. You had your chance to cement your standing in this family when you ruined Jane. Why didn't you marry her? I grant you, Henry wouldn't have liked it much, but he would have supported the match."

David's fair skin flushed. "As I said earlier, I never promised Jane marriage. If she told you I did, she was lying."

"You didn't care about her at all, did you."

"Jealous, Maris?"

"Of course not! I cannot think of anything worse than to be your wife or the mother of your child."

"You're probably too shriveled up at this point to be anyone's mother," he sneered.

Maris eyed the heavy Chinese vase on the mantel, deciding it was too valuable to waste throwing it at David's head. He really was the perfect villain though, almost too cliché. If he always knew the charming words to say to worm himself into favor, he was even better at a cutting, *killing* remark. "You dislike me. I dislike you. And we know my husband despises you. When I think about it, I doubt he'd believe anything you had to say. I'll make alternate arrangements for your quarterly allowance so you will not have to come to Kelby Hall any longer to collect it." She should have done so five years ago.

"Not so fast, my dear. What about your pin money? It does come in handy. One must keep up appearances as heir to an earl."

Maris went to her escritoire and opened a drawer. "Blackmail is such an uninspired crime. It's so . . . banal, don't you think? This will be the last of it, David," she said, tossing him a velvet bag of coins. "Tell Henry whatever you want. I don't care."

The look on his face was almost worth her imprudence. She'd wait to be frightened later. At that moment, she was enjoying herself too much.

"You aren't serious."

"Oh, I am. Who do you think Henry will believe, his devoted wife or his disreputable nephew? He thinks you are a *murderer,* David. Your actions led to the death of his only child. If he could, he'd see you imprisoned for the rest of your days."

David stood, white-faced. "You'll regret this, Maris."

"I don't think I will. And don't think to come back here to Kelby Hall while Henry still lives. I'll have you barred at the door."

He was angrier than she had ever seen him. For a moment, she thought he might stride across the room and hit her. To her relief, he turned and slammed the door behind him, hard enough to wake the dead.

Maris couldn't stop shaking at her brazenness. At first, she'd watched every word she spoke, sure that her newest secret would be revealed to David Kelby. She'd always been a terrible liar. Henry had teased that he'd been aware of her every fib from girlhood on. Those lies had been harmless ones—No, Jane and I didn't steal the last strawberry tart; Yes, our governess let us study in the garden—but now the future of Kelby Hall depended on Maris's ability to dissemble. She thanked heaven she'd washed and perfumed herself again before David arrived. The scent of sex, the scent of Reyn, even to her inexperienced nose, was unmistakable.

She had made a great enemy, and there was a spy in her household, someone on David's payroll. How ironic it was her coin that paid the traitor to report on her. David's allowance had been boosted by her own guilt money over the past five years. She'd given him the last of it to go away.

Could she hold to her resolve and refuse him anymore? The blackmail would never stop unless she found and kept her courage.

If she confessed to Henry, would he understand and forgive what she'd done?

She couldn't do it. Couldn't hurt him. He may have given her permission to have an affair with Reynold Durant, but what she'd done with David was true betrayal.

Maris felt all her carefully basted-over seams begin to unravel, stitch by stitch. She could not go back to the attics and make any sort of order of anything. She needed fresh air.

Her hands were trembling too hard to tie her cloak strings properly, but she managed and would worry about the knot later. She hurried down one of the numerous sets of stairs to the ground floor and went out into the garden through the breakfast room door.

A sharp gust of wind whipped her cloak up. Soon there would be snow on the diamonds and rectangles of the rigidly arranged plantings. The expansion of the original Elizabethan knot garden had been designed by Henry's first wife. It was not to Maris's taste, though she supposed it was impressive enough.

What she loved most was the statuary that kept vigil in each brick or hedge-walled space. They had come from all over the world and some were in better repair than others. There were the obelisk, a fountain with cavorting dolphins, several ancient plinths, a grumpy stone lion, and a young Greek god, amongst others. She didn't mind a missing limb or the creep of moss or the vacant stares of sightless eyes. The statues had been her imaginary friends as she was growing up, and she headed for the garden the farthest from the house where her favorite reigned.

The queen's crown glinted in the sun. Paste jewels—the real ones had been stolen centuries ago—sparkled in the polished marble. The queen's country of origin was unknown. Henry had grown up with her, as had his father and grandfather before him. Family legend had it that she had ruled over this corner of the garden before Kelby Hall had been rebuilt for Queen Elizabeth. Her history was lost.

It was why Henry wanted to account for everything. For future generations, if there were to be any. To share his knowledge and his family's collection with the wider world. Kelby Hall's gardens were open to the public once a year for the local parish fete. It was Henry's intention that the house would also be open, not just one day but many. There were so many things to be learned from studying the relics of the past, and Kelby Hall was crammed to the attics with them.

Maris squinted up at the roofline of the only home she'd ever known. Captain Durant must have given up on her by now. She didn't want to face him. He could not have missed David's insinuations. He must think her an utter hypocrite. All her hesitancy, all her reluctance, the war with her conscience, her tears—all must seem false to him. She'd lost her virtue for far less honorable reasons five years past.

The tears flowed, hot against her cold cheeks. No one could notice her cry but the queen in the center of the garden room, and she had stopped listening to Maris's girlish hopes years ago.

Maris didn't hear the crunch of Reynold Durant's boots on the stone path until he was right above her, thrusting a handkerchief at her face. She took it gratefully, wiped the wet from her face and then blew her nose with all the grace of a trumpeting elephant. Just another reason to be mortified.

"You'd better tell me," he said quietly, "although I think I can guess."

"I'm too ashamed."

"Here, shove over on the bench. All the way over in case there are prying eyes. If I could see you out here, others can. Take a breath."

She had turned into a watering pot around this man. She hadn't ever had a real friend to confide in except Jane, and for obvious reasons she had not been able to confess what she'd done with David. Maris sometimes wondered if Jane had discovered the relationship anyway, and that had contributed to her decision to walk into the lake. Maris wouldn't put it past David to have told Jane and taunted her with it.

Layers of guilt. It was a wonder Maris could stand upright when she was so bent by the weight of them.

"I'm listening. Take your time."

She hardly knew Reynold Durant. Oh, that was absurd. She'd allowed him into her body for the past two days. The handsome stranger who sat beside her knew more about her than her own husband did after ten years of marriage. A limited knowledge, yes, but a profound one.

She hiccupped to hold back a wave of hopeless laughter. She was becoming hysterical at the absurd situation she found herself in. "If you've guessed, you tell me."

He raised a wooly brow. "No indeed. I'm not going to make it easy for you. Confession is good for the soul, I hear. I'll not rob you of the relief of it. It's been hard for you to keep it in, hasn't it?"

Damn him. He was supposed to be ignorant, wasn't he?

"I have nothing to say." She blew her nose again, with a little more discretion.

"Your face said it all upstairs. But tell me in words. I won't judge you, I promise."

"Won't you? Don't you think me the basest sort of woman? I'm an unfaithful wife. A liar."

"You haven't lied so much as not told the truth. I'm not one of those who believes much in the sin of omission. Most people usually have a valid reason to leave out a word or three and keep quiet. You have the greatest reason of all. You wanted to protect your husband. Because you love him."

The simple understanding let loose a fresh assault of tears. Reyn waited patiently while she snuffled and sniffed into his handkerchief. It smelled of sandalwood and starch and was somehow comforting.

"I-I made a horrible mistake." She reached for more words, but they didn't come. She'd tried to explain it all to herself for five years, and had never succeeded. How could she explain to Reynold Durant?

It turned out she didn't need to. "You were lonely, Maris. You love your husband, yes, but he's much older than you are—a bit of a father figure, if you want my unsolicited opinion. By his own account, he's obsessed with his studies, not his young wife. You were looking for something that made you feel alive. Important. It's just too bad you sought it from David Kelby."

She almost smiled. "I thought you were going to let me confess."

"I'm sure I left out some details. I'm not a wizard at mind reading, you know."

"You've come close." She looked at the marble queen, so regal and composed, and took a steadying breath. "When Henry married me, he'd already been afflicted with . . . oh, I don't know how to say it."

"He couldn't exert his husbandly rights."

Maris knew she was blushing. "Yes. He tried, but—" She did not wish to revisit her greatest disappointment and shrugged. "He pleased me in other ways, but we were never able to consummate the marriage despite his desire for a son.

"At first I was fine with it all. I never expected to marry, and I've never really been domestic. Give me a book over a sewing basket any day. I was happy accompanying Henry to Italy and spending time in the library with him. But he grew weaker, and our foreign trips were curtailed. I-I was at loose ends. David was a frequent visitor then, and he was very flattering. *Too* flattering. I should have known better. He made me feel . . . wicked. And I *liked* it."

Reyn was wrong. The confession was not making her feel any better. A horrible silence hung between them. It was suddenly very important to her that he not hold her in contempt. If she continued, it was inevitable that he would.

She lurched off the bench. "I must get back inside."

"Sit down, Maris. You aren't finished."

"I am! I cannot discuss this with you! It isn't proper and I-I hate talking about it."

He rose too. "We left propriety behind quite some time ago, wouldn't you agree? What you felt—what you *feel*—is natural. You are a flesh and blood woman, not like that statue over there. Come, let's walk. It's a beautiful afternoon, much too nice to be shut up in the attics."

"S-someone will notice." She felt eyes were everywhere. David had robbed her of security in her own home.

"Pretend you're educating me about the statuary. Wave your arms about and point. I'm sure if I were really a scholar I'd be interested, wouldn't I?" He grinned at her. Reynold Durant had an easy answer to everything, even if the questions were impossible.

"I really have nothing to add. I betrayed my husband for a few weeks for what was ultimately wretched. When it was over, I was little more informed of carnal pleasure than when I started."

Reyn's grin was wider. "So David was not a good lover?"

Maris wanted to slink into the shrubbery. "I was just there to be conquered. A challenge. David was much too selfish to care about me."

"Nothing like me, then."

"Oh! You are incorrigible." How could he tease her about something so serious?

"Always. Look, you made a mistake over a man. These things happen, more often than you might imagine. David preyed upon your naïveté."

"I was old enough. I was nine and twenty!"

"Well, coincidentally I am too. Today's my birthday. I think I'm still young enough to fall for a pretty face and a sweet lie."

Maris didn't believe him for a minute. "You say that to be kind. And happy birthday. This is not much of a celebratory day, is it."

"Oh, I don't know. This morning was very pleasant." He winked, still keeping his distance.

She remembered to gesture to a black marble plinth as they strolled by it. "How can you be so casual about everything?"

Reyn stopped on the path. "What would you have me do? Whip you with one of the crops from the Reining Monarchs? You've been punishing yourself enough for a long time. What is it now, five years? You cannot change the mistake you made, only learn from it. You haven't been having it off with the gardener or the vicar since, have you? Or perhaps one of the Johns? And seriously, Maris, would it be too much to let the footmen keep their names?"

"What?"

"Never mind. My point is, you are not a serial adulteress. You were taken advantage of by a professional seducer. I recognized his type at once. If you'd had more experience—if you hadn't grown up so sheltered here in this alternate world—you might have been better able to deal with the man. I imagine your husband would even understand and forgive you if you were to tell him."

"No! And please don't say anything."

He looked affronted. "As if I would. It's not my place to get mixed up in the affairs of my betters."

"You know perfectly well you are as good as anyone here. Superior, probably."

"Are you a Jacobin, Lady Kelby? The revolution did not end well. And if you *do* believe in democracy, would you please explain about the footmen?"

"This is the second time you've brought them up," Maris said, confused.

"They're all called John."

"Um, yes."

"Why?"

Maris had never thought about it before. From her infancy, she'd been surrounded by bewigged and green-coated Johns. "I don't know. Does it matter?"

"How would you like it if I called you Harriet? Or Griselda? Antigone? Philomena?"

Her lips turned up a little. "I shouldn't like that at all."

"Of course you wouldn't. Maris is a lovely name, and your parents picked it carefully for you, as you said. You've got a houseful of Aloysiuses and Timothys and Williams all skulking about under false names."

"There can't be more than one Aloysius."

"Perhaps not, but would it be too much trouble to learn the men's given names? Never mind. I guess it would. There are so damn many footmen here I suppose it's convenient to holler 'John' and know for sure someone will turn up. What the devil is that?"

They had come to a stone sarcophagus. A rather short knight lay in repose, his sword at his side and a dog of indeterminate parentage at his feet.

"That's the first Earl of Kelby. Don't worry, he's not inside. He's buried somewhere in the Holy Land."

"How lucky for you. I would hate to worry that every time a bulb was planted the gardeners might unearth a dead relative." Reyn was diverting her, something he was very good at. It was impossible to feel too melancholy in his presence.

Was he right? Should she forgive herself for her stupidity? It had been five long years of scourging herself. Diminishing her pleasure in ordinary things. Feeling inadequate and unworthy. By God, she'd been frightfully boring, even to herself. Henry had not noticed, of course, but she hadn't felt a spark of emotion in years.

Except for her anger at Captain Reynold Durant when he refused to keep his word. He still made her feel something, but it wasn't anger.

If she could find the courage to tell Henry the truth, then David's incessant requests for money would be moot. She didn't believe he wouldn't try for more despite what she'd said to him. Something had snapped when she'd tossed him the coin purse. But she wasn't naïve enough to believe he'd stop importuning her for more money, because eventually he'd figure out she'd been bluffing.

She'd been brave today. And cold. Maris had found words she didn't even know she possessed. Could she find more words to tell Henry?

Chapter 16

Reyn was jealous. He shouldn't be, but there it was. He hadn't shown his irritation to Maris, for what good would that have done her, blubbering on the bench like her dog had died? Speaking of dogs, how could she have fallen victim to a cur like David Kelby?

Well, he'd explained it to her himself. It didn't make it any easier to swallow, however. He wasn't angry *at* her, but *for* her. She really was such an innocent for all her scholarly knowledge.

She had been a twenty-nine-year-old virgin until her misguided affair with her husband's nephew. It was sad, yet somehow touching. The poor woman had never enjoyed what should have been her right by marriage. The elderly Earl of Kelby may have been hopeful when he placed that large diamond on his young wife's finger, but must have known his limitations.

She'd had five years of companionship and affection without intercourse. That may have been enough for some women. Maris had probably convinced herself it was enough for her until the snake slithered into the garden and into her.

Reyn was a firm believer that women deserved as much satisfaction in bed as their partners, but apparently David Kelby did not share a similar generous impulse.

Benefitting from her innocence—her wonder and eagerness were precious—was Reyn's alone. No other man had seen her flame, not even her husband, so Reyn would have to be content with that. In all the ways that counted, he was Maris's first lover.

It was rather daunting. Reyn felt a responsibility, as if he carried a banner to uphold all male honor.

Instinctively, he knew Maris would never engage in another love affair. If they were successful, he was sure she'd devote the rest of her life to their child. That would be a shame, really. She'd already sacrificed her youth to her elderly husband and her aspirations to an unworthy partner. She would never make time for her needs. No wonder she was so highly strung.

At least she wasn't crying any longer. Their walk around the garden was almost normal. She did indeed describe the stone objects at the center of every garden room. Reyn was conscious that despite the brick walls and clipped hedges, their movements were visible from the upper stories of the house. He had spotted her from the attic window—a forlorn figure headed as far away from Kelby Hall as possible. They would have to be more circumspect than ever.

She couldn't outrun her past, just make peace with it. He listened with half an ear as they went through an iron gate to the sweep of lawn above the water. She was talking about the little rotunda perched on the island in the center of the lake. Its design was based on some obscure ruin which Reyn cared not one whit about.

"Enough, Lady Kelby. If I'd wanted to take a degree in architecture or history I would have."

Maris blushed.

He was becoming very used to her pretty pink cheeks.

"I'm sorry. I do tend to go on."

"Is that boat functional?"

"You cannot think to row me out there. People really *will* notice us then."

"You are right. It's too cold anyway. Let's return to the house. You're probably chilled to the bone. Have you any idea who Kelby might be paying to spy on you?"

"No. Henry is a very generous employer. I can't imagine why someone might be tempted to betray him."

"Oh, come now. Money is the universal language, is it not? Temptation enough in its own right. Maybe it's someone who prefers his own name to John and is out for revenge."

"Stop teasing about that. I had nothing to do with the renaming of the servants. I don't even think it was Henry's idea. It's just Kelby tradition."

"Some traditions should die out, don't you think? Do you expect your son to travel the globe and bring back more trash to Kelby

Hall? There's enough here already." He could not see the value in much of what he'd seen over the past two days.

"If he—or she—chooses an interest in history, I would not object," Maris said primly.

"What about the present?" Reyn argued. "Surely one should enjoy oneself in the here and now."

"How do *you* enjoy yourself, Captain Durant? Whipping women?"

"I told you that was not my usual kind of thing!" Reyn sputtered. What exactly had he said about the Reining Monarchs? "I was . . . bored. At loose ends. A friend proposed me for membership and I didn't see the harm."

"You didn't *see the harm*? Perhaps you do need those spectacles after all."

Wait a minute. How had they gone from him trying to cheer her up to this attack on his character? It was she who'd broken a commandment.

Instead of giving her a blistering set-down, he bit his tongue near bloody. She was in a wretched fix and he happened to be a handy whipping boy.

The thought of her whipping *him* made him laugh out loud.

"What is so amusing?"

"You wouldn't understand, Maris. I'm not sure I do myself. Let's cry friends. Go back upstairs to work."

"N-now?"

"It won't be dark for a while."

"All right." She said the words with very little conviction, and would have been even less enthusiastic if she knew what he planned to do to her once she got upstairs.

Reyn had been hired for a job, and a job he would do. He could make Maris forget for a few minutes about David Kelby and the Earl of Kelby and all the Kelbys that had come before them. He was damned annoyed with the Kelbys, men who seemed to revere inanimate objects rather than treat the living well, particularly the Kelby women.

It hadn't taken much, a brush of his lips on the back of her neck and she bent over the desk, his hand squeezing her shoulder. She'd looked up, her questioning brown eyes magnified by her spectacles. Reyn didn't have to say a word to make her drop the pen, rise, and retreat behind the screen. They had undressed each other, hands slow and steady, never breaking eye contact.

It was the most honest interaction he'd ever had with a woman. Maris's trust was a living thing, a gift he could never equal. What he gave her body was nothing to what she gave his soul—her acceptance, her faith, her *respect*. He wasn't worthy, but would work to be.

Reyn let her take charge, placing her over him. Once she realized what could be done, she laughed in delight and proceeded to obliterate all his thoughts but one. He loved her.

That certainly proved what a fool he was. He wasn't in the habit of falling in love. Yes, he enjoyed more than his fair share of women. Who wouldn't, when given the opportunity? But his heart had never been engaged. It shouldn't be engaged now. Maris Kelby was completely wrong for him, and it wasn't just because she was married or a countess. Her intellect was far superior to his own. Would she still like him if she discovered he couldn't even read what she'd been writing in that ledger? He was worse than a child, for at least a child had hope of the future.

Reyn shut his eyes to the beauty of her arching above him, her lush breasts bouncing as she came down smooth and hard on his cock. He would concentrate on what was, not on what couldn't be. He was inside . . . no, temporarily outside . . . the Countess of Kelby . . . *ah, sweet Jesus*. He slipped his hand between them, touching her where she needed to be touched.

Maris bit back a cry and lost her rhythm, but Reyn made up for it by righting her and thrusting deep. He would not let her lose him when he was so close to completion. He pressed and rubbed his thumb against her and felt the jagged tremors start, sweeping him right away with her.

He wanted to open his eyes and watch her come apart, but was afraid to. He didn't need that tempting image in his head, a nagging companion to remind him of what was not his. Was Maris watching him or lost in her own secret world? Reyn wondered if he looked as frantic as he felt. He wrestled his face into a semblance of sanity and buried himself one final time, spending the last drop of seed inside her.

She collapsed atop him, shuddering. Her skin was hot damp velvet. He skimmed her back, coming to rest on her soft bottom. The next time, he'd enter her from behind. He vowed he'd give her as many variations as he knew before he left her. Reyn was still bearing that banner for all male honor, not that he minded. At least, it was something he was considered an expert at.

"Feeling better?"

"Better than I have a right to," she said softly. "Are you too hot? I'm burning up."

Reyn shifted her slightly to the side. "We only live once, Maris. You have every right to feel as good as possible, every single day. Nights, too." He nuzzled her throat.

"Then you are not a proponent of self-abnegation?"

"Self-abnewhatsis? It's not in my dictionary."

She sighed. "Sometimes I think it's the only word in mine."

"Then we must get some ink and blot it out. You can't make other people happy without being happy first yourself." He'd learned that the hard way. Once he'd started following his own drummer, things had fallen into place for him.

"How is it that you're so wise?"

"I'm an old man. Twenty-nine today, may I remind you."

"Happy birthday again. I should have told Cook to bake you a cake."

"Why? So I could eat it all by myself?" Reyn told himself it was just as well that they not dine together. Their growing familiarity would arouse suspicion. And the more time they spent together, the harder it would be for him to leave.

"I-I'm sorry you feel isolated. But now that we know someone is working for David, we must be extra careful."

He kissed her nose. There were a few freckles on it he'd not noticed before. "I'll see what I can do to discover who that is."

She rose up on an elbow, her doubt plain. "How will you go about it?"

"Don't worry. I won't say or do anything to tip my hand. Anyone new working here would be curious about the family, yes? I can ask a few questions." He'd gotten fairly far with Aloysius last night, and there might be someone else loose-lipped on the staff.

Maris frowned. "I don't know. It might be dangerous."

"Have you no confidence in my ability to be an absentminded, yet nosy, professor?"

"David was right. You don't look like a scholar."

"Well, neither do you. You're much too beautiful to be a blue-stocking."

"B-beautiful?"

"Come now, Countess. Don't fish for more compliments. You are a stunner."

She hit his chest. "You are teasing me!"

Reyn sat up. "I am not. When one looks at you—*really* looks at you—one cannot argue that you are not a very handsome woman."

"Oh. Handsome is not beautiful." She sounded a bit disappointed.

By God, she *was* fishing for compliments, and he could provide them all the rest of the afternoon if he wanted to break his own heart.

Her body was glorious. It was criminal that it had been so neglected. Her face—freckles and all—was lovely in animation, her hair entrancing when it was mussed. How sad she did not know her own worth.

Reyn kissed her, letting it speak much more clearly than his words ever could. She relaxed into his arms and kissed him right back. If they kept at it, he would have to have her again, and the hour was growing late. Breathless, he looked down at her flushed face. "Beautiful," he whispered, and made himself get off the chaise and dress.

Chapter 17

There would be no chance meeting with his countess in the garden tonight. Reyn finished his dinner, rang for the tray to be taken away, and actually picked up one of the books Maris had put in his room for his edification. It didn't take long for his eyes to droop and his head to swim. But if he went to bed, he'd be wide awake in the middle of the night with nothing to take his mind off his restlessness.

Best to leave his suite, perhaps cadge another cigar, wander about, and have a word or two with some servants. Maybe even walk down to the village pub. One always picked up a good bit of gossip at a pub.

He put on the smudged spectacles, then removed them so he could clean them with a handkerchief. They were growing on him, not that they improved his vision at all. They gave him something to hide behind, though.

How often was one judged on one's appearance? He thought of Maris, who'd come to him buttoned-up and spotless, obscuring her looks with an excess of respectability. He much preferred her rumpled and flushed from a good fucking.

Enough of that. He was damned lucky to have bedded her twice today. Now that he was almost thirty—well, in another year anyhow—he'd have to anticipate that his capability would diminish, just like the poor old earl. Reyn hoped he still had some good decades left, but one never knew. He'd been lucky so far, despite the ball embedded in his shoulder and the saber scars. Tomorrow he could prick his thumb on a thorn in Maris's garden and die from sepsis, or break his neck falling from Phantom, or be shot dead in a duel by David Kelby.

Hadn't Maris said he was staying in the village? The cigar became even less of a possibility as Reyn clapped his hat on his head, hurried downstairs, and walked through the massive front door that a John held open for him.

He'd ridden through Kelby. It was not very big and not very far from the house, an easy jaunt for a man who'd marched through most of Europe and eastern Canada. A thousand stars lit the clear night sky as Reyn walked between the copper beeches, listening to the owls hoot and the bare branches rattle.

Reyn preferred the solitude of the night. He'd never had trouble staying awake on patrol. Every sense came alive and he could practically hear the universe thrumming all around him. In the dark, no one could read and other skills became much more useful.

He didn't expect to encounter the enemy on the road, but once he got to the pub, he'd have to be careful. Reyn was anxious to hear what the local populace had to say about the Kelby family. And if he was lucky, he'd find the earl's nephew over a pint with his informant.

A haze of wood smoke stung Reyn's eyes as he approached the tiny village. Kelby was mostly dark, but the inn and its front-room pub were lit up like Christmas. He could smell roasting meat and years worth of sour ale that had spilled in the alley.

He pushed open the door and all conversation stopped. He should have expected that, and slouched, trying to look as much like a distracted antiquities expert as possible.

There was no sign of David Kelby. Reyn plunked himself in a corner and ordered ale from a very pretty barmaid. Talk resumed and he wondered which of the men would approach him first to ask for his *curriculum vitae.*

He didn't have long to wait. Two fellows came over to him, both looking somewhat familiar.

"Sir, you're the man the earl hired to go through his attics, ain't you?"

"I am indeed. Do I know you?"

"I'm Bob Hastings. I took your horse when you came the other day. Fine animal. This here's John."

"Francis Smith," the other man said with a black look to his friend.

"Good evening, gentlemen. Night off?"

"We do get them regular. The earl's good that way." Bob took a mouthful of the brew he'd brought with him.

"He seems a very nice old gentleman," Reyn agreed.

"Not like his nephew."

"Shut your gob, Bob!"

That had the effect of reducing Bob the groom to helpless laughter.

Reyn wondered how steadily he'd been drinking. *Well, this is altogether too easy.* He turned to Francis. "I met Mr. Kelby this afternoon. He seemed to think I'd make off with the Kelby fortune. I confess, I was a little insulted. In my line of work, reputation is everything." Hoping he sounded appropriately sniffy, he pushed the glasses back up on the bridge of his nose.

"Counting his chickens before they're hatched, he is," Bob volunteered. "Always coming around the house spying. The earl don't see him anymore. Bad blood there."

"Bob!"

"I'm just stating the facts, Frank."

"You'll be working for David Kelby soon enough if he'll keep a lounger like you on. If I was you, I'd stubble it." Francis Smith went back to the crowded table in front of the fire.

Reyn saw a few other familiar faces, more Johns if he was right.

"Won't you join me, Mr. Hastings?" Reyn waved to the barmaid and pointed to Bob's tankard.

"All right. That's kind of you, sir."

"I'm not being kind. I'm curious. I'll be at Kelby Hall at least a month and I find the atmosphere there somewhat daunting. I'm used to working at big houses, though," Reyn added quickly, "going through, uh, family treasures. Usually to value items for sale." He thought that anyone in "his line of work" might in truth do that. "But I understand everything has to remain in at Kelby Hall."

"I don't know nothing about the house. I've never stepped inside it 'cepting for the kitchen," Bob said. "Worked there all my life. Since I was a boy."

That wasn't so very long ago. Bob's usefulness to David Kelby was considerably less if the young man didn't have free access to the house, though Reyn didn't rule him out as the traitor just yet. "Do you like your job?"

"It's all right. No one rides much anymore, but there are still a lot of horses to take care of. I've got a way with horses, I do."

"So do I. I find them so much more congenial than many people I've met."

It took Bob a few long seconds to get the joke, but then he laughed.

"The staff seems very competent."

"Comp—?"

"Skilled. Good at what they do."

"Oh, aye. The earl wouldn't have it any other way, though really it's the old cove Amesbury what does it all. The butler, you know. Runs a strict household. I'm glad he's not my boss."

Amesbury was probably more terrifying than the earl. If anyone had his finger to the pulse of the household, it would be Amesbury. But Reyn could not see the disdainful butler approving of David Kelby and assisting him in any way.

Reyn spent the next half hour talking horses instead of possible conspirators. Sleuthing business was tricky, especially when one didn't want to tip one's hand. The young groom was nearly poetic in his appreciation of the animals, and Reyn discovered he had more in common with the boy than he expected. The conversation gave him a flickering spark of an idea, which he quickly blew out. He didn't have time to worry about his future away from Kelby Hall, just the next few weeks while he was romancing the countess.

No. *Romancing* was not accurate. Servicing was more like it. Reyn would have to keep his growing feelings in check, for what was the point of yearning for what he could never have?

He'd had too much to drink, but not so much as he could miss the invitation in the pretty barmaid's eyes as he rose to leave. Before he'd come to Surrey, he would not have turned her down, but he was tired, and left the pub. He'd had enough birthday presents for one day.

The moon had risen over the treetops, bathing the road in silvery light. The stars had dimmed a bit by comparison, and the temperature had dropped enough for him to long for his army-issued greatcoat.

He stopped before a curve on the road, alert to a noise ahead. Footsteps, not horse hooves, yet he pressed himself to the hedgerow anyhow, debating the wisdom of calling out. In the end, he decided to whistle a drinking song off-key but stay in place. If his fellow nocturnal traveler had less than honorable intentions, he might underestimate Reyn's ability to defend himself.

The crunch of boot steps stopped. "Who goes there?"

Reyn aborted a high note.

"Come out and show yourself!"

The man sounded imperious, yet Reyn heard the slightest quake in his voice. He decided to round the corner, pulling the knife from his boot first.

Would an antiquities expert carry a knife? Any sensible man would, Reyn decided, expecting to face something similar as he stepped past the hedges. "Good evening!" he said cheerily. "I'm just bound for Kelby Hall. The rest of the party are just behind me." He hoped.

"You."

"Yes, it is I," Reyn agreed.

"Durant."

Reyn knew who was before him. He slid the knife up his sleeve, walked forward, and resumed whistling.

David Kelby stood in the middle of the moon-drenched road. "Why, Mr. Kelby! I did not expect to see you again so soon. A lovely night, is it not?" Reyn deliberately slurred his words.

"You are drunk! I'm sure my uncle would not be best pleased."

"Oh, don't tell on me, I beg you. I'm afraid I have no head for spirits. But I was so b-bloody bored up at the big house. Can't do a proper job when it's dark and there isn't a soul my equal to talk to me there." That was certainly true.

It was preferable that Kelby think he was a pompous idiot rather than someone in thrall to the countess.

"What brings you out this evening?" Reyn asked.

"A walk," Kelby said. "As you said, it's a lovely night."

Had he been meeting with his spy? Reyn was sorry he did not choose to wander about the garden. He might have bumped into them whispering and plotting, but knew he wouldn't find out much by quizzing Kelby on the lane.

Squinting, Reyn noticed that Kelby's cravat was askew, which made him think the spy they were looking for was not a John, but a Mary. *Of course.*

Kelby was a ladies' man. If he'd managed to seduce sensible, virtuous Maris, he was likely to sweep some poor impressionable maid right off her feet.

Reyn tried to remember the girls that had brought him his meals and swept his hearth. They'd made no particular impression on him, but he'd open his eyes and work some of his own charm if he had any left to spare.

The next morning, Reyn was prepared to do his flirtatious best with a housemaid or two, but the breakfast tray did not come at the hour he'd arranged for it, nor was there a response when he tugged his bellpull after waiting rather patiently. Perhaps the bell system was broken, or they'd forgotten about the mad man in the attic.

He'd already washed and shaved with the tepid water on his dressing stand and was fully dressed. Would he be shot if he sought the breakfast room, breaking the earl's fraternization rule?

Reyn decided he didn't care. He needed food in his stomach after all the ale he'd consumed with Bob. It hadn't been hard to play the drunk with Kelby. He *didn't* have a head for spirits. He'd learned nothing of significance from his sacrifice, but at least he hadn't been in his room mooning over Maris.

The house seemed unusually quiet. He noticed at once the absence of the human green wall. The footmen were not in place along the main floor corridor. He'd planned on asking for directions, but like a hound on the hunt, he thought his long nose would track the bacon and toasted bread.

He was wrong. Reyn stood in the cavernous entry hall, uncertain which way to turn.

He wished he'd pocketed that great houses of England guide. He thought there'd been a floor plan, not that he could read the cribbed print on the pages devoted to Kelby Hall. He only knew a few places in the Hall—the earl's library, which he wouldn't dare to enter, Maris's sitting room, his own bedroom, and the attics.

It wasn't the sort of day for walking outside. The bright blue sky of the past few days had faded to gray. A light rain spattered the sidelights surrounding the heavy oak front door. Strange that there wasn't a footman on hand to open it even if he didn't want to go out in the gloom. They were like jack-in-the-boxes, always popping up when you least expected them, only to perform a service you didn't even know you needed.

Maybe they were all on a workers' uprising, Reyn thought with a grin. Inspired by the French Revolution, rioting against injustice on Kelby's sole street—although he hoped the earl and countess kept their heads.

Reyn felt the cold of the hall seep into his bones. It would be difficult to work upstairs. They'd have to light more candles, bring up more lamps, keep the fireplace tended. It would be cozy to lie with Maris on the chaise, listening to the rain on the roof. Perhaps they'd forgo the boxes altogether.

He decided to head left, poking his head into the open doors along the way. There was no sign of footmen or food. Wondering if he had an overlooked biscuit in his saddlebag, he was just about to go up one of the stairways when he met Amesbury coming down.

"Oh! I've just been up to your rooms," the old butler said a bit breathlessly. "Lady Kelby was most particular in wishing to speak to you. Please follow me."

"Is everything all right?"

"No, it is not, sir. The Earl of Kelby is dead."

Chapter 18

Maris was numb. She knew she was supposed to feel *something,* should have expected how to feel when this day came as she knew it would. She had vowed years ago not to cry, for once. Henry would not have liked it. But she felt as if she was wrapped in cotton wool, almost deaf to Betsy and the other servants who had been filing into her room since she discovered Henry's body in the library when she went in to wish him a good morning.

He had been there all night, sprawled facedown on the carpet. He had died alone and in distress. The shame of it was dreadful.

The servants knew better than to bother him, no matter how late the candles burned. No doubt they thought he was working through the night as he sometimes did, and were waiting to be summoned. But Maris herself should have insisted he get himself to bed, even if he wouldn't share hers.

What had she been doing instead of seeing to Henry? Riding Captain Durant, touching herself as he'd touched her, aching for the next day and what would happen between them in the attic. Except it wouldn't happen . . . ever again.

She had to send him away. Hang the inventory. It didn't matter any longer. David could make his own foray into the boxes. She'd told the servants to remove all traces of the office work space. Remove the telltale chaise, too. David would catch one glimpse of it and her dangerous game would be over. He was probably on his way now, woken at the Kelby Arms by the servants' gossip that would fly to the village as fleet as a bird.

She had sent Amesbury to fetch Reyn and dismissed everyone

who had been hovering around her. In a short while, Henry's solicitor Mr. Woodley would be there, and she could arrange for Reyn's payment to be sent to him in London.

She reached into the pocket of her black gown. The emerald was cold and hard, much as she needed to be.

Amesbury knocked and entered. "Captain Durant, my lady."

Reyn trailed after him, looking pale. "You have my sincerest condolences, Lady Kelby."

Reyn is staying a good distance away, thank heaven. "Thank you, Captain. Amesbury, that will be all. Please let me know when Mr. Woodley arrives. Mr. Kelby, too." Maris shivered. She would have to call David "my lord" and curtsey when he came to crow at his good fortune.

"Certainly, my lady." Amesbury left, closing the door behind him. Did he suspect anything? If he did, she sought to quash any talk. Captain Durant was to be packed up and on his way within minutes of their interview.

Reyn was across the room in a flash. "Oh, God, Maris. I'm so sorry."

She allowed him to hold her for a few precious seconds, then stepped out of his embrace. "You have to leave immediately."

A dark eyebrow was raised and she wanted to smooth it down. "Why? I can help you."

"I don't require your help. If you were to stay, how could it be explained? You are not a relative. You . . . you are supposed to be *nothing* to me. The job is over. David won't care what's upstairs. He can't sell anything, so why bother going through it?"

"What if David won't inherit?"

Maris flushed. "I'll know soon enough. I hardly think after only two days that we have . . ." She couldn't say it. Didn't dare to hope it.

He pulled her to him, holding her hands so tightly it hurt. "You'll tell me, won't you?"

"What good will it do to know?" she cried, pulling away.

"You'll tell me. Please."

She really couldn't bear this. Reyn Durant needed to go, and go immediately. She took the emerald from her pocket. "Mr. Woodley—Henry's solicitor—will see that you get your pay no matter what happens. But I want you to have this." Maris shoved the jewel into his hand.

Reyn looked down at it as if she'd given him a poisonous snake. "I'm to be bought off, just like this?"

"Henry hired you for your character. I know I don't have to bribe you. I want you to have it. To take care of your sister. To buy yourself a future."

"I don't want it."

"Don't be so proud. Why shouldn't you have it? You found it. Do you think David Kelby deserves it after all he's done?"

Reyn rolled the stone in his hand. "Was your husband's death natural? I ran into Kelby on the road from the village last night. He was coming from this direction."

Maris felt dizzy. "What? What do you mean?"

"Has a doctor been called?"

"Dr. Crandall is here now." Maris had willingly left him alone, coward that she was.

"I'll go talk to him."

"You cannot! Anything you say will seem odd. You're supposed to be a stranger. Just a temporary employee."

Reyn's mouth was mulish. "He should know to look for what's beyond the obvious."

"Reyn, Henry was an old man. His heart has been weak for years. This day has been coming for a long while." And Maris had still been unprepared.

She was relieved to see Reyn tuck the emerald into his pocket.

"When do you want me to go?"

"They are getting your things together now. You'll want to go upstairs and make sure they don't overlook anything." It was the only way, really. If he stayed, she would not be responsible if she flung herself into his arms and wept her heart out.

Could one love two men at once?

It seemed one could.

Oh, that is ridiculous. She could not possibly be in love with Reynold Durant. She barely knew him. He *was* a stranger. She was just confused by the circumstances she found herself in. The past few days had been too much for her, had made her lose her good sense.

Reyn looked like a stranger, his expression inscrutable, his black eyes dull. She felt his withdrawal almost as a physical thing, as though the air between them was becoming thinner.

"You'll let me know." It was no longer a question, but an order.

"I-I will. But you mustn't come back." She'd have to deal with David Kelby alone.

"As you wish, Countess."

And then he was gone. There had been no kiss, to her hand or any other part of her, no more words. That was what she wanted, wasn't it? A necessary break.

Maris walked to the fireplace. No matter how many coals were burning, she thought she'd never be warm again.

Reyn headed straight for the library. The phalanx of footmen was back at their positions, their green frockcoats augmented with black mourning armbands. That was quick, but he supposed, at a moment's notice, they were ready for anything at Kelby Hall.

He would leave—couldn't wait to leave—but first he'd go against Maris's express wish and speak to Dr. Crandall. He found the man in whispered conversation with Amesbury outside the library door. Both men looked up at his interruption and Reyn rearranged his temper.

"Good morning. I wonder if I might have a word with you, Dr. Crandall."

"Who are you?" The doctor was a portly fellow who seemed annoyed to be ripped away from his breakfast at the early hour.

"Captain Durant is the antiquities expert the late earl engaged," Amesbury explained.

"What do you want?"

"I was just wondering if the earl expired of natural causes."

Amesbury turned a bit gray. The doctor opened his mouth, but it was a while before *"What?"* came out.

"I realize the Earl of Kelby was an elderly man in precarious health. But he seemed quite well when I spoke with him the other day."

"I am sure he did. The earl enjoyed good days, except when he did *not*," Dr. Crandall replied testily. "I can assure you there is nothing suspicious in the manner of the earl's demise. Frankly, I'm astounded that you should think so."

"It's just . . . a feeling," Reyn temporized. "I get them in my line

of work, which is why I've been able to make such valuable discoveries and whatnot." It was true he'd always had a bit of intu-
ition, which had saved his skin a few times. "I wonder, Amesbury,
did the earl receive any visitors last night?"

"Not to my knowledge, Captain. He went into the library shortly
after dining with the countess. *You* were the only one about last
night, according to John." Amesbury meant Aloysius.

Well, I stepped in front of that bullet. Reyn had had a brief conversation with the bleary-eyed young footman when he'd admitted
him into the house. Reyn frowned and considered asking to see the
body, but that really would cause comment. And what would he
know if he examined the earl? Yes, he'd seen many dead men—
hundreds, thousands if he thought about Waterloo, which he tried
very hard not to do—but he was not trained to recognize the signs
of murder.

But he couldn't go away without knowing. "Was there any indication of a struggle?"

The doctor's face turned scarlet. "Captain, you are overstepping
your bounds by a great many miles. I presume people hire you because of your trustworthiness and discretion. If I were you, I'd stop
being such an ass about blighting the family's good name. The Earl
of Kelby lived a long, successful life and His Maker finally came
calling."

"Thank you for your opinion, Dr. Crandall," Reyn said.

The man would never take a second look. Nothing could be
proven anyhow. Unless Henry Kelby had suffered a gunshot
wound, there would be no reason for anyone to doubt why he died.

But Reyn wouldn't put it past David Kelby to have popped out
of the bushes and frightened the old earl through the library windows. Perhaps even entered through the French doors and argued
with him. Kelby had appeared disheveled in the moonlight. Reyn
had attributed that to a tryst, though it could have been something
much more sinister.

There was nothing left to do but go upstairs and round up his
meager belongings. He hadn't known how long he'd stay when he
packed. It turned out not so very.

He was *nothing* to her, Reyn reminded himself. She'd said it.
He'd have to remember it. Reyn was simply a means to an end. It

would be a miracle if they'd achieved what the old Earl of Kelby sought, but stranger things had happened.

Maris was free, but she didn't want him. Why should she? He was *nothing*.

Chapter 19

The Dower House, Kelby Hall, April 1821

"There is no question in my mind, Lady Kelby," Dr. Crandall said, smiling down benevolently at her. "You are quite a ways along now. It's a wonder you did not suspect, though I suppose you've been under shocking stress lately. How pleased your husband would have been."

Betsy gave her a triumphant grin. How humiliating to be proved wrong by a girl who was almost two decades younger than she.

"Yes," Maris said faintly. She couldn't quite believe it. The past few months had been such hell. She had been scrupulous about keeping Kelby traditions alive when all she'd wanted to do was crawl into bed and feel sorry for herself.

Henry's funeral had been a grand affair. Even the king came, which had caused an inordinate amount of fuss. She'd arranged it all from the Dower House, since David had banished her there immediately.

She'd taken Betsy and a few other servants with her—Betsy's John, who turned out to be named Phillip, his friend Aloysius, and Mrs. O'Neill's niece Margaret, who served as housekeeper and cook. A couple potboys and a maid even younger than Betsy rounded out the staff. She could "borrow" people from the big house if she needed to, but a woman in mourning really required very little.

Christmas had been a grim affair, but she had done her duty and distributed baskets to the needy, decorated the church in Kelby village, knit lumpy caps and stockings for the tenants' children. She couldn't leave anything up to David. For all he cared, his people could go cold and hungry.

The New Year's Eve Dance had gone on as scheduled—the servants and tenants looked forward to it every year—and she'd organized the details between bouts of weeping and wishing she was dead. Betsy had said it had gone very well, with a moment of silence for the seventh Earl of Kelby before the fiddling commenced.

Maris had taken Henry's manuscript with her to her own little library, and she'd spent the rest of the winter readying it for publication. Henry's handwriting had become increasingly difficult to read in the last chapters, and she struggled with it even though it was once as familiar to her as her own. The book would be printed in time for the symposium at Oxford. Henry would have been pleased about that, too.

Maris had not felt unwell, but she'd been exhausted and depressed. Battling wits with David when he turned up at Dower House to harass her was enough to give anyone the blue devils. Fortunately he spent most of his time in town, spending his inheritance.

"You truly are sure? I haven't lost my breakfast or had any of the other symptoms of pregnancy." She'd blamed her age for the fact that her recent courses had been spotty and light, too dispirited to hope for anything better.

"Every woman is different, my dear, or so the midwives tell me. Some women still bleed a little in the beginning as you did, but you are in a safe stage now."

Maris didn't feel safe at all.

"You've got an unpleasant task ahead, though, don't you?" Dr. Crandall continued. "I don't envy you, Lady Kelby. Lord Kelby— that is to say *Mr.* Kelby won't like the news."

"It may be a girl," Maris said. Lord, she hoped so. As horrible as David was, she didn't want to cheat him out of his birthright. What she had done she'd done for Henry's sake, but now that he was gone, what difference did it make? She had no heart for true deceit.

"Do you want me to be present when you tell him?" Dr. Crandall's eyes shifted uneasily to a painting of lambs gamboling in a green field.

She couldn't put him through it. "That's very kind of you, but no. I'll manage somehow." Maybe she'd get Mr. Woodley to do it. She'd write to him at once. Woodley had warned David that the title might be held in abeyance waiting for word from the Countess of Kelby, but he'd scoffed and ordered her out of the house.

Maris was only too happy to go, which had surprised her. She'd lived at Kelby Hall her whole life, but now that it was obscured through the woods from vision, she didn't miss it at all. It suited her to be in a smaller dwelling with a *much* smaller staff. She had to remind Mrs. O'Neill it was no longer her place to decide thorny household issues, although Maris believed the woman came to her a few times a week just to be kind. Amesbury and Mrs. O'Neill were perfectly capable of running the house for its absentee owner, far better than Maris had ever been.

Henry had bought a manor house outside the village of Shere for her, in the event she did not want to spend the rest of her life in the Dower House. She could let it for extra income if she wished, and it would serve as a daughter's dowry. Maris had not felt equal to moving to Hazel Grange last winter, but perhaps it would be wise to do so now.

She had seen the house only once when Henry first purchased it for her eight years ago. It was made of mellowed brick, neat and square, with a hipped roof and an Ionic columned entryway. She would have to furnish it, which would be a challenge. She realized she did not even know what her tastes were. She'd been surrounded by generations of Kelby choices. The thought of her very own home with her very own things—*and her very own child*—made her feel somewhat giddy.

Maris looked around the paneled bedchamber with its pastoral pictures of sheep and horses and cows that some previous Dowager Countess of Kelby had selected to adorn the walls. In contrast, there was plenty of land for real animals and a first-rate stable block at Hazel Grange. She could ride every day.

Perhaps not. She'd talk to Dr. Crandall about it when her thoughts were more settled. Maris tied her dressing gown back on and saw Dr. Crandall to the door herself.

When she returned to her bedroom, Betsy was bouncing up and down. "See? I told you so, my lady!"

"Yes, you did." And Maris had not wanted to believe her. She would have to write to Reyn, something that caused her stomach to do a little flip.

She'd heard nothing from him since he'd left Kelby Hall, which was as it should be. Since Henry's death, she had forced herself to be busy at all hours of the day and night. But she had not been too busy to forget the captain, especially as she lay in her solitary bed.

Maybe she wouldn't tell Reyn just yet. The news was so extraordinary Maris wanted to keep it to herself for a little while. Once she moved into Hazel Grange and got settled, there would be plenty of time to notify him. Months. It was not as if he could do anything, and a visit from him to Dower House would only engender gossip.

Maybe he wouldn't want to see her, anyway. She'd been crystal clear about sending him away. *Pushing* him away. That had been for the best. No possibility of anything permanent existed between them.

Maris went to her desk and began to write. Mr. Woodley could take care of the details of telling David about the baby and arranging for her to move some twenty miles away to Shere. She would take her little crew with her if they'd go. Betsy and she might spend a few days in Guildford, buying furniture and other necessities for the new house. Margaret would need to be consulted about kitchen equipment; she should come too.

Actually, Maris supposed they should all inspect the property first. She had been uncomfortable during her only tour of it. The thought of Henry dying and leaving her alone had frightened her. They had been married a mere two years then and he was still a vigorous man despite his difficulties in the bedroom. She'd had hopes . . . but they'd come to nothing.

Now there was reason to feel joy. And trepidation as well. Bringing a child into the world without a father would not be easy. If she had a son, protecting him from a bitter David would require every ounce of strength she possessed.

She couldn't bring up a son at the Grange. He'd have to learn his patrimony, to understand what Henry had intended for the family. The museum he'd been so keen on would come to pass, with Maris at the helm.

Once that would have excited her beyond reason. But oddly, she no longer gave a fig for Henry's grand plans. She was having a baby! She touched her lips to prove to herself she was indeed smiling.

Yes, it was time to move, to start fresh. To surround herself with her own things and her own people. To smile more.

Even if it was just for a few months. All around her things were growing and blooming. Wild daffodils were scattered in the wood, their yellow heads bowing under the sun. She'd take a walk to bid them good-bye, get some roses in her cheeks.

Henry. She hoped he was looking down upon her, smiling himself.

The move was accomplished without any major hiccup. Hazel Grange was found to be solid, partly furnished and well cared for. An elderly caretaker, Mr. Prall, lived in a cottage on the grounds with his two bachelor sons. He had hired day girls from the village to keep the house clean since the last tenant vacated the property, so Maris was not choked with dust on the day she visited.

She had overspent in Guildford. Pretty sprigged and striped paper covered the drawing room walls, plush sofas and chairs were in place to collapse in, crockery had been put away in the kitchen, and a crib was set up in her dressing room. She had bought pictures of her own for her bedroom—no bovine or equine oils, but pastel architectural renderings of famous Italian buildings to remind her of her youth abroad. The garden held no imposing statues, but had been planted lavishly by Mr. Prall and his two sons and was in glorious bloom. The house and outbuildings were really quite perfect.

Dr. Crandall had tutted over a horse, but Maris purchased two and went riding every day with Mr. Prall's younger son, Stephen. They took sedate, quiet country explorations over her own land, no hell-for-leather gallops, which suited her at present. Maris was becoming *bulky*. There was no other word for it. She was quite thick through the middle. If one did not know of her condition, she might appear simply a stout widow.

She had not sought the company of her neighbors, nor had they come to her. The servants had put it about early on that she was in mourning and refusing visitors. Maris was thus spared from making small talk with the local gentry. In fact, merciful heavens, she did not even attend church services. No drifting off while some well-meaning parson tried to explain the universe from one badly translated ancient book. Let them think of her what they would. She knew God had gifted her with a miracle and thanked him from the privacy of her garden and her boudoir every single day.

One grayish cloud was still on her horizon. She had not yet written to Reynold Durant. He might not even be in London for all she knew. The emerald would have opened up the world to him. Perhaps he'd gone back to Canada and taken his sister. She hoped so. An ocean between them would serve her purposes quite well.

Or so she told herself. Not a breath of scandal should be associated with the seventh Earl of Kelby's child.

Chapter 20

May 1821

W*hat were the odds?* Reyn shifted in his seat in St. James's Church and gave Ginny's young vicar a gimlet eye. The man had managed to somehow get the living at Shere and his sister had never said a thing about it, the sly puss. She was blushing as they sat at the back of the church in a patch of stained-glass sunlight, in better health than she'd been in weeks and hanging on the new clergyman's every word.

The move had been difficult for her. Had been difficult for him, too. If he'd known the trouble the emerald would cause, he would have tossed it back at Maris's not-so-dainty feet.

It had been the devil to sell once he'd returned to London. He'd half-expected to be clapped in irons as a thief as he went from jeweler to jeweler. There was no provenance, no bill of sale. His fictional explanations as to how he'd acquired it seemed weak even to him, but he'd finally found a gem dealer who was less than particular.

Less than generous as well. Reyn had known he was being cheated, but he'd had no choice, accepting what the man would give him. Fortunately, it was enough to buy Merrywood Farm, a rather run-down horse breeding operation, from a gentleman who was not particular, either, and rather anxious to get out from under his failing enterprise. The sale had been accomplished in record speed that had made Reyn's head spin with legal logistics and reams of paperwork, and by the end of January he was more or less landed gentry.

If one was not too particular.

Bravo for all those whose standards were low. Reyn possessed a ramshackle house, tumble-down stables, and sufficient acreage to support two dozen fillies of various pedigrees. Phantom, old war horse that he was, ruled the roost, though if he hadn't been gelded would no doubt have been much happier in his new environment. Reyn had been gelded himself. He had no time to return the flirtatious glances of the young and not-so-young ladies of Shere, who fluttered a bit every time he entered St. James's on Sundays or the village when he was absolutely forced to leave his occupation behind. He was up to his eyelashes in hay and muck and repairs and loving every minute of it. He knew he needed to hire more help eventually, but at the moment he was reveling in the backbreaking labor required to set up his new business with the help of only a freckle-faced boy who had seemed to come with the property. Working with his hands kept his mind occupied, almost enough for him to forget a few days last December.

Almost.

He was not foolish enough to call the property a stud farm. Not yet. For one thing, he needed to find a stud horse he could afford without depleting his savings. He had half a mind to write to young Bob Hastings, lure him away from Kelby Hall, and offer him a position as head groom. Reyn might not be able to match his salary, but Bob could be his own man. The large apartment over the stable would be perfect for a fellow to raise a family if they didn't mind the smell of horse.

Reyn's house was sufficient for a family's needs, too. Ginny had directed a great deal from her sickbed, and the old house had been scrubbed clean and simply furnished. The floors might list like a storm-tossed ship, but the dwelling was snug and warm. On her better days, she had replanted the garden, Rufus helping by digging random holes between the lettuces. Mrs. Clark was settled into the kitchen, never once complaining about the primitive range. All in all, Reyn's little household was thriving beyond his humble expectations.

The days were filled with work. The nights, however, were vast oceans of wakefulness, when his hand was called to quell the waves of desire as regular as the tides. Reyn couldn't seem to do anything about his longing for his countess. It had propelled him to buy property in Surrey. He'd told himself Merrywood Farm was a grand bargain, and that Kelby Hall was a fair distance away.

But he would be close enough to be called if needed.

As if he was needed. His job was done, wasn't it? He snorted, causing the old man seated in front of him to turn and give him a sour look. *No snorting in church,* Reyn reminded himself. No talking unless giving the proper prayer book response, no shifting in one's seat, no snoring, God forbid. Ginny's vicar was a serious young man who seemed to be doing his damnedest to be interesting, though that was a losing cause with Reyn. He was there solely—soully—to support his little sister, who did seem to derive comfort from attending church.

Or perhaps it had been the vicar all along. He chuckled, and added no chuckling to his list as Ginny's surprisingly sharp elbow caught him in his midsection.

He endured the rest of the service in relative peace, his mind drifting quite far from ecclesiastical things until he was shuffling down the aisle to shake the vicar's hand.

Ginny dimpled prettily. "I do hope you might join us for Sunday lunch, Mr. Swift."

Swift. Somehow Reyn had blocked the name from his mind. It was not as though the man didn't earn it. The service had gone as fast as possible, he supposed.

Mr. Swift dimpled back. "I should be delighted, if I might postpone that visit until next week, Miss Durant. There is a new parishioner I wish to welcome to the neighborhood, though I confess I feel some trepidation. It is a *lady,* you see. A great lady. She has taken over Hazel Grange, but is not going about in our humble society at all. A recent widow. I fear I am not up to the task of conversing with a countess."

Reyn stilled. *What were the odds?* What were the odds he'd ask himself that question twice in one morning?

"Ah! A countess! How exciting, despite her recent misfortune. Do you know, Mr. Swift, my brother spent some time in an earl's household last fall? Perhaps he should go with you to smooth the way," she teased.

"I am hardly an expert on countesses," Reyn said, gruff. "I barely saw the Countess of Kelby." Damn it all to hell and back.

Forget his sister and her doorstep dance with the vicar. He seemed a good enough fellow, but if he thought Ginny would make a docile clergyman's wife, he was in for a surprise.

Swift's face lit up. "Why, Captain Durant. This is extraordinary! It is the Countess of Kelby I am bound for this afternoon. If she is not up to attending church, it is my Christian duty to bring church to her, so to speak. As I happily did for you some time ago, Miss Durant. It is a pleasure to see you well enough to be here at worship."

"I wouldn't miss it for anything," Ginny said.

Maris was here.

Part of Hazel Grange's land bordered his own. He remembered hearing the name as his solicitor read the deeds to him. *What were the odds?* he thought for the third time.

Reyn hadn't paid attention to anything lately, except repairing the fencing, roofing the stables, and feeding his horses, who were always hungry. Had he passed Maris on the street in Shere and not even noticed?

No. Swift said she was a recluse. He pictured Maris swathed in deepest black, her nose pressed against a window. Hazel Grange sounded like a huge comedown from the grandeur of Kelby Hall. What had caused her to move? Surely David Kelby would have allowed her to stay on at the Dower House.

Unless he importuned her again and she felt she had to flee. Reyn felt a splash of bile rise in his throat.

"Reyn, are you all right? You look quite fierce all of a sudden."

"I'm fine, Gin. Perfectly fine." He would be once he got home and into the brandy. Much against his usual habits, he'd discovered brandy could block out the imaginary scent and vision of Maris Kelby's wavy molasses-colored hair as it spilled over his chest.

"Shall I give the countess your regards, Captain Durant?"

"She would not even know who I am. Good morning to you, Mr. Swift. We'll expect you next Sunday, if not before." Reyn forced himself to smile and wink at the vicar, which caused the fellow to pale.

Perhaps Reyn's eyes and lips weren't working properly. Nothing felt like it was working right as he helped Ginny into their ancient gig—it had come with the ancient house—and hoisted himself up to take the reins. Maris was there and he hadn't known it, hadn't felt it. If he was meant to be with her, surely he would have throbbed like a tuning fork at her nearness.

What rot. He had let himself get carried away over two days. *Two days.*

Reyn's mail was forwarded from London by Gratton, who'd stayed on in his old lodgings with a new gentleman to valet for. There had been no word from her, so their mission had been a failure. Not so surprising, given the limited amount of time they'd had.

Unless Gratton had gotten into the brandy again, and forgot to send the letter on.

No, the countess had not contacted him because there was nothing to tell. For all her reassurances that *she* was no one special, she was the widow of an earl. A great lady, as Swift had said. Why would she want to have anything to do with an illiterate soldier, even if she was free?

Reyn knew Maris was the most proper of women. She would observe a lengthy period of mourning not only because it was proper, but out of respect for her husband. She had loved him, loved him enough to go against all her instincts and lie with a perfect—well, imperfect—stranger. By the time she was out of black, Reyn would just be a blurred memory to her, if that. No doubt she wanted to push the whole unpleasant interlude straight out of her mind.

"You're very quiet. Are you sure you're all right?" Ginny asked.

"I'm fine. Isn't it a lovely spring day?"

It was Ginny's turn to snort. "Something's upset you if you're talking about the weather. Is it Arthur?"

"Who?"

"Mr. Swift, Reyn. I mean to have him, you know. He's been very kind and doesn't mind that I may not li—"

"You will," Reyn interrupted. "You are getting better every single day. The country is good for you. You haven't had a coughing fit in over two months. You're sleeping through the night. You've got roses in your cheeks. You look *pretty*. Too pretty to be a dull parson's wife."

"He is not dull! You really should pay more attention to his sermons. Arthur says some very useful things in a remarkably short stretch of time."

"Arthur. How long has this been going on?"

"Since Richmond, of course. You really need to pay more attention to *everything*."

Undoubtedly that was true, but she'd hit upon the central problem of his life. *Bloody hell.* What kind of a brother was he?

"Has he kissed you?"

"I will not tell you if you're going to make a fuss. You should see your face," Ginny said, quite unruffled. "Remember, I have those eyebrows, too, and I'm not afraid of yours. Though I do pluck mine now."

He would not be distracted by her beauty rituals. "That means he has, the cur."

"Reyn, I am not a little girl. I just turned three and twenty. At my age, you'd been in the army for seven years. Think of the things you did miles away from home and then tell me I have no right to marry where I please."

"Damn it, Ginny! I'm not saying you can't get married!"

"Good. Then it's settled. Summer weddings are lovely, I'm told."

By God, she'd outmaneuvered him. "Are you sure?"

Ginny nodded. "I want to make good use of the time I have."

"Don't talk nonsense."

"It's not nonsense. Everyone should seize the day, even those whose health is good."

"Carpe diem."

"See? And you're always saying school was a waste of time for you. You are much smarter than you think you are."

He didn't bother to disabuse her of her misconception. He knew exactly how smart he was. Not very, if his little sister had been carrying on with Arthur Swift right under his nose.

Oh, he'd known something was going on. But marriage? "Has he asked you to marry him?"

"Sort of, but not precisely. There has been nothing of the dropping to one knee, etcetera. We have talked around it, as it were, agreeing to most of the details. I believe he wants to ask your permission first and is working his courage up before dropping down formally. You do have quite a reputation, you know. War hero and all that."

Lord. He hoped the vicar never found out about Reyn's brief stint as a Reining Monarch. "Will you be happy, Gin?"

"The vicarage is quite lovely, you know. Arthur says I might bring Mrs. Beecham and Molly with me. He already has a house-keeper-cook, so Mrs. Clark is happy to stay with you."

Mrs. Clark knew all this? Napoleon could have used his sister's ability to strategize. Reyn's entire household was privy to his sister's marital plans, but Reyn had been so preoccupied getting his business up and running, he'd been oblivious.

She grinned up at him, looking all of six years old.

"I'm not talking about a house," he scolded. "After getting us settled at Merrywood, I know you can work wonders. I mean, is he a good man? Does he treat you well? Do you care for him? Does he make you—"

Honestly, what was wrong with him? He was about to ask if Ginny burned to bed the man. He devoutly hoped she had not gone that far yet. He would shoot Swift and then himself. "Laugh?" he amended.

Her color had nothing to do with the fresh spring breeze. "I like him very well, Reyn. And yes, he is a good man, but not so good a man that he doesn't know how to kiss."

"Goddamn it, Gin!"

"Not on Sunday." She giggled, then she turned to him, much more sober. "Please be glad for me. I did not think to ever be so happy."

"Your happiness is all I've ever wanted." *Well, almost all.* "If you have fallen in love with him, I suppose I shall have to like him."

In her unthinking joy, Ginny squeezed his bad shoulder. "You will love him too, I know it!"

Reyn envisioned proper Sunday lunches—years of them, if his sister was blessed to live long enough. He would have to reassure himself by speaking with her doctor, though he hadn't thought much of the man when they met earlier. If she was not strong enough for her marital duties, Reyn would forbid the match.

Gah. It was deuced unpleasant to think of his little sister in such a state, with the earnest Mr. Swift so very far from the pulpit. Reyn yearned for some strong soap to scrub his brain clean. He listened with half an ear as Ginny enumerated Swift's many alleged virtues, and was never so happy to see Merrywood at the end of the lane.

The mares were outdoors enjoying the newly fenced pasture,

their coats shining in the sunlight. Smoke rose gently from the kitchen chimney. Mrs. Clark, the cook-conspirator, was no doubt within, roasting a plump chicken for their luncheon. The sky was blue, the clouds were puffy.

And the Countess of Kelby was right next door.

Chapter 21

"I believe it's going to rain, Lady Kelby. You're not still going out?"

"Pooh. Betsy, you are too much of a worrywart for someone your age." Maris adjusted the rather forbidding black bonnet and wished she didn't look quite so crowlike. She would not be able to wear any of Madame Bernard's creations for ages, and by then her figure might be very different. She might not even *have* a figure.

It shouldn't matter. Maris had never cared about what she'd worn, but it did seem a shame those beautiful new clothes might never be used.

"Dr. Crandall said—"

"Dr. Crandall is no longer involved, is he? The new man doesn't seem to be troubled by my riding, if I'm careful."

"The new man is a drunk," Betsy reminded her. "I wouldn't trust him with a litter of kittens."

It was true Dr. Sherman had seemed a bit under the weather when she'd sent for him. So many doctors seemed to have an unfortunate tendency to imbibe. It must be escape from all the grim things they saw in their practices. But babies weren't grim things. Maris had met the local midwife Mrs. Lynch, a calm, grandmotherly woman who'd delivered babies in and around Shere for more than thirty years. Maris was perfectly satisfied with her current arrangements.

She expected David wouldn't be. She fully expected him to haunt her until the child was born. He'd ridden over the day before yesterday, though he was prevented from trying to completely terrorize her by the presence of that shy young clergyman Mr. Swift. She did not have much use for most men of the cloth, but had been glad of the vicar's unscheduled company. He must have sensed her uneasiness, for he outlasted the usual twenty-minute courtesy call and bored David to tears with his random biblical platitudes. Maris had finally pleaded a headache and left both men to their own devices.

Before Mr. Swift turned up, David had been insisting he be present for the birth, so he wouldn't be cheated. "For who knows?" he'd said. "You might get rid of a girl and slip a gypsy brat into the cradle."

If only Henry had thought of that first, she thought with a sour smile. She would not find herself in such straits, yearning for what she couldn't have.

She knew she was remiss about notifying Reyn of the surprising news. She'd picked up her pen a dozen times in as many days, but somehow the words hadn't come. She, who had no difficulty writing about ancient Etruscan society, seemed incapable of describing the simple current event to the man who'd made it happen.

Perhaps when she got back from her ride—her rainy ride if Betsy was right—she'd make herself do it. A letter might not even reach him. Reynold Durant could be anywhere in the world.

She shivered. He might even be standing naked over someone with a whip.

The sky was indeed leaden and damp hung in the air. Stephen Prall waited for her on the drive with her pretty white mare Pearl. The horse was almost too showy. She was a countess's horse, purchased by Henry for her amusement. Maris had neglected her for the last few years, hardly leaving the house as Henry's health had worsened and his work had become paramount. Pearl seemed glad of her new circumstances and the exercise. She tossed her mane and pranced in greeting.

"Good morning, Stephen! Good morning, Pearl!"

"Are you sure you want to ride today, my lady? It's going to rain." He was prepared, in an oilskin jacket and battered cap. If she had those, she'd be wearing them, too. Her black riding habit had been let out at the seams and stretched as far as Betsy's clumsy fingers could make it go, and the hat really was a disaster.

"So Betsy tells me. I'm sure. You won't mind getting a little wet if we don't get back in time, will you? We won't be out long, I promise."

"I don't mind, my lady. You're the boss."

He didn't sound thrilled, but Maris smiled at his words. She'd never really felt like anyone's boss at Kelby Hall.

He helped her mount. To his credit, she didn't feel like a sack of potatoes slung onto the saddle. She took a lungful of heavy air and wondered how long the rain would hold off. Not very, she'd wager. They'd ride to that pretty copse of trees that bordered one dog-leg of her property, then turn back. She hadn't ridden out that way in a week or more.

Maris was too busy watching the darkening clouds to see the man beyond the leafy oaks at first. She raised an arm in a friendly gesture, then froze. It couldn't be. It just couldn't be. The first splash of rain fell on her cheeks and into her open mouth.

Reyn had come to the edge of his property yesterday when the gnawing urge could not be ignored. Twice, actually. Once in the morning, estimating when a gentlewoman might be persuaded to ride, then again near dusk, when he was near to exhaustion. He'd sat atop Phantom like a lovesick schoolboy staring at the empty green space on the other side of a clump of ancient oaks, listening as if he expected a band of Indians to drop from the trees and attack any second.

He'd ridden out again that morning and heard the horses, suddenly paralyzed by hope and fear. Phantom was alert, too, and whickered at the sight of a palfrey that was just missing a unicorn horn.

Maris—for it was she, ink-black against the white horse—waved.

Reyn's throat dried and his wits deserted him completely. All the things he'd planned to say to her when he bumped into her "accidentally" flew from him like scalded birds.

She was as pale as her horse, looking every bit as stunned at the sight of him as he felt at the sight of her. A sudden drop of rain in his eye obscured her for a moment, and then her companion came into view.

Reyn had seen the man before in Shere. He was hard to miss, taller than Reyn and much broader. Some sort of laborer. Good. At least she wasn't accompanied by a swain, or riding alone like a ninny. Anything could happen to an unprotected woman.

He kicked Phantom forward when it was clear Maris was immobile. He watched as the man bent to the countess and said something. Maris shook her head.

When he was just a few feet away, Reyn stopped. "Good morning. I didn't mean to startle you. I collect we are neighbors." The words sounded unsuspicious. Normal. There must be a God.

But she didn't leap from her horse and into his arms and declare he was her long-lost love. In fact she looked at him as if she'd never seen him before.

"N-neighbors?" The shock in her voice was pure.

So, she didn't know. Hadn't been hiding from him. "Allow me to introduce myself. I am Reynold Durant. My property borders this dogleg end of yours. My sister and I make our home at Merrywood Farm."

"Cap—Mr. Durant. I am p-pleased to meet you." She was playing it as he laid it for the benefit of her hulking companion. They were total strangers to each other—which was fundamentally true.

"I bought Merrywood in January. I understand you have recently come to Hazel Grange, Lady Kelby." It wouldn't seem odd that he knew her name. It was probably on everyone's lips in the village, only he'd been too oblivious to listen.

"Y-yes."

The rain was falling with some determination, and Maris's servant shifted uncomfortably.

"Do forgive me for holding up your ride. Filthy weather, isn't it? You must be on your way before you catch a chill. Good day to you then, Lady Kelby. I look forward to meeting you again under more clement skies." Reyn wheeled Phantom away before she could respond.

His heart hammered. He could have reached across the horses and touched her skin. She was so very pale, just as she'd been when she'd found him at the Reining Monarchs Society. He'd shocked her then; he'd shocked her now.

How was it possible they were neighbors? Would she think he was stalking her? Nonsense. He'd come to the neighborhood first, had no idea that Hazel Grange belonged to the relict of the Earl of Kelby. When he first looked in the area, he was told a young family had leased the Grange, but that it was vacant. He'd been much too busy to worry about neighbors and let Ginny deal with visits and so forth.

Maris's surprise had been so intense Reyn couldn't tell if she'd been pleased to see him. Didn't know if she would be pleased to see him again in a meeting that wasn't by chance or rain-soaked. Swift had said she was not receiving. Would she make an exception for him?

She had to. He *needed* her to. His need was a palpable thing, preventing him from thinking clearly.

But there was one thing he *had seen* clearly. She'd been wearing his butterfly pin in the crown of her ugly black bonnet. It had twinkled amidst the raindrops. Totally unsuitable for a widow. If hope had wings—

He squelched his hope. Likely it was the first thing that came to hand when she fastened that monstrosity to her head. The woman needed him to help her shop, even for mourning clothes. Perhaps he should write to Madame Bernard.

His lips curled. By God, he was smiling. He imagined Maris's face when she opened boxes at Hazel Grange and found the most exquisite mourning dresses straight from London. She might have reason to leave her house then. Pretty dresses were always a boost to a woman's confidence.

She'd know at once who'd sent them. Reyn pictured her thank-you note. He'd work especially hard to interpret her loops and curlicues. She would invite him to the Grange, perhaps for tea, that huge servant nowhere around. She'd tell him she couldn't possibly accept his gifts and then fall into his arms and kiss him.

Kiss him with all the ardor and innocence she possessed. It had been far too long since Reyn had experienced a kiss from his countess. He got hard simply thinking of her blush-pink mouth trembling beneath his . . . until a sluice of cold rain slithered down his neck.

Why couldn't they engage in a discreet affair? It would not cause too much comment if he paid her a few visits. They were neighbors, after all. He might be there to advise her on draining her fields or her horse's fetlock or the price of spring lambs. In a year—in less than a year—she might look to marry again, and there he would be, a respectable gentleman with a prosperous enterprise just next door.

He set to whistling. He wouldn't leave Madame Bernard's instructions to a letter. He'd go to London—why not leave in an hour? He was used to traveling light. He might visit Tattersall's while he was there for a day or two and combine business with pleasure. Ginny would be fine. The young stable boy Jack would be elevated in consequence to think Reyn trusted him enough to be left alone with "the girls" for a few days.

Reyn's whistling grew ever more cheerful as he entered the warped entryway of his home. During the winter, he'd planed the front door himself so it would shut properly, but the wood floor still bore evidence of years of incoming rain despite Ginny covering it with a moth-eaten Turkish rug she'd found in the attics. He tossed his riding gloves in a dented but polished copper bowl on the hall table and shook the rest of the rain off like a wet mastiff. "Ho, little sister! I'm home, but not for long," he shouted. "Where are you?"

"In the parlor with Mrs. Beecham."

Reyn found the two women industriously bent over lengths of curtain material. Ginny looked up, cheeks pink. "You foolish man, you are soaked through! And before you lecture *me*, these are for the vicarage, Reyn, so don't think I've spent your coin on stuff we don't need."

Actually most of Merrywood's windows could use new drapes, but he smiled down at his sister, not caring that his lawn shirt was stuck to his chest. "Moving in already? May I remind you, the man has not formally asked you—or me—yet?"

Ginny bit off some thread. "He will. The parish sewing circle is refurbishing the vicarage. It's long overdue. I thought if I helped too I'd get some say in the decoration. You need to get out of those wet clothes."

"You are a cagey one. Poor Mr. Swift."

"He likes me just as I am," Ginny replied.

"He must not know you at all," Reyn teased. "Gin, I've some business in London and will be gone for a few days. You can hold down the fort without me, I know." To his eternal shame, Ginny had gotten along most of her life without his care.

"London? Can't I go with you?"

Reyn considered for perhaps a second. "You've been doing so well. Why risk it? It's raining, too, in case you want to yell at me some more. I'm not taking the mailcoach. Old Phantom will earn his oats tonight."

"Oh. You're probably right."

"It must have cost you to say *that*, little sister. I know I'm right.

Have you forgotten the filthy air? The smells?" Reyn didn't mind them a bit. They were the scent of civilization. Of industry. Of money.

And now that he had some, he was going to spend it on the countess he wanted to woo.

Chapter 22

Maris could not stop shaking once she got indoors. The house was warm enough. The fires were lit against the rain and chill, even in her bedroom. Betsy seemed to think pregnancy was some sort of disease and would have wrapped Maris in fur blankets and hot water bottles all day if she could.

Once out of her wet clothes, Betsy clucking and "I told you so-ing" all the while as she divested Maris of her habit, Maris headed straight for her bed and flopped down into it. She was not tired, but simply confounded.

Captain Reynold Durant was her *neighbor*.

How could she have not known?

Well, that was easy. She'd met no one but Mr. Prall, his sons, and Reverend Swift. She'd deliberately shut herself in—there was even a black wreath on her door—and spread the word she was not to be disturbed.

That had been liberating. She wasn't in charge of a legion of servants or responsible for making small talk with people to whom she was totally indifferent. Henry had ignored his neighbors for the most part, but Maris had felt obligated to receive them when they dared come to call. And it was remarkable how daring some of them had been, anxious to get a look inside Kelby Hall to examine all its treasures.

When she'd retreated to the Dower House, they still came, ostensibly out of sympathy, but Maris had felt like an ant under a magnifying glass, singed a bit by the sun. She'd never been at ease in social situations, even after being a countess for ten years. She'd caused gossip. She was the young adventuress who'd snared the great man Henry Kelby. His secretary's daughter. Henry's eccentricities could be forgiven because of his exalted birth, but she was a nobody.

The fact that she hadn't conformed to anyone's idea of a *femme fatale* had not stopped the talk. Somehow with her plain brown hair and plain brown eyes she'd seduced Henry into losing his good sense and making an imprudent marriage. It was all for an heir, they said, and once she had failed to deliver one, the talk only escalated.

Maris knew she was useful to Henry beyond being a broodmare, and that their partnership had been sincere, their affection for each other real. He had not been an old fool. No one could take away her ten happy years with Henry Kelby.

Except for Reyn.

He'd been scrupulously polite for Stephen Prall's benefit, speaking to her as if she was a stranger. But he was a threat. David would find it very odd that her antiquities expert was now breeding horses right next door.

What was she to do? She trusted her little staff, but that didn't mean David had still not set spies on her. He could have bribed her footman Aloysius Sunday afternoon once she'd gone to bed with her imaginary headache, for example.

She hadn't made her escape—her sanctuary—at Hazel Grange after all, but jumped right from the frying pan into the roaring fire. She'd *have* to write to Reyn now; she had no choice. He must stay away, certainly for the remaining months of her confinement. Maris could imagine him underfoot, being solicitous, bringing her fluffy pillows and sweetmeats. His concern for her well-being would be a disaster.

Could she risk meeting him? To write of her situation would make her even more vulnerable to exposure if the letter went astray. Where could she meet him? The Grange might not be safe.

No place was safe from prying eyes and wagging tongues. Maris squeezed her eyes shut to keep the tears back. She couldn't spend the remaining months crying. That couldn't be good for the baby, nor would it accomplish anything. She was sick of crying, anyway; she needed to be strong for the path she'd chosen.

Reyn might not even want to see her. Perhaps his politeness was just that—a pleasant façade, a social grace. She'd been nearly mute herself.

He had looked . . . *wonderful*. His skin was burnished from the sun, his hair longer, unruly. He'd been hatless and the damp had twisted up his hair into curls at his neck.

Maris rolled off the bed and padded over to her little desk. She'd make the note as innocuous as possible and have Stephen deliver it.

She would write to his sister. Invite them both for tea tomorrow. Get Reyn alone somehow and tell him . . .

What?

She would think of something. She had to. Maybe she'd try the truth.

When Betsy ushered the visitors from Merrywood into her sunny parlor, Maris looked up with a practiced smile. It froze when she noticed the absence of her erstwhile lover. He hadn't come. Did not want—

A girl unmistakably Reyn's sister curtseyed deeply, as did her female companion. Miss Durant was possessed of the same dark hair, and same dark eyes. Same long nose, which should have spoiled her looks, but somehow made her all the more attractive.

"Thank you so much for inviting us, Lady Kelby. I am truly honored. May I introduce my friend and nurse, Mrs. Beecham?"

"W-welcome. Won't you please be seated?"

Miss Durant looked around as she gracefully settled into a wingchair. "What a lovely house this is!"

"Thank you." Maris's tongue felt glued to the roof of her mouth. It had better unstick soon, or the young woman and Mrs. Beecham would think her unfriendly, or so clueless she'd ruin the reputation of countesses everywhere.

"I collect you have not been here long. We are also new to the area. My brother purchased Merrywood in January, and it was a challenge to get it organized. It was in *such* a shocking state. The house had been neglected for years, but Reyn—that's my brother, for his sins—was more interested in the stables. That's a man for you.

"Of course, he was in the army for almost half his life. He tells me he can sleep like a baby in filthy ditches, so a bed is of no consequence to him. Mrs. Beecham, I should be sitting next to you on the couch so you can kick me to keep silent. I'm so sorry, Lady Kelby. I'm chattering like a magpie, but I confess I'm a bit nervous.

I've never met a countess before. I believe you've met my brother, though, haven't you? He did some work for your husband before his passing. My deepest condolences for your loss."

Maris found herself charmed by Miss Durant's nervous prattle. "Thank you. No one needs kicking, save for myself. I've barely said a word."

"How could you?" Ginny's smile was also like her brother's— wide and honest, with a touch of mischief. "I have not let you get one in."

"I must do better. How do you take your tea, Miss Durant, Mrs. Beecham?" Maris kept herself busy pouring and sugaring while Miss Durant commented on the décor.

Maris was quite proud of the way Hazel Grange looked. There was nothing terribly valuable within, but with a baby coming, that was just as well. She took a deep breath. "You are close to your brother?"

"Oh, yes! Reyn is the best of brothers. He sold his commission for me, you know, to take care of me. I used to be very ill, but I'm much better now. Isn't that so, Mrs. Beecham?"

That was the least of what he'd done for his sister.

"Indeed it is, I'm thankful to say. I'm hardly needed anymore." The nurse smiled at her charge.

"Nonsense! I hope you'll live with us forever. I'm to be married soon, Lady Kelby, but it's a bit of a secret just yet. Even my intended is not aware of the date."

Maris laughed. Miss Durant was a delight, every bit as amusing as her brother. "What does Captain Durant have to say about all that?"

"Oh, he's grumbled a bit. But he knows he can't stop me when I make my mind up. I'm very like him in that way. Did you get to know him at all when he was at Kelby Hall?"

"Just a little. Once my husband died, the need for his services ceased. How is he? I-I expected him to be with you today."

"Oh, he's gone off to London. Something about a horse. No doubt he will be very sorry to have missed this afternoon. We are *extremely* honored to be here. I understand you've done very little entertaining, Lady Kelby."

"None, in fact. I was very surprised to meet Captain Durant on my ride yesterday. It . . . it seemed only neighborly I should ask an acquaintance to tea."

A horse. So much for her having dazzled him.

"If it's not too terribly presumptuous for me to ask, Lady Kelby, when is your blessed event?" Mrs. Beecham asked. "I would be honored to assist you in any way I can. I worked in the Viscount Leith's household for a number of years when his family was young."

Miss Durant's face lit. "You're having a baby? How splendid! But how sad, too, that your husband won't be here."

Damn. Damn. Damn.

Damn Mrs. Beecham and her sharp eyes. Surely it was most improper that she, nurse or not, bring up such a thing, but Maris's parlor seemed filled with improper people, most especially herself. Maris's voluminous black dress with its high waist was supposed to prevent such speculation. She really was not showing all that much, she didn't think, which sometimes worried her. What if the baby arrived too small to live? What if there was something wrong with it that she couldn't fix with love and devotion? No matter what, she thought with fierceness, her child would be cared for with every ounce of her capability.

"It's not generally known that I am enceinte," Maris said carefully. "Under the circumstances, I wish to keep my privacy. It *is* sad, Miss Durant. Henry would have been thrilled."

A dreadful thought occurred to her. Reyn must not learn of her condition from his sister's artless conversation. "I would have you say nothing of it to anyone, not even your brother. I—" Maris shook her head—"It's important to me that I not become the latest news of the day. I don't wish people to feel sorrier for me than they already do."

"The baby will be a joy to take your mind off your sorrow," Mrs. Beecham assured her. "I'm sure the people of Shere would be nothing but happy for you. In our experience, everyone has been very welcoming. And everyone does seem to love a baby."

"Nevertheless."

Mrs. Beecham flinched at the steel behind Maris's single word.

"Of course we'll respect your wishes," Miss Durant said quickly. "Reyn wouldn't care anyway. All he wants to do is tend to his horses. Horse-mad, he is, has been since he was a little boy. It's lovely to see him take an interest in something. Be so settled. My big brother is growing up." Miss Durant laughed ruefully. "I did worry for him, you know. He's always been so restless. Up for any lark. Perhaps his brief time at Kelby Hall made him see the error of his ways. He's very serious now. A regular sober-sides."

Maris could not imagine that. But if she was lucky she wouldn't see him in any incarnation. She just had to convince him to stay away, though her scheme for the day was a total failure.

Well, to be fair, Miss Durant was good company. For a young woman who'd spent most of her life in a sickbed, she was cheerful and outgoing, and made Maris laugh out loud several times as they spent the next half hour together. In another universe, Ginny Durant might be her sister-in-law, eagerly anticipating becoming an aunt.

Maris felt a twinge of guilt to heap upon the ever-mounting pile of recriminations. Her guilty conscience had a guilty conscience. But it wouldn't do to dwell on the mistake she'd make with Reyn Durant. A child had resulted, and certainly no child was a mistake, no matter how it was conceived. The baby *was* a blessed event, as Mrs. Beecham said, no matter who your god was or how you worshipped. A miracle.

Maris bid her guests good-bye, refusing, with some difficulty, an invitation to take tea at Merrywood the next week. Ginny's lively presence reminded Maris she had not had a friend since Jane, and the last years of their friendship had been marred by Maris's heavy secret, then Jane's.

Well. Maris still had the problem of finding a way to speak to Reyn. She didn't even know when he would return home. Maybe she *should* go to Merrywood next week. Or better yet, invite the Durants back. A woman in her condition was not expected to go abroad in public, and Ginny would no doubt be thrilled to get another look at Hazel Grange.

Seven days wouldn't matter much; she'd waited this long. Maris went to her desk and began to write.

Chapter 23

Maris *should be going through the boxes from Madame Bernard right about now,* Reyn thought, saddling up Phantom. He could not wait until next week to see her. If he hadn't gone to London, he might have seen her when she'd invited his sister for tea, though if he hadn't gone to London, she would not be in possession of the prettiest mourning gowns Madame Bernard had ever created.

On the off chance she was so overcome with joy and thanks that she'd ride out to where they last met, he went to the oaks and dismounted, crunching rotten acorns underfoot.

The day was spring personified—green, warm, sunny, and sweet-smelling. A little too early for roses, but Maris herself smelled of that particular bloom. Reyn wanted to bury his nose in her loosened hair and breathe her in as though his life depended upon it.

That might be asking too much after all these months. Would she let him kiss her? Not if she was accompanied by that hulking manservant. Reyn hoped she would ride alone—unmolested, of course—slip from her pretty white horse, and into his embrace.

Reyn hadn't taken another woman into his bed since Maris. His opportunities, and they had been considerable, had been easy to dismiss with a shrug and a boyish grin. He hated to hurt anyone's feelings, so he might have given a careless kiss or two and a friendly pat. But his uncareless kisses had been saved for his countess. He simply couldn't imagine being with anyone else.

If she refused to have an affair with him, he supposed he'd have to get used to the idea of celibacy, or change his standards and break his heart. How ironic he'd fallen in love with a bluestocking peeress who was as stern as a governess and as lush as the first rose of summer.

Reyn paced back and forth long enough to wear a trench in the grass. Maybe he should have stayed home and awaited her missive. He was always acting rashly. Why should she come? Maris wouldn't expect him to be doing sentry duty on their border.

He looked to his horse, wondering if he should head back home. Phantom seemed happy enough finding acorns that weren't too rotten. The horse had an iron stomach, anyway. He'd been the ideal warhorse, was a peaceful peacetime companion, and Reyn loved him.

I love that horse almost as much as I love Maris, he thought with a sudden grin.

His life was good—the best it had been since he was a boy. Ginny was well, no one was jumping out of the bushes to shoot him, and his business would take off now that he'd found a good stallion to cover his mares.

At present, Phantom was withholding his approval from the interloper, a bay named Brutus, so things were not as domestically equable with the equines in the barns as they were at the house. Soon, Ginny would leave, however, and then—Reyn wouldn't think that far ahead. But he'd been so busy thinking and juggling acorns and congratulating himself on his good fortune that he'd missed Maris's arrival. His heart leaped. The Prall fellow—he'd asked his name in town—was nowhere to be seen. *Thank God.* Reyn pitched the acorns to the ground and brushed his hands clean on his breeches.

It was impossible to tell from Maris's pale face whether she was pleased with his gifts. She remained seated on her fairy-white horse, clutching the reins tightly. Reyn strode through the trees and raised his arms to help her dismount.

She shook her head. "I cannot stay. But we have to talk."

That sounded ominous. Reyn prepared himself for a lecture. He knew it was improper have sent her the gowns, but hell, there were only three of them, all beautifully made as only Madame Bernard could do. The hat he'd picked out was a vast improvement to what she was currently wearing, too. He was disappointed not to see it or the lacy butterfly again.

"It is *so* good to see you again, but I'll get a crick in my neck looking up at you, Lady Kelby. I swear I'll take no liberties when I help you off your horse."

For a moment he thought he saw naked panic in Maris's eyes, but she regained control. "That won't be necessary. What I have to say shouldn't take long."

Not good, though *I love you* was only three words. How many seconds did they take?

"I am at your service then, Maris. As always. How are you faring? You look . . . beautiful."

She did, too, though she was very pale, her face was slightly fuller, and her breasts swelled under the black riding habit. "I am well enough. I suppose you expect me to thank you for the dresses, Reyn. What were you thinking? If anyone discovers you sent them—"

"Why would they? Mrs. Bernard and her staff keep secrets like bank vaults. They are completely trustworthy. The boxes came express from Mrs. Bernard herself. My part in their purchase will never be detected."

"David has been here. He's suspicious of everything. I think he's spying on me again."

Reyn felt a spurt of anger. "Is the man still hounding you? I will talk to him if you like. In fact, I want to talk to him even if you *don't* like. He's got what he wanted. Why is he bothering you?"

"But he hasn't. I—oh, I don't know how to say it, Reyn. I r-rehearsed and rehearsed." She was shaking as if they were in a swirling snowstorm.

Without thinking, Reyn untangled her hands from the reins and lifted her off the horse. He didn't dare hold her, didn't dare bring her close. He set her down a decent distance away, wondering why her eyes were filling with tears. "What is it? You know you can tell me anything."

"I'm . . . I'm having a baby." She noted the expression on his face and rushed to say, "I didn't tell you earlier because I didn't know. I thought—well, it doesn't matter what I thought. Dr. Crandall told me at the beginning of April that I was pregnant, and then we rushed to move here. I never expected to find you next door."

"The beginning of April?" More than a month ago. What had he been doing then? Painting fences white and shoveling manure. The muscle in his cheek jumped. "You've known for more than a month. If I wasn't right next door, would you ever have told me?"

"Yes. I intended to, truly I did. But I couldn't figure out quite how and—"

"It seems simple enough. Pen. Paper"—he tried to tamp down his anger—"a bit of sealing wax once you're finished. 'Dear Captain Durant, I'm having your child.' "

"But he—or she—*isn't* your child, Reyn."

"Ah." Of course he'd known that. Had agreed to it, albeit with grave reluctance. "You promised you'd tell me, Maris," he said stubbornly.

His child, but not his child. The theoretical had become real, and he was unequal to it.

"I know. I'm telling you now. And you must not come near me. David already thinks I plan to trick him."

"You have." Reyn looked from her face to her figure. She'd felt heavier than he'd expected as he took her from her horse, but not so heavy that his dim brain had been suspicious. She was tall for a woman. Curvaceous. The extra weight looked good on her. "Are you well?"

"Perfectly. That was part of the reason I never thought that we had achieved conception. I never"—she blushed—"have been sick, not even for a day. My courses even came, although they were diminished. I wept for days that there was no baby, Reyn. When they finally stopped altogether, I just thought I was too old. And then when I found out . . . it seemed unbelievable."

"You wanted to keep your secret to yourself." He couldn't help feeling resentful, but in a way he understood.

She nodded. "I knew I should write to you, but I was afraid . . . of so many things."

"I made a bargain with you, Maris. I intend to keep my word." It would be the hardest thing he'd ever do. "So Kelby might be out of the succession. No wonder he's angry."

"He believes I'll smuggle in a boy somehow if the child is a girl. He says he'll stay in Shere when my time comes. He says a lot of nonsense."

"You are not safe." What could Reyn do about it? Lie like some shaggy guard dog across her bedroom threshold? He had no rights to her or their child. Worse, he was supposed to never see her again.

"Shouldn't you go back to Kelby Hall?"

"I don't want to. I love it here. For the first time in my life I have a home that's all mine, the way I wish it to be. I know it sounds stupid."

Did it? It was very like how he felt about Merrywood. "You'll have to if you have a son."

Maris looked mournful. "I know."

"This is absurd, Maris. Henry is dead and his plans with him. Let David Kelby inherit. Who cares about all the piles of rubbish in the Kelby Collection? Marry me. We can raise our child together."

His impetuous words did not have the desired effect.

"M-marry you? I cannot do such a thing. May I remind you I just buried my husband. Not six months ago."

"So, defy convention. Why should you lock yourself up like a princess in a tower? Life goes on, Maris." Reyn knew he sounded desperate. He *was* desperate. Until that moment, he'd not known precisely how deep his feelings—his sense of possession—ran. Hang Henry Kelby and all the earls before and after him. Reyn wanted Maris.

He wanted his child.

"No. I cannot. W-we don't even know each other!"

"That can be remedied. Let me court you. I'll find out your favorite flower, your favorite soup, whatever it takes for you to think we're well-enough acquainted. I should think after what transpired between us at Kelby Hall we have more in common than most couples."

Her cheeks turned scarlet. "That . . . that isn't everything."

He was handling it all wrong. Maris was stepping back farther into the shade of the oaks, looking at him as if he were deranged—which, basically, he was. But he'd never proposed to anyone before, never felt the panic of his future sliding away.

"I know it. Forgive my crudeness. Maris, please think on my offer. I can protect you from David Kelby. I can take care of you and the child."

"I don't need taking care of! I'm older than you are!"

"But not by much. Is that what bothers you? A mere four or five years? The earl was decades older than you."

"I cannot talk about this anymore. Please help me back on my horse."

"See, you do need me, if only for something so inconsequential. I long to kiss you, Maris. Hold you. You've vanquished me completely without even trying. I'm yours to command." Lord, he sounded like some half-baked hero from a gothic novel, but he couldn't seem to help himself. Maris Kelby did something to him no one else had ever done.

"Then leave me in peace, Reyn. Leave me alone." Her voice shook.

In his heart, he knew she didn't mean it. Couldn't. He had to convince her that he was the man for her, without florid love letters or expensive gifts or a title he did not and would never have.

Suddenly he remembered a very minor weapon in his arsenal. "I can't. I've been invited for tea next week, haven't I? It would be impolite not to turn up, and Ginny would be inconsolable. She's talked of nothing else since I got back from town."

Maris stared at him in disbelief. "You're saying you will come anyway, despite my wishes because you don't want to disappoint your sister?"

"I'm saying I want that kiss. That embrace. A cup of tea as only you can brew it. I mean to have them, Maris, and change your mind."

"You are impossible."

"Yes. Just ask anyone."

"Oh, Reyn." She sighed his name and he'd never heard anything sweeter.

"We can figure this out, Maris."

"It's already figured, Reyn. This child will bear the Kelby name. I cannot ruin its life with scandal, no matter what I want."

"What *do* you want?" he asked softly.

"I don't know! I can't think when I'm around you."

He grinned. "That's a very good sign, you know." He felt the same way. The starchy Countess of Kelby made him stiffen in all the right places.

"I need to get back. They will worry about me."

"So they should. You ought not be riding out without an escort, though I'm glad I got this time alone with you. Let me escort you back to the Grange."

"No! What will people say?"

"I'm sure there will be no people along the way to say anything, and if there are, we should shoot them for trespassing. Ah, too bloodthirsty for you? Very well, we can tell these imaginary trespassers the truth. I found you unchaperoned, perhaps a bit faint, and did my gentlemanly duty accompanying you home. There's nothing odd about that. We are neighbors."

Maris looked worried. "If David hears of it—"

"Blast David and all his minions! We're innocent, at least this time. I cannot promise for the future, however." Reyn took her arm and marched her to her horse. "I promised not to take liberties, Maris, but I can tell you I want to. I want to feel the swell of the babe beneath your skirts and know I've done something right for once in my life."

Maris was silent as he helped her back on her mare and nearly so all the way home. Reyn hoped she was thinking about his clumsy proposal, refashioning it in her head into words she couldn't refuse.

He'd have the chance to propose again. He might do better—or worse—next time, but eventually Maris would be his, even if he had to read from a damned book of poetry.

Chapter 24

S he was well and truly ruined. The fragile peace she'd assembled from scraps of her old life and basted together had been torn to shreds. Maris knew she'd been distracting herself over the past months with Henry's work and getting settled into two new houses, but it was time she faced the truth. She had feelings for Reynold Durant. Improper feelings. *Most* improper feelings.

And she didn't know what to do about them.

Last week, he had asked her to marry him, the wretched man, right out of the blue. A widow was meant to remain widowed, at the very least for two years. As she was an earl's relict, it would be expected she might even remain such for the rest of her life. She had an extremely generous widow's jointure, a lovely house, and the prospect of moving back into Kelby Hall if she bore a son. She would not want for any material thing. Her life should be complete.

But there was Reyn over the tea tray, temptation itself. His over-long dark hair was brushed back, his rust-colored coat clinging to his broad shoulders, his buff breeches leaving nothing to her imagination. He and his sister made an attractive pair, and their easy sibling banter made her a little envious. She had grown up with Jane, but the two of them had been naturally reticent, even with each other. Maris had striven to never put a foot wrong, aware she was privileged to be raised in an earl's household. Jane had been painfully shy, more or less ignored by everyone but their governess Miss Holley. It had been much too easy for David Kelby to take advantage of Jane's sweet nature.

The helpful Mrs. Beecham had not come with the Durants. Maris had no intention of discussing the impending birth with a gentleman present, particularly this gentleman. She was absolutely mortified she had discussed her menses twice with Reyn, though she supposed everything about her relationship with him resulted in mortification of the highest order. She wasn't much of a lady, then, even after a lifetime of toeing the line.

To his credit, Reyn treated her like one, like a lady who was more or less a stranger to him. He'd made one reference to meeting her by chance in the garden at Kelby Hall, but said nothing of their working together in the attics.

Maris had been unable to forget those days, and she had tried, feeling so disloyal to Henry every time Reyn, naked and hungry for her, flashed into her mind. She had admired her husband, put him on a pedestal from the time she was a little girl.

Henry could not have been more different from Reyn. Where Henry was all intellect, Reyn was mostly physical. He had been so full of pent-up energy she could feel waves of it across the room as she'd catalogued items from the boxes, energy that was quickly put to use when he took her to bed. His wife would have no complaint in that area, but what would they say to each other once desire was spent?

Why was she being critical? She and Reyn had had no difficulty conversing. True, he'd been self-deprecating about his education, but he'd been charming, was thoughtful and sympathetic. He'd really been so kind when she'd been nothing but a mass of raw nerves.

He was looking at her kindly, one of his dark eyebrows raised.

What had she missed in the conversation? "I'm sorry. I must have been woolgathering. You were saying?"

"My sister asked if she could get you anything from the village shops. She and Mrs. Beecham are going tomorrow. I believe it's all a hum so she can run into Mr. Swift before Sunday."

"Mr. Swift the vicar? He came to see me not long ago."

"Ginny plans on roping the man into marriage. I have not yet given my consent, however," Reyn teased.

"But you will if you know what's good for you," Ginny teased back. "I hope you do not find us very improper, Lady Kelby. Now that my brother is back on British soil I must make up for all the years I couldn't torment him. That's what little sisters are supposed to do."

Maris smiled. "Is that so? I'm afraid I had no brothers or sisters, so I imagine I missed a great deal. Thank you for your offer, Miss Durant—that is, Ginny—but I cannot think of anything you could fetch me." What she really needed could not be found in the confines of Shere. "Have you set a date for your wedding?"

"The sooner the better. I cannot wait to wash my hands of this little baggage. Let poor Swift deal with her," Reyn said, reaching for a raspberry jam-filled tart.

"You know you'll miss me."

"As one misses an extracted tooth, not that I would know. I still have all mine, thank Mr. Swift's Lord."

"If you keep eating jam tarts you won't. Not to mention you'll get fat." Ginny colored, realizing that perhaps she should not be so free with her speech in the presence of a countess. But Maris was quite enjoying picturing Reyn with a pot belly and a missing tooth or two. He wouldn't be such a perfect specimen then and would look more mortal and less like a Greek god.

"Enough, brat," Reyn chided. "Lady Kelby must be bored to death with our bickering. We shall take our leave and promise to do better next time."

Next time? "What cheek! Are you inviting yourself back, Captain Durant?" Maris asked, getting into the spirit of things.

"Not at all. We are hoping you will grace us with your presence at supper one evening soon. An early night. We are complete country mice, now. I can drive the gig over myself and return you safe and sound. I should like you to see Merrywood. It's nothing in comparison to Kelby Hall, of course, or Hazel Grange. But Gin has worked wonders. For all my sister's faults, she is an excellent housekeeper."

"I don't know whether to be flattered or insulted, brother dear. Of course, we'd love to have you, Lady Kelby. Just a quiet evening, no fuss. I know with your recent bereavement you're loath to be in company."

Maris felt a prickle of unease. But it was impossible to withstand the charm of both Durants, and she wasn't sure she wanted to.

If she accepted, would Reyn think she'd accept everything else?

She *couldn't* marry him. It was an absurd notion. She could not embark on an affair with him, either. No man would think she was alluring with her suddenly pendulous breasts and swollen belly. No wonder husbands, the devils, sought amusement elsewhere while their wives stayed home knitting baby caps. It was entirely the husbands' fault their poor wives were as blown up and gassy as a Vauxhall balloon. Damn men anyhow.

Reyn interrupted her mental diatribe. "So you'll come, Lady Kelby?"

"I-I shall be delighted." How easily the lie slipped through her lips. Though she *was* interested in seeing Reyn's property. She had a keen interest in horses now that she didn't have to worry over Henry. Soon, however, she'd just have to talk to Pearl rather than ride her. Though she put the animal through the mildest paces, Stephen was beginning to fret that she would get hurt on their daily outings. He was becoming worse than Betsy, if that was possible. Likely he was embarrassed, too, to be touching her in her present state. Mr. Prall's two bachelor sons seemed shy of the fair sex. "I would love to come a little early to see your horses."

Reyn brightened, making her fear she was only adding to his wishful thinking. "I'd love to show you my girls. My young gentleman, too. Brutus is a new acquisition. He's very full of himself at the moment, showing off for his harem."

Like you, Maris thought. A splendid, viral animal, young and sleek. She felt the blush rise to her cheeks, and fought against the confusion she always felt in Reyn's presence. At least she wasn't stammering again.

She had fallen in lust, she who should know better. Lust didn't last. Would friendship, the kind she had with Henry, ever be possible with a man like Reynold Durant? She pictured him over future tea trays, his dark hair silvering, the smile lines on his face deepening, then shook the homey aspect from her head. She was in no position to anticipate a future with anyone but her coming child.

"It's settled then. Shall we say next Tuesday? I'll come for you at five o'clock. There will be plenty of daylight for you to visit the stables."

Maris meant to object. She had a perfectly good carriage, and Stephen or his brother Samuel could drive her to Merrywood. But if Reyn came to fetch her, she'd have some time alone with him, only minutes really as their properties were so close. She didn't want to deny herself the bliss of sitting close, inhaling sandalwood and leather. She might, if she was very foolish, allow him that kiss he spoke of the other day, One kiss only. Just a taste, like an *amuse-bouche* to keep her lust at bay.

She was a wicked woman—a widow, pregnant and ungainly—desirous of something she could not have. Could never have. For one instant she cursed Henry for placing her in this untenable position. He must have known how it would be for her, awakened and alone, and still his plan to thwart David Kelby trumped all. They knew Henry would not live forever, but Maris had never fully understood what it would be like. She faced a lifetime of self-sacrifice to the Kelby name and collection if she bore a son. What had seemed natural, given her esteem for Henry, was suddenly a heavy burden, robbing her of whatever pleasure she might have discovered on her own as an unencumbered woman.

Resentment against Henry and her own naiveté would not help her get through the next few months, however. She must be as mindful of her humors as to what she ate and how she exercised. The poor baby had endured enough grief in its burgeoning life, but Maris's tears were firmly behind her. They had to be.

"Yes, Captain Durant. I shall be ready." She lowered her eyes so that she would not see the blaze of joy in his.

Chapter 25

Tuesday had inched along all too slowly. It wasn't as if he didn't have a thousand things with which to occupy himself. Reyn was nothing if not busy, nearly overwhelmed with calculations on each of the girls. He was keeping notes and an estral calendar for all of them, having sense enough to know he did not want to be up to his elbows delivering their foals all on the same night. Brutus was anxious to begin his work, but would have to be satisfied with a few mares at a time rather than the whole lot at once.

Some of his horses had already been bred before he purchased Merrywood, and Reyn was anxiously anticipating the new arrivals. He'd even forced himself to sit and get through most of a monograph on the delivery of foals, laboring over each sentence.

He would not see any profit for well over a year, but had enough emerald money left over to keep himself in bread and cheese and his horses in hay if he was frugal. With Ginny married, there would be fewer expenditures on Merrywood, too. He could live with the tilting floors and tattered curtains.

He wouldn't let himself think of Maris moving in.

If she agreed to marry him eventually, they could make their home at Hazel Grange, anyway. He couldn't subject his countess to less comfort than she was used to. The Grange was a very handsome house, beautifully appointed, a fine place to raise a family. The combined acreage of the two properties would be enough to support dozens of horses . . . and children, too.

Bah. What was he doing, dreaming? She couldn't let an Earl of Kelby grow up so far from his birthright, even if Kelby Hall was just some twenty miles away. And he was not fit to be any sort of "stepfather" for such an exalted young personage.

Reyn gripped the reins in frustration, ruing the day he'd ever seen that advertisement in *The London List*. He was tied up in knots, longing for what he could not have. Timing was everything, and he and Maris were its victims. If they had met a mere few months later, once she was safely widowed and settling into Hazel Grange . . . but then he certainly would not be Merrywood's owner. He'd be in London, wasting his life away, doing one damn stupid thing after the next and wondering where his next meal was coming from. Staying up all night at the tables, or bedding some other man's willing wife. He never would have crossed paths with the virtuous Countess of Kelby.

And she would not be bearing his child.

Reyn pulled up to the columned portico of Hazel Grange. Before the groom could rush to hold the horses, Maris stepped out and down the steps. She was wearing one of Madame Bernard's creations, a black moiré that shimmered midnight blue and purple in the sunlight, a gauzy shawl clinging to her shoulders. The hat Reyn had selected, a little crown of iridescent black feathers, was perched on her head like a wayward bird. She took his breath away.

"Good afternoon, Captain Durant."

Reyn wished the old gig was a fairy-tale glass carriage, but at least the seat was newly upholstered and clean. Reyn had stuffed horsehair and pounded the nails in himself after securing a piece of leather in Shere once he knew he would be transporting Maris.

"Good afternoon, my lady." He jumped down and jostled around the groom to help Maris into the conveyance.

"It is a lovely one, is it not? Almost hot."

Too hot for May, and sticky besides. His shoulder ached like the devil, a harbinger of rain to come. Reyn hoped all this weather talk was for the benefit of the boy who stood on Hazel Grange's pea stone drive. They would have to find even more banal things to say over dinner and should not exhaust all of them on the ride to Merrywood.

"Indeed, lovely. My sister has been in a tizzy all day preparing for you."

"I do hope she'd not gone to a lot of trouble," Maris said, frowning. "I'm perfectly satisfied with the simplest things."

"So I told her, but she does not listen to me very often."

Maris adjusted her lightweight shawl. "How goes the wooing with the vicar?"

"You may see for yourself. Mr. Swift is also our supper guest. I hope you do not object. I know you do not relish company at this time." Reyn had argued with Ginny over the invitation, but somehow she'd prevailed.

"He seems a most unobjectionable young man. I think David must have frightened him off, though. He's not come to see me since that first visit."

Reyn ground his teeth. "Has David bothered you again?"

"Only by the post. I don't open his letters, but toss them in the fire. There's a great deal of satisfaction to be had watching the flames, and it's most unlikely he's enclosing bank notes."

Reyn loved the hat. Maris's profile was fully visible to him and he saw the slight curve of her lips.

"I meant what I said, Maris. I will talk to him for you."

She turned to him, feathers fluttering as the gig rolled on the narrow lane that connected their properties. "How could you explain your protective interest, Reyn? I went through a great drama swearing you meant nothing to me. Denying we even *spoke* beyond the merest passing politeness at Kelby Hall. It will be odd enough if he discovers we are neighbors." She bit a lip. "You never should have come for me. I was wrong to accept the supper invitation in the first place."

"One does have to eat sometime," Reyn said, trying to tease her out of her funk.

"I have a perfectly good cook of my own."

Damn it. He didn't want to start their short time alone together off on such a querulous note. "Tonight, let's agree to pretend David Kelby doesn't exist. He's not about to leap out of the hedgerows and catch us together, now is he? In any event, we are doing nothing wrong. You are dining with your new neighbors and a vicar. It doesn't get more boring than that."

She raised a brow at him, but said nothing. Boring was not the word to describe how he felt about Maris and she knew it.

Finally she sighed. "People will gossip."

"You know what? People *always* gossip. What they don't know, they'll make up. I'm afraid you are the most exciting thing that's ever happened to Shere. A real live countess in their midst. If you wanted total privacy, you should have gone elsewhere. The moon, perhaps. The Arctic Circle. But I can't tell you how glad I am you are here next to me."

"Don't expect too much from it," Maris demurred, though she didn't move away.

"Even a countess cannot deny a man his dreams." They were getting close to Merrywood's gate. Reyn had affixed a sign to it just that afternoon; the paint was probably still wet. "Have you given any thought to our kiss?"

"That's a presumptuous question, Captain."

"Presumptuous is my middle name. Or would it be Presumption? I seem to have missed my chance on the road, but the stable will provide the necessary privacy, as long as you don't mind the girls looking on."

"You are being ridiculous, Reyn."

She hadn't said no. He'd have to be careful not to muss her, make sure there were no telltale bits of straw on her bottom. Of course there wouldn't be. He couldn't very well lure her into a stall and toss up her skirts as much as he wanted to. He'd have to refrain from sliding his fingers into her pinned-up hair, undoing the cunning jet buttons on her bodice, nipping her long white neck. And freeing her voluptuous breasts, which seemed a bit larger than he remembered.

And he remembered everything.

"Here we are. It's a pleasant aspect, is it not?" Every time he rode down his lane, he felt a little jolt of pride. The whitewashed stone dwelling at the end of it had begun its life as a humble farmhouse, and several additions had been tacked on over the last century. The roof was thatch, and a clutch of early climbing roses framed the front door. True, he had to duck his head to enter that door, which had taken some getting used to. The outbuildings had been painted to match the house, so everything was blisteringly white and fresh. Reyn knew it was necessary to appear prosperous even if he wasn't yet. His potential customers should be impressed.

His hard work was worth the smile on Maris's face.

"Oh! This is lovely, Reyn!"

"This is more or less my first home, too. My parents weren't much for sticking around to one place. Always fleeing creditors, you know. But I expect that mobility prepared me for the army. I never knew where I'd wake up next."

"That must have been difficult for a little boy. I never lived anywhere but Kelby Hall."

"Do you miss it?"

"Not at all."

Reyn turned to her in surprise.

"It's true. I'm quite content at the Grange. I told you I was happy with simple things."

Excellent. Then there was hope for him. He was simple as they came.

"Let's get you to the stables before Ginny gets her hands on you."

"I don't wish to appear rude."

"Not at all. She knows you're going to tour the barns with me first. I'm anxious to hear what you think."

They rolled into the yard and young Jack came scurrying out to help. The boy was his only help at present, which would soon have to change. Reyn jumped down and helped Maris out, forcing himself not to leave his hands on her too long. They entered the largest cool dark building, horses whickering in greeting. The scent of horse manure was almost entirely absent. As instructed, Jack had been busy.

"Give me a moment for my eyes to adjust to the light before I ooh and ahh," Maris said.

"You needn't try to turn me up sweet. I know Merrywood's limitations." He'd worked like the devil to correct most of them, though.

"Reyn, I can tell already you've done a wonderful job here. Everything is . . . *gleaming*. The boxes are much larger than usual, aren't they?"

"For the foals, when they come. It disturbs the horses to move into roomier quarters once they've given birth. Best to start them out in a larger space." He'd ripped out every original stall himself over the winter, carefully measuring its replacement.

Maris reached for a long cinnamon-colored nose and stroked it. "Pretty girl," she whispered. She opened her reticule and pulled out a lump of sugar.

"Now you've started something. You should have brought an entire cone if you don't want to cause a riot."

"I will the next time."

Her words were heartening. Reyn very much hoped she'd be back again and again.

Sugar gone, they toured the rest of the stable, Maris lingering over each of the fillies with a word or a gentle pat. She had a natural horsewoman's way with the animals and didn't blink when one of the girls excreted a very unladylike mess during her inspection.

They crossed a few grassy steps to the second stable housing the gentlemen's quarters and Reyn's office. One day, the empty stalls would be filled, but only two were occupied at present. Brutus put on a show while Phantom did the equine version of rolling his eyes.

"He is a beauty, isn't he?" Maris said, stepping back to admire the bay in the filtered sunlight.

Jack had done an admirable job scrubbing the windows, too. Reyn would have to give the boy something extra in his pay packet.

"*He* certainly thinks he is. Let's hope his offspring make him worth the price I paid."

Maris pointed to the curtained interior window at the end of the stalls. "Is that your office?"

Reyn nodded. He hadn't planned on showing her the room. His organizational methods left a good deal to be desired. But he wasn't quick enough to stop her from opening the door and peering inside.

It was the one place that wasn't gleaming. Tradesmen's bills were crumpled in a wooden trug, the pasteboard diaries on each horse strewn across the battered desk.

Maris picked one up in her black-gloved hand. *Mother of God.*

He watched her face as she turned the pages.

"Is this in some sort of code to confuse your competitors?"

She had given him the perfect out, but Reyn knew he couldn't lie to her. Wouldn't. He was a man of honor, despite his recent foray into various sins.

A possible marriage to Maris had been a beautiful, impossible dream while it lasted. It was time for him to wake up. Confess. What had he been thinking of to offer her a life with a man such as he? His proposal had been unplanned, reckless as usual. She was far above him and always would be no matter how well he established himself in his business.

"No, Maris, though I suppose that's one way of looking at it."
He took a deep breath, wondering how he would sound as he admitted his greatest fault. "I cannot read well. I write worse. All the
schoolmasters' beatings in the world did not help. You see the result in your hands."

Her brown eyes never left his. Give her credit for more bravery
than he was feeling at the moment.

Even his voice cracked a little as it had in his youth. Reyn gave
her a twisted smile. "I've managed to get by so far on my good
looks and charm, but you have found me out at last. I can barely understand my own notations some days. Now you see how hopeless
it was for your husband to hire me to catalog the contents of Kelby
Hall."

"He didn't hire you for that," she said softly. "Why didn't you
tell me?"

"How could I? I thought it enough to tell you I'm no scholar. No
one knows my limitations, not even Ginny. She thinks I'm just
lazy. Sometimes when I concentrate I can make out the gist of what
I'm reading. I've got a good memory, thank God. If I hear something, it gets filed away. But as a lad, I didn't sit still long enough
to listen to much of anything."

Reyn had trouble standing still, waiting for Maris to give her excuses and leave before partaking of Ginny's eagerly planned supper. He heard the pulse sing in his ears, felt his heart race, and
fought against the urge to flee from his office. From his life. He had
been a fool to think he could cobble together some kind of order to
his existence. Find a measure of happiness. He wasn't worthy. His
tenuous familial link to the ton was far overshadowed by his bad
blood.

What if the child took after him, had his deficiencies? He had
sentenced Maris with a problem that could not be solved. Reyn
should never, ever have agreed to the absurd proposition, but it was
much too late for regret.

She held the open ledger, her trembling hand revealing the impact of his words. He wished he could think of something comforting to say, but the truth was he was doomed and any child of his
might be as well.

"You should have said something. If not to Henry, then to me."

"I know. I was a coward. And you were so lovely I did not want to leave. If the child is afflicted, I can take it and spare you my parents' misery."

"You will not!" Maris was fairly thunderous, her brows every bit as frightening as a Durant's. "There will be no way of knowing for years if the child has difficulties. Was your father—"

"Normal? Oh yes. Even if he was a gamester. He didn't lose because he couldn't read the numbers on his cards, he was just damned unlucky and didn't have the wit to stop. I have no trouble there myself. Numbers are a bit easier for me to manage than letters. And the printed page is much clearer than someone's handwriting."

Her eyes widened. "You didn't read all those desperate letters I wrote because you couldn't."

Reyn felt himself flush, "Guilty as charged. I hoped you'd stop writing once your husband informed you I'd changed my mind. And I *had*. I didn't want to abandon a child, especially one who might need my help, what little I can provide."

Maris sank onto his wooden desk chair. "Oh."

"I've done a terrible, unforgiveable thing to you. The next Earl of Kelby may be as stupid as I am."

"You truly *are* stupid."

"I've told you I am sorry—"

"Do shut up, Reyn! No one knows what the future may hold for any of us. I could go blind tomorrow and then what would my ability to read matter? You have other skills, qualities that have served you well enough. You've made the best of a bad situation. To think you were beaten for what was not your fault. It is horrifying. Look here. See this *d*? Clearly you mean for it to be a *b*."

Reyn stared at the line to which she pointed. "Isn't it?"

"Is that how you see it?"

Reyn squinted, feeling the beginning of a headache take root. "Aye, I suppose."

"Reading for you must be like looking into a fun house mirror. Nothing is as it appears to the rest of us." She dropped the book and seized his hands, forcing his thumbs up and squeezing his fingers into the palm of his hand. "Look there. My governess Miss Holley taught me this trick when I was just a little girl. Jane had problems just as you do when she first learned to write, but she grew out of them. Your left hand makes a lower-case *b*." She traced the curve of one letter, then the next. "The right is a *d*. Do you see it?"

Reyn examined his hands. He did! "How peculiar."

"Isn't it? There must be any number of tricks you can learn to help you. Miss Holley is still at a cottage on Kelby Hall's grounds, retired of course. I bet she would love to help you. I can invite her to come and stay with me. No one would think it odd that I long for my old governess at this time."

"Teach me at my age? Don't be ridiculous."

"It's never too late to learn. I admire you for coping as well as you have, but surely there's room for improvement."

Reyn had been expecting rejection. Contempt. Pity. He had never imagined the Countess of Kelby would be looking up at him with such earnest encouragement when he had done nothing but lie to her. "I—"

"Don't you dare say you can't. Or you won't. What have you got to lose, but an hour or two a day with a sweet old woman who would love to feel useful again? I might even be able to help you as well."

Dear God. He still had some pride left, and would never want Maris to know his shame and frustration. He would go mad sitting in his seat poring over a pile of children's primers. They didn't take the first time. Why should it be any different now? He was nine and twenty, halfway to being thirty, far beyond anyone's help. Reyn had an absurd image of himself crammed into a child's desk, his knees splintering the wood. "I'll think about it." He just had, and it would not suit.

"You'll do more than that if you know what's good for you."

He looked up from his clenched hands. Well, *there* was the Countess of Kelby he'd met so many months ago at the Reining Monarchs Society. It was too bad he could not summon the care-for-nothing man he'd been.

For he cared too much, and it might be his undoing.

Chapter 26

Reyn was stewing. There was no other word for his deportment as he scowled and growled across the table during Ginny's elaborately correct meal. Once he'd crossed Merrywood's threshold, he'd been elaborately correct himself, giving no indication that he was acquainted with Maris beyond their recent civilities. Certainly giving no indication that she knew his sad, dark secret.

But as the conversation continued amongst the women, his silence was a living thing, and the occasional grunts breaking it did nothing to make Maris more comfortable. He'd made no effort to exert his usual boyish charm, staring at his slab of roast beef as if it might rise up and bite him. Any questions Maris had posed to him about his hopes for his stud farm were met with brief syllables. Ginny was becoming increasingly embarrassed by her brother's rudeness, and it was with relief that the ladies withdrew to the cheerful front parlor.

Poor Ginny. Her beau had been unable to come to dinner due to a parish emergency, and her brother was being a boor. She put on a smile and passed Maris a cup of India tea from a gleaming but dented silver tea service.

Maris accepted her cup of tea, wishing the tea leaves would tell her where she'd gone wrong with Reyn. She had shown no horror or disgust when he'd confessed his shortcomings, had truly not even thought what his problem might mean for their child. Now that he'd put the idea into her head, however, it tumbled around with ominous insistence. Could such a trait be passed on, like the family nose or a tendency to baldness?

Maris had never known anyone like Reyn Durant before. He was a man who cloaked himself in good humor and sexual prowess. He had gentled her along like one of his beloved mares, skilled in getting his way, literally charming her out of her petticoats. Such a force of personality indicated native intelligence. In their brief acquaintance, he had surprised her again and again with his knowledge for someone who'd boasted he'd hated school.

But he said he couldn't read, not that he didn't like to. *Couldn't.* The handwriting in his business journal was practically illegible. How had he managed all these years? And how had Henry's careful investigation failed to reveal Reyn's dilemma?

Well, she supposed one didn't have to quote Shakespeare to kill one's enemy. Reyn had been highly decorated for bravery on two continents. Henry had admired his virility and his fearlessness. He had told her once it was as if Captain Durant possessed an extra sense to detect danger. Perhaps that was God's way of making amends.

It was she who was being rude, Maris realized, as Ginny and Mrs. Beecham looked at her with some anxiety. "I'm so sorry. I must have missed your comment."

"It's no wonder. That clap of thunder was enough to deafen us all."

Thunder? Maris set her cup down and it rattled on the table after another clap shook Merrywood to its tenuous foundation. "Good heavens. A spring storm? It was so lovely when we drove over from the Grange." There had been some unusual humidity all day, though Maris had not expected rain.

Ginny got up and walked to the window. The sky beyond had darkened early, not from nightfall but an abundance of threatening gray clouds. She jumped back at a sudden flash of lightning.

"Lady Kelby, you cannot possibly get home in time to avoid the storm. Reyn is a crack whip, but even he would not dare to drive you home now in your condition. Do say you will agree to spend the night with us. We have a spare room, not up to your standards, of course, but it's clean and Molly can get it ready in a trice."

"S-spend the night?" Maris's little contingent would be concerned if she didn't return, and she was not going to ask Ginny to send someone to Hazel Grange to inform them in this kind of weather, even if there was someone to send. She knew from her conversations with his sister that Reyn did most of the labor at Merrywood himself. The halls were not lined with spare footmen waiting to deliver messages. "I couldn't possibly. My people would worry."

"Oh, but you must! Look, it's starting to rain right now."

She rose and joined Ginny at the window and saw the sudden spatter of rain on the wavy glass. "Oh, dear."

"So you see, it's impossible for you to leave." Ginny smiled and looped her arm through Maris's. "We shall take good care of you, I promise. Your people will put two and two together and not expect you to come home in all this. Isn't that right, Reyn?"

He was standing in the doorway, looking blacker than the sky outside. If he'd indulged in a cigar or a glass of port, it hadn't seemed to relax him.

"Reyn, tell the countess she must stay the night. You can drive her home first thing in the morning," Ginny wheedled.

"Of course."

He didn't sound willing to do anything with her. Perhaps that was a relief. All his marriage talk would stop, and that was a good thing, wasn't it?

"Are you going to join us for a cup of tea, Reyn?"

"I think not. I'm headed to the stables. Thunderstorms spook the horses, Brutus in particular. I won't have him kick in his box."

"Heavens, you're not going to sleep out there, are you?" Ginny asked.

"I might. Countess, do excuse me. I'll return you to Hazel Grange at your convenience, tomorrow."

Another rumble of thunder punctuated his words, and he was gone from the doorway before Maris could reply.

Well, *damn.* When Maris had been a girl, she and Jane had shared a pet, a raggedy little terrier much like Ginny's Rufus. The dog had somehow acquired a thorn in its paw, and when Maris held him so Jane could attempt to remove it, the dog had bitten both of them quite badly. Henry had patiently explained to them that wounded animals often turned on those who tried to help them, but had the poor dog put down anyway. Maris had cried for days, and it was the only time in her life when she hated the Earl of Kelby.

Reyn reminded her of that long-ago animal. Somehow she would help him anyway, and pray he didn't decide to bite her, too.

*   *   *

The violence of the storm had subsided, but the rain drummed steadily on the stable roof, reminding Reyn of an endless military tattoo. The horses had finally quieted, and he'd sent young Jack to bed above the mares' building. Reyn lay on a lumpy pallet in his office, the wick of the lantern turned low. The mess on his desk lay as a rebuke to his folly. If only he'd cleaned up before Maris had visited. Idiot that he was, he'd been cleaning himself up, bathing and brushing, buffing his boots, donning a new coat.

It wasn't his body that needed attention, but his mind. Now that Maris knew the truth about him, there was no point in letting himself think about their future. There was none.

It would be all right, or at least good enough. He had a useful occupation and Ginny was on the mend. To look at her, one would never know she'd ever been as sick as she was. Her lungs would never be strong, but if she was careful, that old drunk Dr. Sherman said she might even bear children one day. Reyn would miss her when she moved to the vicarage, but he'd managed most of his life being alone, even in a crowd.

In the midst of his troops, he'd guarded himself, masking his embarrassment at being so deficient. No one had guessed. He was skilled in duplicity. He should have lied to Maris, but his betraying tongue had run away with the truth.

He turned, scrunching up the folded horse blankets he was using as a pillow. He'd need another bath before he took Maris home. And that would be the last he would see of her. There would be no teas or dinners, no "chance" meetings at their boundaries. She would be going back to Kelby Hall eventually to have her child, and he would try to forget them both.

He tossed and turned, knowing he would find no comfort in his own bed, either, so he wasn't asleep when he heard the latch lift and the light footsteps moving across the packed-earth floor. Reyn sat up, smoothing the tangle of his overlong hair.

He could see her peering through a gap in the homespun curtains that gave him privacy in his little office. What did she want? Surely she had not brought books to teach him *tonight*.

She rapped on the window, and gave him a hesitant wave. Reyn fought his desire to put a blanket over his head and pretend he didn't see her.

"May I come in?"

Reyn could say no. Should say no. But he just nodded and watched her disappear around the corner to his office door. The hinges squeaked and she was inside, standing before him like a lost angel, her brown hair plated in a braid that fell over one shoulder. Her borrowed white nightgown showed a great deal of ankle, and more besides. She'd gotten wet on her way to the stables and the garment clung to her in all the right places. He could see the swell of her belly beneath her nervous clasped hands. Her nipples, too. He swallowed hard.

"What do you want?" Reyn knew he sounded surly, but couldn't help himself. He wanted her gone.

"I-I came to talk to you."

"We've talked enough, don't you think? Your hope for my transformation is touching, but rather hopeless, Countess. I am what I am. I don't need a nanny to feel sorry for me."

"No, you don't." She didn't move from the doorway.

"You'll wake the horses. Or Jack. Go back to bed."

"No."

"Good God, woman! Can't you tell you're not wanted? Leave me in peace." Her husband had once cautioned him to be careful with her, but sometimes it was kind to be cruel.

"No."

"You sound like a singularly repetitive parrot."

To his alarm, her mouth wobbled, but then she laughed. "Yes, I suppose I do. Let me say something else then. I want you to make love to me tonight."

His rage boiled over. "A pity fuck? No thank you, Maris. I've got hands and my imagination." Neither of which had come close to assuaging his desire for her all these months.

"Perhaps I want you to take pity on me, Reyn. I am rather ungainly at present. Unattractive."

He snorted. "Don't beg for compliments, my lady. You are magnificent and you know it."

"I am?"

He sprang from his pallet and sat down at his desk showing her his back so he couldn't see her and her magnificence. "Damn it, Maris, let's not play games. You know I want you, and I can't have you. We have nothing in common. I was wrong to ask you to marry me and have the child lose all its advantages. But then I'm often wrong. Anyone could tell you that."

He shuddered as she came up behind him and placed a long white hand on his bad shoulder.

"This is no game, Reyn. I want you to hold me. I want to hold you. If you just give me tonight, I'll understand."

"No."

"Now who's the parrot? Why?"

"Because . . . *because,* damn you! It's not right."

"It was never right, Reyn. From the beginning, we both knew that, but we did it anyway. And it was . . . glorious."

Oh, God. It was torture. He'd finally recovered his scruples, and she came to tempt him. Of course he wanted her. If he looked into her trusting brown eyes, he would not be able to say no again. He racked his brain for a sufficient excuse. "I might hurt you. Hurt the child."

"I-I don't think that can be true." There was a bit of doubt in her voice.

Perhaps it was enough to send her on her way. "If you are desirous of release, Maris, I suggest you use *your* hand as I taught you." Just that morning, he'd thought of her hand between them, his partner in her own bliss. He felt her breath on his neck.

"Perhaps I didn't need you to teach me that particular trick."

Another taunting image for him to dwell on. "You see? You're perfectly capable of taking care of your own needs."

She squeezed his shoulder and he thought he'd shoot straight out of the chair. "You ridiculous man. It's not the same at all. If we are no longer to be friends, I'll face the rest of my life alone. You can give me one last night, surely."

Reyn couldn't help himself. He swung around to face her. "Friends, Lady Kelby? You refused my friendship as I recall."

"Only in the very beginning, Reyn. We became more than friends. We became lovers. From just two days this miracle occurred. Think on it. Anything is possible."

She is at it again. Reyn frowned. "If you think you can turn me into some kind of scholar—"

"Hush," she said, bending over him. "I don't want a scholar. I want a lover."

Reyn couldn't move away as her lips came down on his. Warm.

Demanding. Commanding. His countess was not taking no for an answer, and truthfully Reyn could not have spoken even if his lips and tongue were available.

Oh, hell. He wasn't strong enough to escape the scent of roses or the softness of her mouth. He'd been celibate long enough. "Just tonight," he mumbled when she gave him a moment to breathe.

"We'll see."

He wouldn't waste any more time arguing. Maris might feel sorry for him, but he could not help appreciating the way she chose to express it.

She sank to his rumpled pallet, pulled her rain-dampened night rail up over her knees and then paused. Her lashes flicked. "Perhaps I should keep covered. I don't wish to give you a disgust of me."

Idiot woman. In two steps, he lifted the garment over her head, disentangling her wavy braid from a button. Her skin glowed ivory in the low lamplight, breasts full, belly taut and rounded. He was rendered speechless by her fecund beauty. Without a thought, he placed his hand on the curve that cradled the baby.

She was almost six months gone with child, and not so very large yet. He knew nothing of pregnancy, save he'd always been scrupulously careful not to cause one.

"All is well?"

"I think so. I've felt the baby quicken. It is the most remarkable sensation, Reyn. I cannot begin to describe it."

"Should you still be riding?" What on earth was he about, spoiling the mood of that seductive kiss?

"You sound like Dr. Crandall. I am fine, Reyn. Not sick, just pregnant. And very anxious to have you inside me if you can manage it."

Well. He'd never been able to resist a challenge. Reyn would worry about tomorrow, tomorrow. Tonight, he wouldn't let himself think anymore at all.

Chapter 27

Maris had been unable to fall asleep with the receding rumbling of thunder and the heavy rain falling overhead. All she could think of was Reyn in his misery. No wonder he'd been bored and mocked her fanatic attention to all things historical. My Lord, she had given him books he couldn't read to brush up on antiquities. Yet he'd been convincing, even with David. Reyn was resilient, a master at concealment. She wondered how he'd avoided offering himself up as a spy during the war.

Of course, secret codes would truly be secret to him.

He wasn't stupid, no matter what he'd said. The more she thought about it, the more she admired him for coping with such a heavy burden. If she hadn't picked up that ledger, she never would have guessed.

She'd lain awake in the strange bed until all lights were extinguished and all noises from the household ceased. Restless, she'd risen and gone to the window to watch the storm blow across the night sky. The mares' stable was dark, but cracks of light limned the windows where Brutus and Phantom were housed. Reyn was there, wakeful, watching.

Wounded.

She'd nearly laughed at her alliterative turn of mind.

Maris refused to question why it was so necessary for her to steal down the stairs barefoot, hoping that the door leading to the stable yard was not locked, the key secreted away by one of Ginny's servants. She was almost exultant when the door pushed open freely in the wind.

Closing it carefully behind her, she fled through the puddles and pounding raindrops to where Reyn was keeping vigil. Maris had not formulated exactly what she wanted to say to him; in fact, she really didn't want to talk much at all once she'd said her peace.

She was wicked tonight, and blamed poor Henry for setting this scheme in motion. If she had not ever met Reynold Durant, she would not want his lips and hands on her body. Maris might not want to marry him—yet—but lying with him had been all she could think about since she blew out her candle.

Since she'd met him on horseback scant days ago.

Since she'd first laid eyes on him at the Reining Monarchs Society.

He needed to know she was not disgusted by him. He was, she thought, an amazingly persistent character to have gotten so far in life. Such perseverance was to be commended. Henry had seen it, even if he didn't know the source of Reyn's stubborn success.

Reyn was visible through the gap in the checked curtain on the window of his office, his hair every which way as he sat up on a pile of blankets on the wooden floor. From the frown on his face, she had thought he might deny her entrance, but then he nodded at her with resignation.

And now she was in his arms, where she fit perfectly despite her bulk. He looked at her with wonder, touching the place where their baby grew, making her feel wonderful. No, wonderful was an inadequate word. Treasured. For the first time in her life she lived up to her name. She felt as if she could be a god of fertility.

She'd been bold enough to kiss him first. She was greedy, really, her blood singing with desire.

The night was for him, however. Maris would share herself with no motive except to let him know without a doubt that she valued him. He'd called it a pity fuck, and that was crude and unfair. She would give him the friendship he'd so effortlessly won from her with his charm and kindness.

His problem could have flattened another man, one who gave up and lost himself in ignorance. But Reyn was a fighter, even in civilian life. She seized his fingers and led them to her hollow. She was wet already. Shameless. But before she led him any further, she *would* talk to him.

"*You* touch me," she whispered. "It hasn't been the same when I've done it to myself, only imagining that you are there."

"You think of me?" Through his gruffness, she heard the yearning. What a coil they were in.

"Every night. Every day as well. At first I thought it was the grief and loneliness that led me to fantasy. You know"—her voice hitched, but she went on—"I loved Henry, no matter what I'd done. His death was a shock even though I knew it would happen eventually. But he died alone in his library. You cannot imagine my guilt. It was made worse because I missed you. It doesn't make any sense to me still—I barely knew you but when you left Kelby Hall—"

"As you asked me to," he reminded her, his fingers still circling between them.

It was the most extraordinary conversation of her life. She was naked in a barn, allowing him to touch her. Needing him to touch her. But before she undressed him, she would say what she'd come for.

Maris sighed. "What would you have me do? There was no reason for you to stay. I moved to the Dower House almost immediately and went about my life, mourning many things."

"And then you found out you were pregnant."

"It seemed impossible. But I swear I would have told you. You know now. I am not trifling with you, Reyn. I want you, even if I cannot imagine how to accomplish it."

She hissed as he slid a finger inside her.

"I think you are managing very well, my lady."

"We can have this. If we are careful. I'm so afraid David will find out, but I almost don't care."

He raised a dark eyebrow. "Almost? I have offered you marriage, Maris, even if I'm not worthy. But I will take you as my mistress tonight gladly."

She covered his mouth with her hand, where he proceeded to give it dogged devotion with his wicked swirling tongue. "You are terribly worthy. It is I who am not worthy of you. I'm a coward, Reyn. You invite me to put my past behind me, but I dare not. It's just too soon."

"Crumbs," he said when she withdrew her hand.

"Pardon?"

"You've scattered crumbs for me, but I'm not too proud to lick them up. You give me hope."

And that is exactly what she had come to do.

Parading about as Lady Kelby had never meant anything to her. She was not averse to being plain Mrs. Durant. It had taken Reyn's confession for her to realize what a truly noble man he was.

In so many ways, it would be easier to be the wife of a country gentleman who raised horses. Their properties marched together, could be joined. Their physical joining had always been a thing of wonder to her, so different from anything she had experienced either with her husband or David. But would a son forgive her once he learned that she'd tossed away the Kelby fortune?

She wouldn't think of the necessary waiting ahead, but just the now, with the rain pattering on the roof, lulling her senses. Reyn was taking his crumb-licking seriously, his tongue teasing the edge of her ear, her throat, the crease between her breasts. He cupped one in his free hand as she writhed under him, nuzzled her with a gentleness that went straight to her heart. His path led over her stomach to where his hand already worked feverishly.

And she had thought the night was meant for him.

His mouth was hot, insistent, working in tandem with his work-roughened hands. Maris let herself feel every freeing sweep of his tongue, the tug of his mouth on her core, the glide of his fingers within her. There was nothing in her world but that moment, nothing with more meaning.

She'd had a lifetime devoid of sexual satisfaction. Surely it wasn't too sinful to want just a little before she turned back to duty again? Society might say it was, but Maris wished society to the devil for making her doubt her right to this particular joy. She could not have stopped her reaction to Reyn if all the patronesses at Almack's wandered into the stable to object to her wantonness.

Maris shattered, even before she'd had the chance to remove Reyn's clothes. Tears of gratitude welled in her eyes, but she sat up unsteadily and tore his loose shirt over his head. He had changed from his dinner finery, but to Maris it really didn't matter what he wore. He was too lovely to cover up.

"It's my turn." Her hands shook too badly for her to unfasten his breeches. With a cheeky grin, he helped her. The grin vanished when he realized what she meant to do. "Maris," he warned.

She looked directly into his sin-dark eyes. "I want to."

There had been no time for *this* before, not when his seed had to be spilled into her womb. Maris was no expert. She took his member gingerly in her fist, but he placed his broad hand over hers and squeezed, showing her he couldn't be broken. He was hard and so very warm, so very beautiful. She bent to cover him with her mouth, her unraveling braid falling on his thigh.

Reyn's entire body convulsed with her capture. She had him precisely where she wanted him—flat on his back, at *her* mercy, for a change. She, plain Maris Kelby, could do as she liked with this gorgeous young man and all he could do was groan with pleasure.

He was so large, she divided her attentions to shaft and head, pulsing vein, and heavy stones. Reyn's eyes were closed, his thick brows knit in what looked like agony. Maris knew better. She sheathed as much of him as she could in her mouth as he cupped the back of her head, gently guiding her movement until she tasted the beginnings of salt and sin.

He struggled to push her away in time, then tumbled her on her side, sliding in effortlessly behind her as if they'd practiced the movement a thousand times. He'd been worried, she'd remembered, about crushing the baby, and in this position she was safe. His hand swept with possession over her breasts and belly as he lost his control, whispering prayerful words she didn't catch. With unerring precision he found her swollen center and brought her to climax, yet again.

Maris heard one of the horses snort, the driving rain, and Reyn's jagged breath behind her. She was on the floor of a barn like a common trollop, the itch and smell of the horse blankets no aphrodisiac. Somehow, she didn't mind a bit.

Reyn held her close, their skin slick and too hot. "Are you all right, Countess?"

She wiggled against him. "I could not be better, except if I could see your face."

"This scarred old phiz?" he chuckled. "I can arrange that, but I'm not quite ready to give up your sweet sheath. Nature will deny me, soon enough."

The tension had left his body, and, she hoped, his mind. Her actions spoke to him, did they not? She wanted him to be happy, to know—

Dear God. She had fallen in love with him, and it could no longer be denied.

When Henry died, she'd lost her husband and dearest friend. And she'd had to send her lover away, a man who in such a short time had breached her reserve and awakened her to the possibilities of—what?

There was the baby to consider. And David. And her own conscience. Maris had come to soothe Reyn, but was suddenly as agitated as ants under a quizzing glass in the sun.

They could engage in an affair, as long as her pregnancy was not an impediment. It was not the ideal solution. *That* would be a complete break, but Maris was not brave enough to do it. She wanted Reyn.

Did she still want the earldom for her son? That was not her dream, but Henry's.

To have one's cake and eat it too. Maris had never understood the phrase quite so accurately before. She was a gambler hedging her bets, and it was not a pleasant feeling. She sighed her frustration.

"What is it?" Reyn withdrew and rolled her on her back. She stared at the hatch-work of beams in the ceiling.

"Nothing much. Everything."

He kissed her fingertips. "We must be modern. Don't make things more complicated than they are. I know you cannot marry me. It would not suit. I was impertinent to ask, given the difference in our rank and situation."

Maris wanted to punch him. "Do stop. This has nothing to do with you."

"Nothing? Then why are you here?"

"That's just it. I shouldn't be . . . but I am . . . and I don't want to leave. I don't want to be anywhere else."

Reyn had the effrontery to laugh. "As I said, stop thinking. Let's just enjoy what we have, for however long we have it. It will have to be enough. But when we do this again, we should aim for a bed."

She was heartened by the *when*. Was it enough? Could she have a simple affair with Reynold Durant? Maris didn't know. Things had not been simple for a very long while. She'd spent so much of her life under a thundercloud of guilt, recently, and she wanted to walk in some sunshine.

At least I won't get pregnant from an affair, she thought. And then she laughed too.

Chapter 28

Reyn picked a bit of straw from Maris's hair. Playing ladies' maid had always been amusing, though tonight it was important he take his job seriously. If Maris was discovered re-entering Merrywood, there should be no trace of how they'd just spent the last perfect hour.

"Hold still. How am I to plait your hair if you're hopping about like a rabbit?"

"Sorry. I can do it myself, you know."

"And deprive me of touching the silk of your hair? You are too cruel, madam." Abandoning his ministrations, he bent to kiss the spot below her left ear.

"Stop that or we'll have to begin all over again. Where did the ribbon go?"

"It's in my pocket. I'm keeping it as a token so I may tie it to my lance when I next go out jousting."

"Silly man." She sounded pleased though.

He set his hands on her shoulder and turned her to him. Her cheeks were pink in the dim lamplight and her eyes glowed. She looked like a well-tumbled woman despite the virginal white nightgown and even braid.

"It's not raining quite so hard anymore. You should go."

"I know."

Yet he was loath to release her. The evening had been full of surprises for both of them. Miracles. Maris accepted him for who he was.

She wanted him anyway.

They had spoken just a little of the future. Reyn understood her reluctance to engage in anything else except an affair. How could she betray Henry's memory with a hasty marriage? And what would happen to the child everyone thought was her dead husband's?

Reyn could never go to Kelby Hall and watch his son be raised as the Earl of Kelby. He'd never belong there, would be a useless consort to Maris, and an inadequate "stepfather" to his own child.

So Reyn prayed with all his heart for a girl, a girl not cursed with his long Durant nose or bushy eyebrows. A little girl with toffee-colored hair and wide brown eyes, who was smart and beautiful as her mother. The old earl had dowered a girl child with Hazel Grange and a substantial income. Reyn would have to keep his wits about him repelling fortune hunters.

Yes, a daughter would be ideal. Maris could relinquish her guilt and that damn David Kelby would leave her alone forever. Reyn and Maris could marry after a decent period of mourning and all might be well. If he was writing a book, that's precisely how he'd arrange the plot.

Ha. Write a book? Not likely. Reyn was being fanciful, thinking too far into the future and had to rein himself in. For now, he was having a secret affair with his widowed neighbor, and bloody grateful he was about it.

He fastened the top button of her night rail. "There. All prim and proper. Except for your bare feet. What were you thinking of coming out without shoes?"

"I didn't want to make any noise."

"You are a scandal, Lady Kelby."

Maris blinked. "Oh, I do hope not. We must be discreet, Reyn. I don't want David to catch wind of what we're up to."

"Look, my love, even if he discovers our relationship, it doesn't mean anything. You are a widow. A neighbor. I'm offering you comfort."

"He could take the baby away after it is born, Reyn. Say I was unfit. A harlot."

"How could he do that? Surely Henry didn't make him any kind of guardian or trustee."

"No, of course not. But he's the nearest male relative. The courts are sympathetic to the wishes of men, not women. He could claim he was the temporary head of the family until our son reached his majority. I'd have no say in the raising of my own child."

"That cannot happen, Maris. You are borrowing trouble."

Jesus, no wonder she was so afraid. But if she married him, that would circumvent any nefarious plans David had, surely?

It was too soon to petition her further for a marriage between them. Whatever he had to do to protect her and their child would be done, one way or another. He would be her White Knight, ribbon or no.

He held her close, wishing the earlier glow of the evening would return. Someone should run David Kelby through and spare them all his machinations.

"I'm sorry I'm such a bundle of nerves. But I've had a month to think on all the things that might go wrong. I never expected to find you here, Reyn, and I don't think I can give you up again."

"I won't let you give me up. We'll figure something out, I promise." He was a selfish bastard.

But the best thing he could do for the Countess of Kelby would be to drive her home to Hazel Grange and never see her again.

Reyn couldn't do it. He needed to see her grow large with their child, touch her when she came apart, listen to her worries, and dispatch them as best he could. He hoped he was man enough to manage.

He kissed her forehead. "Let me walk you to the house."

"Someone might see."

"They're all asleep. There was a time when Ginny spent some restless nights, but the danger seems to have passed."

Maris studied his face. "You took Henry's job for your sister, and now she's in health. Are you ever sorry?"

"That I met and fell in love with you? Don't be ridiculous. Things may not be easy for us right now, but they'll come about in the end."

"I wish I could believe that. I don't see how."

He didn't have the first idea either, but wouldn't let that stop him. "Trust me."

She smiled. "I do. I hadn't planned to, either."

"I remember, and who could blame you? We met under rather inauspicious beginnings. But you've improved me, Countess. Who knows? You might even teach me to read at that."

"I'll write to Miss Holley tomorrow."

"Fine." He'd do whatever took her mind off their troubles. He'd subject himself to the schoolroom again and stand on his head if that's what it took to distract her. "Off with you then. Mind the cobblestones. I don't want you stubbing one of your pretty toes."

"Good night, Reyn." She stood on those toes to kiss him—a kiss laced with restraint, mindful that it would not take much for him to get her down on his pallet again.

Reyn stood at the stable door as she disappeared through the misty yard and into the side door. The house was in total darkness, and he hoped her toes would be safe all the way up the stairs and to her room.

Bloody hell. He should consult a solicitor; see what rights David Kelby might have over Maris's child. It had never once occurred to him that the blighter would have a say in anything. But that would arouse suspicion, and that was the last thing Reyn wanted to do.

He sat back down on the crumpled blankets, Maris's scent overcoming horse and hay. He had told her he loved her, and apart from a flick of her long eyelashes, she'd said nothing.

She wanted him. But could she love him? Reyn almost didn't care. It would be enough to have her nearby.

Crumbs. With luck and God's good grace he'd get the whole cake and icing, too.

Breakfast had gone just as it ought, with Maris and Reyn behaving civilized and composed. Toast was crunched, coffee drunk, eggs and bacon consumed over polite conversation, Ginny considerably brighter now that he was not being a rude bastard. Reyn realized he'd been less than a gentleman over dinner, and made certain he behaved himself. No one would guess from his deportment that a few hours earlier he and Maris had rolled around on the floor of his office giving each other unbridled joy.

He intended to drop Maris at her home and continue on to Shere, and they left early, heavy moisture still on the leaves and grass. In less than twenty minutes, Reyn had rolled through the posts at Hazel Grange. Maris's house sat on a little rise, square and neat. As soon as his carriage was spotted on the drive, Stephen Prall lumbered out from her stable and one of the footmen—bearing his own name now—stepped down from the portico.

"Good morning, Lady Kelby. We're so glad you've returned safe and sound."

"I'm so sorry to give you all worry, Phillip. What with the storm, Miss Durant insisted I stay the night, and the captain was kind enough to drive me back."

"You have a visitor, my lady. The Earl of Kelby arrived just after you left yesterday. Told him you were dining with the neighbors. We put him in the blue room when he wouldn't leave. He was in a temper to not find you home."

Maris turned white. Reyn could do nothing to calm her that would not arouse suspicion.

"I hope he did not give you a lot of trouble," Maris said faintly.

"No more than he ever did, my lady. He did get into the best port. Me and Aloysius figured it might be the best way to disarm him."

"W-where is he now?"

"Still abed, my lady. I reckon he's got a head on him this morning."

Maris turned to Reyn. "You'd better go."

"I'm not going to leave you alone with that villain."

Maris squeezed his hand as he helped her descend from the carriage. "But you must! He knows I spent the night at Merrywood, but may not even know it is you who lives there. If he sees us together, it will only fuel his ire."

"You weren't expecting him?"

"Of course not! David always comes and goes as he pleases. Somehow he thinks I will be waiting like a docile schoolgirl so he can scold and bully me." She tried to smile and waggled a finger at him. "Don't worry, I'll stand up for myself and send him packing soon enough after a decent breakfast. At least he has no need to bleed me for money any more. The Kelby coffers are at his disposal, even if the title is in limbo. Maybe you can get a message to Mr. Swift to pay me a visit this morning. He seemed to annoy David quite a lot when they met before."

"I think I should stay," Reyn said, unable to overcome the stubborn feeling that he should remain by Maris's side. What if Kelby tried to hurt her with something other than his tongue? Reyn had never been able to shake the feeling that somehow the man was responsible for the earl's death that dark night, though he would never confess his misgivings to Maris. She didn't need to be frightened any more than she was already.

According to the doctor, there had been no signs of foul play. But one didn't have to raise a fist to a sick old man when one could verbally goad him beyond bearing. Reyn would put nothing past David Kelby.

He had blackmailed Maris for years, keeping her off balance, destroying her peace of mind, and casting a dark shadow on the last years she'd had with her husband. Maris had made a terrible mistake ever trusting him, but her punishment was far more severe than her crime.

"I'm staying."

"You must not!" If possible, she was even paler than she'd been when the footman Phillip told her of her uninvited guest.

"I'm headed for your stables, Countess. Isn't it true that you are looking to acquire more horses? I'm particular about where I sell my stock. Call me peculiar, even. I think I'll just inspect your accommodations. If you have need of me, you know where to find me."

"Oh, Reyn." She spoke softly enough that Phillip and Stephen wouldn't hear her. "All right. But I think it's unnecessary."

"I do hope so. You there! Stephen, isn't it?" Reyn called to the man who held the carriage horse still. "I'm going to take a look at the countess's stables. She's thinking of making some renovations before she purchases some new horses and wants my opinion. Shall we have a look?"

Maris shot him a warning glance, and then disappeared up the steps.

Reyn spent the next quarter hour poking into every corner of every box, asking what he hoped were pertinent questions of Stephen when his mind was really on Maris and whatever indignities David Kelby planned for her. He struggled to keep the bees from buzzing too loudly in his head, but it was a losing battle. When it was obvious that his distraction was alarming the groom, Reyn shrugged with a grin, excused himself, and headed to the house.

He was just being neighborly, he assured himself. Reporting his findings. Bidding the countess good-bye after his inspection. It would be the height of rudeness just to wander off, wouldn't it?

Phillip admitted him and took his hat, and with a friendly wink,

Aloysius appeared as well. The elaborate green Kelby livery and towering wigs had been replaced with simpler suits and their own shorn heads.

"Is Kelby up?"

"Aye, sir. He and the countess are in the breakfast room."

"Take me there, Aloysius." Maris wouldn't like it, but these two young footmen, no matter how devoted to their countess, were not equal to dealing with a man like David Kelby.

Maris's tea cup clattered to its saucer when Aloysius announced him.

"C-Captain Durant! I expected you to be on your way to Shere by now."

Reyn bowed deeply. "My apologies, my lady. I took the opportunity to check out your stables as we discussed, but I see I've come at an inopportune time. Good morning, Mr. Kelby."

"That's 'my lord' to you, Durant. What is *he* doing here?"

Kelby was as bleached of color as Maris, his eyes bloodshot. Reyn noted there was nothing on his plate but plain toast, though the heavy scent of kippers, kidneys, and eggs wafted in the air. Maris's cook was doing her best to unsettle the earl's stomach.

"It's the most amazing thing, Kelby," Reyn said smoothly. "I came into an absolute gem of a legacy and have been able to leave the unprofitable academic arena behind. I purchased the horse farm that abuts the countess's west boundary last winter. Such a small world, isn't it? One could have knocked me down with a feather to discover that Lady Kelby was my new neighbor. She has consulted me on the purchase of some horses and the expansion of her stable block and I've come to give her my opinion."

"Know about horses as well as antiquities? Aren't you the Renaissance man," Kelby mocked.

"I do hope so. My experience in the army has given me insight in what to look for in one's mounts. I should be happy to give you the benefit of my expertise if you should desire it."

Kelby's mouth twisted in distaste. "I'm perfectly satisfied with my horseflesh. My uncle's stable is one of the finest in Surrey."

"Yes, I had occasion to note that during my brief stay at Kelby Hall. What brings you to Hazel Grange?"

"Not that it's any of your business, but I have a care for my aunt's welfare." Kelby tore off a corner of his toast, probably wishing he could do the same to Reyn's head.

Across the table, Maris rolled her eyes but had not spoken again since she'd greeted Reyn when he entered the room.

"Very kind of you, I'm sure. All of her neighbors naturally hold her in the highest esteem, and we all care for her welfare. One might say we all stick together in our little corner of the world. Everyone knows everyone else's business. I'm sure you know what it's like in a small village. The Countess is the center of attention at present."

As far as Reyn knew, no one had laid eyes on the elusive countess except for a handful of people, though it was true she was the subject of gossip. Whether the good people of Shere would lift a finger for her was a matter of conjecture, but he gave them the benefit of the doubt. He pictured the villagers rising up with pitchforks to throw David Kelby flat on his arse.

"I'm sorry if we gave you a fright yesterday," Reyn continued. "Lady Kelby was quite safe. As you know, the storm came on so quickly and was so dreadful my sister insisted the countess spend the night at Merrywood."

Kelby's eyes narrowed. "And where were you, Captain?"

"In the barns, I'm afraid. One of the horses is especially sensitive to noise and it was all I could do to calm him down. What a show he put on. I quite thought I might be trampled to death. I have great hope for Brutus as a stud, but he would have made a miserable army charger. My old Phantom holds him in complete contempt."

Reyn watched Kelby's eyes glaze over as he recited his horses' virtues and deficiencies. Best if the man thought Reyn was too preoccupied with his animals to even notice that Maris Kelby was a woman. "Well, I won't keep you any longer. Countess, your servant. You know you may depend upon me and my sister Virginia should any difficulty of any nature whatsoever arise. Just send us word. We'll talk another time. I'll tell Mr. Swift that you're desirous of his company this morning when I see him. Good day to you, Mr.—Lord Kelby."

Reyn hoped he'd given the impression of a friendly neighbor, a consummate gentleman. But he also wished to convey to Kelby that the countess was not isolated. She had champions, even if they were young servants, a country parson, and a faux scholar and his sister.

"Keep an eye on Kelby," Reyn said to Aloysius as he left. "I have an odd feeling about the man. I don't think he wishes the countess well."

"Of course, sir! He threw me out of the breakfast room, he did, saying he had private matters to discuss with her ladyship. But I've been right outside, just in case. We remember what he was like, always sneaking around Kelby Hall. He's not fit to fill the old earl's shoes. All of us hope the countess has a fine bonny son. That'll fix *him.*"

Or make their problems worse.

Chapter 29

Maris had bitten her cheek raw as Reyn ruffled David's feathers with his neighborly attentions. She couldn't really be angry with him for disregarding her wishes and coming into the house. Like some protective sheepdog, he'd made it very clear to David that she was not alone, even if he was stretching the truth by miles. She was as yet unacquainted with any of her neighbors save those at Merrywood.

"What a bore he is," David drawled once Reyn left.

Maris buttered a piece of toast she did not want. Her stomach was still in knots. "Do you think so? He does seem very devoted to his horses. I do not know him very well, but his sister has been all that is kind since I moved here last month."

"Jumped-up climbers, no doubt. And he's in *trade*."

"Horse breeding is perfectly respectable for a gentleman. And I believe they are in some way connected to the Marquess of Wayneflete, although they do not speak of it." Henry had done an extensive family tree for Reynold Durant to make sure there would be a drop of bluish blood, no matter how diluted, in any future Earl of Kelby.

David snorted. "Wayneflete is as far up River Tick as one can go without drowning."

"Thank goodness one cannot be judged by the behavior of one's relations," Maris said with deceptive sweetness. "Let's get to the point, David. Why are you here again so soon?"

"I thought you might be missing me."

Maris gave an unladylike snort. "Cut line, David. Is it money? Mr. Woodley has assured me you are receiving a most generous allowance while we wait." Involuntarily, she placed a palm across her stomach. "You can't have run through it already."

"Oh can't I have?" David muttered. "But it's not about money. This time." He shifted in his seat, radiating discomfort. Maris had never seen him when he was not in perfect control of his emotions, not that he'd ever displayed anything but pique and cunning heretofore. What could have caused this sudden glimpse into his humanity? Who would have thought he even *had* humanity?

She found she was curious. "I'm listening."

"I don't quite know where to begin."

Maris stopped herself from saying "the beginning." She decided not to make anything easier for the man who had brought such heartbreak to the house of Kelby.

The silence stretched. Maris added jam to her uneaten toast. Finally David sighed.

"There is a woman, you see."

There would be. David had left a trail of broken hearts behind him all his life. Maris looked up from her plate expectantly.

"She may come to see you."

"See *me*? Whatever for?" Maris did not relish acquaintance with one of David's castoffs, even if she did have some sympathy for the woman's plight.

"Well, here's the thing. I've explained the bloody circumstances about the bloody earldom to her, but she doesn't believe me."

"Imagine that. Someone finds you untruthful."

"Don't take such pleasure in my ruin. The woman has her hooks in me and I cannot see a way out."

He did look hunted, less ruddy and cocky. And could it be his russet hair was thinning just a little? "Have you made her a promise of marriage?"

"Not lately." He sounded nearly . . . amused.

"I fail to see what I can do to help you, David. Not that I want to. Mr. Woodley can explain as well as I our current situation. If she is suing you for breach of promise, he is the man to talk to."

"I'm making a muddle of this, aren't I? Here's the thing—when I was barely one and twenty, I made the greatest mistake of my life. And she has the proof."

Maris tried to remember when David was a young buck. He'd

never paid her any attention during his visits to Kelby Hall, not that she'd wanted him to. "What are you talking about?"

"This woman claims she is my wife. Well, to be fair, she *is* my wife. I was of age at the time and we were married in church by her father, who certainly gave his permission."

Maris suppressed a burble of laughter. "*You* married a parson's daughter?" *Incredible.* Whatever she had been expecting, it was not this.

"It was not my choice, I assure you. She was pregnant, and the parson had a way with pistols. For a man of peace, he had a most violent streak when it came to Catherine. I offered them money, but they would not be swayed. Marriage it had to be if I valued my hide."

David fiddled with his unused knife waiting for Maris to speak. When she found she could not think of a thing to say—surely "Congratulations" came too late—he went on. "So you see now why I couldn't marry Jane two years ago when she found herself in the same predicament. Bigamy is a crime, what? Ironic that if I'd only waited to dip my wick in a while, all my problems would have been solved. Marriage to my sweet, stuttering little cousin, pots of money, the earldom secured."

David was *married*. He'd never kept his vows as far as Maris knew. "Did Jane know? Did Henry?"

"Poor Janie did. I had to tell her why I couldn't marry her, didn't I? And look what happened. I know you hold me responsible, and I reckon I am. I never expected her to take her life. I supposed Uncle Henry would send her off to Italy or somewhere for the duration. But she was too terrified to tell him."

And Maris had not noticed the change that had come over her friend. She would never forgive herself for it. "But Henry did not know of your marriage."

"No. It was the one thing I managed to keep from him, but shutting Catherine up all these years was no easy task, I assure you. Your pin money made some little progress there. Odd isn't it? Hush money from one wife to another. Your husband was like a badger digging into my affairs. He kept a list of all my indiscretions, and read it to me every time I turned up. Did you know that? Called on the carpet like an errant schoolboy every time I darkened his door.

Needless to say, I didn't like that." David examined a cuff. "I might have said a few things to him to raise his hackles."

Henry had been nearly apoplectic after his last face-to-face meeting with his nephew. "You threatened to destroy the Kelby Collection."

David shrugged. "I admit I don't care about it. Can't understand why he was consumed with all that old rubbish. But I know my duty. As earl, everything needs to remain for the next generation."

The next generation. Maris pushed her plate away and stood up, too agitated to sit still a minute longer. She walked to the window. Reyn had disappeared down the lane long ago. "You said this Catherine was pregnant when you married."

"Ah, yes. I have a strapping son. He's sixteen this year, I believe."

A son. She turned to David, trying to keep her composure. "You don't know how old he is?"

"Well, I can count as well as the next fellow. He's mine, all right. His damned mother was a virgin and he was born nine months after the benighted night I first took her. We had quite the hot affair for the month I spent in the country. She met me every day, sneaking out of the parsonage like a little spy." He leered, and Maris looked away. "There is nothing like leading a complete innocent astray, Maris, though I don't expect you share my sentiments. I would imagine you believe yourself to be one of my victims, don't you? Unlike you, Catherine couldn't get enough of me then, but no more. We've always lived apart. She and I do not get on very well."

Maris expected not. Who could close both eyes while one's husband carried on affairs as if he wasn't wed?

So Henry had another heir besides his feckless nephew. That knowledge might have done much to soothe his ambition for the title. If Henry had known, he would have offered Catherine and her son residency at Kelby Hall. How he would have loved to watch a boy grow up there!

"Somehow Catherine caught wind of Uncle Henry's death. She's been after me for months now to move to the ancestral pile and set herself up as countess and groom young Peter as the heir. I told her it was no use yet, that you might cut me out of the earldom with the brat in your belly. Quite frankly, at this point I wouldn't mind if you bore a son and saved me the trouble of strangling the woman. She's not aged well at all."

Maris bit a lip to keep from laughing. To think of suave, smooth David Kelby trapped forever in a miserable marriage. While he might be a villain, she somehow couldn't see David's long white fingers around his wife's throat. It would take too much effort.

"Tell Catherine I should like to meet her. Have her bring your son. Is he at school?"

"Who has the money for school fees? I can't send him and support my tailor, too. His grandfather has been tutoring him in that godforsaken village they live in. Catherine brags he's bright enough. There's nothing else for him to do, but study. No amusements to be found whatsoever. That was rather the reason I got entangled with Catherine in the first place. I was visiting my old friend Montague and there she was, fifteen, all blushes and blond ringlets. A regular Eve. A viper in my garden is what she is now."

He had debauched a fifteen-year-old girl. Who was the snake? "Poor David," Maris said, with just a trace of mockery.

"Oh, I'm sure you feel I've gotten just what I deserve for all the trouble I've given you. It's a pity Uncle Henry isn't here to laugh at me." David's face shifted to its usual unpleasant expression. "I warn you, though, should you try to trick me and foist off some local milkmaid's babe as your own son, I'll know. I'll be watching. So, I imagine, will Catherine. Nothing is going to deprive her of seeing her child in his rightful place at last."

"Goodness. I'm quaking." And Maris was. With repressed laughter. The solution to her current agony was plain as the sneer on David's face. A reprieve for her ever-present conscience. But before she made an irrevocable decision, she must meet with Mrs. Catherine Kelby and her son.

Maris wouldn't say anything to Reyn. Not yet. But after last night, the thought of living her life without him in it was impossible. What did she care if she caused a frightful scandal? There would be a new Countess of Kelby, a new heir. At the rate David was going, he was bound to be shot soon by a jealous husband or contract one of the inevitable diseases that ran rampant throughout society for men with his proclivities. Even if he lived a long life and was an unsatisfactory earl, he had a son who might be worthy.

"What is Peter like?"

"I haven't the foggiest." Despite David's blasé tone, the tips of his ears turned red.

"You don't know your own son?" Maris asked, aghast.

"You can't expect me to bury myself in the country to chat up a pimple-faced boy. I saw him a few years ago and he didn't have two words to say for himself. His mother is probably lying when she says he's intelligent. I saw no evidence of it myself."

Poor Peter. But maybe not. No one would think David Kelby to be a good influence on a young man. Perhaps it was a mercy he lived out of the way with his mother and grandfather.

"Anyway, you can judge for yourself. Catherine should arrive at Kelby Hall any day now. I tried to stop her to no avail. She thinks your pregnancy is some sort of trick I've used to fob her off, but one look at you should shut her up. Unless you've got a pillow stuffed under your dress and got that idiot Crandall to lie for you. Do you know he had the gall to accuse me of having something to do with Uncle Henry's death? Just because I was visiting a friend at the Hall the night he died."

"A female friend, I presume." *His spy.*

"Jealous?" David waggled an auburn brow. "We did have some good times, didn't we, my dear? Though you lost your nerve after so brief a time. I never did get to teach you a fraction of what a woman needs to know to please a man. I wonder how you managed to entice my old uncle back into your bed. It was my understanding he was quite beyond performing his husbandly duties."

Maris stood straighter. "Your informant was incorrect, David."

"Was she? I wonder. Maybe you had a fling with the gardener or a footman, perhaps even with Uncle's permission. I wouldn't put anything past the old boy to cut me out. He might even have watched from the sidelines."

"David! You are disgusting!"

He was getting dangerously close to the truth, but he could have no way of knowing.

"So my wife tells me every chance she gets, which, thank God, is not often. I will arrange to send her here when she darkens Kelby Hall's door. As for myself, I'm bound for London this day. The Season, you know. There might be some pretty girls to lure into the bushes. An earldom is so very useful to throw a bit of added glitter into the mix. The mamas have such hopes for their daughters when they see me coming."

He was delusional. At almost thirty-eight, he was showing the years of dissipation. His dark red hair was graying, his mouth bracketed by deep lines, his middle a bit thicker than she remembered. Once, Maris had thought him handsome, but she'd realized too late that his charm had ever been false.

"Happy hunting, then," she said lightly. "How disappointed they will be to discover you have a wife and child tucked away."

"There's no reason yet for anyone to know. If I'm lucky, Catherine's coach will tumble down a ravine and I'll be a grieving widower. Oh, don't look at me like that! Murder is not my style, Maris, else I should have snuffed out Uncle Henry years ago."

"How reassuring." Maris went to the bellpull and Aloysius appeared instantly. "Please see my nephew-in-law out, Aloysius."

The young footman gave David a dark look. "With the greatest of pleasure, my lady."

David threw back his head and laughed. "Such fierce loyalty. I'm gone. For now. But you have not seen the last of me."

Maris collapsed in her chair once he was on his way. It might not be long before she was perfectly safe from him. If she weren't afraid of being able to get up without assistance, she might even get down on her knees and pray.

Chapter 30

June 1821

Reyn was bent over one of the ledgers scratching in information. It had been difficult to settle down to work at his desk, remembering what had occurred on his office floor a week ago. All he could see in his mind's eye was Maris, her head over him, lovely lips on his cock, her dark lashes fluttering as she took him as deep as she dared.

It had been heaven, and now it was hell. He'd heard nothing from her since he left her with that bounder David. Maris had sent Ginny a proper thank-you note for her hospitality the next day, but there was no secret message therein for Reyn. He had not been able to stop himself from riding to the copse of trees every day, sometimes twice. There had been no token from her tied on a tree branch, no letter professing her love tucked into a hollow, no schedule when he might expect to be schooled by the woman, Miss Holley. He had checked, mooning about in the grass until he felt like a complete fool.

Mr. Swift had seen her, however, and by the time he'd arrived after Reyn sent him, David Kelby had gone. Left for London, in fact. At least Maris wasn't being tormented by the man.

Until his next visit.

Blast. There must be something he could do to protect her from Kelby. Reyn threw the pen down, splattering ink across the pages. He looked down as his work-roughened hands, curling his fingers into his palms, raising the thumbs and turning them until his knuckles met. *b* was on the left and *d* was on the right—or was it the other way around? It was hopeless.

He might have stared at his hands indefinitely except he heard the knock on his office door. Hurriedly he closed the ledger. "Come."

It was young Jack, bearing a crisp white piece of stationery, folded but unsealed. *Double blast.*

"What have you got there?"

"A message from Hazel Grange, Captain. One of the footmen brought it. Said he couldn't stay but a second to deliver it. Had to get to the village before something else happened."

Reyn's throat dried. It was much too soon for the baby. "*Something else* happened? He didn't say what?"

"No, sir. In a right tizzy he was. Road off like his life depended upon it. Aren't you going to read it?"

The pristine paper bore Jack's smudged thumbprint. Reyn opened it and struggled to read it. To him, it looked like *You hab detter come at once. The Countess neebs you. A.*

Reyn ran the words through his head, translating what he saw into what was meant. "Aloysius brought this?"

"He didn't say his name, sir. He was just a footman. But he wasn't wearing a fancy white wig or even a bit of braid," Jack sniffed, dismissive.

"Saddle up Brutus for me."

"That devil?"

"Aye, that devil. Do as you're told, sharp." Reyn ran an inky hand through his long hair. Maris would have to take him as she found him. If she was in trouble, she wouldn't care if his hair was unkempt and his tie entirely absent. He rolled his sleeves down, grabbed his old tweed jacket from the back of the chair, and went to help Jack with the tack.

Jack said Aloysius had taken the road, but Reyn rode over the fields hell for leather. When he spotted Hazel Grange over the ridge, all seemed normal. Pastoral. A lazy curl of smoke came from the kitchen chimney. Windows gleamed in the bright June sunshine. Urns of pale pink geraniums flanked the columned portico. The house looked like a gentlewoman's home, and Reyn in his present state was unfit to enter it through the front door.

No matter. He rode around to the kitchen, Stephen Prall huffing to keep up with him and take Brutus's reins.

"Is the Countess well?" Reyn asked as he dismounted. "I received a message."

The man's eyebrows knit. "Far as I know, sir. They'll know more in the house."

Reyn entered the kitchen, much to the alarm of the ladies present. They seemed to be assembling a towering tea tray with dozens of little treats, reminding Reyn that he'd been too busy to eat breakfast or lunch. "Good day. I've come to speak to Aloysius. Is he about?"

The maids looked to Margaret, Maris's housekeeper. "I believe he's gone on an errand, Captain Durant," she said.

"Yes, to fetch me," Reyn said, trying to smile. "Do you know what it's about? His note indicated it was urgent."

"Well, I don't know as I would call it *urgent,* but I'm glad you are here, and that's a fact. My lady has guests."

"Guests?"

"Aye. A person who claims she is the Countess of Kelby, who seems to think *this* house should be hers. And a boy. Poor lamb to have such a mother."

Not David Kelby, then. Reyn allowed himself to relax a fraction. "Has Mr. Woodley been sent for?"

Reyn had had a very discreet dealing with the old earl's solicitor. The emerald was not his only payment for his brief time at Kelby Hall. Woodley professed he did not know the details of the private arrangement Reyn had entered into with Henry Kelby, but had paid him in full.

"Aye. Aloysius was riding into Shere after he went to Merrywood to get word to him by post. But who knows when Mr. Woodley will get here with the proper papers?"

"Perhaps I can help. This woman is not mad, is she? Dangerous?"

"She hasn't whipped out a pistol. But she's making quite a fuss. In her delicate condition, the poor countess should not be bothered." Margaret blushed, recognizing that to discuss such a thing with a strange-ish man was not done.

"I'll just follow you in with the tea tray, shall I?"

"Hold still." In for a penny, in for a pound. As long as Margaret had begun to walk on the edge of impropriety, she smoothed Reyn's windblown hair down and handed him a linen napkin to wipe the sweat off his face. "You'll do, I suppose."

"Thank you, madam."

Who was the guest of Maris's who thought she could move into Hazel Grange? Something very odd was afoot. He followed Margaret and one of the maids up a short flight of stairs to the main floor. Maris's parlor door was open, and a woman's voice immediately grated on his ears.

"If I cannot have Kelby Hall yet, I see no reason why Peter and I shall not have this house."

"Mrs. Kelby," Maris said patiently, then broke off as Reyn and the servants entered the room. She rose in an instant. "Captain! This is a most unexpected visit."

Reyn went to her and kissed her hand, something he'd not done in this sort of context. There was no secret squeeze or sweep of his tongue. "Lady Kelby, please forgive me in all my dirt. I was just passing, and remembered you wished to discuss the renovations of your stable block as soon as possible. Have I come at a difficult time?"

"Oh, no. You are always welcome. That is to say, I know how valuable your time is. If you could join us for tea, I'm sure we can discuss it once my guest and her son leave."

Reyn glanced at the other inhabitants of the room. A youth had risen at his entry, a lad of no more than fifteen or sixteen whose plump cheeks had not yet seen a razor. Though he'd not lost his puppy fat, the boy was tall, with a mop of auburn hair and dark eyes. There was something about him that was vaguely familiar.

His mother remained seated. She was a faded blonde with a great deal too many curls for a woman her age, and possessed of an unremarkable figure. Her blue eyes settled on him with shrewdness. He felt a little like a chop in a butcher shop window.

"And who is this, Maris?"

Reyn saw Maris flinch at the use of her Christian name. "May I present my neighbor, Captain Reynold Durant? Captain, this is my niece-in-law, Mrs. Kelby and her son, Peter. My husband's nephew David's wife and son. My, what a mouthful that is."

Reyn felt the room shift. "How very happy I am to meet you," he said blandly. He found a seat before he fell into it. "I was not aware Mr. Kelby was married."

"Do you know my husband?" From her tone, it was clear that any friend of David's was an enemy.

"A passing acquaintance only. I met him at Kelby Hall when I was doing some work for the late earl."

"What kind of work was that? Stable renovations? I saw no evidence of new construction when I was there."

"Inventorying his antiquities collection. I regret to say I did not complete the task before the earl passed away. An opportunity arose to alter my career path, and so you find me the owner of Merrywood Farm. I raise horses."

Though a trifle pale, Maris was pouring tea and passing plates as if she entertained David Kelby's wife every day of the week. Reyn took a bracing gulp from his cup.

"Peter is horse-mad, aren't you, darling?" The boy blushed as he bit into his seed cake. "We haven't been able to afford a suitable mount for him, but all that will change now that David will be earl. God willing. No offense to you, Maris, but you must realize we pray for the delivery of a healthy girl."

"Mrs. Kelby—Catherine—I do hope your wishes will come true," Maris said, her voice soft.

"Well, I'm due something after the way David has treated me. Treated *us*," she said as her son's blush darkened. "And if my hopes are dashed, I can always move here. It's nothing to Kelby Hall, of course, but better than the rectory, isn't it, Peter? My father is a man of the cloth," she added for Reyn's benefit. "No doubt he'd miss us, but it is past time we had property of our own."

Poor Peter said nothing, looking much like a chubby trapped fox.

Reyn saw his chance to assist. "I was under the impression, Countess, that Hazel Grange is not part of the entail. Didn't your husband purchase it specifically for you and any daughters that might result from your marriage?"

"Exactly so, and that is what I've been trying to explain to C-Catherine. Hazel Grange is mine outright. Mr. Woodley can explain it all."

"That fussy old woman?" Catherine Kelby scoffed. "He tried to turn me out of the Hall yesterday, but I know my rights. It is David's family home, and we are David's family, whether he acknowledges us or not. I have the marriage lines. No one will dare say my boy is a bastard."

"Mama!" Peter Kelby was in agony.

"Stop interrupting, Peter. You've done nothing but contradict me at every turn today. What will the countess think? You've been most impertinent, talking out of turn."

Pot, meet kettle. Reyn found Catherine Kelby outrageously outspoken. For a clergyman's daughter, she was not meek or mild.

"Would you like another biscuit, Peter?" Maris asked kindly.

The boy nodded, mute and miserable.

What a trial it must be to have two such awful parents, Reyn thought. Kelby Hall's butler Amesbury would have a fit if Maris bore a daughter and David and Catherine moved in to ruin the tone of his household.

Reyn caught Maris's eye. The smile she gave him was so dazzling—so *loving*—he was knocked back into his chair.

She might have wanted to thwart David, but depriving young Peter Kelby of his future was an entirely different proposition. An honorable woman like Maris could never do such a thing.

Maris set the china tea pot down. "Captain, do you remember the proposal you made to me the other day?"

"The proposal?" Reyn asked, his tongue suddenly thick.

"Yes. I've been giving it a great deal of thought, and realized I was thinking overmuch. I find I am very agreeable to your suggestion. In fact, the sooner we can plan the *renovations,* the better. Before the baby comes, certainly. I might not have time to make all the necessary arrangements once the child is born."

Reyn knew his mouth was hanging open.

"Why would you care about making improvements to Hazel Grange if you may wind up back at Kelby Hall?" Catherine asked, helping herself to a sliver of candied ginger.

"I have no intention of returning to Kelby Hall."

Catherine Kelby's mouth joined Reyn's. For once, she was wordless.

"Not return?" asked Peter once he had nearly choked on his vanilla-infused biscuit. "What about all those magnificent artifacts? Great-Uncle Henry's Etruscan finds? The library? It's all museum-worthy. I've never seen the like!"

"Do you know, Peter, it was my husband's fondest wish to turn part of the Hall into a museum and open it to the public. He wanted me to be the curator, can you believe it? I spent most of my life working toward that ideal, but now I have other things to occupy me. It's time the Kelby Collection found a new curator. Henry would be so pleased with your interest. Your father tells me you're quite a scholar."

Peter blinked. "He did? My father spoke of me?"

Maris nodded. "He came to war—inform—me that you both might come to pay me a visit, and I'm so glad you did. There's enough at Kelby Hall to keep you busy and expand your classical education for a lifetime. By the time you become earl, you might actually have everything organized."

Catherine put her cup down with a clatter. "I'm afraid I don't understand you, Lady Kelby."

"No, I don't expect you do. There are some days I hardly understand myself. Please enjoy your tea, and if you wouldn't mind terribly, see yourself out when you're done. You must be anxious to get back to the Hall before dark, and there are things I must discuss with the captain. He is so busy, you know. Very much in demand, which is why he rackets about the countryside half dressed and with no neck cloth, but no matter. There is a . . . problem with one of my horses. Captain, you'll accompany me to the stables?"

Reyn stood, a bit unsteadily. "Of course."

Maris stood, too, speaking directly to Catherine. "I'm sure Mr. Woodley will get in touch with you about the particulars of this property. Give my best to David when you see him. Peter is a fine young man. He—you both—should be proud."

The boy was scarlet. "Thank you, my lady."

It was clear Catherine Kelby did not know what to make of Maris's little speech. The last Reyn saw of her, she was frowning, reaching for a strawberry tart.

He hurried alongside Maris as they left the room. "What—?"

"Hush. Not yet."

The footman Phillip opened the front door for them and Reyn followed her outside. The sky was blue and cloudless. Maris's little black lace cap fluttered in the warm breeze as she led Reyn to the rear of the house and a gated garden. She turned the key in the iron lock, moving quickly on a mown grass path to sit down on a shaded bench

Reyn remained standing. "I see no horses."

"I lied. Thank you for coming. Who sent for you? Betsy?"

"Aloysius."

"Bless him. That Kelby woman is insufferable. But I see great promise in her son."

"His mother wouldn't let him get a word in edgewise."

"I had the chance to speak to him alone while Margaret gave his mother a tour of the house. A *long* tour, or as long as it could be in a house of its modest size. I begged off." Maris winked, placing a hand on the black fabric that covered her stomach. "Too exhausting for a woman in my state. So I sat in a comfortable chair and coaxed him to talk while his grasping mother probably pilfered my jewel box, not that there's much in there. The boy is very smart and seems to have inherited neither of his parents' objectionable qualities."

"What are you saying, Maris?"

"I'm going to marry you—if you'll still have me. I must talk to Mr. Woodley about the legalities, but I believe any child born into wedlock will be acknowledged to be my husband's, no matter how brief the marriage. We can raise our child together, Reyn. No more deceit. Henry would have liked Peter, I'm sure of it. If he's managed to remain as pure as he has with that harpy for a mother, we can only imagine how well he'll turn out with some schooling and Mr. Woodley looking out for his interests."

"What about David?"

Maris shrugged. "He may rise to the occasion. If not, how much harm can he do? He should have his hands full keeping his wife under control. Poor man."

Reyn sat beside her and took her hand. "I disagree. How can you feel any sympathy for him? A secret marriage? Deserting his own child all these years?"

"Exactly. One should never desert a child. That was your concern all along, wasn't it? Why you didn't want to follow through with Henry's plan."

"At first. But now there is the small matter that I fell in love with you and can't bear to think of living without you."

She looked up at him, her eyes damp. Damn, but her tears always slayed him. "You won't have to."

"Are you sure, Maris?"

"Oh so very."

Kissing her seemed the right thing to do. The only thing to do. They were to be married, after all, and if anyone saw them through the ornate iron fence, what did it matter? Reyn touched his lips to hers and was lost.

It was all too good—the kiss, the weather, the neat solution to their dilemma. But he had never been one to look for trouble. It had usually found him . . . if he waited long enough, anyway. If Maris thought she could leave her old life behind and marry him, he wouldn't try to talk her out of it.

Or talk to her at all—just kiss—although, to be honest, there was nothing *just* about it.

First Epilogue

September 1821

"I cannot bear it. How can she?"

"Now, Captain Durant, your wife is doing beautifully." The midwife, Mrs. Lynch, handed him a clean damp cloth.

Reyn had lost count of how many clean damp cloths she'd given him over the past twenty hours.

"If you are to remain—it is most indecent of you, really, although it seems Mrs. Durant wants you, though why she does is anyone's guess as you've done your part already and gotten us all into this mess—you must put a smile on your face and wipe hers."

Reyn gave it his best shot, which was more grimace than smile.

"Not like that. You look like you've eaten something nasty. Be brave for the lass as she's been brave for you."

After a career in the army, Reyn had thought he knew what bravery was, but he had been mistaken. Maris was braver than anyone. After almost a day's labor, the baby was not slipping into the world easily, despite Mrs. Lynch's efforts.

There was a reason men were barred from their wives' side at such a time. A reason they drank themselves into a brandified stupor waiting downstairs after listening to the wailing from above. Maris had done her share of wailing, and each cry had pierced Reyn's heart.

"We should send for Dr. Crandall," Reyn whispered as he blotted Maris's brow. Her eyes were closed and she was white as the sheets she lay on, her brown braid soaked. She had given up screaming some time ago and was silent. He thought he much preferred the screams.

"Too far. He'll never get here in time. It really won't be long now."

"Dr. Sherman, then."

Mrs. Lynch tsked. "The man's a drunkard. Be patient, Captain. There's my girl. I think we'll get you up to walk again, my dear. How does that sound?"

Maris's bloodless lips barely moved in response. "Whatever you think best."

"Lean on that strong, handsome husband of yours. Well done, dear. Just to the chair and back. And again. And again."

Reyn felt as if they were marching back and forth to their doom. His wife slumped against him, her body shaking, each step a massive effort. He had never felt so useless. If this child was ever born, he'd never touch her again.

"It will be easier with the next baby," Maris said, causing Reyn to stumble.

"Planning a large family, are you?" Mrs. Lynch asked.

"Yes."

"No!" Reyn growled.

"At least one more after this. We wouldn't want him or her to get lonely." Maris gave him a watery smile.

"You are impossible, wife."

"So you have told me. Oh! *Oh!*"

Reyn panicked at her sharp intake of breath, but Mrs. Lynch smiled. "Ah, well done, Mrs. Durant. We've started up again. Just a few more turns around the room and I'll have you get back into the bed and sit up. Captain, plump those pillows and give her your hand to squeeze. Don't be surprised if she breaks some bones, and anyway, you have another hand, don't you?"

Reyn shut his eyes so he wouldn't see Maris's mouth twist in pain. The contractions were steady now, and very close together. Maris went back to groaning, then screaming. Mrs. Lynch murmured encouraging words, directing Betsy, who had been making herself small in a corner of the bedroom, to help her.

He would never forgive himself if something happened to his wife.

They had been married by special license by Mr. Swift, who was somewhere downstairs with Ginny and Miss Holley, probably not partaking of any brandy while they waited. It had been a quiet wedding in the gated garden of Hazel Grange, with only their servants and his sister as witnesses. Neither Reyn nor Maris cared what the neighbors had thought of the sudden, scandalous union. In time, the gossip would die down and people might even forget that Maris was ever a countess.

Reyn had no idea yet what they'd tell a son or daughter. He only hoped he'd be equal to the task once the time was right.

The Durants had decided to make their home at Hazel Grange. Once Ginny was married to her vicar, the Swifts were welcome to live at Merrywood, if they could stand the comings and goings of horses and foals at all hours.

What had Reyn been thinking of, volunteering for this duty? Just because he'd delivered a few foals did not make him an expert. But Maris had implored him, her eyes huge and wet. He had never been able to resist her tears, not from the first day he met her.

"Lovely, my dear, just lovely. Give a push now, there's a good girl. Yes, just like that. Isn't she doing a splendid job, Captain?"

"Splendid." Reyn felt light-headed.

"Look there. The babe's crowning, Captain."

Reyn was used to following orders, but he was very much afraid the sight of the coming child would be his undoing. Instead, he looked at his wife. "I love you, Maris."

"And . . . I . . . you . . . oh!"

Out of the corner of his eye, Reyn saw something dark and bloody slither onto the bed. His heart stopped.

"Reyn, you are hurting my hand."

Mrs. Lynch moved her hand over Maris's stomach. "Betsy, the twine and scissors, if you please. You have a pretty little girl, Mrs. Durant. Just one more hard push and we'll have the placenta out and your baby ready for you to hold. Isn't she sweet, Captain?"

His daughter made a tiny snuffling sound. Reyn thought babies were supposed to be slapped across their buttocks so they would give a lusty cry. This little scrap looked barely alive.

"Is she all right?" Reyn croaked.

"Of course she is. They both are. Buck up, sir. You're white as a ghost."

There was more blood and mess. Reyn had been in battle countless times, but nothing had prepared him for this. Mrs. Lynch massaged the umbilical cord until she was satisfied, then tied it in two places and snipped between them. She gave the baby to Betsy to clean and wrap up while she tended to Maris. A lifetime seemed to pass before his child made her presence known, objecting to Betsy's ministrations.

"A daughter. Jane. I'm so glad, Reyn."

He was, too. There would always have been some lingering regret and confusion if Maris had born a son.

"You'll have your boy next time." Mrs. Lynch winked at him, and Reyn decided it would be most improper to strike her. To have Maris go through all this again was simply not to be imagined.

"Here she is, my lady." Betsy was beaming. According to her, she'd helped her mam with several confinements and knew all about babies.

Reyn watched as Jane nestled into the crook of Maris's arm.

"The wet nurse is downstairs, I expect," Mrs. Lynch said.

"She is, but I'd like to try myself first."

Reyn had been aghast when his countess insisted on feeding her own child, but Maris had reminded him she wasn't a countess any longer. Her fingers shook as she attempted to unbutton her night rail.

"Let me, my love. Undressing ladies is my specialty."

"You'd better not be undressing any lady but me."

He kissed her damp forehead. "I wouldn't think of it. Are you really all right?"

"How can you doubt? Look at Jane and tell me she is not the most beautiful thing in creation."

Reyn was not entirely in accord with his wife, but he was wise enough to nod. No doubt someday Jane would be a great beauty and drive everyone to distraction, especially her father. She had already frightened him half to death.

"We'll go down and tell the others and give you a little privacy," Mrs. Lynch said. "But Mrs. Durant will need her rest, Captain. Do not tire her out." The midwife and Betsy left them alone in the sunny room.

Reyn didn't even know what time it was. "She's as bossy as you are."

His wife and child began their acquaintance. Jane's little mouth hovered, then latched on with all its might. "Hush. You know I've always got your best interests at heart. How very odd this feels, Reyn. It is nothing like when you kiss me there."

Reyn suppressed a groan. How would he endure abstinence? But how could he not?

Well, there were always French letters. And withdrawal. He'd managed all his life not to get anyone pregnant.

"Reyn, whatever is the matter? You are looking quite gothic."

"Nothing. There is absolutely nothing wrong. I am the happiest man in the world."

Second Epilogue

Maris was so happy she thought it might be criminal. She examined each tiny toe and fingernail once her daughter had drunk her second breakfast. Jane was perfect, with the Durant dimple already visible and a head of midnight hair. Lots of it. Reyn called her his little monkey, which Jane wouldn't like at all once she was older, and so Maris told her husband.

Her husband. Once, she had never expected to marry. Somehow, she'd found two good men to love her. Her life had really unfolded in a most unexpected way.

Mr. Woodley had not batted so much as an eyelash when she'd explained her plans last summer. He had assured her Henry's financial arrangements for her were secure and her widow's jointure—including Hazel Grange—were untouchable by the new Countess of Kelby. He shuddered a bit when he mentioned the name, but perked up when discussing young Peter. The boy had been enrolled at Eton and had a good head on his shoulders, no thanks to either of his parents.

Mr. Woodley had visited several times since. He told her Catherine's father had retired from his parish and was living at Kelby Hall. He was a scholarly fellow who had volunteered to poke around the attics to make himself useful now that he was no longer tutoring his grandson. What might he find in the abandoned boxes? Maris realized she didn't much care.

The new earl preferred to stay in London, which was best for everyone concerned, except perhaps for any young women whose hearts he might break. How long David could play Lothario now that it was known he was married was anyone's guess.

"Your father will keep you safe from any men like him," Maris said to the baby in her arms. "I daresay he is just the man to recognize a rake, as he used to be one before he met me."

"What's that nonsense you're telling our daughter?"

Maris looked up to see Reyn in the doorway. He was splattered with mud and blood, his cheeks chapped red from the cold.

"How did it go?"

Reyn grinned. "We have a fine colt."

"The second this week! Brutus must be proud."

"Not as proud as I am of our little filly. How is Miss Jane today? I won't come in to see for myself."

"It's too soon, but I think she is cutting a tooth." Jane had been frantically chewing everything in sight, including Maris's poor breasts.

"Of course. She is advanced for her age. She takes after her mother."

"But is the image of her father."

"Poor monkey. Let's hope the Durant nose skips a generation. Well, wife, I've been up all night and dead on my feet. I've ordered a bath in my dressing room. Do you think you might join me in a nap this morning once I clean myself up?"

"A *nap,* Captain Durant?"

"You say that as if I have an ulterior motive to get in bed with my wife." He made a show of yawning. Maris wasn't fooled a bit.

"I confess I'm tired too. Jane was fussy last night."

"Excellent. I won't be long."

"Good. Because I'm *very* tired."

"You are incorrigible, aren't you?"

Maris smiled. "I was instructed by a master."

Reyn disappeared down the hall, his whistling of a bawdy tune belying his exhaustion. She rang for Jane's nursemaid, rose from the chaise, and went to her dressing table.

"Damn." There was a new silver hair poking up through the loose brown waves at her temple. She ripped it out and unbraided her hair, brushing it until her arm became weak. What was taking Reyn so long? She really was tired, and would relish falling asleep in her husband's arms.

When they finished loving each other.

He'd been very silly after Jane was born. The poor man had got it into his head that she should never suffer through childbirth again. It had taken some convincing and a consultation with Dr. Crandall, but Reyn had resumed his marital rights a month ago. Maris had missed their intimacy more than she could have ever expressed. For a woman who had mostly lived within proper boundaries, she was afraid she had strayed into wanton territory.

And was glad of it.

She saw him behind her in the mirror, his hair damp and slicked back. He smelled of soap and man, no trace of horse. Reyn raised one wicked black eyebrow and held out a hand. Maris didn't hesitate for a second.

Third Epilogue

It was better this way. Reyn stared gloomily into a glass of whiskey. Still his first, when it should have been at least his seventh. One for every hour of agony upstairs.

He was a dog. A right bastard even if his parents had been married. Somehow he had been unable to keep his vow to himself. For the fourth time in five years, he was waiting for a new child to be born. Jane and her two brothers would shortly—God, if only it *would* be shortly—be joined in the nursery by another little Durant.

This child would be the last of the line. Although she would clout him to say so, Maris was getting too old for this sort of thing. They would just have to be more careful in the future.

Reyn snorted. Good luck with that. It seemed everything he touched resulted in fecundity. His horse farm was a great success. His laborers were building a new barn over at Merrywood even as he sat there not drinking his whiskey.

Childbirth business did not seem to get any easier with practice for him, although Maris uttered not one word of complaint. It was she who had seduced him from his good intentions, and he had to say she made a wonderful mother, as she was wonderful at everything in their domestic sphere. At the age of four, Jane could read already, thanks to her mother's lessons, with none of her father's difficulty. It remained to be seen how Henry and Matthew would fare, but both seemed like bright little boys. Reyn was hopeful for their future.

Perhaps he should go up. It was not his fault he'd fainted when Matthew was born. He'd missed breakfast *and* lunch and was simply hungry. Mrs. Lynch had banned him this time, but this was his home, after all. Surely he had a right to be present at the birth of his own child?

"Reyn! Maris wants you."

His sister Ginny was at the door of his study, quite near the end of her own term. She had requested to be with Maris to know what to expect in two months. She and Arthur had finally been successful in conceiving. She looked none the worse for wear, but Reyn experienced his usual misgivings.

"Is she all right? Is the baby here?"

"You may see for yourself once you stop asking such silly questions." The little baggage stuck her tongue out at him.

Reyn took the stairs two at a time. A baby was crying, the most beautiful sound in the world to his ears.

Maris sat up in bed, her glossy hair tucked up under a nightcap. Her cheeks were flushed and her eyes sparkled. One would never know she'd been writhing in agony for seven hours. "A girl this time, Reyn. Isn't she pretty?"

Reyn peeked at the tiny bundle lying in the cradle. She was clean and pink, and Reyn felt a spasm of guilt. Maris knew how the sight of blood and gore on his newborn babies absolutely terrified him. Odd that he was so adept when it came to equine infants.

"She's a beauty, like her mother." Reyn sat on the bed, noting the sheets had been changed too. He was pathetic, he really was, but the idea of Maris in pain paralyzed him.

There was a word for him—*uxorious*. He had come across it in a book he was making himself read, and had not known the meaning at first. It meant excessively devoted to one's wife. *Guilty as charged.*

She was radiant, and his heart swelled. "Thank you, Maris, for everything."

"I should be thanking you." She grinned, looking half her age. "I can't wait until I'm well enough so we can—"

"No!" Reyn held up a hand in alarm. "Don't say it! Don't even think it!"

"Have a picnic in the garden with the children? Surely you can have no objection to that. The leaves will be turning, and if everyone dresses warmly, we should be fine, even little Juliet. We can bring her along in a Moses basket. I do so love the fall."

Reyn shut his eyes. His wife surprised him daily with her cunning. He was very sure that was not what she had intended to say at all.

Ah, well. He'd worry later. At the moment, he was going to kiss his countess.

Did you miss the first book in Maggie's LONDON LIST series?

Lord Gray's List

From duchesses to chamber maids, everybody's reading it. Each Tuesday, *The London List* appears, filled with gossip and scandal, offering job postings and matches for the lovelorn—and most enticing of all, telling the tales and selling the wares a more modest publication wouldn't touch . . .

The creation of Evangeline Ramsey, *The London List* saved her and her ailing father from destitution. But the paper has given Evie more than financial relief. As its publisher, she lives as a man, dressed in masculine garb, free to pursue and report whatever she likes—especially the latest disgraces besmirching Lord Benton Gray. It's only fair that she hang his dirty laundry, given that it was his youthful ardor that put her off marriage for good . . .

Lord Gray—Ben—isn't about to stand by while all of London laughs at his peccadilloes week after week. But once he discovers that the publisher is none other than pretty Evie Ramsey with her curls lopped short, his worries turn to desires—and not a one of them fit to print . . .

And don't miss LADY ANNE'S LOVER, coming in August.
Here's a sneak peek!

Wales, December 26, 1820

Lady Imaculata Egremont had danced naked in a fountain. She'd eloped to France with a rackety gentleman she'd just as soon forget. She'd sold chestnuts on the street. There was no reason on earth why she could not pick up a dead mouse and dispose of it with her usual élan.

She fought back an unfortunate gag and told herself to stop breathing. To think of lilac bushes in her mother's Dorset garden in the spring. Great purple masses of them, their heavy cones bursting into flower, gray-green leaves shivering in the warm breeze. She was *not* in Wales. It was *not* winter. She was *not* standing bent over a tiny desiccated body in a grim hallway that smelled like death.

And gin.

Somewhere her new employer must have spilled a vat of it and had probably joined the mouse. He certainly had not opened the door to her as she'd injured her hands pounding on it for a full five minutes on the misty doorstep. She'd finally taken the initiative—anyone would tell you Lady Imaculata was bold as brass—and pressed the latch herself, finding the door unlocked. If she were truly a housekeeper, she supposed she should have entered by way of the kitchen, but Lady Imaculata was an earl's daughter, and some habits were hard to break.

The possibly dead Major Ripton-Jones had not sent any transportation to fetch her, either. She'd gotten off the mail coach in Hay on Wye foolishly hopeful, but in the end she'd arranged for a donkey cart herself to bump her along to Llanwyr, hoping her presence had not been noted by her father's spies. She was still almost frozen from the long ride, and the temperature in Ripton Hall's hall was not much warmer than outside. She was probably giving the dead mouse a run for its money with her own *eau de bourrique.*

Lilacs. Think of lilacs. Her favorite flower. No donkeys or dead mice. It was abundantly clear why the old man had placed an advertisement for a housekeeper in *The London List,* and she hadn't even gone ten paces down the dim and fragrant hallway. What would she find when she opened the closed doors? Alas, it was too late to run after the donkey cart.

She may have been raised a lady, but Lady Imaculata was now Mrs. Anne Mont. Anne was her humble middle name, much more suitable for a housekeeper. What her parents had been thinking at her christening was a mystery for the ages. Anyone who named a child Imaculata was asking for trouble. Much like those named Chastity or Christian or Prudence, the Imaculatas of the world were bound to disappoint, and she had been no exception—in fact she had taken a toe or two over the edge of propriety so often she was at a perpetual tilt.

As if a mere change of name would help her with the Herculean tasks at hand, she thought grimly. She'd need to reroute the Welsh equivalent of the Alpheus and Peneus rivers to wash away all this dirt and dust. She was very much afraid she'd gotten in over her head, and not for the first time.

With determination, she set down her portmanteau and got to work. Anne Mont needed this job, at least until she turned twenty-one and became Imaculata Egremont again to come into her funds. Two years was not so very long to endure isolation and filth, and anyway, she'd fix the filth or die trying. She closed her eyes, gingerly scooped the dead mouse up with her handkerchief and tossed it out onto the frost-covered drive, the handkerchief right along with it. Let the poor mouse have its embroidered shroud. She couldn't imagine ever blowing her nose delicately into it again, even if she knew how to do laundry. Mrs. Anne Mont didn't have the first idea how to wash a handkerchief or anything else, but supposed that was one of the things a housekeeper would have to learn. The major was apt to have handkerchiefs and clothes now, wasn't he?

Her benefactress Evangeline Ramsey had pressed upon her an ancient copy of *The Compleat Housewife* before she left London, and Anne had plenty of time to read it and become dismayed on her journey west. The title page alone had been daunting—"*Collection of several hundred of the most approved receipts, in cookery, pastry, confectionery, preserving, pickles, cakes, creams, jellies, made wines, cordials. And also bills of fare for every month of the year. To which is added, a collection of nearly two hundred family receipts of medicines; viz. drinks, syrups, salves, ointments, and many other things of sovereign and approved efficacy in most distempers, pains, aches, wounds, sores, etc. never before made publick in these parts; fit either for private families, or such publick-spirited gentlewomen as would be beneficent to their poor neighbours.*" The author Eliza Smith must have been wonderfully efficient, but then she'd never had to deal with Major Ripton-Jones's house and his dead and living pests. The major's house was a dismal wreck and she would earn every bit of the pittance he'd promised to pay her.

Anne batted the worst of the spiderwebs away with her wet black bonnet, hoping none of the spiders decided to take up residency in her hat. Satisfied she could now walk the gauntlet of the hallway, she opened a shut door. It revealed a monstrously large cold double drawing room, big enough to host a cotillion, badly furnished. Great swaths of cobwebs hung in every corner, Dust lay thick on every surface, windows were so smudged one could not see the frigid rain-washed fields beyond them. The fireplaces at either end were heaping-full of cold ashes. No one had sat on the mice-shredded satin sofas in a long while.

Next was the monstrously large colder dining room, in worse repair—not a chair looked able to hold her weight, and she was quite a little thing. She could have written her name on the dust on the long dining table, if she could remember that she was Anne Mont now.

The door at the end of the hall was locked, but she swore she smelled peat burning beyond it. And gin. She took a long sniff, filling her nose with the distinct aroma of drink and unwashed man.

Definitely no lilacs.

Her elderly employer was behind it, most likely, and he was snoring. He must have doused the room in alcohol—she may as well have been outside a ginhouse. Anne damned her new friend Evangeline Ramsey and her newspaper *The London List* with an extremely naughty oath for sending her here to the back of beyond to cater to a drunken old man.

But, Anne reminded herself, Major Ripton-Jones was better than her father, and if he wasn't, she would bean him on the head with a kettle if she could find one in the kitchen. If she could find the kitchen.

Everyone thought her papa was a saint. If they only knew what he had tried to do with his only child once the candles were blown out, they would soon change their mind.

Anne was still a virgin. Her father had attempted but not succeeded in getting very far. Nor had the rackety gentleman she'd run off to France with, although he'd tried to alter her not-quite-innocent state before they had gotten to an altar. She'd actually been relieved when the private detective her father had hired found them, even if she had punched poor Mr. Mulgrew in the nose.

She had faced her demons for the past four years, at first wondering what it was about her that brought the devil to her doorstep. Her father, she knew, blamed her for his unnatural lust and beat her for it. He had looked at her oddly after her mother died, when she was so lost in grief and had turned to him for comfort. But when he'd finally taken her in his arms, it was not as a father, but a man. Anne had been shocked and confused, then sick with fear. She supposed she could have countered him in any number of ways—leaping to her death from the roof, chewing up some foxglove, shooting herself—or better yet, him—with her pearl-handled pistol.

She had done none of those things. Instead, she had fought him off and made herself a byword of scandal from the moment of her debut, and had the newspaper clippings to prove it. As a debutante she had been very naughty indeed. Lady Imaculata had sought low, even subterranean society in order to escape her father's predatory attentions, thinking that he'd let her have her mother's fortune and wash his hands of her if she misbehaved sufficiently. But no matter what foolish—and sometimes dangerous—thing she'd done, he had kept her a prisoner.

So fiery, flame-haired Lady Imaculata Egremont was no more. In her place was frowsy brunette Anne Mont, reluctant and incompetent housekeeper. Anne had noted some of the brown color had rubbed off on her pillows as she'd spent the night in coaching houses. Whatever elixir Evangeline had used on her was fading fast. Unless she could find some Atkinson's Vegetable Dye, she'd have to confess to the major that he'd hired a red-headed imposter. Maybe the old man was so blind he'd never notice. If he could bear to live in his current squalor, appearances could not possibly matter to him.

Anne gathered her courage and used her most confident voice. She was a good mimic, and it was necessary for the major to think he had hired a forthright woman rather than a foolish, inexperienced girl. She had played a part or two in her time. Surely she could convince an old sot that she was a housekeeper, even if she didn't know how to remove mouse excrescence from a handkerchief.

"Major Ripton-Jones! It is Mrs. Mont, your new housekeeper. Please open the door so we may become acquainted."

The string of muffled words coming from behind the door that her governess would have forbidden did not shock her. Anne had said them anyway for maximum shock value, as often as possible, and actually just a few minutes ago. Stepping back, she lifted her chin and awaited her employer's displeasure at being torn from his inebriated slumber.

The door was wrenched open by a towering scarecrow of a man, bearded, shaggy-haired, disreputably dressed, indubitably drunk.

And one-armed. His dirty linen shirtsleeve hung empty, flapping a bit as he had listed toward the doorframe.

He wasn't old. Not old at all. There was a little gray in his beard—though that could very well be dust—but he could not have been much above thirty years old.

"Good afternoon," Anne had said briskly, masking her surprise and keeping her chin high. She was bound to get a crick in her neck if she had to address him for any length of time. "I believe Mi-uh, Mr. Ramsey from *The London List* sent word to you that I was coming."

He looked down at her, *way* down as he was so very tall, with blood-shot blue eyes. "You can't be the housekeeper."

He did not slur a word, although his breath nearly knocked her over. She would light no matches anywhere near him or he'd go up like a Guy Fawkes effigy.

"I can indeed, sir. I have a reference from Lady Pennington." She pulled the forged letter from her reticule.

"How old are you, *Mrs*. Mont? Twelve? And where is *Mr*. Mont?"

Evangeline had wanted her to lie and say she lost her husband at Waterloo—which would have made Anne a fourteen-year-old bride—but the man in front of her had probably lost his arm to war so that did not seem at all sporting. Anne knew she looked young—she *was* young, her freckles forever marking her just a step from the schoolroom. She had decided to be reasonably honest. If Major Ripton-Jones dismissed her, she'd go back to Evangeline and try for something else. Tightrope walker, street walker, it really didn't matter as long as she escaped her father's predatory attentions and beatings.

"Housekeepers are always addressed as 'Mrs.,' Major Ripton-Jones. Surely you know that. And I am old enough. I've been in service for—ages."

Ever since she walked into the house, anyway.

The man snorted and caught himself on the wall before he fell on her. "You'll have your work cut out for you, as you can see. Your room is off the kitchen. You'd best get started." He then shut the door in her face.

Well. T'was more or less still the Christmas season and Anne felt she should be charitable. She would carry her own bag to this bedroom—there wasn't much in it since her flight from London had been somewhat spontaneous. She'd gone to Evangeline Ramsey's house anticipating a very different outcome than her current employment. Fortunately, she'd had her savings stitched into her fur muff, and the coins had come in handy on the journey west. Anne did not want to spend a penny of them going back east. She challenged herself to make it to the New Year. It was only a few days away.

If she didn't kill the major first with her cooking or her pearl-handled pistol. She patted her reticule to assure herself it was still there. It wasn't loaded, for with her luck she'd shoot herself in her well-rounded derriere. But the gun would be a deterrent should the man try any of her father's tricks.

He was not at all what she'd expected. She'd seen the letter he'd sent to *The London List* requesting the services of a housekeeper.

Both she and Evangeline had assumed from his spidery handwriting he was an older gentleman. White-haired. Wrinkled.Weak.

Major Ripton-Jones did not seem weak at all, except when it came to his sobriety. Despite his missing arm, Anne would almost call him handsome beneath his grime if she let herself.

That would be inappropriate. He was her employer, at least for the moment. How long she could last here was anybody's guess.

Printed in the United States
by Baker & Taylor Publisher Services